Cauldron of Fire

Blood on the Stars V

Jay Allan

system 7
publishing

Also By Jay Allan

www.jayallanbooks.com

Cauldron of Fire

Cauldron of Fire is a work of fiction. All names, characters, incidents, and locations are fictitious. Any resemblance to actual persons, living or dead, events or places is entirely coincidental.

ISBN: 978-1-946451-04-0

Chapter One

Excerpt from the Funeral Missive for Katrine Rigellus

It is with the gravest respect and honor—and a grief I can hardly describe—that I stand before you today on this solemn occasion. Commander-Altum Katrine Rigellus was a hero of the Alliance, a warrior for us to emulate. She represented the ideal of the Palatian warrior. But she was more to me than that—more than a comrade in arms, more than an inspiration to those of us who had the fortune and honor to follow her into battle. She was my friend.

Katrine and I *were* friends, despite the great differences in our stations and the fact that she was my commanding officer. Though we were born into vastly different realities, never once in all the years I knew Kat did she treat me as anything but a close friend and companion. All I have achieved, all I aspire to one day attain in service to Palatia and the Alliance, I owe to her.

I could regale everyone here today with a recitation of her many victories and honors, but I will leave that to others more suited to such tasks. I shall, instead, indulge in a display of affection and loyalty, one perhaps beyond that common between warriors and comrades in arms. I will dwell not on the many battles Katrine won, but instead on the final one...the one she lost. The one that took her from us. The one I was compelled to miss. The one that has gone unavenged.

My words are not those spoken in acclamation by the men and women who served under her, nor the language of admiration and respect from the senior officers who commanded her.

No, I speak rather as a childhood friend, and my message is a personal one, sworn with all the intensity that resides in my soul.

I, Optiomagis Jovi Grachus, speak now, to this august body of mourners, and swear this oath to all of you, and to the shade of she who was as a sister to me. I shall not rest. I shall avenge my friend. I shall destroy those who took her life, and no force or power will stop me.

Interplanetary Space
Athenae System
Year 62 (311 AC)

"Dragons, pattern Epsilon-2. We're going in, cutting around the fringe of that attack formation." Jovi Grachus sat wedged into the cramped and uncomfortable cockpit, directing the moves of her Palatine fighter as though the sleek, eighty-ton craft was an extension of her own body. The Palatines were powerful ships, but sometimes treacherous to fly, at least for inexperienced pilots. But Grachus was an ace, and she worked her fighter the way a virtuoso coaxed melodies from a violin.

"Acknowledged, Optiomagis." Her second-in-command answered first, but Optio Gillus won that race by only the slightest of margins. Every pilot in Red Dragon squadron snapped out his or her reply within a second or two, the efficiency of the small war machine Grachus had built evident in both the tone and speed of the acknowledgements. She was proud of her people. Damned proud.

She rolled her head around on her shoulders, trying to force out the knots. Fatigue was creeping in from the edges of her mind. This was her peoples' second sortie of the battle, and she already had two kills to add to her roster. *Illustrious's* flight crew had turned her ships around in what had to be close to record time. She'd been breathing down their necks the whole time, of course, but that didn't take away from the good work they'd done. And nothing changed the fact that Grachus had been going full bore for twelve hours under combat conditions.

She'd popped a small handful of stims to keep her going, but that wasn't the same thing as being fresh.

Fresh isn't in the cards now…

"I'm going to count down. On one, we're going to overpower our thrusters. I want reactors at one hundred ten percent." The extra burst of thrust would allow her small attack force to reach the enemy's bombers before their interceptors could interfere. Then her people could swing about and meet the fighters coming back at them on something like even terms. And at even odds, the Red Dragons didn't lose dogfights.

Grachus leaned forward, bringing her lips closer to the comm. The unit extended out from her console on a small telescoping arm. It was a special setup, one she'd gotten *Illustrious's* crew chief to rig up for her—a special accommodation for the ship's top pilot. She hated the normal headsets. Her head was small, and she'd never managed to get one of the things to stay put on her, especially during the wild maneuvers she pulled in battle. Just one small privilege of her rank and notoriety.

"Three," she said, coldly, with the almost-monotone delivery that told her pilots even their celebrated commander knew she was pushing things to the limit.

She tightened her hand around the throttle, feeling the rough, slip-resistant material under her slightly moist fingers. She had a reputation as a stone cold warrior, one who was afraid of nothing, and she'd done all she could to encourage that useful fiction. Such foolishness had its uses, of course, certainly in terms of career advancement in a service like that of the Alliance, but still, it was nonsense. She was afraid in the cockpit, as scared as any other pilot who climbed into a fighter and blasted off into battle, and she had the clammy hands and sweat on her neck to prove it. She just never let it interfere with her actions.

"Two."

She centered herself, banishing the fear, the doubt, pushing it all back into the place she kept it in combat. She'd resolved long ago that duty would always come first, and she'd sworn, to herself at least, she was willing to die in battle without complaint if that was her fate. It was who she was at her core, but even more, it was a debt she owed to her mentor. Grachus knew she would still be on the estate now, working in a menial job, or at best serving as a bottom grade trooper in a garrison legion, had it not been for her unlikely childhood friend, Katrine Rigellus.

"One." She moved the controls with her right hand, even as her left dropped down to the small lever that regulated her ship's reactor. Her fingers moved lightly, pushing it to the side and then up, ignoring the AI's almost immediate warning that the system was now operating beyond its rated capacity.

She could hear the familiar hum behind her grow louder. It wasn't an enormous difference, probably nothing most pilots would even notice, but Grachus was painstakingly familiar with every aspect of her fighter. She'd tried to train her people, even intimidate them into following her lead, but for all their skill and aptitude, she'd never had much success getting them to emulate their leader's almost uncanny connection to the Palatine craft. There was a rhythm to a fighter's sounds, and more than once her singular affinity for her ship's idiosyncrasies had saved her life. But that gift was one she'd found difficult to share effectively with comrades who didn't naturally possess it.

She glanced over at her scanner, confirming what she already knew. The vector change her people had just executed was taking them around the enemy interceptors. Her adversaries were good, she knew that much. She'd served with some of them before, in the Alliance's many battles with its enemies.

But now it is Alliance warriors who are the enemy…

The opposing interceptor squadrons were already adjusting, attempting to match the maneuver her people had just executed. She nodded, a perfunctory acknowledgment that the squadron lined up against her was likely almost as good as her own.

Almost…

Grachus checked her ships, making sure they were all in the tight formation she'd ordered. Her maneuver, and the risk she was taking abusing the reactors of the squadron's vessels, would buy her people a jump, but only a short one. Those were Alliance pilots out there against them, even if they served the false Imperator, and they wouldn't be so easily fooled again.

Imperator Tarkus I. Once, the very idea of Tarkus Vennius in the Alliance's highest office would have thrilled her. Vennius had been a frequent visitor to the Rigellus estate, and a good friend to Kat—even somewhat of a father to her after Lucius Rigellus was killed in battle. Vennius had even been respectful to Grachus, accepting her as Kat's friend when most others of rank and privilege either barely acknowledged her existence or actively shunned her.

Katrine had been at the pinnacle of the estate's ecosystem, the sole heir to her patrician family's vast wealth and power. Grachus, on the other hand, had been near its bottom, the child of a once moderately prosperous Prob clan that her grandfather's disgrace had reduced to poverty and Pleb status. But despite the enormous gulf between the young girls, they had grown up together, and as an adult, Katrine had not forgotten her friend. She'd used her considerable influence to obtain a place for Grachus in the Ordeal, and then later at flight school. On graduation, Kat's sponsorship had resulted in a commission for Grachus, and a chance at a real career in the Alliance's military. Years later, when Katrine took command of *Vindictus*, she'd had Grachus transferred to her wings, where she'd groomed her ward for eventual squadron command. In due course, Kat had even managed to secure Grachus's advancement to Citizen status, an almost unheard of leap for the scion of a disgraced Pleb family.

But Grachus's respect for Vennius was gone. It had become shaky as she wondered what role the old man had played in the decision that led to Kat's mission to Santis, and to her death. But when word had reached her that Vennius had allied with the Confederation—not only the Confederation, but with the very officer that had killed Kat—her shaken respect turned quickly to hatred.

She hadn't wanted to believe, at first, that Vennius had started the civil war with his grab for power, nor that he'd abducted and later murdered the Imperatrix, but seeing him consort with the Confeds who'd killed Kat had convinced her. She had sworn to avenge her friend, and she would do whatever it took to fulfill that oath. Even side with a pig like Calavius, and acknowledge him as Imperator.

"We're coming in now, Dragons. Let's do what we do best. I want this bomber formation shattered, and I want it done before those interceptors get to us. That gives us…" She glanced down at the chronometer to check, though she already knew the answer. "…ninety-five seconds. That's not long, so make your shots count."

She gripped the throttle tightly and took a deep breath. "Break," she said into the microphone, as she jerked her hand hard to the side, bringing her fighter around and angling the vector of its thrust. There were almost forty bombers on her display…and twelve interceptors in her squadron. But the heavy assault kits slowed the attack craft, and denied them any weapons beyond the large-payload plasma bombs. They were sitting ducks for a force of ships fitted for fighter to fighter combat, especially one as tight and capable as the Dragons.

Grachus angled her ship again, continuing to alter the vector of thrust, closing on her first chosen target. She thought for an instant about holding her missiles, attacking the bombers with lasers only and saving the heavier weapons for the interceptors she knew were coming. But strafing runs took time, especially for ships burdened with bulky missiles, and her people had to take down as many bombers as possible in a very short time. Twenty-four missiles would go a long way toward getting the job done.

"Missile attacks…now." Her pilots had no doubt considered the same facts she had, but she figured a few of them might have held back the heavy weapons anyway, at least without a clear command to launch.

Her eyes were focused on the scope, tapping the throttle gently, locking her first missile on one of the bombers. Her finger tightened on the firing stud, and the fighter bucked hard as the weapon blasted out of its cradle, streaking toward the enemy ship, accelerating at 25g and adjusting its thrust angles every few milliseconds in response to its target's maneuvers.

She swung her hand hard to the side, feeling the g forces slam into her again as her engines blasted with one hundred ten percent of her reactor's standard energy production. The dampeners absorbed some of the force, but not enough to avoid a considerable amount of pain, especially in her chest, where the two ribs she'd broken weeks before were still tender. But pain meant even less to her than fear, and she gritted her teeth and powered through.

Her eyes were fixed on her second target, even as she saw out of the corner of her eye that her first missile had claimed its victim. She felt the usual burst of excitement at the kill, if a weak one. Shooting down bombers was almost child's play, at least to a pilot of her skill. Something about it had always felt subtly wrong, and she much preferred going up against other interceptors, despite the increased difficulty and danger. Alliance culture was based on victory at any cost, but there was a heavy adherence to honor as well, and little of that was to be gained destroying nearly-helpless targets.

She pressed the firing button again, sending her second missile on its way, looking almost immediately afterward at the long-range display. The enemy interceptors were inbound, about fifty seconds from entering range. Her hand tightened on the controls, and her mind shifted to the coming danger even as she fired her lasers, destroying a third bomber. Most enemies would have broken and fled by now, but she knew her former Alliance comrades would fight to the end.

This civil war will be the bloodiest conflict in history. The very thought of two sides fighting each other, each raised and trained to Alliance ideals, adhering to the way, was terrifying in its implications. The way is the way. How many times had she said it, thought it? But never against fellow Palatians. Never before now.

But she didn't care. The cost was irrelevant. She had one goal, and one goal alone. To avenge her lost friend. To kill those responsible for Katrine Rigellus's death. And Tarkus Vennius and his Gray Alliance followers had become the proxies for her vengeful rage.

She brought her ship around, nodding approvingly as the scanner confirmed her people had taken out almost half the bombers. The rest were trying to move away, breaking their formations and expending massive amounts of fuel to do it. The evasive maneuvers would cost the survivors their chance at completing their attack runs. By any measure, the mission was a success. Her people had done their duty for *Illustrious* and the other battleships. Now they would be fighting for themselves.

"Enemy fighters coming in. Let's go get 'em. And watch yourselves...they've got missiles and we don't." She stared ahead, eyes narrow and focused. The lead wave of interceptors had launched their heavy weapons. Grachus watched as three streaked toward her, their onboard AIs adjusting the missiles' vectors to home in on her fighter. But she was already responding, blasting hard to port, putting every bit of thrust her ship could produce into a series of wild evasive maneuvers. Missiles were no joke, and she concentrated hard, knowing one of the deadly drones could finish her in an instant. But she knew every aspect of the Alliance's weapons, their acceleration capacity, tactical programs, range. There were dangers in fighting other Alliance warriors, but there were advantages too, familiarity with their systems being one.

She brought her ship around hard, watching as, one by one, the small dots on her screen began flashing—missiles that had exhausted their fuel. Those weapons were still deadly, but with no more thrust, they were stuck on constant vectors and velocities, and thus were easy to avoid.

She spared a quick glance at the screen. She had lost one ship to the barrage. No, two. But Sestus had managed to eject, and his beacon was transmitting. *So, only one dead. So far.*

"Let's go, Dragons. It's down to lasers against lasers." Her tone was cold, focused. This was a knife fight...and she almost pitied the pilots coming up against her pack of ruthless killers. "Let's do what we do best."

Chapter Two

Communique from Tyler Barron to Admiral Striker

As I sit here and record this dispatch, we are preparing for another raid. *Dauntless* and *Repulse* will join a force of Gray Alliance ships attacking a Red Alliance supply convoy, while *Illustrious* and *Constitution* remain with the Sentinel-2 defense fleet. I dislike splitting my forces, but I know the loss of the Cilian system and its fortress would mean the destruction of Imperator Vennius's cause. Our ships are the heaviest and strongest, and I feel it is important to have a presence both on the defensive and also accompanying the attacks against the enemy logistics.

The previous missions were successful, though not without cost. *Dauntless* took moderate damage in the last raid, as did *Repulse*, though in both cases, Commander Fritz was able to direct the damage control teams in herculean repair efforts. Despite the hard duty my fleet has endured, all four of my battleships remain fully-operational. Though I have documented this more times than I dare to count, I must again note that Commander Fritz deserves an enormous share of the credit for what we have achieved. I have seen few officers so dedicated, so capable, so tireless, in the implementation of their duties.

I am less sanguine about the overall prospects of the war. We continue to inflict greater losses than we take, almost without exception, but with the enemy still controlling over two-thirds of the Alliance fleet, even a moderately favorable loss ratio becomes negative.

I continue to be amazed at the combat power of the new

battleships, and I can say without reservation that, had you not sent them, the Gray Alliance cause would have been lost already. I can only imagine how much they were missed on the Union front, and I deeply regret what I must now report. I have analyzed our operations to date, and I have come to an inescapable conclusion. Unless additional forces are sent here—soon—I believe Imperator Vennius will be defeated, despite the best efforts of the forces under my command. If this is allowed to happen, the Alliance will fall under the effective control of the Union.

I have no plan or stratagem to offer, no tactics I believe can lead to victory with only the current ships deployed to the theater. We are relegated to operations against supplies and lightning raids on isolated enemy forces, but we are running out of time. We are cut off from effective communications with any areas outside those we control. The Red Alliance high command undoubtedly uses every passing week to consolidate its forces and prepare for the final battle.

I do not know when that will come, and I can promise you most assuredly that, when it does, we will fight—Imperator Vennius's Grays and my own Confederation forces both—with all the strength we possess. But I must also report to you that I see no outcome of such a conflict but utter defeat. Calavius is a pompous and arrogant man, but he is not a complete fool. He has been burned several times by premature attacks on Sentinel-2, and the long delay we have seen since the last attempt only confirms my notion that he has resolved to amass an invincible force, and only when that is ready, to return and seek to finish the war in one bloody stroke.

As I noted previously, I can only imagine how desperately the soon-to be-launched battleships are needed on the main front, and I understand completely if you must turn down this request for further aid. But if Vennius falls, I believe a Union-controlled Alliance will not hesitate to invade. Such a war against an external enemy will only aid Calavius in solidifying his hold on the Imperator's seat, and, of course, it is the end result his Union paymasters have sought all along.

You know as well as I do how thinly our forces are spread in the target sectors. The Alliance forces will slice through our barely defended Rim frontier, on to the populated worlds beyond. Even to the Iron Belt and the Core Worlds. The Confederation's very existence will face a dire threat.

You have my oath, Admiral, that the forces under my command will fight to the end, and that we will do everything possible to degrade enemy forces that might be used against the Confederation. You also have my assessment, given not only to a superior officer, but to one I have come to consider a friend: what we do here, unassisted, will not be enough. We will fall, and I fear, not long after, you will be struggling to defend Megara and the other worlds of the Core.

Bridge
CFS Dauntless
Athenae System
Year 311 AC

"Full power to primaries. Bring us around hard, Commander. Aim right for that big bastard up front." Barron leaned forward in his chair—*Atara Travis's chair now, by rights*. He wore the insignia of a Confederation commodore, and his authority extended well beyond the hull of his beloved *Dauntless*, but he was having trouble with the transition. He'd wondered more than once if he'd been wrong not to transfer his flag, to move to *Repulse* or one of the other new ships, and leave *Dauntless* to his longtime exec and friend.

God knows she deserves it. She should have had her own ship a year ago. More, even.

Travis had chosen instead to stay with him, passing up offered promotions, as had virtually all of *Dauntless's* crew. He appreciated the loyalty, so much so that the thought of leaving ranged somewhere from the far side of difficult to damned near impossible. He knew he'd have to go eventually, but for six months now the thought in his mind had been the same. *Not today*.

"Primaries are ready, Commodore. Entering range in thirty seconds." Travis's voice was unchanged, the same firm, immediate type of response she always gave. If the very concept of competence had a sound, it would have been that of his first officer's cool tone.

Travis hadn't displayed the slightest sign of resentment that Barron had not moved to one of the larger, more powerful ships and opened the way for her to command *Dauntless*. In fact, he'd thought he'd detected a hint of relief from her once or twice, as if she was as content to keep things the way they had been as he was.

"Very well, Commander. Authorize the gunnery to fire at will as we come into range."

"Yes, sir."

The target wasn't a battleship. Not even an escort. It didn't have a beam on it hot enough to make a pot of coffee. But if Vennius's intel was correct—and for all that the Gray Imperator was outnumbered by his opponent, he retained enough contacts and influence to produce a steady stream of mostly-reliable intelligence—the freighter, and the other two lined up just next to it, were packed to capacity with advanced quantum computer components destined for Palatia. For the ships of Calavius's fleet.

Barron didn't like chasing down convoys like some kind of privateer. His people were combat veterans, perhaps the best the Confederation had, and blasting cargo ships to scrap seemed beneath their pay grade. But warriors did what duty demanded, and right now the best way the overmatched Gray forces could fight their enemy was by picking at their supplies, keeping them off balance.

"Admiral, we just got a communique from *Repulse*. Captain Eaton advises that they are heavily engaged."

"Very well, Commander. Advise her we are about to engage the enemy freighters." Even as he finished his sentence, the bridge lights dimmed for an instant, and the familiar hum sounded throughout the ship. *Dauntless*'s primaries lanced out, one of the two beams slamming into the target. The other missed, but one hit out of two was solid shooting at such long range—and it was more than enough to take out a cargo ship. The freighter was large, two-thirds *Dauntless*'s length, but she hadn't been built to withstand battleship-killing particle accelerator beams. Barron watched on the display as the dot flickered for a few seconds, and then disappeared entirely.

His eyes darted down to the small screen on his own workstation, where his AI was reconstructing the demolition of the enemy vessel. The beam had struck directly amidships, and an instant later, a massive series of internal explosions had erupted, splitting the stricken vessel into two nearly equal-sized sections.

"Recharge primaries." Barron's words were as robotic-sounding as they were unnecessary. Travis had already sent her own equally superfluous command to *Dauntless*'s veteran gunners, who had begun to reset their weapons without being told to do so. "Lock onto target number two."

"Already locked, Commodore." Travis had only slipped up once, perhaps the fifth or six time she'd addressed Barron, and even then, the word "captain" had only partially escaped her lips before she'd pulled it back. "Entering range, and ready to fire as soon as charging is complete."

"Very well." *When you finally do transfer off Dauntless, you couldn't be leaving her in better hands…But not today.*

His eyes darted up to the main display. It had been an instinctive move, a cursory glance at the incoming data from the other fight, the one where *Repulse* and a flotilla of Vennius's ships were taking on the escorting force intended to protect the freighters. But now his eyes froze, locked on a small column of numbers scrolling down the side.

Fighter data. Specifically, loss figures. Vennius and Eaton's squadrons were suffering far higher casualties than expected, even in the worst-case scenario. The enemy force had been larger than anticipated, and Eaton's massive new battleship was crewed with raw squadrons. But still, that didn't explain what was happening.

What's going on over there?

He looked up as the lights dimmed again, the heavy guns momentarily soaking up every available watt produced by *Dauntless*'s reactors. Another hit. The second freighter was mortally wounded. This one endured a more tortured ending, as small explosions rippled through it, blasting out parts of the vessel and tearing huge gaping rents in its hull. The ship was still there, more or less, but energy readings were dropping rapidly toward zero. The freighter was dying, but Barron wasn't going to assume anything. Undamaged cargo could be reclaimed from a dead hulk, after all. "Recharge weapons, and target the third ship. Then bring us around to finish off number two."

"Yes, Commodore."

Barron's eyes moved back to the screen, to the troubling loss figures. "And then set a course back to the main fleet, maximum speed."

"Yes, sir."

Barron paused, trying to figure out what was causing the heavy fighter casualties. Then he decided it didn't matter. What mattered was how he responded.

"And scramble all fighters. Prepare to launch on my command."

*   *   *

Kyle Jamison stared at the small screen on his ship's control panel. The long-range display was full of icons and symbols, each representing a warship or a squadron of fighters. The battle had begun as a hit and run assault against a supply convoy. But the escort force here had been far more powerful than expected, and things had escalated to a full-fledged pitched battle.

Did the Reds get tipped off? Or are they just being more careful with their convoys after we picked off half a dozen?

Jamison nodded, grinning cynically as he thought about how quickly the two sides in the Alliance civil war had assumed distinct identities. The Grays were named, informally at least, for the colors of their uniforms and the flags they had quickly designed to match. They fought for Imperator Tarkus Vennius, and they stood in opposition to their more numerous adversaries, the similarly anointed Reds. Jamison wasn't sure of the source of the enemy faction's color, though he'd heard it was drawn from the scarlet standards of the rival Imperator's house. Which seemed as likely an explanation as any.

The fighting had been fierce, far more intense than expected. The plan had been for the main force to draw off the escorting battleships from the freighters, allowing *Dauntless* to come around from the cover of the system's second sun and take out the cargo vessels. Everything went according to plan, save for one thing. There were more Red ships than there were supposed to be. And, perhaps worse, their fighters were tearing into the Gray squadrons with a ferocity he hadn't seen…at least outside of his own veteran wings.

He reached down and toggled the comm unit. "Raptor, we've got Red fighters cutting up a Gray bomber force. The Blues are closest. We may be too late, but see what you can do."

"On it, Thunder." Jake "Raptor" Stockton was *Dauntless's* ace pilot…hell, he was the whole fleet's top fighter jock, the role model of the thousands of new recruits being rushed through flight school to take their places in the line of battle.

Jamison watched on his screen as Blue squadron, his most elite, reacted almost immediately to its famous leader's commands. "Raptor" Stockton was wasting no time, and *Dauntless's* strike force commander was gratified to see his friend back to form. Stockton had suffered horrific wounds when his fighter crash-landed in the bay, and even after he'd recovered physically, the psychological scars had nearly destroyed him.

The two men were nothing alike, not really. Jamison was cool, calculating, almost entirely lacking the bravado so common in the fighter corps, while Stockton had long been almost a stereotype of the wild fighter pilot—fearless, reckless, oblivious to all but victory over an opponent. But they had been friends for many years, as close as brothers, and Jamison was thankful not only that his best pilot was back up to form, but that he had his friend back as well.

Jamison's eyes flicked back to his display. *Dauntless* had launched its squadrons just as the big ship had started back toward the main fight, but now the old battleship was moving into the combat zone. It would engage the enemy in just a few moments. He glanced at the readouts coming in, the damage to *Repulse* and the Gray battleships fighting alongside her. He didn't know what was making the enemy fighters so effective, but he had no intention of letting those squadrons anywhere near his mother ship. Stockton's people were already on the way, blasting full on their thrusters. Jamison had been planning to hold the other four squadrons in reserve, watching and deploying them as opportunity presented itself. But he had a feeling in his gut, one he didn't like. More on instinct than the analysis he so favored, he decided not to wait.

"Red, Yellow, Green, Eagle leaders…form up your wings. We're going in on Blue squadron's heels."

He barely heard the expected acknowledgements. Stockton's singular brilliance didn't take away from the fact that all Jamison's squadrons were commanded by crack veterans. He knew he didn't have to tell them anything twice.

He reached down and grabbed the fighter's controls, pulling back and blasting with maximum thrust, even as he saw half his birds already doing the same.

They were doing what they had done so many times. Bringing the fight to the enemy.

Chapter Three

Excerpt from the Personal Log of Kyle Jamison

Alliance pilots are highly-skilled. I remember that well enough from the deadly fighting at Santis...my God, was that more than four years ago? The losses from that terrible fight still cut deep, the wounds as painful as if they had been inflicted yesterday. But for all their skill and courage, the Alliance squadrons we faced then were hampered by the technology of their craft, out-powered and out-gunned by our own fighters. That is true now to a far lesser extent, if at all. Their new ships—Palatines, the Gray officers told me they're called—are a huge step up in capability, incorporating technology seized from conquered worlds. They are nearly a match for our own Lightnings.

I know this is a capable enemy we dare not underestimate, but still, I cannot shake the edginess I feel, the strange feeling that something greater is at play. This enemy, so capable and deadly already, has become even more dangerous. There is something there, something unforeseen...perhaps a new leader inspiring them to excel. I see it in the way they fight, in the crispness of their maneuvers. In the losses we have suffered.

I know the odds are against our allies, the Grays, that the entire war is likely to end in defeat. But that is not my problem to worry about now. Such concerns are the province of Commodore Barron and the new Imperator. My duty is in the cockpit, at the command of *Dauntless*'s squadrons and, now, those of the other three ships in the expeditionary force. And I fear we face a new danger, one that is like to cut a bloody swatch through our ranks.

One that could destroy us.
    Unless we destroy it first.

Bridge
CFS Dauntless
Athenae System
Year 311 AC

"We're closing, Commodore. Several enemy fighter wings have changed course and are moving to engage us. Commander Stockton's squadrons are about to intercept."

"Very well, Commander." Barron leaned back and took a deep breath. He knew, more perhaps than anyone, just what his squadrons could do. He tried to avoid hubris, struggled to maintain his caution at all times, but with Kyle Jamison in command of his strike force and Jake Stockton back to form—not to mention Olya Federov, Dirk Timmons, and the rest of his crack pilots—he couldn't help but feel confident his ship had little to fear from an equal number of enemy fighters.

He thought for an instant about pulling back, delaying *Dauntless*'s move toward the battleline until his squadrons had completed their work. But his trust in his pilots was absolute, and the rest of the ships of the line looked like they could use the help.

That alone is cause for concern. We should have crushed the escort force easily. There are more ships here than we expected.

Barron tried to resist the thought forcing its way into his mind, but to no avail.

They knew we were coming. Somehow, they knew…

"Maintain full thrust, Commander. Change vector 109.210.007." He stared at the huge 3D display in the middle of *Dauntless*'s bridge. "Directly toward the enemy line."

"Yes, Commodore." Travis was staring at her display, a rare moment of distraction delaying her response. A few seconds later: "Course set, sir." Then: "Commodore, *Repulse* is under attack from two enemy battleships. She has suffered significant damage."

His eyes snapped around, fixing on Captain Eaton's ship on the display. The new battleship out-massed and outgunned *Dauntless*, and by extension anything either Alliance faction possessed, but she'd been bracketed by three enemy capital ships, and at least half a dozen escorts. She'd held her own, reducing one of the enemy battleships to a lifeless hulk, but the other two were pounding away, and even her immense armor plating could only hold back so much destructive force.

"Adjust course, Commander. Directly for *Repulse*. Full thrust."

"Yes, sir." Travis worked her controls, leaning forward and relaying commands down to engineering. "Course set for *Repulse*, Commodore." Then, a few seconds later: "Sir, that course takes us almost directly toward the approaching enemy fighters."

"I'm aware of that, Commander. But Captain Eaton and her people need some help…and all our squadrons are in a position to intercept the approaching attack force. I doubt many of those bombers will get through."

"Yes, sir."

Barron glanced over at his first officer, but he didn't say anything. There was concern in her voice. Barron understood. He understood because he had the same feeling. He felt as though he was letting his cockiness, his overconfidence, loose. But *Repulse* needed the help, and that was that.

He flipped the controls on his comm, pulling up the point defense gunnery channel. "This is Commodore Barron." He still felt ridiculous every time he said that. "I need all of you at one hundred percent right now. No, one hundred ten percent. We've got bombers inbound, and if the fighters don't get them all, I'm counting on you to finish the job."

"We're here, sir. You can depend on us." It was Commander Christian, *Dauntless*'s top gunnery officer. Christian's responsibilities went far beyond just the small anti-fighter turrets. He ran *Dauntless*'s primaries and her secondaries—every beam on the ship hot enough to light a candle. Barron let out a small sigh. The defensive weapons were in good hands.

"I know I can, Charles. I always have."

He cut the connection, and he turned back toward Travis. "Let's go help *Repulse*. Full thrust…now!"

*   *   *

The explosion was silent on the small display, just a flash of light, but it was enough to divert Jake Stockton's attention from the enemy fighter he was pursuing. It was the second of his Blues he'd lost, it seemed in as many minutes. The first had hurt, but he'd written it off to bad luck. His veteran pilots were well able to handle anything they encountered, at least that was what he'd thought. But now, as he watched the battle unfolding all around, he could see more of his people were in trouble. Riggs had an enemy on his tail, and Beauvais was bracketed by three, coming at him along different vectors.

What the hell is going on here?

He pulled his arm hard to the side, angling his thrust and blasting away from his target. There was nothing Stockton hated more than letting his prey go. Except watching more of his people die.

He felt the g forces slam into him as his engines fired at full power, overwhelming his fighter's compensators. His eyes were still fixed on the display, and with each passing second, he felt his concern ratchet up.

This lead squadron is…

He didn't finish the thought. It wasn't in him to admit, even to himself, that another squadron was as good as his Blues. Or better…

He reached to the side of his head, toggling the squadron-wide channel on the comm. "Heads up, everybody. This squadron running interference for the bombers is good. I mean *good*. Stay focused…and don't underestimate them." He felt strange scolding his people for not taking their enemies seriously enough. There were few pilots in the Confederation service with a reputation for cockiness and bravado to match Stockton's, though since his accident he'd become more controlled, methodical. The recklessness of his youth had died in the fire on the landing bay and, once he'd learned to adapt to what had happened to him, it had been replaced by cold confidence. Still, he wasn't able to wrap his head around his Blues having an adversary as good as they were, and he didn't think any of his pilots were either.

But there they are...

He stared straight ahead, picking out the closest target. He eased his controls to the side, moving to match the enemy fighter's vector. His hand was tense around the controls, his finger poised over the firing stud. His approach vector was wild, unpredictable, designed to fool his prey. But before he could get a shot, the Alliance ship blasted its own engines, an unexpected maneuver that came close to putting the intended target on Stockton's blind spot. His hand shifted, almost by instinct, breaking free of his enemy's move. Barely.

Watch these guys, Raptor...

The next words stalled in his mind, some internal resistance fighting to hold them back. But they were still there. *They're as good as your Blues.*

He swung around yet again, moving in on another fighter. His first target had broken free cleanly, and their vectors were near opposites, sending them away from each other at 0.005c. He slammed his throttle back hard, pushing his engines again to one hundred percent output. His fingers squeezed tightly, his dual laser cannon firing at the extent of its range. Stockton liked to close with his opponents, attacking only when he'd seized the advantage of position. But that wasn't going to happen, not here. These pilots were too good, their own instincts too sharp. There would be no finesse in this battle, only a brutal struggle to the finish.

He fired again, and again as he closed. The ship in front of him jerked around wildly, the pilot altering vector constantly. Stockton's shots went wide, the target moving even as his fingers closed on the trigger.

C'mon, Raptor…no one flies a fighter like you. It's part of you, like an arm or a leg…

He felt his body relax, his mind extending out, like the eyes of his craft. His hands loosened on the throttle, but his control remained sharp, tight. He imagined his enemy, considered the moves he'd make in the same situation. He ignored the targeting computer and breathed deeply, slowly.

His hand jerked to the side, then back. He fired with each burst of thrust, almost in rhythm, and his laser bolts closed in on the target, zipping by mere meters from the Alliance ship. He could see—feel—the desperation growing in his enemy, even as his own serenity endured. He was Raptor, death in a fighter, and he'd come to kill.

He fired again. Another miss. Then again. Miss.

His will was iron, and he fought off the frustration and fear. He fired again, and as he did, he saw another Alliance fighter breaking off from an engagement and altering vector to close with him.

Time was running out. He'd never be able to handle two of these enemies. He had to finish his target in time to come about and face the new attacker. Or he'd have to break off. Run. And that was a language "Raptor" Stockton didn't speak.

"C'mon, you bastard," he muttered under his breath, even as he struggled to maintain the sense of calm. He fired again. Almost! Then the enemy blasted hard to port, and unexpected move. But Stockton didn't delay. He didn't lose a second. Almost faster than his rational mind could follow, he angled his own thrusters, matching the enemy's maneuver, hanging onto the target's tail.

His eyes narrowed, and his hand tightened. He could feel his heartbeat, a steady pounding in his ears, even as he drew in regular, focused breaths. He felt his finger moving, almost without conscious thought. The button was smooth plastic, slick now with his own perspiration. It moved, slowly, steadily…until he heard the familiar click, and the sound of the lasers firing.

He was watching the display when the enemy ship vanished. A hit! He'd taken his enemy down. But there was no time to savor victory. The second Alliance ship was coming on hard, almost in firing range.

*   *   *

Jovi Grachus leaned forward, her shoulders hunched over her fighter's dashboard.

That ship is *Dauntless. I* know *it. Captain Barron is here.*

Grachus's squadron had landed and rearmed after their first sortie, and now they were escorting a bomber strike force toward an enemy battleship.

Not just any battleship…

Her first instinct had been to go for the Confederation ship because she considered Vennius's allies to be weak and easily defeated. If they suffered enough losses, they would turn tail, leaving their ally, the pretender Imperator, to his own resources…and near-certain defeat. But then she reviewed the scans in greater detail.

The mass, shape, primary components. All matches.

She had studied *Dauntless*, reviewed every scan and document the Alliance possessed on the Confederation's most famous vessel. Now, she was sure. Her greatest enemy was here, and if she could get enough bombers through, she just might taste the vengeance she had craved for four years.

"Dragons, stay tight. We've got to get the bombers through." She felt the danger in her gut. She'd expected her Dragons to obliterate the sole Confederation squadron engaging them, but the fight had been far from one-sided. Her people had the edge, perhaps. Slightly. But this was no normal squadron. She'd been holding back the other wings, keeping them ready to deal with the rest of the approaching Confed force. But now she wasn't sure what to do. She didn't command the Fire Hawks and the War Cats, but she didn't doubt her fellow squadron leaders would do as she asked either. She might be the jumped-up offspring of a disgraced family, but she'd made her bones in the fighter corps, and there were few pilots who refused to heed her advice in battle.

As she approached her chosen target, one of her fighters vanished from her screen. Deserius. Grachus felt as though she had been punched in the gut. He was one of her newer replacements, but he'd been a veteran already when she'd gotten him, and he'd honed his abilities since then. She'd had great hopes for him, but now those were gone. There was no sign of an escape pod, just the empty space where his ship had been, and a small cloud of radiation with elevated, but dropping, energy readings.

She felt a surge of anger, and she focused intently on the ship that had killed him. The pilot was already changing vector, shifting course to pursue another of her people. She could see in the moves, the swiftness and determination…this was no normal pilot.

She watched for a few seconds, her eyes darting all across the enemy formation. *No, that is no normal pilot…and I'd bet a fair bit he's the squadron leader.*

Grachus knew well how her death would affect and demoralize her own Dragons, and she suspected it would be the same for the Confed pilots. She was about to send two of her closest pilots after the enemy leader, but she hesitated, watching his wild and unpredictable maneuvers. No, she couldn't send anyone. This Confed was too good, too capable. She would have to take him down herself.

She eased her controls back, feeding power to her engines. Grachus knew how good she was, but she'd never let pride or arrogance rule her actions, and she wasn't about to start now. This was a worthy opponent, one who wouldn't hesitate to vaporize her if she gave him the chance. *And it won't take much of a mistake to get killed by this one…*

She reached out to her board, activating the AI. She wanted to know everything she could about this squadron, and particularly about the pilot she was about to engage. She tended to ignore enemy communications in battle, feeling it was a waste of time to obsess over mostly secure encryption. But she knew her ship's computer was working constantly, trying to decode even the smallest bits of information. And right now, she wanted everything she could get.

Unfortunately, Confederation codes were sophisticated, and her AI had so far gleaned only a single piece of intelligence, one of dubious utility. Still it was something, even if only the name of this formation.

Blue squadron.

All right, Blue Leader…and I'm sure that's who you are. Let's do this.

She pulled back hard on the throttle, her body slammed back into her seat as her engines blasted at full.

I'm coming for you, Blue Leader…

Chapter Four

"Commodore, the dogfight…"

Tyler Barron was already staring at the display, even before Commander Travis's warning. *Dauntless*'s fighters were engaged. And they were taking heavy losses.

Barron hadn't seen his people struggle so badly against a force that didn't outnumber them, not since…

Santis.

But at Santis his forces faced the elite of the Alliance, their flagship and the pick of their squadrons. This was just a raid against an enemy supply convoy.

Or is it? The whole thing had started to feel almost like a trap. *Don't underestimate this enemy…*

Dauntless shook hard, a lucky long-ranged shot from the approaching enemy line. Barron had ordered his ship to join *Repulse*, and the enemy had responded by sending another two battleships forward. *Dauntless*'s primaries had riddled one of the ships, and it had fallen behind, now unable to match its companion's acceleration. But the second vessel was entering its own firing range, and it was clear the ship's gunners knew their craft.

He checked the damage report, though he was so attuned to his ship he could almost tell by the way she lurched from the hit. Some external damage, one secondary battery disabled. Nothing too bad. *Nothing Fritzie can't handle.*

He looked up at the small chromometer next to the main display. The countdown clock read 64. Just over a minute until the ship's fearsome primary batteries would be charged and ready to fire again. Barron had gotten used to his gunners blowing away targeting norms and raking enemy vessels with deadly effectiveness, even at the longest ranges. But the Alliance crews' evasive maneuvers were far better than those of the Union, and he was still adapting his expectations to the realities of this enemy. His people were going to miss more, and he couldn't count on one marksmanlike shot after another pulling him out of trouble.

He looked back toward the 3D display that dominated the center of the bridge. Kyle Jamison had brought up the rest of *Dauntless*'s squadrons, but the enemy had also thrown reserves into the fight. He watched, silently, his eyes moving back toward the cluster of enemy bombers coming up right behind the fighter battle. He'd been confident that none of the attackers would make it through his fighter screen…but now doubt began to creep in from the edges of his mind.

Maybe he could reinforce his squadrons. He looked all around the long-range display, searching for fighters he could redirect to join the fight. The Alliance wings were all too far away, most of them deeply engaged in their own dogfights or executing strafing runs on the Red battleline. *Repulse* had sent half of her own birds to the far flank of the line. That was almost an hour's flying time to adjust their vectors and return… and by then they'd be almost out of fuel. The other half of Captain Eaton's fighters had just landed, their tanks and power banks empty. She might get a dozen ships out in twenty minutes or so, but that would still be too few and too late. For better or worse, *Dauntless*'s pilots were on their own.

He pushed back against the growing doubts. His squadrons would do the job. And if they didn't completely turn back the enemy bombers, Commander Christian and his gunners would be ready. But despite his efforts, he felt edgy. Fighting off a bomber attack while engaged with enemy battleships was difficult, one of the situations the "book" warned about. Fire control would become a nightmare and, in the end, he would face a choice: slack off against the enemy battleships or mount a hampered defense against the bombers. It was bad either way, and he hoped to avoid the need to make the decision.

But as his eyes moved back and forth, he could feel the truth in his stomach. At least some of those bombers were going to get through. And all he could do was inflict as much damage as possible on the enemy battleships before they did.

The countdown clock was in single digits. Five, four, three...

He watched intently, and even as the numeral '1' was blinking out, his mouth was pressed against his comm unit, and a single word was forming, his tone grim, determined.

"Fire."

*   *   *

Watch your ass, Raptor, or you're going to get it blown off...

Stockton could feel the sweat on his arms, his back. His heart was pounding, so hard he'd have sworn he could hear each thunderous beat.

He'd seen the enemy fighter approaching, and he knew the pilot had targeted him. He'd had more than enough time to prepare, and he'd been ready to teach the Alliance flyer what it meant to come after "Raptor" Stockton.

But he'd gotten the lesson instead...and almost a lot more. He could still feel the shiver between his shoulder blades. The laser bolt had been close, too close. He suspected when he got back to *Dauntless*, he'd see the scar on the side of his ship. And he'd know just how close he'd come to his last mission.

If I make it back...

He was still in a fight, and a damned nasty one. He'd been sure he had his target, but the Alliance bird had pulled off a series of maneuvers he'd never seen before. One second, the ship was in his sights, seconds from destruction. Then, sud-

denly, he was watching a wild sequence of turns and unpredictable bursts of thrust that ended with him as the prey.

His arm moved to the port, then starboard, then port again,
in his own series of bizarre moves. He couldn't take anything for
granted, not with this enemy. Part of him respected an adversary of such ability, but mostly he felt apprehension, tension…
fear.

He was coming around, moving away from his opponent.
He was going to swing back from a distance, and close at full
speed. His enemy was in pursuit, no doubt convinced he was
running. That gnawed at him, not the least because part of him
wanted to run. Stockton didn't flee from battles, and he knew
he'd fight this one to the end, but that didn't stop the visions
from creeping in, moments with Stara, good times with Kyle
Jamison in the officers' club. The reckless bravery of his youth
was long gone, and now his courage carried baggage—a full rec-
ognition of all he had, all he would lose, the day his skills failed
him for just an instant.

Damn.

Stockton was pulling every maneuver he could, but his
enemy was still hanging tight. His ego was part of what had
always made him the best, the source of the confidence that
allowed him to fly the way he did. It wasn't in him to admit he'd
met a pilot as good as he was, much less one better, but it was
getting harder to avoid that conclusion.

He jerked the throttle hard and then cut the engines, hitting
the positioning thrusters to swing his ship around. It was a
dangerous move, he knew, one that made him an easier target.
But it would be unexpected, and in fighter combat, surprising an
enemy was everything.

He squeezed his fingers hard, gritting his teeth as his cockpit reverberated with the whine of his laser cannons. He fired
again, and again. Close! As close as his enemy's shot had come
to his ship. But he'd missed, just as his foe had.

He felt the urge to stay where he was, to keep shooting, but
he was already pushing his luck. He angled his controls again
and blasted at nearly full thrust, as a burst of enemy laser fire

ripped through the space his ship had just occupied. He gasped for breath against the g forces as he pushed to full power, changing his vector slightly every second, or even half second. Stockton had always been almost one with his fighter, his stomach cast iron against even the wildest maneuvers, but he could feel the unease in his gut as the wild gyrations made the bile rise up to the back of his throat.

Stay focused, Raptor.

He was in the toughest fight of his life, and he knew it. The cool confidence that dominated everything he did was long gone, and now all he could feel was the coldness…and the grim focus that would save his life.

If anything could…

Then, his comm came to life.

"Raptor, hang on…I'm on the way."

Dirk Timmons's voice was clear and crisp on Stockton's comm, but he could hear the tension in his comrade's voice. Timmons and Stockton had long been rivals, arguably the two best pilots in the Confederation service. And two men who'd, for many years, detested each other.

War and shared sacrifice had gone a long way to erasing years of bad feeling, and the two men had become, if not exactly friends, at least something close to that. But enough of the rivalry remained to make Timmons the last person Stockton wanted rushing to save him, and the feeling of relief that greeted the Timmons's words told him just how scared he was.

"Roger that, Warrior. I'll be here." *I hope.*

Stockton moved his arm forward and to the port, cutting his thrust and angling his vector yet again. He'd been surrendering the initiative to his adversary, but now the realization that Timmons was rushing to his aid poked at his pride, and he felt a wave of aggression. He was the top ace in the Confederation fleet. No Alliance pilot was going to take him down. No way.

He brought his ship around, firing a burst with his lasers. More near misses before his target reacted, lurching away from his assault. His eyes were trained on the Alliance ship, but now his enemy was pulling back.

Running?

He couldn't believe the enemy he'd faced for the last twenty minutes was suddenly fleeing the battle. *Low on fuel, maybe? No, if that squadron was escorting those bombers…*

The bombers!

His eyes shot down to the display. The assault force was heading right for *Dauntless*. Yellow squadron was moving to intercept, but they were going to be late. All along the line, the Alliance ships were moving back, trying to coax the Confed squadrons to pursue, and move farther from *Dauntless* and the wave of bombers heading toward her.

"Blue squadron, cease pursuit. All fighters, come about and pursue those bombers. Now!"

You damned fool! You let those interceptors hang you up. All the while, they were just opening a lane for that assault force.

Stockton was angry, with himself mostly. Not only had his flying been matched—he wasn't ready to acknowledge he might have been outflown, not yet at least—but he'd been hoodwinked too. *Dauntless*'s entire strike force was out of position to intercept the incoming attack.

He slipped his hand down to the side of his chair, opening the cover that enclosed his override controls. He flipped the switches, ignoring the warnings from the AI as he increased his reactor's output to one hundred ten percent.

He felt the increased power as the g forces slammed him back even harder into his acceleration couch. It was more than discomfort now. It was pain. But he didn't care. It took his enemy by surprise, and he managed to break completely free. He'd let himself be suckered into a battle when his main job had been to protect *Dauntless*. He'd be damned now if he was going to let those bombers get through, at least not without doing everything he could. Taking any risk necessary.

"Blues, switch off those safeties. We need velocity now." Stockton was one who frequently took heavy risks, but he was far less likely to order his pilots to follow his lead. More often than not, he was trying to stop them from emulating him. But *Dauntless* was on the line now, and every bomber that delivered its plasma torpedo payload would tear into her hull, kill her crew.

"Roger that, Leader."

"We're with you, Raptor."

The responses came in one after the other, every one of his pilots snapping back their answers without delay.

Everyone who is still here.

He'd lost four pilots in the fight, and more than one of his people were flying a damaged bird right now. They'd drawn blood too, but a stalemate was the best Stockton could convince himself the battle had been, and in the back of his mind he suspected something worse. His Blues had been bested...and that was intolerable.

He flipped the comm to Jamison's direct channel. "Thunder...those bombers..."

"I know, Raptor. The interceptors tied us up, pulled us off course."

"They pulled on over on us, Thunder." Stockton didn't find it easy to admit he'd been bested, but the realization was sinking in.

"Do what you can, Raptor. We've got to get at least some of those bombers."

"We're inbound, Kyle. One ten on the reactors."

There was a short pause, and Stockton half expected Jamison to order his people back to normal energy levels. But the next words came across on the main comm line, and Jamison's voice was stone cold as he uttered them.

"All squadrons...go to one hundred ten on your reactors. We've got to get those bombers. Whatever it takes."

Stockton felt a chill inside. Kyle Jamison was his best friend, closer than a brother, but the two men were very different. Where he was cocky, sometimes arrogant, Jamison was like a rock, steady, unshakeable. "Thunder" Jamison didn't order his squadrons to engage in reckless maneuvers. At least not until now.

The Blues were the best *Dauntless* had...but ordering the rest of the wings to cut their safeties too was *dangerous*. Stockton took a deep breath, as he looked down at the display. He moved the center of reference, pushing it back, farther behind. He had a hunch…and a second later he realized he was right.

The Alliance fighters had reversed course again. They were following his people. The Blues would get a few shots at the enemy bombers—if they were lucky—but then the enemy interceptors would be on them again.

He stared at the dots on the screen for a few more seconds, one question running through his mind again and again as his eyes focused on the tiny dot he knew was his recent opponent's ship.

Who the hell are you?

Chapter Five

"Bombers entering range of our defensive batteries, Commodore. They're moving at 0.012c. We'll have roughly three minutes before they reach launch range."

Barron nodded, and then he said, "All batteries, open fire." He knew his order would shut down *Dauntless's* primaries. The massive particle accelerators sucked up almost every watt of power the big ship could generate, effectively shutting down all other weapons systems.

Barron could see the status indicators, showing his orders being obeyed. The small anti-fighter batteries didn't make any sound, at least none that could be heard all the way inside the ship, on her well-protected bridge. But that didn't make them any less deadly. He watched as the first enemy bomber vanished, and then a second. But there were nearly thirty left, even after the Yellows had attacked, taking down a respectable eight of the attacking craft.

Dauntless's Yellow squadron had been the closest, best positioned to intercept, but she was also the ship's most junior at present, with most of its veteran personnel transferred to Blue and Scarlet Eagle squadrons to replace losses. The Yellows had been a crack unit once, when Tillis "Ice" Krill had been their

34

commander, an ace pilot who'd made it his business to drive his pilots until they were almost a match for Stockton's Blues. "Almost" to anyone except Krill, who'd insisted to anyone who would listen that his people were every bit the equals of Blue squadron.

Krill had been one of the losses at Santis, and in the years since, the squadron had gradually declined in the hierarchy of *Dauntless*'s strike force. They were more than respectable by the standards of the fleet at large, but they were Barron' last choice as a final stand against an approaching torpedo attack.

Maybe *the final stand*...

His eyes were on the display. The AI had declared that none of *Dauntless*'s other squadrons would reach the bombers in time to intercept. But Barron could see the Blues closing fast. He rechecked the calculations. They were right. Then he realized, Stockton and his people were accelerating beyond their maximum thrust capacities, overloading their reactors. It was a dangerous move, downright reckless and forbidden by navy regs. But he'd never been happier to see his brilliant rogue pilot showing his flagrant disregard for rules.

Come on, Raptor...

Dauntless could endure a moderate torpedo attack, but if Stockton and his Blues didn't get some of those assault ships, his beloved vessel was going to get pounded badly...and a critical hit or two could mean...

He watched the scanners again. The bombers were ninety seconds from launching their torpedoes. The defensive batteries had gotten seven so far: three destroyed outright, four more damaged and forced to veer off. But that wasn't enough...and ninety seconds more of fire wasn't going to make it enough.

His eyes moved to the large display. The battleships *Dauntless* had been facing were both heavily damaged. One was immobile, a cripple drifting in space. The other was accelerating, at maybe one-third power, pulling away. With the primaries out of action, the enemy would be out of range right around the time the enemy bombers launched. That, at least, was a break. If he'd had to worry about closing battleships as well as bombers, things could get ugly fast.

"Commander Travis, starboard secondaries are to open fire. As many batteries as power supply allows."

"Yes, sir." A few second later. "Seven batteries firing, sir."

Barron knew the range was long for his secondary guns, that the fleeing enemy would likely escape, but he had to try something. Anything was better than staring at the approaching wall of bombers, knowing he had already done everything he could. When the ships launched their warheads and converted them to fixed-course plasmas, he would order evasive maneuvers, but with that many weapons in space, some were going to hit, no matter what he did. Too many.

"One minute to projected torpedo launch, sir." Then, perhaps ten seconds later: "Blue squadron, sir. They're engaging!" Atara Travis rarely showed emotion, at least not on the bridge during combat. But even *Dauntless*'s stoic executive officer was clearly surprised that "Raptor" Stockton and his squadron had reached the bombers in time. They didn't have long, and some of the attackers would almost certainly get through. But if they could get enough…

"C'mon, Jake," Barron muttered softly, only to himself. "You can do this."

*   *   *

"Let's go, Blues. These bombers handle like pigs, and everybody who bags one gets a drink on me. Take down two, and I'll drink you under the table." Stockton's encouragement was more bluster than reality. He'd be happy to buy his people rounds for their kills, but despite his occasional bluster to the contrary, he wasn't really much of a drinker. Blue squadron had at least half a dozen pilots who could put him away at the officer's club without even trying.

He grinned as he heard the acknowledgements, and the healthy chatter on the main channel. The Blues had suffered, and the less his people thought of their dead friends now, the better. They still had work to do. There would be time later for mourning and remembrance.

And Zucker and Tobias are still back there. He'd lost two ships to reactor overloads, but in both cases, the units scragged before going critical. His pilots were still out there, zipping through space unable to decelerate or change course. They'd be okay; the rescue boats would retrieve them. At least, they would if the battle was won. If *Dauntless* had to retreat, the cold reality was that she'd have to abandon most of her ditched pilots. If there was one thing every man and woman in the fighter corps knew from the first days at flight school, it was that capital ships were more important than fighters. If it was the mothership or you, well, you were shit out of luck.

Barron was a ship commander who'd pushed that rule to the limit before, taking risks most captains wouldn't to save his pilots. But in the end, he would do what had to be done to save *Dauntless*. Whatever it cost him personally.

Stockton was bringing his ship around, coming up behind a pair of bombers. The two craft were close to each other, at least by the standards of space combat, just over one thousand kilometers. One was farther forward, perhaps four hundred kilometers.

He targeted the first ship, opening fire almost as soon as he entered range. A hit! The tiny icon on his screen hovered there for a few seconds, and then it winked out, leaving nothing but blackness behind.

That's one...

Stockton was already changing course slightly, bringing the second target into his sights. He fired. Close, but the bomber managed to evade at the last instant. He stared intently, tapping the throttle, adjusting his vector slightly. The bomber pilot was highly skilled, Stockton didn't doubt that, but the heavily-laded craft was ungainly to fly. It was only a matter of time before he took the target down, he knew, but time was something in very short supply right now.

He fired again, a sustained blast, one lance of concentrated light after another ripping out, across the twelve thousand kilometers to his target. One of the shots hit, a glancing blow, but it only took a few seconds for Stockton to realize he'd knocked out the ship's engines. He'd have moved on to another target, but the attack ship was still on a vector toward *Dauntless*. Stockton knew the shot would be a hard one for the Alliance pilot, that hitting the battleship would be difficult without engine power. But he couldn't take the chance, not where *Dauntless* was concerned. The ship was his home, and everybody who meant a damned thing to him was onboard. Commodore Barron, Commander Travis…Stara.

He looked at the small symbol on his screen, his stare frozen, like death. He might have let the enemy pilot escape in other circumstances, but now he knew what he had to do. It was almost too easy. Without its engine, the bomber couldn't evade. A first-year cadet could have scored a hit. The deadliest pilot in the Confederation navy could hardly miss.

And he didn't. The first blast was a direct hit, and the ship disappeared immediately from his screen. He felt the urge to go after another, but a quick glance told him it was too late. Fourteen bombers had completed their runs, and they had all launched. His first impulse was to hunt them down, destroy them before they could return to their base ships. But he had something more important to do. The Alliance interceptors were coming up behind his Blues, and a quick look at the data on his screen confirmed that they were overloading their own reactors, as his people had done.

Who are you? He thought about this enemy, about the relentlessness and skill being directed at his people. He was silent for a few seconds. Then he clicked on the comm. "All right, Blues, we've done all we can here, but our work's not done." He paused, his eyes dropping to check his fuel status. He already knew it wasn't good, and a quick glance confirmed that it sucked. *But theirs can't be much better…actually, it's probably worse…*

He sighed. "Let's go," he said into the comm, wondering if these Alliance pilots were as suicidal as some of the ones he'd faced at Santis.

His focus was total, his attitude grim.

Yes. He was sure they'd be as crazy as those he'd fought at

Santis…and, if anything, even more dangerous…

*   *   *

Grachus watched as the plasma torpedoes streaked across her screen toward *Dauntless*. She'd expected more of the attack ships to get through, but the Confed interceptors her people had fought had proven their skill yet again, closing despite the fact that she'd lured them out of support range. They'd taken a terrible risk to get back there, but they'd pulled it off. All she could do was hope fourteen torpedoes was enough.

Enough to destroy that accursed battleship and her commander. To avenge Kat.

She cut her own thrust now, altering her course slightly, moving toward the Confed squadron that was already in position. She'd hoped to take the survivors by surprise, but they were too good for that. There was no easy way to win this fight, not against this enemy. Her people would have to do it the hard way, and she knew they would pay in blood.

"Dragons, attack. We take this squadron down, and we do it now." She checked her display. The other enemy wings were closing, but she had parity in numbers for at least a few minutes. And she intended to make the most of that time.

She shot a glance to the screen, checking the status of the torpedoes. She wanted to beat these fighters…many of them had probably been at Santis, and they carried their own share of the responsibility for Kat's death. But mostly, she wanted *Dauntless*, and she would do anything, endure any sacrifice, to gain that victory.

Damn.

Dauntless's gunners picked off two of the inbound torpedoes as she watched. She cursed under her breath, angry that the bomber crews hadn't converted their weapons to energy yet. She knew her anger was misplaced, that guiding in a successful bombing attack meant balancing factors correctly. The plasma torpedoes were almost impossible to intercept once they had fired up their reactions, but then they would be on a fixed vector, the thrusters that allowed course changes incinerated by the conversion.

She pulled her eyes from the long-range screen, back to the tactical display. There was no time to watch the attack on *Dauntless*. Those fighters were coming on. She could defeat them, she was confident about that, but she also knew how dangerous they were, that if she relaxed her guard, let down her intensity one iota, this Confed squadron would cut her people to ribbons.

She looked over the display, her eyes seeking the ship she'd engaged before. She'd put a tracer on him, and now her AI was searching the incoming scanner data, looking for her target. She hoped for an instant the pilot had been one of those stranded by an overloaded reactor, but then one of the symbols on her screen glowed. There he was.

The ship was at the far end of the enemy formation, not an ideal position for her to engage. But that pilot was too good. He could kill a lot of her people…unless she took him down herself.

She hit her turbos and was pressed back into her seat by the force of acceleration. She took a deep breath, at least as deep as she could manage with an effective force eight times her body weight pressing down on her. Grachus believed in the way, with all her heart and soul. She was an Alliance warrior. She didn't acknowledge fear, and she didn't let concern for danger interfere with her actions.

She felt a droplet streaking down her neck, then another. She might not acknowledge fear, but that didn't mean she didn't feel it. It was there, now more than ever. She'd never met her match before in the cockpit, never encountered a pilot she couldn't best. Until now.

This Confed was good. Really good. She thought she might have the edge, slightly, but then she wondered if that was just ego driving her analysis. Whatever the final score, the tally of skill and talent, she knew this Confed *could* best her. She needed all she could manage right now, every scrap of instinct and experience she could deploy to face this deadly foe.

She took another deep breath. She was ready.

*   *   *

"Seal off breached compartments. Reroute main port power conduit." Barron was snapping out commands, fully aware of the redundancy of every word coming out of his mouth. He knew Fritzie was on top of all of it, that she had likely already dispatched crews to do everything he was ordering. But she remained silent on the other end of the comm line, respectfully listening to his every word.

"Yes, sir," she replied as soon as Barron paused long enough to allow her to get out a word without interrupting him. "All being done, sir. The hit was a solid one, but I think we've got most of the damage contained."

"All right, Fritzie. I hear you. Carry on." Barron's tone was as apologetic as a ship commander's was ever likely to be in action. He knew his engineer was in control, but damn it anyway, *Dauntless* was *his* ship, and he'd sweat every detail, especially when she was hurt.

She's only your ship because you won't give her up to Atara as you should...

He shut the comm line. His engineer had more important things to do than humor her captain's interference. Fritzie had brought *Dauntless* back from the blackest pits again and again. If there was one person in the crew who deserved his utmost trust to do her job, it was Anya Fritz. And, despite his tendency to micromanage upon occasion, the truth was, she had it. There was no one Barron trusted and relied upon more than his extraordinary engineer.

"Commodore..." Barron heard Travis's voice, even as his eyes fixed on the last group of torpedoes. There were five, coming in at better than 0.05c, and the spread pattern was a problem.

Damn these Alliance pilots.

Barron's mind raced, looking for an evasion pattern, one that would allow him to avoid all five incoming weapons. But there wasn't one. The cluster of plasmas was perfectly placed, and approaching along every possible escape route.

"Hard to port, full thrust," he yelled, gripping the armrests of his chair against the expected force.

"Hard to port, sir," Travis snapped back. *Dauntless* swung hard, and a wave of pressure hit Barron and the rest of the bridge crew.

Barron's eyes were fixed on the display, watching each of the approaching plasmas. He was sure he'd evaded two of them, but that wasn't enough.

"Cut thrust to fifty percent. Full power to starboard positioning thrusters."

"Yes, Commodore." Once again, Travis executed his orders faster than he'd thought possible. The ship shook again, and the force shifted, and lessened in intensity.

Barron watched as two more torpedoes zipped by, one missing the ship by less than five hundred meters, a very close shave by the standards of space combat.

He wanted to breathe a sigh of relief, but he was too distracted watching the last torpedo, the one he hadn't managed to evade. The one that was about to slam into *Dauntless* amidships.

The battleship shook hard once, followed by silence, for perhaps ten seconds. Then a series of internal explosions rocked *Dauntless*, the sounds reverberating through the hull. A shower of sparks flew across the bridge as a series of panels burned out one after the other, and a section of plating fell from the ceiling, landing with a loud crash.

Barron was on the comm again in an instant. "Fritzie..."

This time the engineer did interrupt. "It's bad, Commodore...but I can get it under control. We're looking at some temporary power losses...and you can forget about primaries *or* secondaries for at least an hour, and probably longer." There was a pause, a few seconds where the only sound was the static of the damaged lines. Then, as if reading his mind, she continued, "The landing bays are salvageable, sir. Alpha's in better shape than Beta, but we should be able to land the entire strike force."

That was good news, at least, tinged a bit darker by the fact that *Dauntless*'s combined wings were going to be quite a bit smaller landing than they were taking off.

"Okay, Fritzie. Priority to keeping the bays open. Our squadrons are going to be on fumes by the time they get back." *If they get back.* "And I want the rescue boats ready to launch. A lot of our people had to ditch out there, and we're not leaving them behind."

"Yes, sir. Don't worry…we'll get them all in."

"I know you will, Fritzie." Barron hit the comm unit, cutting the line again. He leaned back in his chair and took a deep breath. *Dauntless* was out of the fight, at least for some time. But she'd done her part, battering two enemy battleships to scrap.

Tyler Barron hated sitting there, watching, leaving his fate in the hands of others. But there was nothing to do but wait.

And hope his ship had done enough to tilt the battle into the win column.

* * *

Grachus did the calculations again, as though her AI—and she, herself, the other three times she'd done the math—were wrong, that some repeated miscalculation had reared its head instead of the simple fact that she didn't have enough fuel.

Turn back now. That's what the book says.

Grachus wanted to ignore regs, to stay in the fight as long as she had fuel in the tanks and watts in her lasers. But it was about more than her right now, more even than her own Dragons. There were three full squadrons engaged with the Confeds, and as unofficial as it might be, she was as good as the commander of the whole lot. They'd followed her here, they'd thrown themselves into the fight with abandon, without the slightest reservations. Could she really decide on suicide, not just for herself, but for all of them?

Because it would be suicide. *Our battleships are losing, they'd never be able to send a rescue after us.*

She'd sparred with that Confed pilot again, another twenty minutes of pointless maneuvering and close calls on both sides. Every stratagem she tried, every trick to get a second's advantage, had been countered. She'd come close once or twice to taking him, she was sure of that. It was harder to acknowledge the reverse, that he too had nearly taken her out, that more than one of his attacks had almost finished her. The two had ended up on sharply divergent vectors, causing a momentary break in their death struggle. Now, she had to decide whether to stay and finish the fight—and risk running out of fuel—or to return to the ship. She knew what she wanted to do, and also what she should do. The two were contradictory.

She stared at her display. The battleship, that accursed ship *Dauntless*, had taken significant damage, but the bombing strike had failed to destroy her. That pilot was as much to blame for that as anyone. Somehow, he'd gotten his squadron back in time. His people hadn't been able to turn back the whole assault force, but they'd thinned it enough. The whole battle had been close, but looking at the screen, she knew her comrades would be retreating soon. The Grays had the clear edge now, another injury caused by *Dauntless*.

She felt the rage growing again, the hatred for that ship and its commander...and that ace pilot. She respected his ability, but he had thwarted her vengeance, and for that he would have to pay.

She knew what she had to do, but she swore silently, an oath to herself, that they would all meet again. And when they did, it would be a reckoning the likes of which could hardly be imagined.

I failed you here, Kat, but I swear on my honor, on my life, that I will still avenge you.

Chapter Six

Imperator's Palace
Victorum, Alliance Capital City
Palatia, Astara II
Year 62 (311 AC)

"We knew they were coming, we devised a plan to surprise them...and yet the result is still the same. Defeat. The freighters were destroyed, and a precious cargo of vital electronics obliterated. We outnumber the traitors, yet all my admirals deliver to me is lost battles, even when we risk a king's ransom of precious supplies as bait in a snare. Who did we trap? Ourselves?" The Imperator Calavius I sat on his seat, looking out over the officers and courtiers gathered before him on the polished marble floor.

No, not a seat. Ricard Lille, the architect of the current regime's rise to power—and its financier as well—stood quietly in the corner of the room, watching as his creation roared at his subordinates with a fury that increasingly seemed to verge on the irrational. *That is not a seat. It is a throne.*

Calavius had pushed hard since Lille had helped engineer the coup that had put him in that...chair. He had relentlessly secured more and more power for himself, ignoring the very tenets of the Alliance's "way" even as he gave speeches praising Palatia's early heroes for their virtues of honor and duty to the

45

state. The Imperator had never been an absolute monarch in the Alliance. In fact, the Imperator had been somewhat of a figurehead, a senior warrior to lead his or her people by example, not by unquestioned edict. But Calavius didn't want only the respect and the trappings of power. He wanted it all.

Still, he needs to move more slowly. Foolish opulence like that chair will cause more damage to the loyalty of his followers than three lost battles...

"Your Supremacy, I assure you that we inflicted as much damage as we suffered in this last exchange. Indeed, we were close to victory...before the Confed flagship returned and joined the enemy line." The officer's voice changed slightly as he mentioned the Confederation vessel.

"Flagship? Do you fear that wretched craft so much that you cannot utter its name? Must I do it for you? *Dauntless.*" The last word dripped heavily with venom. Calavius paused, glaring down with such focused rage, his commanders were struck silent. They watched their leader with varying degrees of concern, fear...and some growing resentment as well. "Or its cursed commander. Tyler Barron."

Lille had been well aware Calavius was a man driven by ego, that the tool he had chosen to secure control of the Alliance would become difficult to handle once in power. Calavius was far from an ideal choice, but his friendship with Vennius had meant he was the only one with the ability to sabotage his friend's possible responses to a coup. At least, the only one corrupt enough to be susceptible to Lille's overtures.

The fool had botched the initial move against Vennius, of course, allowing the Alliance's top military commander to escape from Palatia with the Imperatrix in tow. Vennius had been able to mount a defense against the coup, turning an effective fait accompli into a full-blown civil war. Lille was angry his tool had allowed that to happen, but in spite of the complications, there was no question Calavius had delivered some solid value, especially in securing the allegiance of fleet units and utilizing his control of the communications networks to declare his adversary a traitor. Lille was continually amazed at just how naïve these Alliance warriors were. Propaganda that wouldn't fool indentured workers on any Union world was taken as unquestioned fact, even by the Patrician elite. And that fact had been used to great effect, turning many against Vennius who otherwise would have enthusiastically supported him.

Vennius, cornered in Sentinel-2, clinging to just under thirty percent of total Alliance forces, was a much preferable situation to the Commander Maximus at his desk in Victorum, reputation intact and the whole fleet under his command. And while Calavius's people had failed to kill the Imperatrix in her palace as he'd ordered—*suggested*, Lille reminded himself—they'd managed to wound her. And though she'd taken her time about it, by all accounts, the infuriatingly stubborn old woman had finally had the decency to die. That left Vennius alone, isolated, his claim to the Imperator's scepter lacking the Council approval Calavius had managed to buy...and coerce. All in all, things were still moving in the right direction, and if an easy and quick victory had been squandered, it still seemed likely his plan would succeed.

But now he's going too far. These are Alliance officers, nobles and members of distinguished families. They were raised on the cult of duty, but they are also proud and arrogant in their own rights. If he pushes them too far, acts too much like a king...

"Perhaps more could have been done to win the outright victory." Lille stepped away from the wall, interjecting himself into the exchange. He'd almost kept silent, fully aware of that most of the Alliance officers despised him. But he was afraid of how far Calavius might go if left unattended. *If he starts executing his top officers...*

The last thing Lille needed was a coup within the coup.

"But there is no question this last battle was far more successful than those that preceded it." He could feel the eyes of the assembled officers boring into him as he spoke. He wasn't one to allow hostility to distract him, but the success of his mission depended on keeping these men and women in Calavius's camp, something the Imperator was beginning to prove to be beyond his own abilities. "I believe we can learn from this last fight, and continue to push this destructive conflict to the end we all seek." He paused for a few seconds, then he continued, "All present despise Tarkus Vennius as a traitor, a collaborator with the Confeds…" Always worth reminding them of the image his propaganda had created of the previously popular Commander Maximus. *There is nothing so powerful as a fallen hero, nor anything so readily despised by weak-minded fools.* "…but we must not allow ourselves to underestimate his tactical skills, nor those of the butcher, Tyler Barron. Hate them both, swear to destroy them…but never forget how dangerous they are."

Lille could see the anger in the officers' faces. It was reflexive, he knew. They might agree with every word he said, but they would never show that to him, the foreigner, the outsider. Still, he could feel the tension ratchet down, and he knew he'd managed what he'd set out to achieve.

Now, something positive…

"And one more thing. Your fighter squadrons battled the enemy to a standstill. This is a marked change from previous battles, is it not? Perhaps there is someone to reward, a warrior whose skill and valor has set an example to all the wings fighting alongside her own." He knew already, of course, of whom he spoke…and he was well aware the admirals all did as well. But his words weren't for them. They were for Calavius, whose adherence to old social standings was most definitely subordinate to the fight to secure his throne.

"Ambassador Lille is correct," the Imperator said after an overlong silence. "We must reward heroism and success, wherever it arises in our service. We need role models. Our fighter pilots were inspired by one who set the standard for courage and skill. I will reward that hero."

"A Pleb from a disgraced family as a hero?" Commander-Altum Battarus spoke first, though Lille knew the gruff old man was only saying what the others were thinking. "I do not question the piloting skill of this Optiomagis—what is her name, Grachus? Nor do I doubt that her exploits have provided limited inspiration to members of her squadron, and even some among the lesser-born in the other wings. But, I cannot believe you would elevate such a lower…"

"You may believe it, Commander-Altum. If you or any of your associates had devised and executed a winning strategy, none of this would be necessary. But Optiomagis Grachus— no, Commander-Princeps Grachus now—is the one beacon of success in an otherwise lackluster series of operations. We must seek to build on her accomplishments." Calavius glared at Battarus, almost daring the officer to disagree before he continued, "Commander Grachus will henceforth be designated as fleet fighter commander, and she shall lead all squadrons deployed to the next operation."

Battarus glared back, his expression itself almost an act of defiance. But in the end, he remained silent, finally croaking out a weak acknowledgement. "Yes, Your Supremacy." It was as close to a surrender as Calavius was likely to get from the ancient, grizzled warrior.

"Commander Grachus's valor in combat has more than proven her loyalty, and expunged the treachery and cowardice of her grandfather. Henceforth, her name shall be cleared, and Commander Grachus, already a Citizen herself by prior acclamation, shall become hereditary in that status, and pass her Citizenship to her heirs, and their heirs, in perpetuity. I shall also grant her estates befitting one of her rank, from among the state-owned lands in the capital district."

It was a major award, and Lille had never heard of such largesse being granted to a Palatian of Grachus's standing and dubious family history. He'd studied the subject of Calavius's largesse sufficiently to know, almost for certain, that her grandfather's treachery had been all too real. He knew the other officers would grumble about her elevation, but he was also confident they would accept it, or at least pretend to. And the whole confrontation that had been brewing before was disarmed, the direct struggle between Calavius and his senior officers forgotten amid the stunning news that a disgraced Pleb had been placed in command of the fleet's fighter wings.

Lille had hoped to divert the discussion, but even he was

surprised at the extent of the Imperator's actions. He'd come nearly to despair the prospects of his creature making intelligent choices, but now he saw a glimpse of the ability he'd recognized earlier in Calavius. Jovi Grachus was, by all accounts, an almost astonishingly gifted pilot, one whose skill had overcome the prejudices against her family history and gained her a large and loyal following, at least in the fighter wings. And there was no doubt that wherever she flew, not only her own squadron, but all the wings in the vicinity vastly overperformed. She was a weapon, one that could very well help end the destructive civil war before the Red Alliance forces were too degraded to invade the Confederation.

Which, after all, was the entire purpose of all of this.

*   *   *

Jovi Grachus sat on the edge of her crisply-made cot, staring at the small tablet in her hands. She'd read the orders three times—no, more like five—and they still said the same thing.

And she still couldn't believe it.

Commander-Princeps. It was a rank she'd never imagined she could attain, and certainly not now, with her primary patron gone. She'd fully expected to spend the rest of her career as a squadron commander, and her only regret about that was it limited her chances to avenge her friend.

She put her hand up to her face, wiping away a tear. Kat had been gone for more than four years now, but the pain still felt fresh, every recollection of her old friend slicing into her like a blade. This promotion was another reminder of just how much she owed Kat…and it stoked her rage, her grim determination to make all those responsible for Kat's death pay. She allowed herself a fleeting, almost sinister grin. Command of all the fleet's fighters would certainly help in that goal.

She reached down to the cot, scooping up the small box that had come with the new orders. She popped it open and looked at the platinum insignia inside, the mark of her new rank. She took one look and snapped it shut again, setting it aside. She needed a few minutes to get used to the idea before she could even think about clipping the small bits of platinum to her collar.

The box had been laying on top of another tablet, one she had been looking at when the mail call arrived. Her eyes again caught the image it displayed, a small boy, about four years old, his golden hair long, in the fashion currently fashionable among Palatian Patricians.

Varus.

Her son.

Kat had arranged the match for her. *Of course. How else would someone of my background pair with anyone but a gutter rat or criminal?* The father of her son, Jarus of the Omegii, was vastly above Grachus in social status, an utterly unattainable mate by any normal standards. She'd genuinely liked Jarus, finding him to be pleasant and witty…and very easy on the eyes. He had been kind to her during their couplings, a good lover who didn't let on to the slightest sign of disapproval at pairing with a mate so far beneath him. Grachus had known there was more at play than she could see, most likely the repayment of some grand old honor debt the Omegii owed the Rigellii. There was some hurt in that, twinges she felt from time to time wondering what had really gone through Jarus's mind as he had worked off his family's obligations in her bed, but such nonsense was beneath the dignity of a Palatian warrior, and she suppressed the thoughts ruthlessly when they appeared. She was grateful to Kat for the pairing, as she was for almost everything worthwhile in her life, and that was all that mattered. She wasn't some weak-minded Pleb, riddled with senseless emotion and insecurities, sobbing in the night about a bunch of hair-pulling nonsense.

She loved her son, more even than she'd imagined possible, though the thought of him carried pain with it as well. For one thing, she'd never forget that, save for her pregnancy, she'd have been with Kat on *Invictus*. She realized she couldn't have changed the outcome of the battle—at least most of the time she realized that—but in many ways, it felt wrong to have survived when Kat had died. She had the same impulse to live as anyone did, but in ways it also felt wrong, even disloyal, for her to be alive.

Survivor's guilt was only one source of pain. There were others. There had been no arguing with either Jarus's rugged good looks or his immaculate DNA sequencing, but she'd underestimated the pain of giving up her child so soon after his birth. Palatian law was clear that the offspring of any Citizen pairing were to be raised as members of the higher-ranked family. The courts were clogged with disputes between parents, each arguing that their own lineage was the greater, but in Grachus's case there was no argument to be made. Jarus was a Patrician, among the Alliance's elite, and she was the granddaughter of a disgraced traitor. For all she wished she could have her son with her, she'd never have done anything to cost him his birthright as a member of the Alliance's highest rank.

Her face tightened, a wave of anger sweeping through her. *The birthright he should have had.* The Omegii were longtime allies of both the Rigellii and the Vennii, and the entire family, Jarus included, had declared for Vennius, abandoning their estates and defecting with their ships and fleets to rally to the traitor. The thought of friends of the Rigellii siding with Vennius enraged her. Vennius's hands were as good as stained with Kat's blood, and the noble Rigellii were reduced now almost to extinction by his foolishness—or worse, his treachery. Kat's son and daughter, both underage, years even from the Ordeal, were all that remained of one of the Alliance's great families. At least Vennius hadn't been able to take them with him when he escaped. Kat's children were safe on Palatia. Imperator Calavius had even had them escorted from the Rigellus estates to his own fortress in Victorum for their protection.

And my son is bound to a family now turned traitors.

It had been nearly a year since she'd seen Varus. Though Jarus had always remained cordial with her during her visits, the rest of the Omegii had made little effort to hide their disdain. She'd done her best to ignore it, but as the years began to pass, she'd resigned herself to the fact that her son's future was best served by limited contact.

Until Jarus and the rest of the Omegii took him to follow a traitor.

Her son would be lost, his lineage tainted from both sides now. If he even survived the destruction of Vennius's rebellion. Unless she could use this promotion, gain sufficient renown to reclaim Varus, and to beseech Imperator Calavius for a pardon for her young son, who'd had no say in the choices of the Omegii.

Now she had even more reason to fight. To avenge the past…and to save what remained of the future. She tore the Optiomagis rank markers from her collar and opened the box again. She picked out one of the new insignia, and she moved it into place. Then she put the second one on.

She stood up, looking in the mirror, her eyes fixed on the small pieces of platinum that had, until moments before, seemed so unattainable.

I will do what must be done. I will lead our pilots to victory. And I will achieve all I must, for the Alliance, for Kat…and for my beloved Varus.

Chapter Seven

Free Trader Pegasus
Ibulan System
Deep in the Badlands
Year 311 AC

"Something's not right. There are fuel traces all around the orbital track of that moon. Someone was there, and not long ago." Andi Lafarge was sitting on *Pegasus's* bridge, her eyes darting back and forth at the screens and scanners crowded all around.

"Those are faint readings, Andi. Maybe it's something natural. Or even a small miscalibration of the scanners." Vig Merrick turned around and looked at her across *Pegasus's* cramped bridge.

"Well, is it a miscalibration? Maybe you should check the scanners before you write off a potential threat as a malfunction." She was sorry for the tone, even as the words slipped out of her mouth. "I'm sorry, Vig. It's not you. I'm just nervous."

"No problem, Andi. I understand. Checking the scanner suite now."

She knew Merrick was serious. He *did* understand. There were few people who knew her as well as her second-in-command, though, of course, no one *really* knew her. Not even *him*.

Her thoughts shifted, from her steadfast friend to someone

else, the one person who had truly been a match for her in all things. Her parting with Tyler Barron had been an uncomfortable one. She'd fully intended to be the one who left, but she'd waited too long, and he'd raised the issue first. He'd said it delicately, shrouded in expressions of concerns for her safety—which she knew were sincere—but it still gnawed at her that she'd waited until he had sent her away.

She wasn't the type to get distracted over such foolishness, but she'd found Barron difficult to forget. Perhaps forget was a strong word. She'd probably see him again, at least if he didn't manage to get himself killed fighting in the Alliance. But she had no illusions about their futures. Tyler Barron would follow in his grandfather's footsteps one day, leading the Confederation's fleets...or he would die in this horrible war. Either way, there was no place for fantasies of hearth and home and happily ever afters. Barron was a fling, and a friend too. But she didn't do "romance."

Still, deep down she knew she'd driven this far into the Badlands as much for distraction as profit. Her habitual hunt for wealth was good cover, and she even fooled herself a little, at least sometimes. She hadn't lost her drive to amass riches, and if she also pushed a certain Confederation officer out of her mind in the process, well, killing two birds with one stone wasn't such a bad thing...

She took a deep breath, checking the scanners again. Her people had never been out this far, and she was having trouble shaking the eerie, haunted feeling of the place. Space travel so far from any ports or support was dangerous. Any malfunction a ship's crew couldn't handle was likely a death sentence, which was one reason most of the explorers and adventurers based out of Dannith and the other border ports tended to stay a bit closer in, within the range a damaged ship might at least hope to be found and rescued. Everybody had heard at least one story of a ship that had ventured out too far...and was never heard from again.

But Andromeda Lafarge had never been afraid to take calculated risks, and her ship had both double stores of replacement parts and Lex Righter. Her engineer had saved their asses more than once, and she'd come to have enormous faith in him, despite his occasional personal struggles. Righter had fought a long war with the bottle, one he seemed to be winning at long last. She was happy for him, and as much as she could have done without the added stress of his addictions, she knew full well that she'd never have had him on her small ship at all if she hadn't found him face down in the gutter.

Still, for all her caution and careful preparation, she knew she was taking more risks than usual, not just for herself, but for her people as well. Getting away from Tyler Barron was her own affair, but the search for something significant—not just scraps of old tech, but an artifact that would make them all filthy, stinking rich—that was something for all of them. They'd come close before, and even the trinkets they'd discovered along the way had added up to enough to live on comfortably. But Lafarge hadn't crawled out of the filthy slums of Hephaeseus to be comfortable. She intended to live like the Oligarchs of her homeworld, who resided in gold-plated luxury high above the misery of the masses. She would never allow herself to end up helpless again, whatever it took. No danger was too great in the pursuit of that goal.

She felt a wave of resentment as she thought of finding that big score. She'd already discovered the old tech that should have made her goal a reality. The planet-killer. Her people had gotten there first, but the maggot informant who'd sold her the information had also given it to Union spies. She'd fully intended to kill the bastard in payment, but in the end, she'd given him to Gary Holsten and Confederation Intelligence. She suspected her informant had encountered less gentle treatment than he might have liked at their hands…but it was a damned sight better than what he'd have endured if she'd kept him.

That's all in the past. Leave it there.

She had new information, rumors of a major imperial ruin somewhere in this deep sector. This time she wasn't relying on a single, untrustworthy informant. She had multiple sources of info, and if they were vague on an exact location, they all agreed on one thing. There was something out here, something major. Maybe in this system, maybe the next. Maybe three or four from here. But somewhere close.

"How's that systems check going, Vig?" He tone was softer than it had been earlier. "We need to figure out if those fuel trails are real. We're a long way from home, and if there's someone else out here, we need to know."

She took another breath, suddenly feeling very alone and exposed. "We *need* to know now."

*   *   *

Gaston Villieneuve stood along the edge of the bridge, looking out over the battleship's command crew. *Banniere* was one of the new ships, fresh out of the yard and bigger and stronger than anything the prewar Union fleet had possessed. It was desperately needed along the main battleline, as were any fresh forces, to counter the output from the Confederation's shipyards, but Villieneuve had found a better use for his new vessel. The front line offered only stalemate and eventual defeat, a slow and steady loss of ground to the Confederation's superior production. But what he'd found here could lead to victory.

He'd been silent, standing quietly and not interfering in *Banniere*'s operation, but he could see the tension in Captain Mies, the way her shoulders were hunched forward. His presence clearly unnerved her, though he had been nothing but proper and even downright pleasant since he'd come aboard weeks before.

Good...when they're no longer afraid of Sector Nine, then we are truly lost. Villieneuve believed profoundly in the use of fear as a motivator, and he placed its effectiveness even above the other pillar of encouragement, greed. Sector Nine had mastered the art of causing fear...and, when called for, manipulating greed as well.

There was mercy of a sort in the intelligence agency's fearsome reputation, in that it discouraged disobedience and treachery. What terror could accomplish, blades and electrodes and noxious drugs would not have to. Villieneuve had presided over a fifty percent reduction in executions and torture cases, not because he was unwilling to employ extreme sanctions, but because he'd mastered the use of preemptive fear the way an artist did his medium.

"Status, Captain?"

"Unchanged, sir. The entire system has been explored. No apparent installations on any other worlds or moons, and no signs of any vessels other than our own, either Confederation or other."

"Very well. Maintain full alert status. I don't want anything to interfere with what we're doing here." Then, with a coldness that hadn't been there before, "Like last time." Mies wasn't responsible for the debacle the Union forces had suffered at the hands of Tyler Barron and *Dauntless*, of course, but Villieneuve wanted to be clear he had no intention of tolerating a repeat of that sorry episode.

"Yes, sir." Mies's edginess was clear, despite the officer's clear efforts to hide it. Villieneuve couldn't fault the captain. *A crucial mission deep in the haunted Badlands with the head of Sector Nine breathing down her neck. Any sane man or woman would be on edge.*

Good.

"Proceed with operations."

"Yes, sir. All work teams are on or ahead of schedule."

Villieneuve nodded, more to himself than *Banniere's* captain. He looked around the bridge, his eyes focusing for a few seconds on the main display. He detested leaving his comfortable office in the capital, and even more venturing into an abandoned wasteland like the Badlands. But the reports had been irresistible, just maybe another chance to alter the deteriorating trajectory of the war. Lille's operation in the Alliance offered the potential to outflank and overwhelm the Confeds, but he wasn't about to count on it until it was done, especially with Barron out there, apparently leading the Confederation expeditionary force. Meanwhile, if he could secure the old tech he needed, Alliance support would be extraneous. They would be next on the list.

He'd hesitated coming out this far himself, but only for a short time. There had been too many lost opportunities, mistakes that had cost chances of victory. He'd trusted subordinates to secure the planet-killer, only to see the astonishing superweapon destroyed by Captain Barron. This time, Villieneuve would see to the completion of the mission himself.

Commodore Barron, he reminded himself. The intel reports had been confirmed. Barron had been promoted and placed in command of the Confederation forces aiding the Gray Alliance faction. *That makes him Ricard's problem...*

Villieneuve knew Barron was a dangerous man, but Ricard Lille was no less brilliant and deadly. If anyone could outmaneuver the Confederation's most famous captain, it was the calm, methodical assassin. Villieneuve didn't trust anyone, but if he was choosing one person to rely upon, it would be Ricard Lille. He had no one better to match against Barron, and if reports coming in were accurate, for all the Confederation officer's damnable skill—and luck, he suspected—the Union-backed Red faction seemed close to victory.

I'll count on that when I see it. Lille was the best assassin Villieneuve had ever known, but half a year had passed since his friend had sworn to kill Barron, and the Confederation officer was still alive. That was partially his own fault, he suspected. His earlier, clumsy, attempt at assassination had failed, and now Barron's fanatically loyal crew was on a hair trigger, protecting their beloved commander around the clock. If Lille hadn't been able to get to him, no one could. And that meant the victory would have to be won in battle, where Barron and his people were at their best.

The Reds outnumber the Grays by better than two to one... even Tyler Barron will have his hands full against that many fanatical Alliance warriors. And while Dauntless and most of the Confederation's new ships are tied down on the Rim, we will be deploying this...

He looked at the screen on the far wall, at the images of the work crews down on the surface. The excavation site was massive. He'd shipped ten thousand workers to the planet, all the while maintaining absolute secrecy. It was a major endeavor, and one that had been successful to date. He still hadn't decided what he would do about his transplanted workforce when the job was done. Minimizing the number of ships traveling back and forth reduced the chance of encountering a Confederation patrol or even a rogue adventurer's ship, but he couldn't leave them here either, not alive. That would be too great a security risk.

Villieneuve wasn't bloodthirsty like so many of his predecessors, but he wasn't squeamish either. And if he had to leave the workers on this planet when he left, he was going to make sure none of them could divulge a word about what his expedition had found here.

He turned, glancing at the long-range display. Nothing but his own ships on patrol, just as Mies had reported. But he was still edgy. He simply didn't have the resources he'd had the last time his people had sought victory from the ancient ruins in the Badlands. The flotillas of battleships he'd sent then weren't available now. The remnants of the fleet were barely sufficient to garrison the front, and most of the new construction was lagging, despite the severe repercussions he imposed on those failing to meet deadlines. *Banniere* was the only battleship he had on this mission, backed up by ten smaller escorts. Not much of a fleet to protect a find of such importance. He had no reason to expect the Confeds knew anything about what he was doing here, but that was far from a guarantee.

At least I know Barron and his miserable ship won't show up. They're months away at full speed, and neck deep in their own mess...

His people had found this site—bought the information that led them to it, actually—along the Confederation's border with the Badlands, from the lowlife adventurers who'd discovered it but lacked the means to unearth the precious equipment buried there. He'd not only bought it, he'd bought it cheap, for an amount of coin that no doubt seemed vast to the ragtag group who'd stumbled onto this system but was a pittance as far as Villieneuve was concerned.

One they'll go through in a year or two of drinking and whoring...

He couldn't help but smile, thinking that the Confeds had this information within their grasp. Sector Nine had long plied its trade among the rogues who scavenged the Badlands for scraps of old tech, while the Confeds discouraged their activities, even hunted them down as criminals when their activities were too overt. The Union was a party to the same international treaties banning exploitation of the Badlands, but the Confeds actually adhered to the terms of the agreements, at least most of the time. Villieneuve couldn't think of anything more totally ignored in the Union—and in the other nations, too, he suspected. Once again, he gave thanks for the foolish ideals that so often turned to destructive self-flagellation in the Confederation.

With their tech and their production, they'd be unstoppable. If they weren't their own worst enemies...

"Captain, send a communique down to the surface. I want rest periods reduced by one standard hour." He paused. "No, two hours." The crews were already on a grueling schedule, but Villieneuve intended to have the artifact retrieved and back in the Union before someone wandered into this system and discovered what was going on. Whatever it took.

"Yes, sir." He thought he caught a hint of sympathy in Mies's voice. The thousands of workers down there were Union citizens, after all—but he ignored it. The misery of those ten thousand men and women was irrelevant measured against the implications of the work here. They were doing their duty for the state, and if that meant working three hours for each hour of rest, so be it.

Villieneuve looked back at the display, at the icons representing the ships of his small fleet. He'd come here to make sure there were no failures this time, and he had every intention of seeing that done.

Even if he had to work a few thousand laborers to death to do it.

Chapter Eight

"Commodore Barron is correct. It is exceedingly unlikely the enemy simply guessed, not only what convoy we were going after, but when and where that attack would take place." Vennius looked over at his ally, and the two shared a glance. He turned back to the Alliance officers—Barron was the sole foreigner present, as representative from the Confederation's expeditionary force. As the Confederation's top commander in the theater, Barron was perfectly suitable to represent his people, but Vennius made a note to invite at least Captain Eaton to the next strategy session, just so Barron wasn't so alone.

His initial contact with Barron had been a tense one. It hadn't been easy for him to acknowledge he needed foreign assistance at all. The fact that the provider of that aid was the man who had beaten Kat and caused her death seemed like fate toying with him. He had enough honor to acknowledge that *Dauntless* had defeated *Invictus* in straight up fight, but Kat had been like a daughter to him, and honor only went so far to staunch an old man's pain.

Nevertheless, in spite of everything, the two men had learned to work well together, and even with his prejudices and the burden their histories placed on their relationship, he'd begun to think of Barron as a friend. He'd also gotten a glimpse of the brilliance that had defeated Kat. He'd heard stories of Barron's grandfather, and he'd mostly written them off as propaganda, but now, he was starting to believe them.

Vennius stood at the head of the conference table. The Gray Imperator's garb was modest, the standard field uniform of an Alliance commander. He had eschewed all trappings of the office he'd so desperately hoped to avoid, behaving simply as a senior officer directing his forces in war. A gray sash, like the ones worn by all his officers, was the only ornamentation on the uniform he'd worn as Commander-Maximus.

He shook his head as he looked out again over his top commanders. The men and women present were split between those who had declared for his claim themselves, and those who had followed more senior commanders in their support of the legitimate ruler of the Alliance. *Or a pretender, depending on which side's propaganda you listened to.*

He wondered if he should be more suspicious of those who'd followed others here. *Almost certainly.*

"Never," he said grimly. "I never imagined it would be possible that I would be looking for a traitor among our top-ranking officers." He paused and took a deep breath. "Yet, no one below the highest levels was aware of our target. Someone with that knowledge betrayed us." He hesitated again, not wanting to say what he knew was necessary. "We must find the traitor, whatever it takes. We must prevent this from happening again, at all costs." His eyes moved slowly down the table, and he wondered if the one he sought was in the room now, one of his closest allies and confidantes. The thought sickened him, though he realized that was almost certainly the case.

"You speak wisely, Your Supremacy. We find ourselves facing the greatest crisis since the founding of the Alliance. Now is not the time for weakness. We must move decisively, as I have urged you to do before. We must root out disloyalty. We must find those who conspire with our enemies, and we must destroy them."

Vennius turned his gaze on the speaker. Hirtius Longinus had been one of his earliest supporters, a retired fleet commander who had returned to arms to support the Gray claim, bringing several ship commanders along with him. Longinus was a hardliner, his views founded on the bedrock of Alliance orthodoxy. To a man like Longinus, the perpetrator of a coup like Calavius's was not just a traitor, he was a virtual heretic, and any rules of honor or war simply did not apply in the extermination of such vermin. Vennius wondered how Longinus's hard attitudes addressed collateral damage, loyal officers harassed and disgraced by overzealous prosecution, for example.

Vennius had listened to his supporter's tirades before, but he'd been reluctant to allow Longinus to enact any of his schemes. The Alliance's was a harsh culture, demanding on its warriors and civilians alike, but the measures Longinus had been pushing for sounded more like the ways of the Union—setting his people to spying on each other. But now, Vennius knew he didn't have any choice. His Gray forces were outnumbered, penned in at Sentinel-2 while their enemies controlled Palatia and all the Alliance's main communications nexuses. He simply couldn't allow Calavius to have access to his secrets and plans as well.

"Commander Longinus speaks the truth," he said, trying to keep the doubt and regret from his tone. "I do not like such measures, but we *must* find the source of these leaks, and we must plug it. The future of the Alliance itself depends on it... and nothing is more important than that. *No one* is more important." Vennius took another breath, wondering just how much of himself this conflict would claim before it was done. Death in battle wouldn't be so bad—at least if it didn't also mean the failure of his cause and Calavius's victory. There were worse losses than of life. To endure, but to become something he couldn't recognize, a creature his current self would pity and despise; he feared that potential future most of all.

"At last," Longinus said, then, perhaps realizing his words and tone verged on the disrespectful, he added, "You speak wisdom, Your Supremacy. Nothing is more vital than saving the

Alliance we all serve. We must do what we must."

Vennius just nodded. Then he looked out at the assembled officers. "I need all of you to pay close attention to your subordinates. I know this is distasteful, but we have no choice." *As I must watch all of* you.

A ragged chain of nods and softly spoken acknowledgements went around the group. It was clear his people didn't like the idea of spying on each other any more than he did. But they would do it. They would do whatever victory demanded.

The way is the way...

*   *   *

"I am putting you in charge of this effort, Hirtius. You were the first to warn of the dangers of such leaks, that..." Vennius paused, seeming to struggle to even utter the words. "...traitors might be in our midst."

Barron sat quietly, feeling that the current subject was one best left to the Palatians. He'd come to understand them better over the past half year and, for the most part, to admire them. They could be brutal, and they were certainly warlike, but a comprehension of the horrors of their national past went a long way to blunting condemnation on that accord.

He'd particularly begun to admire Vennius. The man had a lifetime of blood on his hands, and billions lived in virtual servitude because of his military campaigns. But the man was something different than Barron had expected, devoid of personal lust for power. In fact, Barron was fairly sure Vennius would have preferred retirement to his estates, hunting and fishing and canoeing on Palatia's fast, cold streams, to bearing the burdens and obligation fate had placed on him.

Barron suspected that of all that cut at the Gray Imperator and tormented him, it was the realization that the tactics of deceit and corruption had proven more effective than the bonds of honor he had followed his whole life. Calavius's scheming had brought him within a hair of total victory, and by any measure the enemy was still likely to prevail in the current fight. And now, even among Vennius's own people, he had to fear every careless word, every whisper in the dark. For all the combat and loss Barron had suffered over the past several years, he'd never had to endure the betrayal of those closest to him. Vennius had, first with Calavius, and now again, with some as yet unidentified traitor.

"I will start at once, Your Supremacy." Longinus sounded a little too eager for Barron's tastes and, from the expression on his face, for Vennius's as well. Barron knew Longinus was a proud man, and he wasn't surprised at the anger directed at those engaged in treachery...but he was aware, as he suspected Vennius was, at how such energies could go to harmful extremes. He wanted to say something, but he knew his place was to remain silent, and rely on Vennius to handle his officer.

"Yes, Hirtius, by all means, start at once. It is vital that we find the guilty party." A short pause. "But, I must entreat you to exercise restraint and caution. The fury you feel is directed at the guilty, not at the innocent and loyal who might be hurt by overzealousness. Investigate, by all means, but be sure of yourself before you denounce any officer."

"Of course, Your Supremacy." Longinus replied, with rather less conviction than Barron would have liked.

Vennius looked like he was just as concerned, but he let it go. "There is one other matter I wish to discuss." He looked around the room, as if checking to make sure again that the six officers present were alone.

Barron looked at Vennius, his curiosity peaked. He and Vennius had met alone before this meeting, and they had discussed appointing Longinus to root out the source of the intelligence leaks, but the Imperator had made no mention of any other significant news.

"I have received a private communique, one that made it here through a rather torturous series of relays." He paused, looking around one more time. "It was from Commander-Altum Mellus." The name was vaguely familiar to Barron, but he didn't know anything of note about the officer, save that she was highly regarded in the Alliance service. He could see the reactions of Vennius's officers, however, and he realized this was indeed news of some note.

"She has communicated her intention to declare for us, along with her entire fleet. Six battleships, and over twenty escort vessels."

Barron exhaled softly. This *was* news.

There were smiles around the table, and more than one variation of, "Congratulations, Your Supremacy." Six battleships would still leave Vennius's forces heavily outnumbered, but it would go a long way in the right direction, especially as Calavius would lose those vessels.

"I cannot express the need for complete and total silence on this. You are not to discuss this with anyone not present in this room. Commander Mellus is planning to move her fleet under pretense of carrying out her orders from Calavius. Several of her senior officers are involved in the decision to defect, and she believes she has control of every ship. However, though she in confident the vast majority of her crews will join her, she is not going to disclose her plans to her fleet personnel at large until she is too close to Sentinel-2 for the Red forces to intervene. Just in case any disgruntled warriors are able to signal Calavius's forces. So, not a word, to anyone. Friends, trusted officer, lovers. No one. Is that understood?"

Vennius's question prompted a round of acknowledgements. He'd waited until he was with his inner circle to make the announcement, and the tiny size of the gathering told Barron just how seriously Vennius was taking the leak threat.

Calavius had the presumption of legitimacy, by his possession of Palatia if nothing else, but Barron suspected a high-profile defection could lead to more commanders switching sides. Vennius had been discredited by his enemies lies, but he'd been enormously respected for decades, and such things tended to build on themselves. The defection was a crucial development, one that had to be protected at all costs. Secrecy was essential. If the Red forces found out about Mellus's plan, they would attack her fleet with everything they could muster.

The Imperator turned toward Barron, his gaze interrupting

the Confederation officer's thoughts. "Commodore, I request that you accompany the force sent to meet Commander Mellus, perhaps with two of your four capital ships."

"Is that really necessary, Your Supremacy?" It was Vian Tulus speaking. Barron knew Tulus was one of Vennius's oldest friends, and he'd surmised that the officer's loyalty, to the Imperator at least, if not his Confed allies, was total. "Commander Mellus is an Alliance officer. She should be met by Alliance forces. We have more than enough strength to…"

"To challenge your Imperator?" Vennius's tone turned harsh, cold. He paused, his hard stare fixed on Tulus. "Commodore Barron and his people have come to our aid. They have fought with us and bled with us. I know the way. I have followed it all of my long life of service. But ways change, even ours. Without Commodore Barron, without the Confederation ships that have come to our assistance, we would have been defeated by now. Feel shame, if you must, that we find ourselves in need of outside aid. But do not commit the additional dishonor of accepting such assistance, profiting from it, and offering disrespect to your ally."

Barron was surprised at the outburst, at the intensity of Vennius's defense of the Confederation personnel…and certainly at the admission that he would have been defeated without the aid. He thought he'd won Vennius's respect, at least, and he knew the Imperator desperately needed the support of his ships, so he tried to remain unprovoked by the words of the other officer. Vennius didn't need any more on his plate, not now, and Barron believed the Alliance leader's promise to join the Confederation in the war when his own conflict was over. Barron could endure having his pride dinged by the likes of Tulus if that was what it took to win.

That didn't mean Barron wasn't tired of the surly attitude he encountered with so many Alliance officers, but so far he'd maintained his discipline and managed to look the other way. Most of the time, at least. He'd let a few of them have it here and there, when his own frustration overwhelmed his self-control. Weirdly, the officers he'd exploded on, and in one instance, come close to blows with, were now the ones who accorded his people the most respect. Alliance culture was very different from that of the Confederation, but he was beginning to grasp its tenets. He was learning how to fight alongside his new allies. He figured, in time, the Alliance warriors would find their way to accepting the help they needed.

"I meant no disrespect, Your Supremacy. It's just that..." Tulus hesitated. He turned toward Barron. "I did not intend to denigrate the abilities of you or your people, Commodore." Barron just nodded. Of course, that was exactly what Tulus had done, or at least expressed his unwillingness to trust the Confeds. But Barron decided to leave the matter to Vennius.

"If you mean no disrespect, Tulus, perhaps next time do not show any...either to our allies, or to me, whose orders you were defying." There was no discernible anger in Vennius's voice now, no increase in volume, but Barron could see the scythe-like way his words cut into Tulus.

"Your Supremacy...I would never defy your orders. I..." His voice trailed off, and he looked plaintively toward Vennius.

"Then stand by those words, and do as I say. Commodore Barron will accompany our forces to the rendezvous point..." He paused and looked over at the Confederation officer. "...if that is acceptable to you, Commodore."

Barron could feel the discomfort the other officers felt about Vennius's deferential tone toward him. They had been raised on the cult of obedience, and none of them had any significant experience dealing with allies. Neither did Vennius, for that matter, but the Imperator was showing his ability to adapt to the changing situation, far more deftly than most of his officers. Barron nodded. "Certainly." He tended to avoid addressing Vennius whenever possible. "Your Supremacy" was the only term of address used when speaking to the Imperator. The Alliance had been so insular for so long, there was no verbiage for allies, or any foreigners, to use, and "Your Supremacy" was a little strong for foreign officers. "I will do as you need me to do." It wasn't obedience, strictly speaking, but Barron figured openly submitting to Vennius's request would help satisfy the other officers.

"Thank you, Commodore." Vennius turned his head. "And you, Commander Tulus, you will lead our contingent. You will be in command of Alliance forces present, but you will remember that Commodore Barron and his people are our allies, not our subjects, and you will conduct yourself accordingly."

Barron felt a tightness in his stomach. He knew Tulus was one of Vennius's closest friends, but the Alliance officer had also been one of the most skeptical toward Confederation involvement in the war. Barron understood to a point, but Tulus's lack of respect for the Confederation men and women fighting, and dying, for the Gray cause, didn't sit well with him. He'd held his tongue, another concession to duty, but if Vennius's victory hadn't been so important to the Confederation, he would have resolved the situation in a different way, one he suspected would come as a surprise to the arrogant Alliance officer.

Still, for all his control, he didn't relish the thought of dealing with Tulus without Vennius around, and the fact that he had no idea what to expect from Commander Mellus made the whole thing worse. *Two* fools treating his people like unwelcome interlopers would be too much to handle. But he knew Vennius was trying to make a point to his officers, and while he was far from confident it would work, he was willing to play along.

If he had to.

Chapter Nine

Excerpt from the Log of Ginia Mellus

I have sealed this log, under an access code known only to myself and Commander Sasca. I trust Ilius Sasca with all things, my life, this fleet, our mission. But all others, I must view with at least some degree of suspicion. It is a sad state of affairs, one that digs at me deeply, that I cannot fully trust men and women with whom I have shared the rigors and dangers of war.

How did our precious Alliance come to this terrible pass? By what sadistic twist of fate are we, after sixty years of uninterrupted victory and strength, now tearing at ourselves, as some great beast, driven to insanity, digging into its own flesh with pointed talons?

I can ask such questions, though I daresay I possess the answer myself, even in my own thoughts and actions. It is foolishness, arrogance. Why are we so willing to accept lies as truth, propaganda as news? I have served Tarkus Vennius my whole life. My first ship command was under his leadership. My promotion to Commander-Altum bore his signature. I watched with my own eyes as he led our forces, worked tirelessly, held himself up as the selfless ideal of the Alliance warrior.

And yet, when this struggle began, I believed what I was told about him. How he'd betrayed Katrine Rigellus, warned the Confederation of *Invictus*'s invasion, and conspired to align the Alliance with the Confeds, to sell our great nation and its ideals. What utter nonsense. Yet I listened. Worse, I acted on the lies I was told.

It was only by fortune that I received Tarkus's communique, that somehow, amid war and secrecy and tumult, it reached me, and it spurred me to sober thought. I was struck, by the tone of his words, by his lack of condemnation for my actions, as though he understood how I had fallen under Calavius's spell. I felt shame...for my failure, for his forgiveness of my folly, for the way our Imperator was driven from her palace by traitors to die on another world, trapped like an animal. Only Tarkus Vennius stood by her, remained loyal. He showed us by deed the ideal of the Palatian warrior.

I cannot undo what was done, not even my own misguided actions. But I can control what I do from now forward, and I swear here, for myself and any who one day read this, I will atone for my idiocy. I will serve Imperator Vennius, and with all my power I will fight to see him restored to his rightful place on Palatia.

Or I will die in the effort. I ask only one mercy from the fates. If I am to meet my end in this conflict, let it be a warrior's death. Let me face my end with courage and conviction and regain the pride I have sacrificed through poor judgment.

AS Viribus
Pergara System
Inbound from the Capria Transwarp Link
Year 62 (311 AC)

"All ships report systems fully-operational, Commander. We are inbound from the Capria link, accelerating at 2g."

"Very well, Commander Sasca. Proceed according to plan." Ginia Mellus sat in the center of *Viribus*'s bridge, trying to maintain a calm demeanor despite the acid threatening to burn through her stomach. She was unsettled for sure—scared, she suspected, if she were able to truly admit that to herself—but she wasn't going to let it interfere in her actions. She wasn't going to let *anything* stop her from doing what she knew was right. She'd been late to see things clearly, and she wasn't going to be dissuaded now.

She glanced over at Ilius Sasca. Sasca had been her first officer from the day she'd taken command of *Ursa*, more years ago than she cared to count. He had followed her from the escort ship to her first battleship command, and when she'd received her Commander-Altum's stars, she'd seen to his parallel promotion, and his appointment as her aide. They'd been together ever since, a team honed to a fine razor sharpness by time and the heat of battle.

Sometimes it seemed to her that little had changed since those early days, at least in the dynamic between them. Alliance fleet leaders also served as commanders of their flagships, and their aides filled in as their executive officers in addition to fleet operations duties, so despite the massive increase in responsibilities over the past four years of fleet command, on some level things still felt even more familiar.

She shifted in her seat, trying to control the edginess that continued to distract her. Mellus didn't like feeling uncomfortable, not on her own bridge. Part of her job was to radiate confidence to the men and women serving under her. But now, she struggled to hold on to her own.

She wasn't sure what had her on edge more—concern that something would go wrong, or the fact that she was hiding her true intentions from almost everyone in her fleet. Officers and spacers who had served her unquestioningly, who had fought and bled for her...she was as much as saying she didn't trust them, or at least it would seem that way to them. It was an insult to their honor, and it pained her to exhibit such disrespect to warriors loyal to her.

It was more complicated than that, of course. She *did* trust her people, enough that she had no real doubts that most of them would abide by her decision, and accept her rationale for supporting Vennius. But disaster didn't require all her warriors to oppose her choice, nor even a significant number. One Calavius stalwart and a comm unit could lead to catastrophe, and since she was virtually certain the Red Imperator had assigned spies to her ships, her hands—and her tongue—were tied. However she felt about it, there was no choice but to keep her secret as long as she could.

Until it's too late for anyone to intervene.

There was more to the gnawing ache in her gut though, a pain more deeply personal. She'd had to act quickly, taking advantage of her orders from Calavius to get close enough to Sentinel-2 to pull off the defection. There had been no time to return to Palatia, to her family estate on the Rigora coast.

To her children, Ila and Tia.

She had sent someone to the children, at least, to get them off Palatia. Torba, her servant since youth, a Mellus family retainer, and as loyal to her as any of her warriors. He would get to them, find a way to slip them off Palatia…or he would die in the attempt. She was sure of that, but for all her confidence in Torba, she couldn't banish the fears of failure, of her childhood friend dead and her children held prisoner, hostages Calavius would almost certainly use against her.

How is it so much easier to face death for yourself, and so much harder to endure the danger of those close to you?

Concern for the children had almost stopped her from deciding to declare for Vennius, but in the end, she'd been a Palatian before she'd been a mother, and whatever happened, she would not bequeath shame and disgrace to her son and daughter. Continuing to serve Calavius, ignoring his lies and propaganda, was unthinkable. It would be a stain on her name, and on her children's.

It killed her that her actions placed Ila and Tia in danger, and it took all she had to control the fears and focus on what she had to do. There'd been no other choice. If she'd tried to reach them herself, they all would have been caught, with consequences she could hardly imagine, both to the family and to the Alliance itself.

Torba will get there. He will get them off Palatia.

But then where? She knew she was joining the weaker side in the conflict, that for all Vennius's tactical brilliance, he could very well lose the war, even with her ships added to his roster. Would lose, in all probability.

"Status report, Commander?" She was edgy enough to check again, just a few minutes after Sasca had reported everything clear.

"Still clear, Commander."

"Very well." She arched back in her chair, trying to get comfortable as she pulled up *Viribus*'s operations reports. She wanted her ship ready for action...her whole fleet.

And she wanted to keep her mind occupied.

*   *   *

"Commander Tulus...requests...that we take position on the extreme right of the fleet and conduct an intensive scan of the area around the Porea transwarp point."

Barron felt a flush of anger, quickly doused by a bit of unexpected amusement. He doubted Tulus had "requested" anything from him. No, more than that, he was sure the arrogant fool had issued something that he had referred to as an order. The smile he had to fight to keep from his lips was for Atara Travis, for the creative editing he suspected she had done to the incoming communique. Travis was far more than his exec. She was his other half, an integral part of the machine that had made his command of *Dauntless* the success it had been. She was a friend too, closer even. The sister he'd never had. And she knew how to manage him, probably better than anyone else he'd ever known. He wondered sometimes if she knew he realized when she was pulling his strings...assuming he did know every time she did it. He had to allow for the possibility he didn't.

"Very well, Commander. Advise Commander Tulus that we will do what he *asks*." He wasn't sure if the emphasis was a dig at Tulus or just his way of letting Travis know he was well aware of what she was doing. He wasn't sure it mattered.

He pushed the last of his resentment for Tulus aside. He was not subject to the Palatian's orders...he wasn't even under Vennius's command. His force was allied to the Gray Alliance fleet, and that meant he had the final say on their dispositions and actions. It was annoying that the Imperator could manage to accept that arrangement and accord his allies respect, but his subordinates so often could not. Nevertheless, "annoying" didn't really factor into any of this. He was a Confederation commodore, and a Barron. Reason ruled his actions, analysis. He wasn't an Alliance officer, born into a warrior culture that placed personal honor and pride above all things. So, why was he starting to act like one? He did admire much about the Alliance, and since the battle at Santis, he'd studied their ways. But he didn't intend to become one of them.

"Set a course toward the Porea point, Commander." A pause. "And order Red squadron to the bays. I want a patrol sent out to back up the scanners." Barron didn't much like Tulus, but the Alliance officer wasn't wrong to want the link from Porea carefully scouted. The rendezvous point with Mellus's fleet was in the next system, Pergara. The transit point to that system was straight ahead, but the link to Porea was part of a secondary line leading to Palatia. The danger of a Red scoutship, or even a whole task force, emerging behind the fleet from the Porea link, was very real.

"Yes, sir." Then, a few seconds later: "Commodore, launching and retrieving a fighter force will put us behind the rest of the fleet."

"I realize that, Commander. But we've got an acceleration advantage over the Alliance ships. We should be able to catch them before they get to Pergara." He paused. "Even if we lag behind, they've got enough force to meet Commander Mellus and her ships…and as much as I hate to agree with Tulus, I just don't like the look of that Porea link. There are dust clouds all around it, and the system's asteroid belt comes awfully close to the portal itself. The enemy could have a scoutship hiding in there, and we'd never detect it, not without conducting a thorough search." Another pause. "Hell, there could be a whole fleet in there." Barron was cautious and suspicious by nature, but now his mind was focused on a specific memory, that of Captain Eaton and her vessel *Intrepid*, hiding in the Arcturon system after the disastrous battle there three years before. The Union fleet never did find *Intrepid*, and Eaton and her people had survived to come to *Dauntless*'s support, saving his vessel from certain destruction. That Union failure had led directly to the loss of their massive supply base and the halting of their great offensive, with incalculable effect on the course of the war.

The clouds in Arcturon had been even heavier than the ones here in Tarantum, but that didn't mean enemy ships couldn't be hiding out there, powered down, watching with passive scanners as the Gray fleet passed through the system. It wouldn't take more than a scoutship to send a warning to the Red fleet that Gray forces had passed through the system. That wouldn't necessarily expose Mellus's defection, but it could still bring a dangerous response.

"Commander, Lieutenant Federov advises Red squadron is ready to launch."

Barron nodded his head, glancing at the chronometer as he did. Less than four minutes. That was an astounding time, even for a squadron on standby alert, their ships armed and ready.

Olya Federov's Reds would be the elite squadron on any other ship in the fleet, and she'd have her commander's wings and probably the strike force leader's slot. He wondered if she ever second-guessed her service on *Dauntless*, if any resentment surfaced about being overshadowed by pilots like Stockton and Timmons.

There was something of the big-fish–little-pond and little-fish–big-pond debate to his questions, but he put it all aside. Federov had never expressed any indications of resentment or the desire to serve elsewhere. She was part of his team, his family, and he treated her accordingly.

But when this campaign is over you need to see she gets her promotion. She should have had it long ago…

"Very well, Commander," he said slowly, his thoughts still on Federov. "Launch Red squadron."

*   *   *

Jovi Grachus twisted her body to the side, stretching out her legs, at least as much as she could manage in the cramped confines of her cockpit. She'd flown deep space patrols before, but this was the longest she'd ever spent in her fighter without a break. The sleek craft had always felt like home to her, but now even she wished she could get away from the thing, at least for a few minutes. A short walk, a shower, a fresh uniform...they all seemed like unattainable treasures. But despite her discomfort, she remained focused. The plan had been hers, her first orders as fleet fighter commander, and if her people could endure it, so could she.

As she watched the scanner, a smile crept onto her lips. It wasn't the happy grin of good times or relaxed conversation with friends. It spoke more of the instinctive satisfaction of the predator, about to lunge forward at its prey.

The intelligence reports were accurate. A major Gray fleet was indeed moving through Tarantum. It was a significant force, perhaps even too much for her squadrons to take on alone. But she wouldn't have to defeat them on her own, just delay them.

But what's this?

Her smile sharpened.

The main force was continuing on, again, just as the reports had said it would. She'd planned to slip in behind, to harass the enemy, delay its transit to Pergara. But the enemy had detached a pair of battleships while the rest of the force continued toward the Pergara transit point. The strategy was sound. Someone over there wasn't easily fooled. The dust clouds were an ideal place to hide a few ships, at least, and scouting the area carefully was the smart play.

But it will backfire here...

The clouds weren't thick enough to hide an entire battle-fleet, at least not with any degree of certainty. Large capital ships could be detected too easily. But Grachus didn't have any battleships. She didn't have any escorts either. Just fighters. Squadron after squadron...over two hundred in total. Stripped from five of the fleet's capital ships, vessels that were needed elsewhere.

It had been a difficult mission for her people, but they were Alliance warriors, and no hardship was too much to demand in pursuit of victory. Three days. They'd been sitting there for three days, enough to drive normal men and women mad. But these weren't normal men and women. They were Palatians, and officers all. They would endure. They would do their duty.

The enemy has sent out one squadron to scout the cloud.

The two battleships are heading this way behind the fighters. Wait…wait until they're closer.

She was tense, ready, waiting for the right instant. Her communique to her squadrons would announce their presence. *Wait…not yet…*

She had the approaching squadron on her screen. The capital ships were too far out for positive IDs, but she could tell they were both big, and one of them was downright enormous, though she couldn't get much more from the weak passive scanners on her fighter. But that didn't matter. Any Gray battleships were the enemy.

And Jovi Grachus had no mercy for her enemies.

Chapter Ten

"The artifact is loaded aboard, Minister Villieneuve. All components are secured for transport." Captain Mies didn't manage to hide her edginess very well, despite what sounded like a major effort. Villieneuve knew the officer's tension had to do with more than just her baseline fear of him and of Sector Nine. The space around *Banniere* was littered with debris from the battleship's bays and holds—fighters, crates, and spare parts jettisoned to make room for the pieces of ancient technology. Villieneuve had ordered his people to take everything they uncovered from beneath the grayish brown sands of this dead alien world, whether it seemed like part of the artifact or not. All old tech was valuable, and he wasn't going to take any chances on leaving behind any key components. This expedition was too important to take chances, so the end result was, everything not absolutely vital to getting *Banniere* back to Union space had been thrown out...including every one of the battleship's fighters.

Villieneuve didn't like it any more than Mies did. *Banniere* lost much of her fighting strength, with her fighters gone and her pilots sitting on their bunks staring at each other. It was a long way back to the Union, and he knew despite its secrecy, despite every precaution he had taken, his expedition could still find itself in a fight before it got home. He'd have preferred to have a much larger fleet, one that could deal with any threat, but the Union simply did not have that many ships to spare. Not anymore.

He *was* nervous about the trip home, but he was gratified too, and glad he'd come to supervise the expedition's work himself. He was going back with what he'd come for, something that very well might change the course of the war.

He smiled, perversely amused at how strong the Confederation could be, and also how weak. The information that led his people here had come from within the confines of Confederation space. His people had made their payoffs in bars and hotel rooms on Confederation planets. For the most part, the sellers were Confed citizens, though few of them knew the mysterious adventurers and rogues buying their intel with untraceable platinum bars were Sector Nine agents.

The Confeds had proven to be capable adversaries, their battlefleets formidable, the courage and steadfastness of their spacers truly admirable.

But now they defeat themselves…

He scolded himself for some of the earlier plans that had failed. He'd gone right at the Confederation's strength before, seeking victory in the field, ship against ship. This time he was exploiting his enemy's weakness. The Confederation had a direct border on the heart of the Badlands, and the explorers they hounded and imprisoned—and his people paid—were the best sources of information on potential finds.

What fools. They could have had this artifact. They could have had the planet-killer. And who knows what else is out here. Yet they did nothing. They made no effort to seize this power.

Why? To actually honor an international agreement? To be the only signing power that paid more than lip-service to the treaty?

"All ships report ready, Minister Villieneuve. The fleet can depart on your order."

He'd always known that foolish ideals were the Confederation's weakness, that, and their population's unwillingness to see things through. He didn't fool himself that their politicians were any less corrupt than those in the Union, but they were compelled to act as though they were, to speak of fairness and ethics while making little effort to follow through on any of it. Voters were fools, easily tricked, Villieneuve had no doubt about that. But it was still easier to keep the masses under tight control, and to respond to any resistance with fear. The Confeds had never learned that lesson.

Though they will when they are conquered. Their fat, lazy civilians will learn what it is to serve the state.

Villieneuve took a last look at the main display, at the semi-circular representation of the planet below. He wished there was more time to explore the planet and the system, and the whole immediate area of the Badlands. This was farther out than the planet-killer had been, but the trend was clear. More than a century of random exploration may have finally led to a concentration of ancient tech. Villieneuve knew in many ways, the future lay in the past. The Union would come back here, as soon as the war was over, before any other power could exploit the wonders of the ancients. The prize for uncovering more artifacts was nothing less than total dominance. And he liked the sound of that.

But now it was time to go back home and win the war.

"The fleet will move out, Captain Mies. At once."

*   *   *

"There was definitely someone here, Andi, just like in Ibulan. But these readings are all over the place, much heavier. Multiple vessels, and at least one a damned sight larger than any Badlands adventurer's ship I've ever seen. If I didn't know better, I'd say…"

Lafarge was staring at the small display on *Pegasus*'s bridge, and now she turned to her exec. "You'd say what? Spit it out,

Vig." But she already knew what he was going to say.

"I'd say there was a battleship here in this system. Something as big as…"

"As *Dauntless*," she finished for him, holding back a small sigh. "But *Dauntless isn't* here, we can be damned sure of that. So, if there was a large warship in this system, we'd better start figuring out what it was. *Whose* it was…or is. Any signs of anything here now?"

She looked back at the screen, reading the AI's analysis for herself, and flipping to the direct scanner feed. She came to the same conclusion as Merrick. There *had* been ships here, and a significant presence at that. But there were no signs of any current activity, at least none *Pegasus's* passive scanners could detect at this range.

It could have been a ship from the Confederation, she thought, with more hope than conviction. But her gut told her whatever ships had been there were not friendlies. The Confederation was struggling to support two fronts right now, and while she certainly wouldn't be privy to any expeditions into the Badlands, she'd have bet a tidy sum the trails her scanners had picked up were not made by Confed ships. There were a number of possibilities, some less dire than others, but if there truly had been a *battleship* out here, that quickly narrowed the usual suspects down to one.

The Union.

Dammit. Are they back out here?

She remembered the terrible combat around the planet-killer—*my God, was that almost two years ago already?*—the nearly hopeless struggle that Barron had somehow managed to win. *With a little help…*

Did they find something else out here? The planet-killer had been a once-in-a-lifetime discovery, something monstrously powerful and relatively intact. But it wouldn't take something that large to make a difference in the war.

She'd known all about Sector Nine's presence along the Confederation's Badlands frontier, about the payoffs they offered, years before war had broken out. The totalitarian Union often looked farther ahead than the reasonably democratic and often tumultuous Confederation, planning and executing long-range plans while the Confederation Senate stumbled by year after year, pandering to the shifting moods of the populace.

The Union operatives thought they were acting in secret, and with most of the rogues and smugglers on the frontier they probably did. But Lafarge knew the *real* denizens of the scummy ports and ramshackle taverns where such business was conducted, and Sector Nine agents waving around cases of pristine platinum bars were a damned sight more obvious than they seemed to think they were.

Of course, the Confed navy was always more interested in harassing ship captains than cleaning up the enemy agents infesting the frontier.

Andi hadn't been above dealing with Sector Nine once or twice, at least before the war, though never with anything more than routine trinkets. The Union operatives *always* paid the best, and discretion was even more important to them than to the ship captains operating somewhere between smuggling and piracy.

She hadn't gone near any of her old Union contacts, not since the war started. Not since she'd met Barron. She wasn't a traitor, nor a disloyal Confederation citizen, even for all her scrapes with the law. She didn't feel good about the deals she'd made earlier, not now that the Union was the enemy, but she was sure nothing she'd sold them had cost the lives of any Confed spacers.

Pretty sure…

"Cut the engines, Vig." She was suddenly nervous, more so than she had been. "Let's coast in. Minimal power output. I know it will slow us down, but let's not take any unnecessary chances. If there's something here, we don't want to make it easy for them to find us."

Of course, if there is a task force of some kind here, they'll have scanner buoys or some type of picket force at the transit points. The Union navy wasn't a match for the Confeds, but they weren't incompetent either.

"Yes, Andi." She could tell from Merrick's tone he agreed with her.

She looked back at the long-range display, her eyes darting around the system's features. Six planets and a yellow primary sequence star. She moved her fingers across her station, bringing up a star map next to the system display. "It could be this one, Vig," she said softly. "Or this one." She reached out, pointing toward one of the small star icons.

Pegasus wasn't out here wandering aimlessly. Andi had her own intelligence, clues about a particularly juicy piece of old tech. But, like most things in her trade, her data was hopelessly partial and vague. She had basic descriptions, but this far out there was little familiarity with the system cartography. Even the names were spotty, with each star having three, four, even more designations. They were outside the borders of the charted and notated areas of the Badlands, and that meant they were feeling their way through the unknown.

"It could be this one here, also." Merrick stood up, extending his finger toward yet another icon. "There are half a dozen systems on here with six planets confirmed, more even that *might* have six." The partial map they had listed specific planet totals for some systems, and ranges of numbers, notations like "4-7" for others. A good third of them had nothing listed at all, which really cranked up the degree of difficulty in figuring where they were. They could backtrack and find their way home without a problem, but tracking down what they sought was proving to be difficult and frustrating.

She'd promised herself one thing. If she found what she was looking for, she'd offer it to the Confed authorities for use in the war. She had her resentments for the way she, and the other adventurers combing the Badlands, had been treated by the authorities, but she was still a patriot, in her own way.

But they would pay for it this time…and they would pay what it was worth. If they could pour billions of credits into R&D and ship construction to fight this war, she was damned if she'd be a charity again, especially when she and her people were risking their lives doing what the Confederation government should have been doing all along.

In fairness, the last time *Pegasus* had been out here seeking an old tech artifact, her people had been in trouble, and it had taken significant Confederation intervention to save them…and keep the planet-killer out of Union hands. And Admiral Striker hadn't exactly stiffed her people. They'd been paid, a nice sum if not the king's treasure the antimatter they'd brought back would have fetched on the black market. And Striker had fixed up *Pegasus* for her too, gratis, doing such a first-class job, she'd hardly recognized her old vessel.

"Andi…the system is still clear, but we're getting more readings. The third planet seems to be the center of whatever activity took place here. We've got multiple drive trails and lots of residual energy readings."

She looked back at the scanner, staring intently. Still nothing. "Bring us to the third planet, Vig. Minimum possible thrust. Just enough to alter our vector." This wasn't the system she was looking for. The map said she was seeking for a binary star with just one planet. But she had to at least take a look. If the Union was out here and had gone, that could mean they'd given up on whatever they were looking for.

Or it could mean they found it.

She felt the burst of thrust as Merrick fired the engines, just for about thirty seconds. Then *Pegasus* returned to minimal power output. "We should be in orbital insertion range in… twenty-three minutes, Andi."

"Twenty-three minutes," she repeated, sighing softly as soon as she did. With any luck, she'd find evidence of a clearly abandoned search site, a wild goose chase that had drained away Union resources for no gain. She could hope at least.

But Andi Lafarge wasn't one for unfocused hope. She preferred cold, rational analysis…and that was telling her something she didn't want to hear.

Her people had stumbled onto something here, something bad.

Chapter Eleven

CFS Dauntless
Tarantum System
Near the Porea Transit Point
Year 62 (311 AC)

"Lieutenant Federov reports no contacts, Commodore. She is..." Travis's voice stopped cold. Then she spun around, looking right at Barron. "Sir, Red squadron is reporting multiple energy sources from within the dust cloud."

"Battlestations." Barron wasn't surprised, not really. After five years of war, his caution had morphed into a sort of fatalism. He retained his basic confidence in himself and his crew, but otherwise he expected the worst at all times. *And how often have you been wrong?* "Notify *Illustrious.*"

"Battlestations, sir." The klaxons sounded an instant later, and the bridge was bathed in the all too familiar red light of the lamps. A few second later: "Captain Reardon acknowledges." Then, almost immediately, "*Illustrious* confirms battlestations."

Barron glanced down at his screen, his eyes moving over the series of readouts. A red alert triggered a whole series of automatic responses, from the activation of combat duty stations, to the manning of all fighter squadrons in the bays. But a launch would require his expressed order, and he wanted to be sure what was out there before he gave it.

87

"Lieutenant Federov reports…"

"Put her on main comm, Commander."

Travis flipped a switch, and Federov's voice blared from the speakers. "…fighters. Multiple squadrons, coming out from all along the clouds…"

Barron leaned forward, putting his mouth to the comm unit to ask Red squadron's commander to be specific, but before the words came, his screen lit up with contacts, the data relayed automatically from Federov's ships. Fighters. Hundreds of fighters.

"Status in the bays?"

"Commander Sinclair reports Blue and Scarlet Eagle squadrons will be ready to launch in…four minutes. Yellow and Green four minutes after that."

Barron shook his head. He'd been careful and careless at the same time. His ships were too damned close to the clouds. He'd been concerned about scoutships and escorts, not fully-deployed attack squadrons.

"Lieutenant Federov, pull your squadron back now. You can regroup with the Blues and Eagles when they launch." Federov's fighters were outnumbered twenty to one. Barron had faith in his people, but a battle at those odds would be a slaughter.

"Commodore, I think we can delay them, make them brake their acceleration to engage…"

"Negative, Lieutenant. Pull back. That's a damned order."

He didn't even hear her acknowledgement. He was deep in thought, checking out velocities and vectors, trying to decide if her people even *could* break off before they were fully engaged. A lot depended on what the enemy did, but his best guess was right around 50-50. The odds of *Dauntless* and *Illustrious* getting away before the enemy fighters reached them were rather less.

"Active scanners on full power, Commander. There are motherships out there somewhere, and we've got to find them." *We should have gotten some kind of readings before now.* He knew the fighters were small, and already launched as they were, it was no surprise his people hadn't picked them up until they were so close. *But hiding battleships is a different matter entirely…*

"Scanners on full, sir. No contacts but fighter squadrons.

We're picking up two hundred forty-two ships now."

"That's impossible, Commander. How can this many fighters be here with no base or mother…" He suddenly felt sick. Enemy battleships would only make the fight more uneven… but the lack of them could only mean one thing. They had dropped the fighters here before proceeding somewhere else…

They knew we were coming.

Again.

"Send a flash communique to Commander Tulus before the fleet transits." The Gray Alliance ships were light minutes ahead of *Dauntless* and *Illustrious* now, and it would be almost half an hour before a message could travel there and back. His first instinct had been to call for help…but those fighters would reach his two ships long before Tulus could get back.

"Yes, sir. Sending now."

"Commander Tulus, we have encountered large numbers of enemy fighters. This is a trap. They were waiting for us." Barron's words were cold, matter-of-fact.

"With no motherships?" Travis turned to face him.

"It seems so, Commander. They must have dropped the fighters here."

"How long can pilots operate in a fighter without a break?"

"These are Alliance pilots, Commander. They're born and bred to follow orders." Barron was struck by both the stark strangeness of Alliance culture, and how much he admired it. He didn't want to live in such a society, and the Alliance was certainly cruel to those they conquered, but he'd be damned if he didn't respect them on some levels. As allies or enemies. It was a refreshing change from the utter and complete vileness of the Union.

"But why operate here without battleships? They could have ambushed us just the same with their mother…"

"Because they needed their motherships somewhere else." Barron paused, just for a second, his face going pale as realization set in. If the traitor in their midst had struck again, if Calavius's people knew they were coming through here, they knew why as well. "Priority comm channel to Commander Tulus.

Now!"

Travis spun around, her hands flying over the controls. "On your line, sir."

"Commander, this is a trap. The enemy fighters attacking us...everything. They know we were coming. They know about Commander Mellus. You have to get through to her fleet before they're attacked and destroyed." His words were hasty, not carefully chosen. Normally, he'd have handled Tulus with a softer touch, one that sounded less like orders. But there was no time.

He glanced down at the scanners, at the range display. Tulus's ships were ahead of schedule. He did a quick calculation, one that told him his Gray Alliance counterpart would jump before his messages arrived.

He was on his own here...and Tulus and his people would face what was waiting for them without warning.

Barron considered the whole situation, and with each passing second his conclusion grew glummer, more ominous.

If this leaked, that means the traitor is...

"Commodore, Blue and Scarlet Eagle squadrons requesting launch authorization."

"Launch," he spat, robotically. His thoughts were elsewhere.

There were only six of us there that day. That means the traitor is in Vennius's inner circle...

The implications were terrifying. But the soft vibrations of fighters launching pulled him back to the present. His ship was going into battle...and nothing else mattered. Not right now.

*   *   *

"Bearclaw, Kraken, Direwolf, Banshee squadrons, engage enemy interceptors. Red Dragons and all other interceptors on me. We're taking the bombers in. We've got two battleships picked off from the main force, and we're going to take them both down." Grachus pulled back on her controls, kicking in her turbo thrusters, even as the acknowledgements began pouring in on her comm. There wasn't a doubt in her mind her people would follow her orders. All her life she'd been shut out, treated as an outsider, despite Kat Rigellus's mentorship. But the fighter corps was different. Her promotion, given directly by the Imperator, and her reputation as a stone cold killer in the cockpit, had made her a legend, at least among the pilots. It was an odd feeling, for once to be the subject of admiration. She liked it, she could admit that to herself at least. But she intended to get more from it than personal satisfaction. She couldn't be sure, not until she got closer scanner reads, but her gut—and the preliminary mass readings—told her those were Confederation ships out there. And if there were Confeds here, Tyler Barron was probably with them.

She brought her ship around, plotting a course to skirt the flank of the incoming formation. The four squadrons she'd detached to meet them would be outnumbered, but Alliance pilots paid no heed to such things. They would fight. And they would hold their own.

And I will lead these bombers right into attack range…

She glanced down at the screen again. One of the battleships was immense. *That has to be one of the new Confed ships.* The other was somewhat smaller, though still massive by Alliance standards. *Dauntless?*

She punched at her controls, pumping up the power of her scanners. She was going beyond the posted maximums, but she had to know. She had every particular of Tyler Barron's flagship in her AI. In just a few seconds, she'd be sure.

It didn't matter, not really, not strategically at least. Destroying two Confed battleships would be a major victory, whether or not Barron was there. Killing Barron would be useful to the Red cause, of course. He was a highly capable officer and his loss would hurt the Grays badly. For all her discipline, she couldn't take her mind off the revenge she craved so powerfully.

She felt invigorated as the screen display the positive ID. CFS *Dauntless.* Tyler Barron *was* here.

It's time, Kat. Today you will be avenged, my friend. My sister.

"Keep your formations tight," she said into the comm. "We've got multiple waves coming in." She'd taken the Confeds by surprise, though perhaps not as much as she'd hoped. She had planned to get in behind them as they passed and attack from the rear. But for all she hated Tyler Barron, she was painfully aware he was no fool. He'd launched a scouting force to check the dust clouds…forcing her to launch her attack prematurely. She still had the edge, but she was facing two powerful ships, and she knew she had one hell of a fight on her hands.

She checked her display. The bomber squadrons were dropping in right behind her screening fighters. She hoped her blocking force would divert most of the Confed interceptors, that they would waste squadrons on bombing attacks targeting her non-existent battleships. But as she watched the last of the Confed fighters clear their platforms, she realized that part of her deception, at least, had failed. Every one of those Confed birds was outfitted for fighter to fighter combat. And that meant her people were heading into one serious melee.

Part of her wished she was with the blocking force. She didn't like ordering her people into a fight at such a disadvantage, especially not when she wasn't with them. But success here would come from killing battleships, not fighters. Nothing was more important than getting the bombers through.

Nothing.

*   *   *

"Yellows, Reds, Mustangs, Jaguars…keep those ships in the center occupied. Blues, Eagles, White Condors…with me. We're going for those bombers."

Stockton nodded to himself as he listened to Kyle Jamison snapping out orders over the comm. Jamison was officially *Dauntless*'s strike force commander, but he effectively commanded all Confederation fighters in the battle. Right now, that included *Illustrious*'s six largely-raw squadrons. Stockton didn't envy his friend right now. Sending those green pilots up against Alliance flyers was almost murder. But there was no choice. *Dauntless*'s wings could hold their own—they could even outmatch the Alliance pilots, on anything like even terms. But they couldn't win outnumbered four to one.

And if that squadron is out there. That *pilot…*

Stockton had been thinking about the last battle pretty much constantly from the moment he landed back on *Dauntless*. The Alliance had one hell of a flyer out there somewhere, one he had to find—and kill—before any more of his comrades found themselves outmatched and blasted to atoms.

The threat wasn't theoretical. Stockton had faced off against this enemy, and the experience had shaken him. Winning the victory he needed would take everything he had…and perhaps for the first time, he wondered if that would be enough. He'd fought many battles, but this was new. He'd never doubted his ability to defeat a single enemy in a one on one matchup. Until now.

"Roger, Thunder. Blue squadron with you." He paused, just for an instant. Then: "All right Blues, we follow the commander in. Take out as many interceptors as you can, but remember, that's a big force of bombers, and they're our primary target." Ignore the interceptors, go for the bombers…it was often the right call, but there weren't many situations pilots hated more. Nothing made enemy fighters deadlier than ignoring them, ripping by to attack the attack bombers, leaving flanks and rear exposed. But every man and women understood, before they every launched for the first time, that their first and overriding purpose was to protect the battleships.

Stockton had heard it put a dozen ways, some of them impressive exercises in diplomatic phrasing, but he preferred the bluntness of "expendable." Which was exactly what he and every pilot flying with him was, at least compared to the four million tons of *Dauntless* and her thousand crew.

"Blues, on me. Let's go. Arrowhead formation, full thrust… now." He blasted his engines full, feeling the g forces slam into him, pushing the breath from his lungs. The enemy had a screen of interceptors out in front of their bombers, and on the flanks as well. Stockton's mind raced, looking for a vulnerable spot… but there wasn't one. At least none his squadron could get to in time. However Blue squadron approached, they'd have to fight their way through…and they'd have to leave enemies behind them.

"We're on your flank, Raptor." Dirk Timmons's voice was cold. It was clear he knew as well as Stockton what they were up against.

"Roger that, Warrior. We just cut through these interceptors...straight through to the bombers."

"We're with you, Raptor."

Stockton stared at the controls, his eyes fixed on the enemy formation on his scanner. There were half a dozen interceptors right ahead. A quick glance to the side confirmed that Timmons's Eagles had a larger number than that in their path, a dozen or more.

"Looks like we've got the weak spot," he whispered to himself.

Weak being a relative term of course...

He moved his hand, his fingers sliding along the arming controls for his missiles. He wanted to save the heavy ordnance, blast through the interceptors with just lasers, but he found himself shaking his head even as he was still considering it.

No, the Alliance pilots were just too good. Trying to hold back missiles would cost him in casualties, and he suspected he would lose enough of his people in the best circumstances. *Maybe launch one?*

He shook his head, at least as well as he could under more than 8g. A fighter armed with missiles was cumbersome, harder to handle, especially in a dogfight with experienced interceptor pilots. And one carrying a single one of the heavy weapons was off-balance besides. It was something he'd try against Union squadrons, maybe. But the Alliance pilots were just too good.

"Blue squadron, arm all missiles." He had a passing vision, his squadron launching their barrage, blowing away every enemy fighter in its path. But he knew better. Nobody blasted Alliance squadrons away like that.

"All right, listen up. We hit that first line as hard as we can, but we don't stop. So, make those missiles count...because anything you don't take out is going to be coming around and following us in." Whoever had set up the enemy formation knew what they were doing. The Alliance Interceptors were moving at low velocity, their vectors nearly perpendicular to his approaching craft. It wouldn't take the survivors long to reorient their courses and come up behind his people.

"Maintain full thrust. We're going in hot." It was the only choice. The velocity would make it harder for the enemy fighters to follow. It would buy some time before his people had Alliance fighters coming at them from behind, though it would also take his people right past the bombers before they could decelerate. They'd have to make their attacks count...and quickly.

The enemy fighters were growing on his screen. It was almost time. He flipped the two switches on his control panel, activating the final arming sequence for his missiles. Then: "All right Blues...let's go get 'em."

He swung the stick around, hard to starboard, picking out one of the Alliance fighters. His hand tightened, his finger pressing down on the firing stud. But he stopped. His target had blasted its thrusters hard, upsetting his target lock. When *Dauntless* had first arrived on the Rim, he and his people had been accustomed to the lower proficiency of the Union squadrons, but they'd gotten a lesson quickly. Now, he didn't even react. He just readjusted his thrust, picking out another target. He didn't have as hard a lock as he'd have liked, but he didn't have time to waste either. His ship was moving at almost 0.005c, and he'd be out of engagement range in less than a minute.

He moved his hand over the controls, adjusting his course slightly with each tap on the throttle. He pushed to the port, then again. And he fired.

The fighter lurched as the missile broke free of its hardpoint and blasted out for the enemy fighter. The drone had a far higher rate of thrust than his fighter, and it accelerated toward the target at 25g.

The Alliance ship reacted immediately, swinging around, firing its engines in an attempt to escape the deadly warhead. Stockton watched for a few seconds, as his prey struggled to elude the missile, to keep away long enough for the madly-accelerating weapon to exhaust its fuel supply. Then he turned back to the scanner and started to look for another target. But before he found one, his own warning system buzzed.

"Incoming missile," the fighter's AI said, in its annoyingly calm tone.

It'll blow you to atoms too, he thought pointlessly toward the AI.

Stockton's hands moved almost by themselves, even as he focused on the screen, getting a read on the missile's approach. It was coming directly toward him, and he angled the throttle and blasted at full, changing course, even as the missile reacted.

He counted under his breath as he watched, and as he shifted the angle of his thrust again. The AI was doing the same thing, rattling off ranges and times to contact, but Stockton worked by feel as much as hard data. The Alliance missiles were shorter-ranged than the Confederation weapons, and their acceleration topped out around 21.5g, a pair of facts that Stockton knew had saved more than one of his pilots over the past six months. But he'd let this enemy get too close, and the missile was closing hard.

He flashed a glance to the attack screen, checking on his own weapon. He thought he'd had the enemy dead to rights, but now he could see that the Alliance pilot had managed to evade the missile. He couldn't be sure, not on such a quick glance, but his gut told him the warhead would run out of fuel before it caught the enemy ship.

Damn.

He wasn't sure if the thought was spurred by his own miss, or by the fact that he was wasting time and attention on tracking his missile when he needed to put all his focus into escaping the weapon closing on him.

He slammed the throttle hard, back and to the side, radically altering the vector of thrust. His ship's course changed far more slowly, as momentum carried him forward. The inability to make wild and immediate course changes, as a flyer in an atmosphere could do, was one of the toughest aspects of space combat. It was difficult to evade a faster projectile, but enough random moves could mess with the AI guiding the thing, and he only needed to stay away from it for another…forty seconds or so.

He knew it would be close, all the more so for the sweat he could feel pouring down his back in rivulets. He'd let his pride get the better of him, turned his focus almost purely to the offensive instead of watching out for enemy attacks. It was an error he swore not to repeat. Assuming he got the chance.

He angled his ship's thrust yet again...and then he hit the positioning thrusters and spun the small vessel around one hundred eighty degrees, blasting his engines again, decelerating at full. It was a move than made no sense, mathematically at least. But he was counting down the missile's fuel supply, and he knew the abrupt reversal would confuse the AI, briefly at least. And every second counted.

He could see the missile getting closer, its trajectory bringing it toward his ship...or, more accurately, near his ship. The drone was blasting its own thrusters, correcting its course, locking in on his fighter. It was close now.

But it's almost out of time...

His eyes were locked on the scanner display as he swung the throttle yet again. Now he was buying mere seconds. The missile would have him in half a minute, maybe less. But he'd just bet his life the thing would run out of fuel before that.

He watched, waiting to see the engines cut out, each fraction of a second stretching out, feeling like minutes. He kept up the evasive maneuvers, but this close they were increasingly ineffective. The missile was reacting to every change of vector, refining its targeting. It had him.

He stared, but the drone's thrusters kept blasting. He'd counted down, but now he was past zero, his guess on the thing's fuel capacity proving inaccurate. Still, he knew he couldn't be off by much...could he?

His confidence surrounded him like a wall, high, thick, impervious. Almost. But each passing second wore away at it, doubt growing, pressing in on him. Could he have made that much of an error?

He was staring at the screen, watching his death approach when the energy output from the missile dropped off. It was still heading straight for his fighter, only seconds away now. But the thrust was dead.

He gripped the throttle, angling it to the side, blasting his engines again. It didn't matter where…any change in his vector would do now. The missile was zipping through space at better than 0.01c, but its course was fixed now, its engines silent. He watched as the tiny symbol went by, less than a kilometer away. That was "sweating range" in space combat, and he had the drenched flight suit to prove it. But a miss was a miss.

Pull your shit together, Raptor…and don't underestimate these people again.

The Alliance pilots were flying better than he'd ever seen them, and deep down he knew what had changed. His thoughts drifted to the phantom pilot, the one he'd dueled with so intensely. The Red Alliance fighter corps clearly had more than just a new ace.

"Watch your asses out there, Blues." *And you too, Blue Leader.* "These are some sharp pilots we've got here."

They have a new leader…and they're fired up.

Chapter Twelve

"We've got more ships transiting, Commander. They're demanding we surrender at once."

Mellus sat in her chair, fighting off the shock that had begun with the first vessel emerging into the system. She'd known then, almost immediately, without scanner reports, without any communication, that her effort to defect had failed. Calavius knew all about it...and he'd sent ships to stop her. Enough ships to wipe out her whole fleet.

She sighed softly as she saw more and more symbols emerge from the transit point. There was no way her fleet could escape, and no way it could win either. Whatever she did now, she was dead.

She felt the urge to fight to the end, to go down as she had lived, as an Alliance warrior. She had made her gambit, and now it was time to face the consequences. But thousands of her people would die too, all of them innocent, unaware even that they'd been in the act of switching sides. If she ordered the fleet to stand down, if she took full blame for what she had done... maybe Calavius would pardon her officers and crews.

The pain in her gut told her how little she believed those hopeful thoughts. Calavius might believe some of the crews didn't know…but he'd never believe she'd managed to keep it as much a secret as she had. Her senior officers would find themselves under arrest, disgraced, and very likely executed. Even her crews would suffer. Calavius might not shoot or imprison the entire fleet's complement, but he would reassign them, replacing them with less tainted personnel as quickly as he could. The men and women of her fleet would find themselves manning remote stations, or discharged entirely. For the common spacers, men and women of no wealth or resources, they'd end up little better than Plebs, working the rest of their lives for whatever scant wage anyone would pay them.

And Calavius will regain these six battleships…

No, I can't let that happen. I can't let him get these ships back. I erred once…I was weak. I supported the wrong side. Never again.

"Commander, get me a fleetwide line."

A few seconds passed. "You're live, Commander."

She took a deep breath, suddenly at a loss of what to say. How could she explain the situation she'd put her people in? She'd had the best intentions, but how could she explain now why she hadn't told them, without saying as much as she didn't trust them?

"Officers and spacers of the fleet, this is Commander Mellus. As many of you no doubt see on your scanners, there are ships emerging from the transwarp point. Alliance ships, sworn to the Red faction, as we…were."

She took a breath, suddenly feeling the stares of *Viribus's* bridge crew boring into her. She knew it would be especially painful for them that she hadn't included them. They would see it as a lack of faith, which was far from the truth. "Some weeks ago, I received a communication from Commander Vennius… Imperator Tarkus I. He sent me evidence…of Calavius's plot to seize power, of his attack on the Imperatrix. Of the Imperatrix's death…from wounds inflicted by Calavius's forces when they attacked the palace."

She struggled to keep her voice firm, but she could hear the cracks despite her efforts. "I was wrong to swear fealty to Cala-vius. I was wrong to lead all of you down that road. I believed what I was told, to my everlasting shame. And, worse perhaps, when I decided to repent, to support the rightful ruler of the Alliance, I didn't tell all of you. I took it as my mistake to cor-rect, my obligation, and I tried to shield you. But in my efforts to protect, I did every man and women in this fleet a terrible dis-service. I denied you the right to choose your allegiance. And I failed to show you the trust you deserve, that each of you has earned, through long service and shared sacrifice."

She turned her head, pushing herself to look at the faces of the officers surrounding her. She felt a fear more terrible than any she'd ever known, not of death and defeat, but of what she'd see in those stares, in the eyes of the men and women who had served her.

But it wasn't the hatred she'd expected. There was pain, certainly, hurt at what she had said and done. But there was defiance too, and support. Loyalty.

"I am with you, Commander." A lone voice, from the far side of the bridge. Optio Bellus, she realized, a tactical officer.

"And I, Commander. I understand what you did."

"Yes…you have my trust, now and always."

"We're with you, Commander."

She was stunned, and she felt a wave of emotion stirring inside. There wasn't a dissenting voice, not on her bridge at least. And then she saw the comm board all lit up, officers and spacers from every station of the ship, checking in…all with her. She had *Viribus*, at least.

"Ships of the fleet, hear me now. I believe Imperator Ven-nius is our rightful ruler, and for me to ignore his call would be the blackest of treasons. But you must make your choices now, either to follow me, to declare at this moment for Vennius and the Grays, or to reaffirm your loyalty to the Red cause. Known now, all of you, that following me, joining the Grays, is likely to end in your deaths here in this system, for I fear we are trapped, soon to be surrounded. I will fight, *Viribus* will fight, to the last if need be. But each ship's commander and crew must make their own decision. Whatever course you choose, you all have my deepest respect and admiration. And my gratitude for the service each of you has given."

She turned and made a gesture across her throat, the signal to Sasca to cut the line. She'd done all she could. She didn't even know what she was hoping for them to do. To join her now, and die here? Or to crawl back to Calavius, hoping for his dubious clemency?

"Commander Sasca, bring *Viribus* to battlestations."

"Yes, Commander." Her aide's voice was firm, almost eager. Whatever fear and uncertainty he felt was well-hidden.

She paused a second, her eyes on Sasca. *A model of the Alliance warrior. Fare thee well, Ilius Sasca, wherever this dark fight leads us.*

"Commander! We're getting messages from the ships of the fleet. They're with us!" A short pause. "They're all with us!"

Mellus turned and looked at the main display. All six battleships remained in formation, and all but two of the escorts. She was transfixed, watching a single pair of frigates blasting their engines, moving away from the fleet. The rest of her force stood, resolute. She was almost overcome by her peoples' loyalty.

And now you will reward that faithfulness by leading them to their deaths...

Her eyes moved up, toward the screen displaying the newly-arrived fleet. Nineteen battleships, the lead units already launching fighters. And on the flanks, more than thirty-five frigates. Her fleet was doomed. They would never reach Sentinel-2. Their only service to the Grays would be here, now, causing as much damage to the Red fleet as they could before they were destroyed.

She looked around the bridge again, at the men and women who had so recently shouted out their support for her. She still felt shards of gratification, but the guilt and sadness had mostly taken over. If she could have saved them all, she would have given herself up, yielded to death and disgrace. But she knew that would serve no purpose. And they could do some good, at least, for the side they now all served. There were worse fates for an Alliance warrior than to die in battle, serving a just and true cause.

"Scramble all fighters."

"Yes, Commander."

"And full power to all batteries. All personnel to combat stations. Fleet order...prepare for battle!"

If she couldn't save her people, she would see that they died as they had lived. As Alliance warriors.

The way is the way.

*   *   *

"Commander Tulus..."

"Yes, Ingus, I see." Tulus had seen that something was wrong the instant *Ferox*'s scanners had cleared the usual interference from the jump insystem. He'd expected to find Mellus's fleet waiting, but there was more happening in the Pergara system. Much more. There was a battle going on, a big one.

And fierce, from the look of it.

It took a bit longer, perhaps a minute, before he confirmed what he'd guessed from the start. Commander Mellus's fleet was under attack. And they were outnumbered, almost surrounded.

"Battlestations, Ingus. All ships, prepare to launch fighters." He hesitated for an instant, almost taking back that last order. His eyes were moving all across the display, getting a good idea just how large the Red fleet was. Understanding dawned quickly. Mellus's people were doomed without help, that had been obvious from the first seconds after his scanners reactivated, but now he could see the true extent of the trap. Even with his fleet, the situation was just about hopeless.

"Get me a line to Commander Mellus."

"Yes, sir." A few seconds later. "On your line, Commander. Transmission time one minute, twenty seconds." Tulus nodded, holding back a sigh. He'd known Mellus's forces were significantly farther in-system, but even though he'd expected it, a nearly three minute lag between round trip communications wasn't going to do anything to help the two forces coordinate against a superior enemy.

"This is Commander-Altum Vian Tulus, calling Commander-Altum Mellus. We are moving into the system toward your position. Please advise on the status of your force and prepare a plan to fall back on the Tarantum transit point. We will form up and attempt to provide cover as you withdraw." Tulus said the words, but even as he spoke, he felt the leaden feeling growing inside him. The attackers were too close, coming along a vector that would put them almost right between the two Gray forces.

"All ships report battlestations, sir. Our fighters are ready to launch, Commander. *Mico* also reports ready to launch."

"All fighters launch." He looked back to the screen, at his four battleships. Even with his forces added to Mellus's, the enemy still had almost two to one odds.

Where the hell is Barron with those two ships of his?

Tulus did not count himself among the small number of officers who had come to embrace Confederation assistance. The strategist inside him knew the Gray cause needed the help, indeed, he might even acknowledge the possibility that they would have met total defeat already without the Confeds. But the old line warrior in there still stood on pride, resenting these new allies. And considering them inferior, despite the distinction they'd shown in battle.

Confeds or not, those ships are big...especially the newer one. If they were here now...

Tulus had sent Barron to investigate the Porea transit point, but now he was wondering where the hell the Confed and his people were. They should have scouted things out by now and rejoined the fleet. Especially with their higher thrust levels.

He felt anger, frustration...a growing sense that his allies were letting him down. Were they cowering in the Tarantum system? Or was it worse? Were they in on the treachery?

There was nothing he could do about it now. Perhaps Barron and his people were just slow, inefficient. He was measuring their expected performance by Alliance standards. But whatever it was, he'd have to fight without them, at least at first.

"Bring us forward twenty light seconds, and then cut thrust."

He couldn't leave Mellus's forces without trying to save them. He would not suffer the dishonor of abandoning allies without even fighting. But he wasn't about to get his own force too deep into the system. If he let the Reds get around his flank, interpose between his ships and the transit point back to Tarantum, none of his people would make it back to Sentinel-2.

"Commander Tulus, greetings." Mellus's delayed response was loud in his headset. "Your aid is appreciated, but I warn you. We are likely trapped here and outnumbered. We will fight, but you must seek to preserve your force. Imperator Vennius cannot lose more ships this day than can be avoided."

Tulus heard the strength in Mellus's voice, but also the acceptance. She'd given up on escaping herself—Viribus was on the far side of her formation, the most distant from the Tarantum transit point—but perhaps she clung to hope that some of her people might escape.

"I urge you, Commander Tulus, to assist my people, those closest to your force, to escape. Victory is not an option here, only survival. For some, at least."

It filled Tulus with rage to hear such a valiant officer broken, resolved to her death even as she fought on. For an instant, he felt a flush of determination, an urge to find a way to save her. But even as he indulged it for a passing moment, his eyes drew in the reality the scanners were showing him. Viribus was already almost cut off, waves of Red fighters moving in, slicing toward the battleship and its two nearby companions. Mellus was trapped. But half her fleet had a chance. At least a small chance.

"All ships continue to launch as squadrons are ready."

"Yes, Commander."

"Then power up main batteries...and bring us right toward the right flank of Mellus's position."

With any luck, we'll bracket the attackers between Mellus's three closer in battleships and ours. Maybe we can give the Reds enough of a bloody nose to pull out.

Maybe.

He looked to the side, toward the long-range screens covering the transit point.

Where the hell are you, Barron?

Chapter Thirteen

CFS Dauntless
Tarantum System
Near the Porea Transit Point
Year 62 (311 AC)

"Commander, we've got another wave coming in. Red squadron's on combat space patrol, and Blue squadron is coming in behind the bombers." Travis looked around, back toward Barron. "Lieutenant Timmons's Eagles are engaging the second wave of interceptors coming in behind the assault squadrons." A pause. "They're outnumbered more than three to one."

Barron just nodded. He knew exactly what Stockton and Timmons were doing. His two elite squadrons should have joined forces and held back the Red interceptors together. But Federov's Reds weren't going to turn back this assault wave alone. They'd lost too many of their people repelling the first one. More than half of Federov's people were back in the landing bays now, standing around as the flight crews struggled to get their damaged and depleted craft repaired and refueled enough to launch. Or they'd ditched, and they were floating in the space around *Dauntless*, waiting and hoping there would be enough time for the rescue boats to recover them before they ran out of life support.

And three of her pilots were dead. At least, *Dauntless*'s scan-

107

ners had failed to pick out any lifepods after their ships had been destroyed.

Stockton's Blues would cut down on the number of bombers getting through—if they made it in time—but even with his top ace leading his people into the fray, Barron knew the strike wave was likely to draw blood. Not to mention the losses the Eagles would suffer as the forlorn hope, fighting to buy the few moments the others needed.

His eyes darted to the side, to the screen displaying the space around *Illustrious*. The new battleship wasn't quite the shiny beauty she'd been when Sara Eaton had first arrived at Sentinel-2. Eaton had fought at his side three years before, when *Dauntless* had returned from the Rim to find the Confederation fleet beaten and retreating...and his own vessel trapped behind enemy lines. She'd been *Intrepid*'s commander then, and the two battleships had pulled off a desperate mission to destroy the Union's supply base, a victory that halted the enemy invasion in its tracks. Eaton was back at Sentinel-2 now, in charge of the other two ships of the expeditionary force.

Illustrious had been in several fights out here now, and gone through the all too familiar routine of battle damage followed by hasty repairs. Still, she was bigger, newer, and more powerful than *Dauntless*.

But the pilots defending her were raw, and the Alliance flyers were cutting through them with far greater ease than they were against *Dauntless*'s veteran squadrons. The big ship had already taken two hits, once of which looked quite serious. And she had her own second wave of enemy bombers coming at her.

Barron had to keep reminding himself he was responsible for both ships. James Reardon was an experienced captain, one who'd been at the helm of a battleship before Barron had ever set eyes on *Dauntless*. But that did nothing to lessen the responsibility.

He felt the urge to reassign one of his more experienced squadrons, but a quick look at his screens told him he didn't have a ship to spare. *Illustrious* already fielded a larger complement than *Dauntless*, which meant they could lose more and still maintain a defensive line. Barron didn't like the idea of throwing numbers at a problem, of making his people cannon fodder, even when it was the only choice…but right now, it *was* the only choice. At least for *Illustrious*.

And Reardon knows that. Which is why he hasn't asked for support.

Barron's hand moved down the armrest of his chair, toward the comm controls. He flipped on the intraship line, switching to the main engineering channel. "Fritzie?"

"Yes, Commodore?" The response was almost immediate, but Barron could hear a hint of distraction as well. Wherever she was, Fritz was working on something.

"I just wanted to get a status report before those bombers come in." *And what the hell are you working on already? We haven't taken any real damage yet.*

"Everything's good, sir. I've got response teams stationed at all crucial points, and double crews at the landing bays. Wherever we get hit…" Barron noted she hadn't said "if" we get hit. "…we'll be ready." A pause. "Is it true, sir, we're facing only fighters?"

"It looks true enough. No sign of anything larger." *And it's my fault for not predicting the hardship these Alliance pilots can take. I should have seen this coming…or at least been more prepared in case it did.*

"If you're sure of that…" Her voice trailed off.

"What is it, Fritzie? You've never had any trouble speaking your mind to me."

"Well, sir…I was just thinking. If we're *sure* there are no enemy battleships out there, I could take the primaries offline completely. We could cut the power leads entirely, and get some fire suppressant all around the main equipment. It will protect them against any overloads caused by hits we might take."

"Makes sense. Do it."

"You have to understand, sir. I'm talking about physically severing a dozen connections. I'd be doing as much damage as a direct hit, but it would be more controlled, easier to reverse. Still, if we do it, we're looking at six hours at least to get them back online."

Barron heard her words, and he understood the hesitancy

she'd shown.

"It would make it a lot less likely they'll suffer significant damage…but then they're effectively out of this battle."

Barron paused, his eyes panning across the scanners again, looking for any signs of an enemy vessel larger than a fighter. He almost ordered Travis to run a new scan, but he realized it was a waste of time. He'd have found anything out there by now, at least anything in range. And if the Alliance had found a way to hide capital ships this well, another concentrated search wasn't going to find them.

"Do it, Fritzie."

"Yes, sir." The line was still live, but she didn't say anything else. Barron sat for a moment, and then he cut the connection. He looked up at the main display, just as Blue squadron slammed into the rear of the enemy bomber formation.

*   *   *

Stockton brought his ship around, firing a final blast toward the closest bomber. It had been a last hope, a long shot to try to take down one more attack ship. But his lasers went wide—barely—and the bomber continued on. *Toward Federov's Reds. And then* Dauntless…

Stockton's Blues had managed to get back for an attack run against the bombers, but their velocity and vectors precluded them from staying in the fight. By the time they could decelerate and come around again, the surviving assault craft would already have launched their torpedoes.

He paused, cursing under his breath as he watched his would-be prey slip from his grasp. But the distraction only lasted a few seconds. His gaze shifted to the mass of icons and symbols on the display, Timmons and his Eagles, surrounded and almost overwhelmed.

The Eagles had held the enemy back, bought Stockton and his people the chance to cut into the bombers. It was normal procedure—battleships came first—but it was still hard to watch his comrades and friends facing the prospect of imminent destruction. The Blues had done what they could for the mothership. Now, it was time to back up Timmons and his Eagles.

"Let's go, Blues. I know fuel's getting a little low, but we don't have time to waste here. Full turbos...the Eagles need some help, and we're the closest right now." Fuel was getting more than a little low, and he knew his pilots would burn half of what they had left getting to the enemy formation. But the only alternative was to watch the Eagles get wiped out.

"Hang on, Warrior. We're heading your way now."

"Hurry, Raptor. We could use the backup about now."

Stockton would hear the tension in Timmons's voice. It stood out, perhaps because he'd so rarely heard his former rival seem afraid. Like he did now.

He looked at the display. Timmons was blasting hard, a series of wildly evasive maneuvers, with an enemy ship on his tail. Stockton knew better than anyone how good a pilot Timmons was, but the Alliance fighter was glued to him, matching his every attempt to break free, almost as though its pilot was reading his mind.

Could it be? Stockton remembered the pilot he'd fought weeks earlier. He hadn't been able to get the recollections from his mind, even lying in his bunk at night, thoughts of the enemy who'd come so close to defeating him swirling around in the darkness. He'd almost asked Commodore Barron to see if there were any databases with listings of Alliance aces, but he'd held back. On *Dauntless*, with days and then weeks filling the gap between him and the fateful struggle, his paranoia seemed sillier, more like wounded pride than cautious curiosity.

Until now.

He pulled back harder on the throttle, as if it could somehow coax more thrust from his straining engines. He almost reached down and cut the safeties to crank the reactor up to one hundred ten, but he held back. He'd resorted to that too many times, and he knew each had taken a toll on the ship. If he burnt out his power source now, he'd never get there. And Warrior could hold out a few more seconds.

I hope.

He knew the leader of Scarlet Eagle squadron was a great pilot, one of the very best in the fleet. But Stockton was the Confederation's top ace, and he could still remember the icy feeling between his shoulder blades as that mystery pilot clung to his vector, firing all around, missing him by only the slightest of margins.

He saw enemy fighters coming up on him, slowly moving into range. Stockton wasn't interested…his mind was focused on one target only, the ship affixed to Warrior's tail. But if he didn't engage, they'd just slip in behind him. And dragging along a string of bogies was not the way to help Timmons.

Not if it is that *pilot on his tail…*

He cut his thrust and hit the positioning jets, whipping the ship around. He eased the throttle to the side, his fingers squeezing tightly on the firing stud. A series of blasts ripped out from his lasers…and the closest ship disappeared. The attack had been lightning quick, unstoppable. Stockton was in his element right now, the state of mind that made him as deadly as any human being who'd ever manned a fighter.

He was already spinning his fighter around again. The second nearby bogie was trying to get a lock on him, but he tapped the controls a few times in rapid succession, evading the shots coming toward him as he pulled the trigger again…and another Red fighter was gone. His mind was clear, focused…he was like a man possessed.

He had to save Timmons. He *had* to defeat that pilot, before more of his people ended up dead.

Hang on, Dirk…

He spun around again, blasting toward Timmons's ship. He dropped his hands to the side of the throttle, flipping open the override controls. He'd held back before, and his rationale had been valid. But this time there was no choice. Timmons was barely hanging on, his every evasive move countered. And each time the next attack came closer. For all Timmons's extraordinary skill in the cockpit, he was like an animal corralled, penned in by the hunters.

The hunter. Only one.

Stockton grabbed the small safety control, pulling it as far as he could to the side. The AI started warning him about impending overloads, but he just watched the energy output on his screen. One hundred ten. One hundred twenty. It was more than he'd ever tried to coax from his engines, more than he'd ever heard of anyone achieving.

One hundred twenty-three. He could hear the reactor now, and the radiation alarms in the cockpit joined the unending cacophony of warnings and klaxons. But he ignored it all. He could get a radiation cleanse after he landed, and any damage done to his ship could be fixed. But if he didn't get there in time...

He saw the first shot graze Timmons's ship. The fighter shook hard, and its thrust dropped to half what it had been. The explosion exerted considerable force, but the ship's existing momentum reduced the rate of change to a barely measurable amount. It was enough to evade laser blasts...at least until his pursuer could adjust. But Timmons's maneuverability was way down.

Stockton knew he was watching the final stages of the hunt. His eyes locked on the screen. He was still out of range...or perhaps, just at the very extreme edge. He fired, an act of desperation more than anything based in the rational or even in the gut feeling that drove his true skill. The shot went wide, if it even reached the enemy with enough power to do any damage.

Maybe it will be a distraction...

But even as the thought drifted through his mind, he recognized it for what it was, a straw he grasped for pointlessly. This pilot was far too good to be rattled by his ineffectual potshots. Especially with a target of Timmons's obvious stature so close to within reach.

Stockton felt anger, frustration. He had done everything he could, pushed all he had to the brink. He just needed time, a tiny, pointless, instant of time.

But in his gut, he knew he wasn't going to get it.

*   *   *

"Commander!"

Travis's tone assumed an almost physical manifestation, reaching inside him like a shadowy claw gripping his spine. His normally-controlled first officer had let the horror she felt loose in her voice. And the instant Barron turned around, he understood.

The right side of the main display focused on *Illustrious*, and on the fighters swirling all around her. The big ship's squadrons had fought to protect the great ship, but her pilots were mostly young, fresh out of the Academy before this deployment. They might have held their own against Union fighters, but the veteran Alliance flyers cut through them like a warm knife through soft butter.

Illustrious's squadrons fought—it was not their courage that was in question—but they were outnumbered and outflown. They took down almost two dozen bombers, sacrificing themselves in many instances to do it, but more than twenty attack ships got through.

Illustrious had an impressive array of defensive turrets, almost half again *Dauntless*'s complement, but as with her fighters, that impressive armament was manned largely by green crew. Even with the impressive AI-directed fire control built into the Confederation's newest ships, the seasoned hand of a veteran gunner was invaluable…and sorely missed on the massive battleship.

Barron stared, his eyes following what Travis had clearly seen. Two dozen bombers, coming in fast, their formation amazingly tight. *Illustrious*'s guns fired, taking down one, then a second. But the attackers came on, still accelerating. They were well within firing range, but Captain Reardon had maneuvered his ship out of the paths of almost a dozen plasmas during the earlier attack, and these pilots had clearly decided to damn all the battleship could throw at them and drive home for the point blank shot.

A third bomber vanished in the fire of *Illustrious*'s massed batteries, but then the remaining ones launched their missiles, the whole salvo surging forth almost as one.

The missiles accelerated at once, blasting straight for the battleship at 25g, but only for a few seconds, far too short a time for *Illustrious* to target them. Then, in an instant, they all converted to plasmas, the roiling balls of impossibly hot energy heading right for the ship.

Barron knew his own vessel was under assault as well. Federov's Reds had completed their runs, and they'd hit the bombers that had endured Blue squadron's fury with their own not inconsiderable intensity. *Dauntless*'s gunners were now firing, trying to take down as many of the incoming weapons as possible. Barron knew it was almost time for evasive maneuvers, but he couldn't take his eyes off the tragedy he saw unfolding before his other ship. Reardon was a good captain, but there was nothing for him to do. The Red bombers had paid the blood price to close to killing range...and now the battleship would endure the consequences.

Barron could see the readings, *Illustrious*'s engines firing, the great ship trying to evade the approaching plasmas. But even as the battleship's vector began to change, the first warhead slammed hard into its starboard.

Then another three, in rapid succession.

Barron watched as the damage assessments flowed in, one wild, blurry series of numbers, racing by one after another. The energy readings were almost off the charts, and the reports that followed were grim. *Illustrious*'s engines were down...that meant no more evasive maneuvers. Her energy transmission system was a wreck, and most of her batteries that were not outright damaged or destroyed were cut off from the reactors and powerless.

Barron closed his eyes for an instant, unable to make himself watch. The great vessel was moving along steadily, its vector unaltered. One plasma after another hit it, vaporizing armor plate, gouging great rents in the side of its hull. Barron didn't want to look, but the darkness was worse. His mind filled the emptiness with images, ones far starker than the antiseptic symbols on the display. Compartments collapsing, broken and twisted girders whipping around, crashing through bulkheads.

Men and women dying…crushed, burned, blown out into space. He didn't have casualty reports from *Illustrious* yet, but he could fill in the blanks, and he knew they'd be bad when they came.

"Commodore…bombers approaching."

Travis's words pulled his attention back to *Dauntless*. There were seven enemy ships coming in, far fewer than the hordes plaguing *Illustrious*. He knew he had his veteran pilots and gunners to thank for that. Blue squadron had ripped through the attack force like the wrath of God, gunning down bomber after bomber, and Federov's Reds had done hardly less. And the gunners at their stations, veterans of dozens of hard battles, had fired relentlessly, their triple turrets taking down ten of the attackers.

Barron watched as yet another bomber fell victim to the precise targeting of his fire crews and then, almost as if in response, the remaining ships launched and began to accelerate away, struggling to get out of range of the deadly guns. But those weapons were no longer firing at them. Barron's people had needed no order, no direction. As soon as the torpedoes were launched, they trained in on them instead of the now harmless ships, firing at maximum.

The small warheads were faster than the bombers, more maneuverable. Their wild gyrations at better than 25g made targeting them extremely difficult. But there were only six left, and every one the gunners could hit was one less that could smash into *Dauntless*, tearing apart the structure of the ship and killing its people.

Barron watched as one of the tiny icons vanished, a last price extracted by his gunners before the other five converted. Now, it was up to him, and to his nav crew.

"Engines ready, Commander. I'm going to want fifty percent thrust, course 104.191.333 on my command."

The sound of Travis's hand on her keyboard. "Yes, Commodore. Course laid in. Waiting for your order."

Barron sat, his eyes fixed on the approaching plasmas. The

enemy's targeting had been excellent. It would be difficult, maybe impossible to dodge all the warheads. But he would do what he could. "Now, Commander."

"Yes, sir," Travis replied, even as she executed the command. The bridge shook from the abrupt change in thrust angle.

"Repositioning jets 3a, 4a, 4b…fire at full."

"Firing now, Commodore." The ship shook again, as its starboard jets blasted, shifting its facing.

Barron watched as two plasmas passed by, one of them close enough to fry a few external antennas, but far enough to spare his ship any real damage.

"Back, Commander. Jets 17c, 18c, 18d…full."

"Yes, sir."

Barron held onto his armrests. *Dauntless* shook hard, as the chosen port jets blasted out, offsetting the momentum from his previous maneuver, and sending the ship spinning around the other way. Another plasma zipped by, farther away than the first two. A clean miss.

The last two were coming on fast. He wasn't going to clear them, not quickly enough. He almost ordered full thrust forward, but something stopped him. *Dauntless* wasn't going to escape the incoming plasmas…and forward thrust would push the impact point backward, toward the engines.

Any damage was bad enough, but losing the engines now, with hundreds of enemy fighters still out there, would be disastrous.

"Secure for impact," he yelled, and a few seconds later, the ship shook wildly, the sounds of muffled explosions vibrating up through the hull.

His hand was down on his comm, his fingers punching up Fritz's damage control line. But his eyes were on the display, its projection wavy with power surges moving through. The image was blurry, but it was clear enough. *Illustrious*, thrust completely dead, wracked with explosions…with yet another flight of bombers heading right for her.

"Commodore?" Fritzie's voice was haggard. But Barron didn't hear her, not for a few seconds, at least. He held his gaze on *Illustrious*, on her desperate struggle for survival. Then he shook his head and looked down.

"Commander?" Fritz repeated.

"Fritzie, sorry. Damage report..."

Chapter Fourteen

Tulus sat like a statue, eyes fixed forward as he watched his ships battle nearly twice their number of enemy vessels. He felt fear, of death certainly, but more, of failure, of defeat. Of disgrace.

He'd made the decision to stand and fight, to do what he could to extricate even some portion of Mellus's fleet from this trap. It remained to be seen whether he would succeed or not, but he'd made his choice, and that was the end of that.

It was an open question if even if his own ships would escape.

His force had held its own so far, but the ships they were facing were the same as his, crewed by old comrades, their training identical. It was comforting to think of his crews as veterans with an advantage against most opponents, but they were facing other Alliance warriors now, Palatians just like them. The superiority he'd come to take as a given in war was gone. The men and women trying to kill his people were their equals.

He fancied himself a skilled tactician, but despite his intense direction of the fight, his warriors were struggling to gain even

119

a temporary respite. The split between Mellus's forces had widened. The Commander was trapped with the flagship and two of her other battleships, plus a cluster of escorts, almost completely surrounded and under relentless assault.

He'd been wracking his brain for a way to cut open a path, to clear the way for Mellus and her ships to escape. But there was nothing he could conceive, at least not without Barron's ships. It galled him to feel he needed the Confed vessels, but his prejudice didn't blind him completely to their combat power. Maybe…just maybe, they could be the spearpoint, using their superior range to surprise the Red forces, and slice open a hole for Mellus's battered ships to escape.

But Barron's ships were nowhere to be seen. Tulus turned and looked at the display again, his frustration growing. But this time something came through the transit point as his eyes were fixed on the screen.

For an instant, he thought it might be one of Barron's ships, but that hope only lasted a second or two. The vessel transiting was far too small.

It was one of his escorts, the scoutship he'd left behind to report on *Dauntless* and *Illustrious*.

Maybe they came through to report that Barron is on the way.

"Commander, Optiomagis Dyanis is…"

"Put her through."

"Yes, sir…on your line."

"Optiomagis, report," Tulus snapped.

"Commander, *Dauntless* and *Illustrious* were attacked by Red forces hidden in the dust clouds near the Porea transit point. The last communication we received advised they were heavily engaged with multiple attack squadrons."

The words hit Tulus like a sledgehammer. He'd been concerned about Red scouts hiding in the clouds, but a force large enough to engage two battleships? Two large and powerful Confed ships?

"Your report is neither complete nor conclusive, Optiomagis. What did your scanners pick up? You must have gotten readings from attacking battleships."

"Negative, sir. We detected no battleships. We were too far out for detailed scans of fighter groups, but what we could read, plus the information in *Dauntless*'s transmissions, suggests more than twenty squadrons."

"Twenty squadrons?" Tulus tried to bite back on the shock in his tone, but he couldn't hold it all.

"Yes, sir." A short pause. "At least."

"With no battleships?"

"None that we could detect, sir."

Tulus looked across the bridge, silent, his mind racing. There were no bases in Tarantum, no inhabited planets. Not even an outpost or refueling station. *How could that many fighters operate there without battleships?*

Unless the battleships are hiding somewhere…

He had no idea how the Reds could have assembled the force his people were now fighting plus another five or six battleships besides. But if there was a fleet that large, behind his ships…

On the only route back to Sentinel-2…

"Get me a line to Commander Mellus immediately." He felt his throat tighten. If the Red fleet here could pursue his people…and a blocking force was waiting for them…

"On your channel, sir. Twenty-three second transmission time."

Mellus's ship was closer than it had been, but the distance was still considerable. "Commander Mellus, we have just received a report of substantial enemy forces in the Tarantum system." He hesitated. *If you had the guts you like to think you do, you'd tell her flat out, you've got to get your people out of here. Now. You've got to leave her to die.* "Commander, I urge you to set a course for the transit point at maximum thrust, regardless of enemy activity. Immediately." *Coward. You know she'll never make it. You might get the three closest ships out. But Mellus is trapped. She's as good as dead.*

He turned back toward his exec. "Set a course for the transit point. Maximum thrust." The words were thick, forced from his throat. "Fleet order…all ships proceed to the transit point at top possible speed." The thought of running from any fight was hard enough for a Palatian warrior to swallow. But fleeing and leaving comrades behind? *Worse, pretending they have a chance, that you're not just abandoning them...*

He felt the urge to retract the order, to stand and fight against the overwhelming forces in front of his ships...and whatever dire threat lay behind. He could control his fear of death in battle. But a warrior's creed went beyond bravery, to duty. It was at the core of everything that made him, made all of his officer and spacers, what they were. They were warriors, yes, but soldiers as well, parts of a greater whole. It would appease some primal need for him to stay and fight to the end alongside Mellus and her people. But the honor in such a course was false, overcome by the shame of failing his cause. Imperator Vennius couldn't spare his ships, nor Barron's Alliance craft. The Gray cause was on the verge of defeat already. If Tulus's entire fleet was destroyed, the war would be as good as over.

"Commander Tulus...Vian." Mellus's words were somber as her response trickled into his headset. "You have done all you could, more than honor and comradeship demand. To share our fate would serve no purpose, for my warriors and I shall have sufficient company in death. Go, now. Extricate what forces you may. Half of my ships have a chance at escape. I entrust them to you. My sole request is for you to take them... do what you can to enable them to escape." A short pause. "As I will do my best to create a diversion, to distract the enemy while you withdraw."

Tulus sat bolt upright, still hearing the last words of Mellus's message. *Diversion? What is she going to do?*

"Commander..."

His exec's voice drew his attention, and he looked up, eyes finding their way to the main display, to the symbols representing *Viribus* and the ships around her.

Oh my God...

*   *   *

"I want damage control teams diverted to the reactors and engines, Ilius. We need that thrust." Mellus had always referred to Sasca formally on the bridge, in front of other officers. She had a reputation as being a bit stiff, perhaps not a martinet, but tight in the way she conducted herself. But there didn't seem to be a point now. Perhaps it was okay to let a little of the human being out from behind the grim warrior's façade…before death came for them all.

"Yes, Commander." Sasca's tone was as firm as ever. Almost. Mellus's ear caught a hint of emotion. Her aide knew as well as she did, their long partnership was almost at its end.

Every warrior must face that final battle…

"Maintain full fire, all batteries." The longer the enemy was confused about her intentions, the better.

She looked at the display. Tulus's forces were already blasting at full thrust. *Good.* It would take some time for the ships to offset their current vectors and establish a course for the transit point—and even more time for her three battleships, which were the farthest from the jump point. *At least the farthest with any chance of getting out.*

She felt a burst of uncertainty, a renewed round of hope that perhaps there was something she'd overlooked, to save her people. But rationality reasserted itself almost immediately. Mellus had never been one to believe in fantasies, and she wasn't about to start now. There was no escape, not for her, nor for the crews of the vessels lined up around *Viribus*.

Still…there are different ways to die.

"Put me on the fleetwide comm, Ilius."

"Yes, Commander…on your line."

"All ships, please broadcast this over your intraship comm." She paused for a few seconds. "This is Commander Mellus. As you know, *Viribus* and half of the fleet is cut off, surrounded by enemy forces. Most of you are unaware that there are enemy forces operating in the Tarantum system as well. This necessitates that Commander Tulus and his forces, along with the ships of our fleet close enough to retreat, depart at once." Another pause. "For those of you within range of the transit point, it is my final order to you that you retreat with Commander Tulus. I know such things are…difficult…for us, that many of you would choose to stand here, to fight to the finish. But there is more to a warrior's soul than courage. There is duty."

She looked around the bridge, at her officers watching her. They were staring in rapt attention. "For those of you who can reach the transit point, your duty is not to die here with us. It is to carry on the fight. In many ways, I know I lay a greater burden on you than on those of us trapped…but I urge you nevertheless to find the strength you need to continue the fight. For only in your ultimate triumph can our deaths be vindicated. I know most of you followed me into the service of the Red fleet, and then again in our attempt to correct that error, to join the Grays, and the legitimate Imperator. I have one final request of all of you, for it is not something that I can command. Go, escape this trap and join the Grays. Serve Imperator Vennius, and win the victory, not only for yourselves, or for me, but for all our people. Each of you carries with you my gratitude and my undying respect. It has been the greatest privilege of my life to command you all in battle."

She cut the line, and she took a deep breath. "All right, Illius…" She looked around the bridge. "…all of you. Let's do this." She sat silently for a few seconds, then she said, "There." She pointed toward the display, to a single small circle. "*Tempestas.*"

She turned and looked right at Sasca. "Increase reactor output to one hundred twenty percent. Ramming course directly for *Tempesta*s."

There was a brief silence, not a sound on the bridge save for the background hum of the engines. Then, "Yes, Commander. One hundred twenty percent."

Mellus leaned back in her chair, trying to ignore the crushing pain of acceleration as the engines fired, driving a massive overload of thrust. She looked to the side, with considerable difficulty, checking on the rest of her officers. They were all focused on their stations, not a single one allowing themselves to be distracted by the g forces pressing against them.

She felt as though her ribs were breaking in her chest, and she turned slightly, trying to find a more comfortable posture.

"Maintain maximum possible laser fire, Commander." She knew there wasn't enough spare power for all her guns to fire, but she wanted every bit of destructive force she could get now. She couldn't win the fight. She couldn't even survive it. But she could see what filled the spine of her adversary.

"Forward batteries firing at maximum, Commander."

Even as Sasca was finishing his report, she saw a pair of shots hit the target. Her hand in her lap balled into a triumphant fist. Her people knew they were doomed. They were working under terrible conditions, being crushed even as they raced toward their deaths. But they were at their stations, giving all they had. She felt the weight of guilt for leading them to this... but pride as well in who they were, the warriors they'd become under her command.

She glanced over at the display. Her ships closest to the transit point were following her orders. She could see the energy readings as they blasted at full thrust. They were all under attack...but if her plan worked, she might...just...take some of the pressure off. For long enough, at least.

She watched as her two closest battleship companions, and the small cloud of escort vessels trapped with her, pushed forward. She hadn't given them explicit orders, but they'd fallen in around her ship, running interference as well as they could, trying to protect her flanks. It was clear they knew what she was attempting...and they were with her.

She winced as one of the frigates blinked from the scanner...and a few seconds later, another. Her eyes were still fixed on the screen when *Viribus* shook. Her abrupt course change—and the recklessness of running her reactors and engines on critical overloads—had confused her attackers, but now they came on with renewed vigor, her terrible purpose all too clear to them now.

Viribus lurched hard again...and then once more. The rumble of distant explosions shook the bridge, but Mellus ignored them. She could feel the engines still blasting, and as long as her ship had thrust, nothing else mattered. She imagined her engineers, rushing around the reactors, and the network of conduits that fed power to *Viribus*'s colossal engines. The reactor operating at one hundred twenty percent would be overloading its radiation control mechanisms. Her people down there were probably getting massive blasts of radiation, even lethal doses. But the continued operation of the engines attested to their diligence at their posts.

An engineer who stands at his post, tools in hand, dies no less a warrior's death than a fighter with fingers gripped tightly around his rifle. There were no non-fighters aboard an Alliance vessel, and certainly not on hers. Medics charged into the flames and radiation to tend to the wounded. Stewards backed up their technician comrades, fighting fires and shoving structural supports back into place.

Her body snapped forward as the ship took another hit, a bad one this time. She felt the relief of freefall as the engines cut out completely. Though she savored the physical respite from the grinding pressure, she felt a sense of despair as well. It was too soon. *Viribus* was still too far out. Worse, her ships moving toward the transit point hadn't gotten close enough… and they were still under heavy attack.

She'd made peace with her impending death, but not with sitting in space, crippled, as her enemies destroyed *Viribus* at their leisure. She was struggling to hold off the darkness, trying to focus on what she could do, when the thrust resumed, slamming her hard into her chair.

It wasn't as strong as it had been, not quite, but it was enough. *As long as we can maintain it.*

She didn't need to actually make it to her target, though she relished the thought of taking the enemy flagship down with her. No, she just needed to get close enough. It was a test of wills. She had given herself over to fate. She would die here, no matter what. But her counterpart, whoever was commanding this enemy fleet, did not expect to meet destruction here. *That was the true test of courage. Will you stand and face what is coming toward you? Or will you blink? Will you call the rest of your ships in to stop us?*

She stared at the screen, trying to imagine who she was facing off against. Calavius had a number of senior officers serving him, at least three or four of whom would have fought for this assignment. She had some idea of the ones likeliest to hold firm, but in the end, she was well aware, you could never know what someone would do until you put them in that position.

Are you ready to risk *Viribus* getting through? Are you ready to die, as your forces win the victory?

She glanced back at the screen as her ship shook again, and a shower of sparks flew across the bridge. Still nothing. *Tempestas* was blasting hard now, firing its thrusters to move away from the onrushing *Viribus*, but the rest of the fleet had not changed course. *Damn.*

She knew not every ship would react, not even if the opposing commander completely lost his nerve. But she didn't need them all...she just needed enough to give her people an opening, to get them to the transit point before they were blasted to slag.

Viribus shook again, and a section of the ceiling came loose and crashed into the rear wall, into two of her people. She was about to call for a medic, but she managed to turn around under the intense g forces, and she could see immediately there was no reason. Her officers had been crushed against the bulkhead, one of them sliced literally in half by the steel girder. The gory scene struck at even her veteran's resolve, and she felt nauseous.

She let herself fall back into her seat, wondering if it was more her stubbornness or the intense pressure slamming into her chest that held back the vomit.

Come on...come on...call for help...

The fleet sent to attack her forces had changed its codes. All of Calavius's ships would have done so once they'd gotten news of her defection, so she had no idea what was being said in the intrafleet communications channels. She wouldn't know her opponent had called for aid until she saw the actual course changes on the scanners.

The screens on the bridge blinked off and then back on, as *Viribus* took yet another direct hit. *Assuming we have scanners by then...*

She was running out of time. Her ship couldn't take much more. *Viribus* had already given her more than she had a right to expect, and the fact that the engines were still blasting so near to full thrust was a virtual miracle. One she knew she owed at least in part to her sweating, struggling…dying…engineers. She couldn't imagine the nightmare down there, the rad leaks, the heat from insulation breaches, the hastily jury-rigged structural supports holding the whole engineering section together. *Viribus* could go at any time. One hit in the right spot, one blast to her tortured reactors, and it would be all over.

She could see her three battleships from the far wing, each of them moving toward the transit point. They were under attack from their flanks and rear, but they might just make it. If she could divert some of the attacking ships, even just the few closest to *Viribus*.

She stared straight ahead, frustrated that there was nothing more she could do except watch, and hope. Most of her escorts were gone now, the few that remained fighting six or seven times their number, desperately trying to provide what cover they could to the flagship. *They'll be gone in another minute, two at most.*

She was about to turn away when a flash lit up the display. She knew what it was, even before she looked. *Murus*. The battleship had been on *Viribus*'s port, deflecting as much fire as possible while Mellus's vessel continued its relentless approach to the enemy's flagship. But *Murus* had given all she had to give, and now she had vanished in a blaze of thermonuclear fire.

Almost a thousand men and women. Though she doubted more than half of them had been alive by the end. She almost checked *Viribus*'s casualty reports, but she stopped herself. There was no point.

She felt the shaking all around her, as a series of hits slammed into her ship. *Viribus* was dying, there was no question of that. She felt herself giving in to despair. Her gambit wasn't working. There was some iron inside whoever she was up against. *Tempestas* continued its reverse thrust, but the rest of the Red fleet continued its relentless attacks against her other ships… and Tulus's. She'd taken her gambit, done all she could think of to buy time for some of her people to escape. Now, the bitter taste of failure closed in on her.

She struggled to maintain her focus, to do her duty to the end, but she couldn't keep other thoughts away. Torba, her children. Had her childhood friend succeeded in his mission, had he done better than she had here? Were her children safe? Or were they prisoners, the captured offspring of a soon-to-be-dead traitor?

She thought of the last time she'd seen them—*my God, was that more than a year ago?* She loved her children, as thoroughly and deeply as any parent could, but she was a Palatian Patrician. A mother's love, her touch, her attention…all of that was subordinate to passing them the family honor, intact. She'd fought for Palatia, of course, but also for Ila and Tia, to bequeath them a stronger Alliance. Now, that was all gone. Whatever happened in the war, things would never be the same. *I am so sorry, Ila, Tia…for so many things. I strove to bequeath you a better future, yet all there is now is ruin.*

"Commander!"

She heard the voice. Sasca's. It was coming from far away… no, not far. She was on the bridge, the pressure still intense. *Viribus*'s engines were still blasting at full. The compartment was a shambles, half her people dead or wounded, entire sections of wall and ceiling caved in. But the engines were still firing. Somehow, though her flagship was little more than a ruin, it pushed relentlessly forward, directly toward the enemy.

"Commander…"

"Yes, Ilius?" She turned her head as far as she could manage under the pressure.

"The display. Look at the display."

She swung her head around, almost out of strength to combat the crushing g force. But, as her eyes came around, she saw it…and a new burst of energy filled her aching limbs. Ships. Red ships. Firing at full thrust, changing their vectors. Heading for *Viribus*.

It was death, more certain and final than even that which stalked her ship already. But in that annihilation lay the seeds of hope. Hope that her death, and the death of her crew, would not be in vain. The ships coming for her were breaking off from her three farthest battleships. Those vessels still faced a fight to the transit point, there was no question about that. But they had a chance now…and that was all she could give them.

She had done what she had set out to do, given her people the diversion they needed. *Go, my warriors, escape this trap. Live to fight again, and bring with you to Imperator Vennius what strength I could send him…and my fealty, even beyond death.*

Viribus shook again. There were shouts from around her. Sasca fell hard out of his chair, and she could see burns across the side of his face and body. She pushed forward against the g forces, struggling to rise, to rush to her friend. But then she realized it was too late. He was dead.

She felt pain, but it was muted, hazy. They were all finished, and Sasca had gone quickly, without suffering. *Fare thee well, Ilius Sasca, my friend. I will be with you in a moment…*

Her eyes checked the display again, as a sudden doubt took her, a worry that all she had seen had been hallucination. But the Red ships were still pulling away from her people. Half the Red fleet was converging on *Viribus*. Her planned had worked.

She smiled, her eyes locking on the small circle that was *Tempestas*. *You blinked*, she thought, as a manic laugh escaped from her lips. *You blinked.*

Viribus shook again, almost throwing her from her chair. The force of the engine thrust lessened immediately, and a few seconds later it vanished entirely, replaced by the relief of free fall.

She looked around the bridge, her eyes moving from one station to another. Most of her people were down, the others sitting silently at their stations, waiting for the end. Her ship was dying. *Viribus* would never make it to *Tempestas*. She would never ram her enemy. But the noble vessel had done what she had to, endured long enough to give the rest of her people a chance.

A quick look at one of the few functioning screens told her all she needed to know. There was hardly an operational system on her ship, not a gun hot enough to heat a bowl of soup nor a power plant capable of energizing it. There was nothing to do now but wait for the end.

She glanced around the bridge one more time as the ship shuddered with yet another hit. She exchanged glances with her surviving officers, silent farewells. Then she leaned back and closed her eyes.

They were there, her children, sitting at the big table behind the family manor. They were happy, animated, enjoying one of her far too infrequent visits home.

She felt the shaking again, heard the sounds of distant explosions. She had moments left to live, perhaps only seconds.

She would spend them with the children...

Chapter Fifteen

CFS Dauntless
Tarantum System
Near the Porea Transit Point
Year 311 AC

"That last hit was bad, sir. I think we can get the fires under control, but we'll have to cut oxygen to a dozen compartments to do it. That's going to cost us the port batteries…for at least a few hours."

"Just do what you need to do, Fritzie. How about the bays? Can we get any of Federov's Reds launched?"

"Doubtful, sir. Honestly, I don't even know if we've got fighters down there or slagged wreckage. Both bays were hit hard, and we're not getting a response from Beta flight control. It's probably just a cut comm line, but…" A pause. "I'll do what I can, Commodore, but I've got to focus on the main structure first. If we don't protect the reactors, we'll be in a world of hurt."

"Do it, Fritzie." *But we're already in a world of hurt.* Barron was watching the next wave of bombers coming in, toward *Dauntless*, but perhaps even more ominously, right at *Illustrious*.

He felt a wave of helplessness. *Dauntless* was damaged, and Fritz and her people had their hands full…but at least the ship had something close to full thrust, and some of its weapons were still operational. From what he could see, Reardon's ship had no engine power at all, and a deeper review of the data coming in suggested *Illustrious* had only a couple guns still capable of firing...if they had the power to fire any at all.

"Activate the positioning jets, Commander. Spin us around. Bring the starboard batteries to bear."

"Yes, sir." The order took longer to execute than usual, likely the result of comm lags and damage to the realignment thrusters themselves, but finally, Barron felt the lateral force of the compressed air jets swinging his ship around. A few seconds later, the force reversed, and *Dauntless's* facing had flipped. The need to keep the ship's starboard to the enemy would restrict his evasive maneuvers, limiting options mostly to deceleration rather than acceleration. But the exchange was worthwhile to bring the fresh starboard defensive batteries into play.

Barron glanced back at the display. *Illustrious's* course was unchanged, and there were no signs any of her guns were powered up.

Damn.

"Atara, plot us a course toward *Illustrious.*" Barron's recent series of orders had been those of a captain, seeking to get his ship through the fight. But now, his commodore's stars were weighing heavily on his shoulders. He couldn't focus on *Dauntless* and ignore his other ship's struggle for survival. *Illustrious* was in trouble, real trouble. Barron knew there wasn't much he could do, but what there was, he intended to try.

"That will degrade our field of fire from the starboard guns, sir."

"I know..." Barron's voice was raw as he responded. "But they're not going to make it if we don't do something." He'd said it out loud, the fear that had been gnawing at him since the first bomber attack had slammed into *Illustrious.* Barron had been a commodore for more than six months now, and in that time, he'd become slightly more accustomed to the realities of flag rank. But he'd never lost a ship under his command, and now the thought was stark, real. It terrified him.

"Understood, sir." Travis looked across the bridge for a few seconds, the expression on her face one Barron knew well, the one that told him she knew exactly what he was feeling. He didn't know how he was going to manage when she got her own command. With any luck, she'd end up commanding *Dauntless* under him...but even then, he knew he'd have to transfer the flag. There was no way Travis could act as captain if he was still aboard *Dauntless*. If he was stationed on the ship as fleet commander, everyone would look to him. There was no way—*no way*—a ship's captain could function effectively in that situation.

Barron felt the thrust kick in again, and one glance at the display told him Travis's angle of approach kept half *Dauntless*'s starboard broadside facing the approaching bombers, while heading almost directly toward *Illustrious*.

"Nicely done," he said, grinning. Then: "Get me Captain Reardon."

"Yes, sir." A moment later. "Sir, Captain Reardon has been wounded. Commander Hachet is in command."

"Commander," he said into his headset.

"Yes, Commodore?" There was shouting in the background, a cacophony of voices.

"We're heading for your position. You've got bombers inbound. What is the status of your defensive batteries?"

"We're trying to get one of the reactors restarted, Commodore. We've got two squadrons ready to launch, assuming we can get power." A short pause. "What's left of two squadrons." The officer hesitated again...clearly there were people on the bridge shouting to him. "The defensive batteries are mostly operable, sir. The reactor and the transmission lines are the problem."

"Whatever it takes, Commander."

"Yes, sir." Barron could hear the tension in Hachet's voice. He tried to place *Illustrious*'s second in command...until he realized Hachet was third. Commander Jorvis must be wounded too. Or worse.

Hachet was a well-regarded officer, but he'd spent most of his career behind a desk. Barron didn't like the proportion of previously non-combat officers among the crews of his new ships, but then he understood well enough the losses the navy had suffered. It was easier to build ships than the men and women to run them.

"I can hear the chaos on your bridge. She's your ship, Commander. You need to take control." Barron wished he could be on *Illustrious*'s bridge, even for a moment. "Whatever state that reactor is in, you've got to do the restart now."

"But, sir...the engineer..."

"I don't give a damn about the blasted engineer, Commander. You're *Illustrious*'s captain. You've got bombers incoming, and if you can't put up a defense, that ship is as good as lost. Do you understand?" Barron's words were hard, firm. He knew it was a delicate balance, shocking the inexperienced commander into doing what the moment required...without driving him over the edge.

"Yes, sir." Barron could hear Hachet barking out orders. The voices died down in a few seconds, as the officer took control. "Restarting reactor in thirty seconds, Commodore."

Barron allowed himself a little smile at the strength he heard growing in Hachet's voice. He was used to managing subordinates on the ship with him, not officers thousands of kilometers away, commanding their own vessels. It had been a difficult transition for him, but he felt good about how he'd handled Hachet. "See to it, Commander."

"Yes, sir."

Barron cut the line. "All right, Atara...we've got our own flight of bombers coming in, and our fighter cover is all but stripped away. We need to be ready. Report from the bays?"

"Six Red squadron ships ready to launch, sir. Fully armed and refueled."

Barron's eyes turned toward the display. *Dauntless* had eighteen bombers inbound. His fighter cover might have been pulled away, but the attack force seemed to have lost whatever escorts it had originally had as well. "Launch," he said, staring at the approaching phalanx of bombers. He smiled, knowing six of Federov's Reds, fresh and armed with missiles, would take one hell of a bite out of the unescorted attackers.

Maybe even enough…

He looked back toward *Illustrious*. He was worried enough about *Dauntless*, but he could feel the fear for his other ship growing in his gut. It was alleviated, slightly, a moment later when Travis said, "Commodore, *Illustrious* reports a successful reactor restart. They've got thirty percent thrust and they're powering up their defensive laser grid."

Barron let out a breath. *Illustrious* was still in trouble, but at least she wasn't completely helpless.

He watched on the screen as the six fighters, all his ship had left to throw at the incoming attack craft, shook down into formation and blasted off, accelerating directly toward the bombers.

"Power up our defense grid, Commander. I want all batteries to open fire the instant those bombers come into range…"

*   *   *

Stockton's eyes were locked on his display, watching the Alliance pilot closing on Warrior. The last assault, the one that had damaged Timmons's ship, had taken his attacker on a wider arc, buying a few extra seconds, time that would have been precious…if Warrior's fighter weren't shot up, capable of producing less than half its normal thrust. Now, it was just a matter of time. And not much of it, Stockton realized, as he watched the enemy ship blasting at full, modifying its vector right back toward the wounded Confederation fighter.

Stockton was coming on hard, his hand tight around the controls, as if force of grip would somehow coax more thrust from his straining engines. The g forces slamming against him were brutal, almost unbearable. His reactor somehow stayed online, operating on a wild overload, producing far more power than it had been designed to generate.

He fired twice, feeling a slight lessening of the force as energy from the reactor diverted to recharge the laser cannon. He was still too far out—a hit at this range would be akin to a lightning strike—but it was all he could do, so he did it. He knew from his own experience that being fired upon was a distraction, whatever the likelihood of being hit. It was all he could do, so he did it.

He stared at the screen as the Alliance ace came around, the fighter's vector almost perfectly aligned with Timmons's. Its guns were silent...but Stockton knew that would change any second. Timmons was trying to evade, but with one of his engines gone, he was at a massive disadvantage.

Stockton knew a pilot of Warrior's skill and ability might very well defeat an enemy of normal skill, despite the handicap of a wounded fighter. But this was no normal pilot. Timmons was a cripple, hunted by a sleek, deadly predator.

And I'm going to be too late...

The frustration was almost unbearable. He fidgeted around in the cockpit, despite the great pressure pushing down on him. He swore under his breath...and he kept firing, angling his ship slightly, trying to nudge the laser blasts closer to his enemy.

He watched as the Alliance pilot closed on Timmons...and opened fire. Close! But Timmons managed an evasive maneuver, his ship jerking to the side, avoiding the series of blasts by perhaps three hundred meters.

Stockton felt a jolt of elation at the maneuver...a brilliant move, and one that reminded him why Timmons had long been his rival. But the enemy was still on Warrior's tail, still firing. And the shots were getting closer.

He fired again, helplessly. He needed two minutes, maybe three. Then he'd be close enough to truly engage the enemy, to save Timmons.

But he wasn't going to get two minutes...

*   *   *

Grachus's eyes were cold, fixed, staring straight ahead. The fight had been a difficult one, her adversary highly skilled. If she hadn't put the tracer on her earlier opponent, she'd have wondered for a moment if this was him. But her instincts told her what the scanner lock confirmed. It was a different enemy.

This pilot was good, one of the very best she'd ever faced—perhaps the second best.

There had been something about that other enemy, a feeling she hadn't been able to place. He was good, certainly, and dangerous, but there was more there, a sensation she'd never had in any of her battles. That pilot reminded her of…herself. It was a strange sensation, an odd thought to grasp, but on some level, she'd felt like she was fighting herself. Whatever made her the pilot she was, put her above so many of her comrades, that Confed pilot had it too. She'd thought about that encounter many times since it had happened, and the emotions she felt were strange, unsettling.

That pilot can defeat me.

It was hard for her to accept such a thought. She knew she could be overcome by multiple attackers, by a systems failure on her ship, by a dozen of other mishaps. The realization that death could find her on the battlefield was nothing new. But only now did she understand how deeply she'd believed she could best any foe in one-on-one combat. And how much her overall confidence drew strength from that sense of being the best.

The thought of a rival out there, a pilot who could match her head to head…it was deeply unsettling.

She gripped the firing control tightly, her stare fixed on the target. There was no time to think of other battles and future matchups. It wasn't the way she conducted herself. But since that fateful battle, she'd been unable to keep the thoughts from intruding on her, even pushing in on her focus and concentration.

She fired, feeling satisfaction as the sound of the lasers reverberated around her cockpit…and then frustration as she saw that her opponent had…barely…managed to evade her shot again. She'd thought that was *the* shot, that she'd finally run her target down. But the Confed ship was still there, evading wildly, using its limited thrust to full effect.

I'm running out of time…

She took her eyes off the enemy in front of her, just for a second, glancing over to the mid-range display. There was another fighter, on a direct trajectory toward her. She'd have known it was him, even if her AI hadn't confirmed the tracer readings. The other pilot, the one she hadn't been able to forget, was coming for her. Coming to save his comrade.

He is doing exactly what I would do…

She shook her head. She wanted to meet this pilot now, to fight the final duel between them here. But that was impossible.

She fired again, closer this time. Her quarry was enormously skilled, but she had him. Her eyes flashed to the scanner, to the position of the approaching Confed fighter. She had enough time to finish her current target off. The Confed ace was still too far to be a serious threat.

But then you have to break off. You have to pull away before you get tied down in another fight here.

She wanted to stay. With every fiber of her being, she wanted to fight that battle now. Pride was on the line, and, perhaps more pointedly, the knowledge that this pilot was out there, that sooner or later she would have to face him, had weighed heavily on her. She was scared—something difficult for her to admit, even to herself—and the longer their duel was delayed, the more those feelings ate away at her.

Enough. You have duties waiting for you.

Her eyes narrowed, and her hand tightened around the controls, her finger pushing down slowly…

Chapter Sixteen

CFS Dauntless
Tarantum System
Near the Porea Transit Point
Year 311 AC

"My compliments to your people, Lieutenant Federov. Their performance was nothing less than brilliant." Barron had felt compelled to congratulate Federov immediately. He'd just watched six of her people, the ones who'd managed to get their craft landed in moderately good condition to rearm and refuel, cut through the enemy bombers like the wrath of God. The half dozen fighters had destroyed five bombers outright, and they had damaged and turned back a remarkable eleven more. Barron watched on his screen as the two surviving ships continued their now almost hopeless attack run.

He couldn't help but admire the courage and dedication of the Alliance pilots, but that wasn't going to stop him from blowing them to bits. The chance of a mere two ships getting through to launch range was pretty poor, especially against a roster of gunners like *Dauntless's*. Barron wasn't prone to over-confidence, but he'd also expected his batteries to face a lot more than two targets.

He turned his head, looking toward the far end of the display. *Illustrious* was facing greater immediate danger, though even her inexperienced squadrons had rallied to hit the approaching bombers hard. They hadn't shattered the attacking formations the way *Dauntless*'s pilots had, but they'd done far better than they had before.

This is where heroes are forged. Barron didn't want to think about the losses *Illustrious*'s wings had suffered, but he couldn't avoid the realization that half the battleship's fighters had been destroyed or damaged.

"Commander…Red squadron is to move toward *Illustrious* and do anything they can to intercept the approaching bombers." Barron hadn't done detailed calculations…he didn't know if the Reds who had just performed so well would be able to adjust their courses and reach *Illustrious* in time. He wasn't even sure if *Dauntless* would reach *Illustrious* in time. But his gut told him it would be close…and, regardless, it was all he could do. The screen was clear of fresh attackers, and the newly-launched Reds had plenty of fuel, even if they had expended their missiles already.

"Yes, Commander." Travis relayed the order. "Projected one minute thirty seconds until remaining two bombers are in launch range. Four minutes forty-five seconds until we enter firing range of the squadrons attacking *Illustrious*."

Barron leaned back, taking a breath. There was nothing to do now but wait. Wait and see if his gunners could pick off the last two attackers…and if his efforts had been enough to save *Illustrious*.

*   *   *

Stockton watched in horror as Timmons's ship took another hit. He was sure his comrade was dead, that the purpose of his efforts to intervene had morphed hideously from saving a friend to avenging one. But the dot on the scanner, the electronic avatar of Timmons's fighter, didn't blink out of existence as he expected.

He checked the readings. Power dead, radiation leaking all around. The fighter was done, little more than a floating chunk of debris, with perhaps half its mass remaining. But somehow it was still there.

Stockton felt a burst of rage, tempered by fragile rays of hope. Could Timmons still be alive?

He was shaking with anger, his mind focused on one thing… to chase this Alliance pilot down. To blow that fighter to bits. He *knew* it was the same enemy. He had no evidence, no way to prove it, but he didn't have a doubt. This pilot would keep killing his people unless he did something about it. He had to end this.

You don't have nearly enough fuel…

The Alliance bird must be low too, he answered himself, with more determination than sense.

He'd envisioned a fight right there, but now he could see the enemy pulling away, blasting at something close to full thrust.

You coward…

But even as the thought entered his mind, he knew this pilot was no coward. It was more than fear driving this adversary to evade combat right now. It was discipline.

And what about Warrior? If there's any chance…

"Warrior, respond. Warrior, this is Raptor, please respond." Nothing but static.

His ship is badly shot up…he could be alive, without comm…

Stockton imagined his comrade, floating alive, in the ruins of his cockpit, desperately trying to contact *Dauntless* with his comm and transponders dead.

Fantasy. You're just trying to tell yourself he could be alive.

He stared at the screen, watching the Alliance ship accelerate away. If he was going after his enemy, it had to be now. He knew he might not have enough fuel, but every fiber of his being cried out to him to try. It was time to destroy this adversary.

Before more of my people die…

But he couldn't get the image of Timmons out of his mind, trapped, cut off, without even the means to call for help. *And your people…you think the words, but do you understand the meaning? They need you here, not chasing a vendetta.*

His hands were clenched hard, pale white from the tight grip on the controls. He was conflicted, a battle raging in his head, his heart. He wanted to chase down his enemy...but he knew what he had to do. Vengeance would have to wait. The show-down would come another day.

"Warrior, do you read me?" He loosened his grip on the controls, letting his ship's thrust drop off. His vector was close to Timmons's, and he angled the throttle now, adjusting his course to match.

The dot on the scanner blinked slightly as he got closer. Whatever was left of Warrior's ship, it was still putting out trace energy. Stockton had thought the fighter was completely dead, but now, closer, his scanners were definitely reading something.

C'mon, Warrior...

He brought his ship around, matching vectors and increasing velocity, coming up behind Timmons's crippled ship.

"Rap...th...you..."

Stockton's face tightened as he listened to the comm. Was he hearing words in there somewhere...or was it just the static?

"Warrior, is that you? Do you read?"

Another blast of static. Stockton looked down and exhaled hard. *I must have been hearing things.*

Then: "Raptor...do...read..."

"Warrior, I read you." Stockton slammed his hands down on the control panel, a wave of excitement taking him as he recognized his comrade's faint words. "I read you, Warrior. Relax. I'll get the retrieval boat out here now."

"Roger th...Raptor." A pause, and a burst of static. Then, "Thanks...friend. Thanks."

Stockton smiled as he dialed up *Dauntless*'s flight control line. *Yes, we are friends, Warrior. I wonder when the hell that happened?*

*   *   *

"Both targets destroyed, Commodore." Travis's words were unnecessary, but he didn't begrudge her making a report she clearly enjoyed so much. Barron had been watching the action, his eyes focused on the screen as *Dauntless*'s aft starboard batteries opened fire. He'd been tense, despite his confidence in his people, but once the firing started, it was over in less than a minute. The first bomber went down almost immediately, hit head on and almost completely vaporized. Barron had initially thought it was the first shot that hit, but the AI confirmed it was the second battery to open fire.

The second bomber evaded several salvoes, before a glancing hit tore off a large section of its tail. The ship had retained some maneuvering power, but it was clearly too damaged to continue the attack run, and it turned about and tried to flee. Barron almost ordered his guns to stand down, but something held his tongue. An instant later, a pair of turrets fired almost simultaneously, blasting the Alliance ship to atoms.

Barron didn't like gunning down crippled enemies, but he hadn't told his batteries to stand down either. Honor and mercy were all well and good, but there was no question that anyone his people allowed to escape would come back at them. Would kill more of his people. These were Alliance warriors...and if he didn't crush them when he had the chance, he knew he had no hope of beating them.

"Very well," he said, gesturing toward Travis. "That's our last immediate threat...so let's focus on *Illustrious*. We've got to get her through this." He could see the bombers moving directly toward the other battleship. *Illustrious* had a few handfuls of fighters, perhaps a dozen in total, lined up in a disorganized and scarttered defensive position. It was more than *Dauntless* had had defending it, in numbers at least if not in skill and experience. But the bomber forces heading toward *Illustrious* had half a dozen interceptors out in front and, as Barron watched in horror, the experienced Alliance fighters ripped into *Illustrious*'s green pilots.

He winced as a pair of Confed fighters vanished one after the other. *Illustrious*'s squadrons were paying a fearsome price, but they were still in the fight.

"Forward defensive batteries entering range of attacking bombers in twenty seconds, sir."

Barron nodded silently, his eyes fixed on the display. His batteries would get some shots at long range before those bombers launched, but it wasn't going to be enough. *Illustrious* was operational again, to a point, but he knew how fragile her repairs were, and how badly damaged the ship actually was. She couldn't take too many more hits from plasma torpedoes, and unless his six fighter pilots could get there in time—and get past the defending interceptors—at least a dozen ships were going to get to launch range. And with her engines maxing out at thirty percent power, *Illustrious* and her green commander weren't going to evade that many projectiles.

"Entering…"

"Open fire," Barron interrupted. There wasn't a second to spare.

He watched as *Dauntless*'s defensive turrets opened up with an almost synchronized broadside. He nodded his head in satisfaction at the readiness of his people, but he wasn't surprised when the shots all came up misses. His ship was still at extreme range for hitting targets as small as individual bombers, and even his skilled gunners were pushed to their limits.

"All batteries, focus on the rear wave of bombers." It was counter-intuitive. Most gunnery protocols specified firing at the bombers closest to the target. But his people weren't going to get them all no matter what, and they had a better chance of honing in on the ships that would be in range longer.

"Yes, sir."

Barron watched the lopsided fight as *Illustrious*'s ragtag line of interceptors fought against their more skilled and experienced Alliance adversaries. The fight was far from an even matchup, but a small cheer went up on *Dauntless*'s bridge when the second Alliance fighter in ten seconds vanished. The raw Confeds were losing two or three for every one they killed, but they held their ground and fought hard.

Barron's respect for the young pilots grew, but he also realized the dogfight was serving the Alliance force's purpose, drawing off *Illustrious*'s combat space patrol and opening the way for the bombers to get through.

The six Red squadron fighters zipped in from the edge of the close range display, blasting at full acceleration directly toward the Alliance bombers. The fighters were in moving fast, close to 0.005c now, which meant they'd be in range of the attack ships for less than a minute before they overshot their targets. The bombing run would be long over before they could decelerate and return.

Barron watched, counting down. The half-dozen fighters were perfectly formed up, like a deadly blade slicing through space toward the enemy bombers. *Illustrious*'s ships were suffering in their exchange, but they had managed to pin down all the enemy interceptors, which meant that Federov's six Reds could focus solely on the bombers.

The fighters zipped into range, and almost immediately, their lasers opened up, strafing the cumbersome but fast-moving attack ships. The first blast was at long range, and only one shot scored a hit, a glancing blow that was nevertheless enough to knock one ship out of the battle.

The interceptors fired again and again as they zoomed into close range, obliterating two bombers and damaging three others. Then, almost in an instant, it seemed, they were past the formation. Barron smiled as they cut their thrust and spun around in almost perfect unison, bringing their lasers to bear on the targets they were rapidly leaving behind. Another three bombers went down.

Federov's pilots had done an amazing job, far better than he could have expected. But he still wasn't sure it would be enough. Nine bombers remained on target, and they were going to launch any second.

His eyes were on the display as *Illustrious*'s gunners got one—and his own people hit two more—but then the remaining six jerked slightly on the screen, and a smaller dot moved forward from each bomber.

"Six torpedoes launched," Travis said, her tone attesting that she knew how needless the announcement was.

Barron's stomach tensed. *Illustrious* wasn't going to dodge them all. Not six. Not shot up like she was, limping along on less than one-third thrust.

The next thirty seconds seemed to stretch out, almost without end. The tiny dots streaked across the display, and Barron stared as *Illustrious* fired her thrust, blasting straight ahead with all her wounded engines could give. A pair of torpedoes zipped right by, one so close he was sure it had hit until he saw the speck of light emerge on the far side of the battleship.

A third weapon missed an instant later, as the big warship abruptly changed its vector and fired its engines again. Barron could see a fourth was also going to miss…but the other two slammed into *Illustrious*'s side, one right after the other.

Barron stared, aghast. The bridge was silent, every pair of eyes bolted to one screen or another, waiting for an update. The seconds passed, slowly, agonizingly, and Barron realized he was holding his breath. He let out a loud exhale, even as images went through his mind, scenes of *Illustrious* splitting in two, torn apart by massive internal explosions. But as he took a deep breath, and then another, the small blue icon remained on the screen. *Illustrious* was still there. She was dead in space again, and her side was wracked with explosions. Barron couldn't imagine the suffering, the number of her spacers lying dead, wounded, struggling to escape from shattered compartments. But there were numbers next to the icon, a small column of blue figures attesting to the fact that the ship retained detectable energy production. She was still transmitting, at least from her ID transponders. And, an instant later, Travis turned toward Barron, a smile on her face.

"I've got Commander Hachet for you, sir."

"On the main screen, Commander."

Dauntless's main comm display lit up. A man in a torn uniform stared back at *Dauntless*'s bridge crew. He had a long cut down the side of his face, with a small crust of mostly-dried blood tracking its length. The air was hazy with smoke behind him, and the sounds of several klaxons rang in the background. He looked half in shock, but he was standing in front of the battleship's command chair.

"Status report, Commander." Barron was nodding slightly,

his approval of how this desk officer had handled his initiation into the ranks of combat officers.

"It's bad, sir. We're on emergency power. Reactor B is still operating, but at less than ten percent. Our power transmission lines are torn to bits, and landing bays beta and gamma are hopeless wrecks. Internal comm is spotty, but mostly operative. And I think we can have alpha bay open in half an hour."

"That's good news, Commander." He wasn't sure he'd really characterize it as *good*, but it wasn't the worst it could have been, and for now he was willing to call that a victory. "Casualties?"

Hachet's face dropped. "I don't know, sir. We've got a lot of areas cut off...and a lot of people...trapped." A pause. Then: "They're bad, sir."

"I know it's hard, son." *When the hell did you get old enough to call other officers "son?"* "Focus on the people who are still alive, Commander. You brought them through this far, but they still need you." Barron took a deep breath, holding it for a few seconds. "The dead will wait."

"Yes, sir."

Barron wasn't sure how much good his words did for Hachet. It had taken some time, and no small number of casualties, before Barron himself had been able to compartmentalize his thoughts effectively. Hachet seemed like a good officer, a good man. And Barron knew that meant he was likely torturing himself.

"Stay on your damage control, Commander. Power and maneuver are most important...that and getting at least one bay operational."

"Yes, sir."

"And, Commander?"

"Yes, Commodore?"

"You did a good job here. Your people were lucky to have you."

*   *   *

Grachus felt strange. When she'd taken that final shot, she'd been positive it had finished off that last opponent. Now she wasn't so sure. The recollections of those seconds gelled in her mind now, solidified. She'd had him dead to rights, but then he did...something. The ship shimmied, at the last second. It wasn't engine thrust, not anything she'd expected.

Could he have ejected some of his atmosphere? Just enough to adjust his vector a fraction of a degree? The thought had just popped into her mind, but the more she thought about it, the more she was convinced.

She sighed to herself, coming face to face with the troubled thoughts in her mind. She'd fought against a number of the Alliance's enemies, and now, even against former Palatian comrades. But she'd never been pushed as hard as she'd been by these Confeds.

She'd seen the other Confed coming after her, still out of range when she'd fired her final shot at her opponent. She'd felt the urge to engage the other fighter as soon as possible, an almost overwhelming need to finish things with the ace she knew was truly a match for her. But, she didn't have enough fuel, and while she couldn't imagine her approaching enemy did either, that made any fight now a figurative coin toss, to determine who ran out of power first. Grachus took calculated risks, but she didn't gamble. Especially not now.

She was still struggling with the realization that she was no longer just a pilot, nor even the leader of a single squadron. She was responsible for hundreds of people here, in Tarantum... and hundreds more with the main fleet, in Pergara. The whole operation was unorthodox, difficult, and extremely complex. The only reason it was happening was because Calavius—the Imperator!—had listened to her plan. He had ordered it implemented, and placed her in charge of all fighter operations. She couldn't just go get herself killed and leave her pilots leaderless. Vengeance demanded she fight *Dauntless* and its warriors, and honor compelled her to match against this Confederation ace. But duty stood above all, and she had work to do.

The fleet was coming, and the motherships for her squadrons with it. Her mission had been to wait here and to slam the door shut on the retreating enemy forces, to slow them and help close the trap that would sign the death warrant of the Gray cause. But *Dauntless* had interfered again, and she'd been forced to attack early, lest her hiding squadrons be discovered. Now, her ships were depleted, low on fuel and energy.

Fortunately, she'd planned for the eventuality. There were tankers deep in the dust cloud, hidden beyond easy detection range. She had to get her squadrons back there, and refuel them. It would be chaotic, a difficult operation. Few, if any, of her people had experience with anything of the sort. But, if her squadrons couldn't get back into the fight in time, the fleeing Gray and Confed ships would escape.

"All squadrons...disengage. Commence operation Black-Three." She didn't suspect the Confeds had a fighter operating on more than fumes right now either, but the codes she'd put in place still made sense. *Let them think we're done, that we're running off to some pickup point. Then, we'll hit them again.*

She glanced at the display, at the damage assessments on the two Confed battleships. She couldn't help but feel disappointment at the data on *Dauntless*. She'd let herself hope her assaults would finish the old vessel, but despite signs of significant damage, the battleship appeared close to fully operational.

The other ship was a different story. It was clearly newer, larger, and more powerful than *Dauntless*...but her squadrons had sliced through its defenders and launched one devastating assault after another. She couldn't be sure—long range damage assessments were unreliable—but her best guess was her people had come close to taking that ship down.

She checked the scanners, confirming that her squadrons were executing the order she'd just given. They looked great, their formations perfectly ordered—save for the great gaps in the ranks. She'd taken heavy losses in this battle, especially in the fighting around *Dauntless*. Her assault squadrons had been gutted trying to get through to Tyler Barron's ship, and her lost crews joined the ghosts screaming for vengeance against that cursed Confed vessel.

She would get that vengeance, for Kat, and for the rest of

her comrades. But to get to *Dauntless*, she had to get through its fighters, and that meant first, she had to fight that pilot. He was too good, and he inspired *Dauntless*'s wings.

Grachus was methodical, cold, calculating...almost amazingly so for a fighter pilot. She believed in doing her homework, in being ready for what she had to face. And so, she'd studied. Every record she could get on *Dauntless*, on the fateful battle four years before. Her new rank gave her access to more files than she'd had available before.

She couldn't know, not for sure, who this enemy pilot was, or even whether he'd been in the combat at Santis that had claimed Kat. *Dauntless* had many skilled pilots, then as now. But she had a pretty good hunch. One of *Dauntless*'s fighters was truly special. He had killed many Alliance pilots at Santis, contributed mightily to Kat's defeat...and since then he had cut a bloody swath through the Union fighter corps.

She tried to be cautious, to hold back from making any assumptions when she couldn't be certain, but somehow now the doubt was gone. She could feel it. She knew her enemy. Knew his name, at least.

Jake Stockton.

Chapter Seventeen

Free Trader Pegasus
Carnasus System
Deep in the Badlands
Year 311 AC

"It was a big operation down there, Andi. Massive excavation, lots of debris…in orbit, at least. Whoever was down there didn't want anybody snooping around on the surface. They blasted the whole area with a nuclear barrage, and a dirty one at that. Anybody going down to snoop around would need level one protective gear, and even with that they might need a cleanse when they got back."

Lafarge was looking at her screen as Merrick spoke, watching the image from one of the drones she'd sent down. *Pegasus* had launched four, but the first three had flown too close to intense hotspots, and the radiation had scrambled their systems. She'd managed to pull the last one back, but the downside of that was data was limited to what the device could gather from ten thousand meters above the site.

"Careful with that drone, Vig. We've only got four left, and we're going to need them if we find what we're after." *Or should I burn them on this? Is what we're looking for as important as…whatever this was?*

"Got it, Andi. I'll keep it at ten-k, at least until we've got all we can get from there. Then, maybe we'll ease it in, see what other data we can collect before it gets fried."

"Good." Her thoughts were focused on the planet below, on her wild guesses about what had happened there. She hadn't expected to find anything at all this far out. Nor could she guess with any level of fact-based reliability. But despite all of that, she was still certain. The Union had been there.

And they took something significant with them. They weren't here digging for rock samples.

She felt the urge to order Vig to set a course back to the Confederation, to warn Admiral Striker. She shook her head, still trying to understand how she'd gotten where she had over the last two years. A Confederation admiral as a trusted friend, a captain—no, commodore now—as a lover. Lafarge had spent most of her adult life dodging naval officers and other government officials. She liked Striker, and her feelings for Barron were still there, but she still couldn't quite reconcile with having one foot in the harsh light of the navy—and the regulations and government interference that entailed—and the other in the shadowy world of Badlands rogues and adventurers. She'd always had a clear idea of who she was and what she believed, but for the first time, cracks had begun to appear in that certainty.

"Any guesses, Vig?"

"On what they pulled out of there?" Her friend turned and looked across *Pegasus's* cramped bridge toward her. "No idea. Nothing to even base a guess on. It could be nothing. Maybe they just dug and didn't find anything."

"And they unleashed a couple hundred megatons of thermonuclear bombs to cover up the dirt they disturbed?" Her words were directed at Merrick, but they worked on her own doubts as well. She'd been thinking the same thing, that perhaps the Union had been out here on a fruitless chase. The truth was, most Badlands tips turned out to be a waste of time. But the bombardment told her they were trying to hide something.

And that means they found something. Something important.
Damn.

"We'll collect as much data as we can, Vig…and then we

have to make a decision. Do we turn back, warn the authorities that the Union was out here, and that they likely found something significant? Or do we track down what we're out here looking for?"

Merrick hesitated for a few seconds. "Andi, assuming we were willing to give up our own quest, what would we say when we got back? We think the Union might have found something in the Badlands? It's not like we know anything. For that matter, who would we tell? Are we talking about risking our lives with another unauthorized visit to Grimaldi in the hope that Admiral Striker is there and we can reach him?"

Lafarge nodded slowly. "You're right, Vig. Part of me feels like we should report this...but report what? Chances are, no one would listen to us. And even if they did, what could they do about it? We don't know where the ships that were here are now. We have no idea what they found." She paused. "It's important information in a sense, but also in a way, useless. At least unless we can learn more."

"If we try to land anywhere within a hundred kilometers of those hotspots, we'll risk frying the navcom. We could end up stranded...or worse." Merrick shook his head slowly. "There's no way to get more information, Andi. Not with what we've got here. We don't have the protective gear we'd need, even if we landed far away and headed in on foot. And, chances are there's nothing to find anyway. You don't blast something that hard so you leave meaningful clues behind."

Lafarge looked back at her screen. The data from the drone was still coming in, but it wasn't telling her anything she didn't already know. If she had the resources to truly explore this site, she probably would have done it. But there was nothing to be gained staying, and nothing material to report, even if she managed to reach Admiral Striker.

"All right, Vig. Let's bring that drone in a bit closer and see if we can get anything else before we lose it."

Merrick turned and flipped a pair of switches. "Done, Andi."

She leaned back and sighed. "Meanwhile, let's get ready to blast out of orbit. I've been studying the charts, and it looks like the inner transwarp link is our best bet. Lay in a direct course."

"On it."

She took a last look at the screen, watching as a stream of closer-ranged, but essentially unchanged, data scrolled down, stopping perhaps half a minute later when the link to the probe was lost. Then she turned back to her navigation charts.

*   *   *

"Minister Villieneuve, welcome home, sir. It is a joy to see you." Pierre Coulette was clearly on his best behavior, his fawning tone bordering on obsequious. He was wearing an exquisite suit, perfectly pressed, a hypersilk blend that likely cost ten times what the average citizen of the Union earned in a year.

Villieneuve just nodded. He was tired, and his head was pounding. He despised space travel, and this had been the longest trip he'd ever taken. He was so happy to be back on the firm ground of the capital, he was even willing to overlook whatever mischief and self-dealing Coulette had been up to in his absence.

Assuming it wasn't too bad…

He didn't have a doubt in his mind that Coulette could shift in an instant from an attentive and admiring subordinate to a dark figure standing over his corpse, blood-soaked blade in hand. Villieneuve had no illusions about what drove people, and he strove to keep that understanding always foremost in his thoughts. The human mind ached to believe…in people, causes, trust. People were so easily lied to because they longed for what they were told to be true. Villieneuve had long ago sworn to himself he would never fall into that trap. He would recognize corruption, see it wherever it lurked—which was everywhere— and he would use it to his advantage.

Corruption was rampant in the Union, of course, but he knew it was nearly as endemic in places like the Confederation or Alliance, nations that considered themselves purer in such ways. *As it no doubt was in the old empire. Likely that is what led to the demise of that great polity…as it has with every nation that has ever existed.*

Villieneuve had worked harder, pushed farther, to drive the Union to total hegemony than any government minister anywhere. But it was nothing so childish as patriotism that pushed him, nor any unrealistic beliefs that the Union would stand forever. His lust for power, if less overt and blatant than those of some of his peers, was centered on himself. The Union government was his means to an end. If it couldn't prevail in its current form, he would gladly see it changed to something more successful.

The Confederation was a threat to the Union, and the Union was the basis of his own power and position. Therefore, the Confederation had to be subjugated, the danger it represented neutralized. It was that simple. He'd tried a number of strategies to attain that goal to date, all unsuccessful. This time he had sought a new kind of ally, not the unreliability of foreign warriors bound to service by treaties, but the fearsome technology of a long-dead empire.

And he'd done it.

The shipment was unloading even as he stood there, bound for the secret facility he'd prepared. He had found what he'd sought, but it wasn't ready. Not yet. There was work to do… and he had to address the issue of a power source. The device required antimatter, in quantities orders of magnitude beyond that he could obtain. But energy was energy, and he was sure his engineers could adapt fusion power to the role.

That's a lot of fusion…dozens of reactors, even hundreds…

He'd been preoccupied with the power, even as the small team of researchers he'd brought with him had recited the myriad of other problems to be solved. But he wasn't going to allow that to stop him, not this close to finding the way.

To winning the war.

I will see it built, however massive a chain of reactors we need. Then we will deploy this device…and the Confeds will fall. They have no defense against this onslaught.

He turned away from his fawning companion. "See that this entire area is closed off, Coulette. No one, I mean no one, gets in here without my express authorization." He swung his head around, glaring back toward the minister. "Understood?"

"Yes, sir. Understood."

That means you too, Coulette.

Villieneuve sighed. He'd already set up his own security. If Coulette snooped around too much, he'd disappear. There could be no slip ups now. Not this close to victory.

*   *   *

Lafarge was watching as the system data came in. *Pegasus* had just emerged from the transit point, and her systems were still coming back online. The early information was promising. Lafarge had done her best to calculate the location, to make sense out of the clues her people were following. Her best guess had been this would be the system, but she wasn't going to let herself believe it, not until she was sure.

Her thoughts kept drifting back several systems, to the site of the Union expedition. She still had no real evidence it had been the Union, but she didn't have any doubts either. She'd been second-guessing her decision to move on...she should have explored the planet more aggressively, she should have gone back and told Admiral Striker. But the answers were still the same. She didn't have the equipment to inspect the radioactive hell the Union bombardment had left behind, and she didn't have anything useful to tell Striker either. *What would I have said? The Union is up to something, but I don't know what?*

"I think this is it, Andi." Merrick's voice was crisp, focused. Her first officer seemed less troubled by the decision to move on. *Just as you would have been before...*

She shook her head, trying to clear her mind. She found herself astride two worlds, half of her still an outlaw at heart, and the other half now neck deep in Confederation business. Her people had stuck with her, spent most of the past two years pursuing ventures that, with the exception of the payment from Admiral Striker, had been essentially profitless. That wasn't what they'd signed on for, and she knew they had stayed purely out of loyalty to her. But now it was time for her to return to her roots, to come through for her crew. Her friends.

"Let's hope, Vig. We could use the payday. The site is supposed to be on planet number three, so let's get over there and get some close-in scans. We're still just guessing we're in the right place, so let's run down the checklist before we pop any champagne corks."

"You got it, Andi." Merrick turned toward his workstation. "Locking in course toward planet three, fifty percent thrust." A few seconds later: "Ready."

Lafarge looked at the screen, and the system details continuing to appear as her active scanners blasted out on full power.

"Let's go," she said, feeling a touch of the old explorer's excitement. *I'm back*, she thought. *The old Andi Lafarge.*

But there were doubts still lurking, and a feeling in the pit of her stomach that whatever the Union had been up to, she hadn't heard the last of it.

Chapter Eighteen

CFS Dauntless
Tarantum System
Year 311 AC

Alarms were wailing all over *Dauntless*'s Alpha flight deck. Fighters were coming in, landing any way they could amid the twisted wreckage and firefighting equipment cluttering the normally wide open area.

Stockton saw that there were no fires still raging, though the sections of melted and rehardened metal told him there had been conflagrations there. He wondered what herculean efforts *Dauntless*'s damage control teams had made to suppress the fires...to keep the bays open.

Stockton's bird was out of fuel, at least according to his readouts. But he'd long known the designers of the Lightning fighters had built in a bit of a reserve that didn't register on the gauges. He understood the rationale, but he wasn't a fan of such measures. He wanted to know exactly where he was in terms of resources, but considering the psychology of the typical fighter pilot—himself included—he couldn't argue with the logic of leaving a little something there.

Of course, we all know it's there, so we plan for it. Just like now.

He hoped he'd saved enough of it this time. From the looks of the bay, the last thing *Dauntless* needed right now was another uncontrolled landing in the bay.

He felt a shiver between his shoulders, and he tried to push the thought away. He'd crashed in this bay before, and he'd come as close to dying in the searing flames as a man could and still live. The pain had been indescribable—even his memories and nightmares failed to do it justice. But the worst thing, the recollection that had come closest to costing him his sanity, had been the smell. Burning flesh was never a pleasant odor, but to lie there, writhing in agony, knowing it was your own body searing, charring…

He shook his head, trying to clear it. There was no time for this now. The retrieval boat was right behind him. He'd stayed with Timmons, protecting his comrade's shattered ship with the last of his fighter's resources. Now, they were almost back, both of them.

He started straight ahead, choosing his spot to land. It would be tight…but he could manage it. *As long as I have ten more seconds of fuel…*

He tapped the throttle slightly, and then began pushing forward, decelerating. He was glad no one was grading the landing…it was likely to be less elegant than usual.

He felt the fighter slowing, dropping…saw the deck ahead of him. His eye caught the remains of another fighter, cracked open, partially charred. He wondered if the pilot had survived that landing. His gut told him it was fifty-fifty.

His ship glided in slowly, even gracefully, his fuel holding out until his landing gears hit the deck. The landing was, if not soft, not rough either. He felt a flush of near-panic just before he came in, the last vestige of the emotional scars that terrible crash had caused. But, he pushed it aside almost the instant he felt it, and now he let out a deep breath and closed his eyes, just for a few seconds.

He opened his cockpit and climbed out onto his fighter. Two of the flight techs were pushing the ladder up to his bird, and after waiting a few seconds, he scrambled down, watching as the retrieval boat came in, the shattered wreck of Timmons's fighter clamped to its grappling arm.

Stockton's face went white. The ship was worse than he'd

imagined. Far worse. There was less than half of it left, and the front and back both ended in mangled webs of twisted metal. He was amazed now, looking at the remains, that Timmons was alive. He wouldn't have thought any pilot could have survived in that ship.

He saw the crew scrambling out of the retrieval boat...and the urgency in their motions. Then he heard the shout, even as a group of white-clad medics rushed toward the ship. "We need a trauma team here...now!"

He cursed his own ignorance. Timmons hadn't said a word about being wounded...and Stockton hadn't considered it any further. But now it was clear his comrade *was* injured...badly.

He remembered that day, when *he* had been the subject of the frantic calls for medical aid. He remembered the panicked cries of the flight crews, or at least he thought he did. Much of what remained in his mind now was hazy, uncertain, more vague twinges of fear than clear recollections.

Now, he was watching his comrade, almost as though he was floating over his own crash, looking down as *Dauntless*'s flight staff pulled his own, mostly dead body from the ruins of his ship.

He raced across the deck, toward the remains of Timmons's ship. One of the med techs tried to hold him back. He could hear the words, but they had no meaning. "Sir, please...stay back..." All he could really hear was the sound, the sick popping in his ears, his own flesh burning, charring, dripping off his body.

He could see Timmons, still in the cockpit of his fighter. He looked okay. At least he wasn't immersed in flames, as Stockton had been.

He felt a surge of hope, that maybe Timmons was only lightly wounded. But there were flight crew and medical staff all around, and their shouts and body language told the real story.

Stockton stood and watched, and then, for an instant, he made eye contact. He could see the agony in Timmons's expression through the opening in his helmet, but also, somehow, through the pain and fear, a brief smile. He knew it immediately for what it was. A thank you, a salute between rivals…adversaries of a sort, now become true friends. Stockton nodded in return. Then he winced as Timmons screamed in pain. One of the med techs gave the wounded pilot an injection.

Stockton lost track of time, standing there, frozen, watching as a half a dozen people struggled to free Timmons from the twisted wreckage of his fighter. He stared as they worked, as sparks flew around the plasma torch, the crews cutting through the blackened metal of the cockpit.

He was still watching minutes later, when they started to pull Timmons out, slowly, carefully.

When his friend's body came out. What was left of it, at least.

Stockton stood in the middle of *Dauntless*'s savaged landing bay, his breath stilled, eyes fixed, staring in horror at the bloody, legless clump of flesh that was all that remained of Dirk Timmons.

*   *   *

"Commander…*Illustrious* reports thrust up to twenty percent. She's got one landing bay open, and she's managed to recover thirty-one fighters." Travis's voice was hoarse, gravely. *Dauntless*'s bridge crew had been on duty for thirty hours straight, and the fatigue was beginning to show. Barron had ordered everyone to take a dose of stims, but he'd held back from authorizing a second, except for the damage control parties. As much as his people needed the boost, he knew the fight wasn't over, and his combat officer, gunners, pilot…they had to be ready when the next assault came.

"We've managed to land all our own fighters, sir, and we've got eleven of *Illustrious*'s too. Flight control is working to refit the squadrons, but damage is heavy, and progress is slow."

"I need better data than that. Get me Commander Sinclair."

A few seconds later: "On your line."

"Commander, I'm getting vague reports up here…not what I usually expect from you." He kept his tone even, not too aggressive. Stara Sinclair was a good officer, and she'd done wonders running flight operations since he'd bumped her up to the top control job. He couldn't imagine the chaos she was dealing with right now, but that didn't change the fact that he needed to know when he would have fighters ready to launch.

"My apologies, sir." He could hardly hear her over the noise in the background. "I'm following up on that now…we'll have the Eagles ready to go in twenty minutes, sir." There was a hitch in her voice, one Barron understood all too well. The Eagles were Warrior's squadron, and news of Dirk Timmons's injuries had spread like wildfire through the ship.

"Where are you, Commander? I can barely hear you."

"I'm on Alpha deck, sir. I had to leave flight control…our internal comm lines there are down. I couldn't stay on top of things at my station." A short pause. "I'm sorry, sir…I should have requested permis…"

"None of that, Commander. Stay on top of your duty, however you have to."

"Yes, sir."

"Twenty minutes…" Barron didn't like having his ship naked, unable to launch even a single fighter. But he could only imagine the herculean efforts it had taken for Sinclair to get even one of his top squadrons rearmed. Still, though they were veterans all, he wondered how the Eagles would perform without their commander. He worried, for a few seconds, if they might be distracted, but then he came to a different conclusion…and he almost pitied any enemies who got in their path. Those pilots would be out to avenge their leader. The more Barron thought about it, the more convinced he became. "Well done, Commander," he finally said, realizing she had done yeoman's work keeping things moving down there. "What's the status on the rest of the strike force?"

"It's hard to be precise, sir. We've got a lot of damage down here…and more up the line. We're having trouble getting reloads from the holds, and we're down to a single fuel line from the reserves."

"Your best estimate, Commander." Sinclair was fastidious

by nature, precise. He knew she hated guessing, but he needed something.

"I think we can have Blue squadron ready an hour later, maybe an hour and a half. The Eagles took all the supplies we had on the deck, and we're waiting to get more missiles and fuel up here. I'm afraid the internal cargo hauling systems are all out of operation. We've got crews manually carrying reloads up from deep storage."

"What if we launch without missiles? Can you shave any time from that?"

"Maybe, sir…I'm sorry, I don't mean to be vague. It depends on whether that fuel line holds out. Commander Fritz has it restricted to half capacity. It runs through some damaged sections, and one blowout could shut us down, not to mention feed some nasty fires."

"Do what you can, Commander." He looked at the display. Tulus's ships—plus the three of Mellus's that had managed to escape into Tarantum with him, were managing to stay ahead of their pursuers. But he had to keep the way open behind them… and despite his inability to find any motherships or refueling stations in the clouds around the Porea transit point, he had a feeling in his gut he hadn't seen the last of those enemy fighters. "Do what you can," he repeated, feeling far too helpless as he did.

*   *   *

"This is taking too long." Grachus extended her right leg, as far as she could, at least, in the cramped confines of her cockpit. She'd just taken another dose of stimulant, which helped her alertness, but made her even more fidgety. She'd been in the cockpit for days now, and it was starting to get to her. She could only imagine how her pilots were dealing with it.

"My apologies, Commander, but few of our people have ever conducted a refueling operation like this, certainly not under field conditions." She heard the officer's words over her comm, and she couldn't argue with the logic of what he said.

But she didn't care. All that mattered to her was launching another strike, before *Dauntless* and the other enemy ships managed to escape from the trap.

"Yes, Optiomagis, I understand...but we are Alliance warriors, are we not? The way is the way. We have no time for excuses."

"Commander, I do understand, but if we push your pilots too hard, we're going to have accidents...fatalities."

"And you think no one will die in this battle? That no one has already? I don't care about the risk, Optiomagis." She paused, feeling her hands ball up into frustrated fists. She could *feel Dauntless* slipping away.

She'd ordered the tankers to begin refueling fighters as they arrived. Many of her squadrons had been hopelessly intermixed, and it would have taken hours more to reorganize them. Some ships had refueled and rearmed, while others from the same squadrons were still waiting in the queue. Ideally, she'd launch her attack with a crisp, reordered formation, but that wasn't going to happen. Her people would go in—now—but they would be one big mob, bits and pieces of squadrons intermixed, mostly interceptors, but a few refit bombers thrown in as well.

"Faster, Optiomagis. Work faster." She cut the line, switching on the channel to all her squadrons. "All rearmed fighters... we're going in now. There's no time for anything fancy...no plans at all. We just go in, like the warriors we are, and hit as many of those ships as we can. If we can slow them all down enough, the fleet can close and finish this here and now. You all know what you must do, and why we are here. The way is the way. All ships...follow me."

She pulled back on the throttle, her body thrown back into the cushioned chair as her refueled fighter blasted out at full thrust. It was time to finish this.

*   *   *

"All right, Eagles...mount up." Kyle Jamison stood in the

center of the launch bay, with Stara Sinclair standing to his side. "Commander Sinclair's people have you cleared for launch." Jamison didn't like sending out one of his squadrons alone, but *Dauntless*'s scanners had already picked up the incoming Alliance fighters. With any luck, Sinclair would have Blue squadron out in time to join the Eagles before the renewed fight everyone knew was coming. But at least this way he'd have some interceptors out there. *Dauntless* was surprisingly operational for the amount of damage she'd taken, but Jamison was enough of a veteran to realize how fragile that status could be.

"We've got an extra fighter, Commander." Sinclair turned toward him as she spoke. "I didn't think we'd get it repaired on time, but Chief Evans and his people managed it somehow."

"I'll take it." The words came from the direction of the lift. Jake Stockton was walking across the deck, his face white as a sheet.

"You just come from sickbay?"

"Yes." Stockton's eyes met his friend's. "He's bad, Kyle. He's lost his legs for sure…and Doc Weldon's not even sure he's going to make it."

"I'm sorry, Jake." Jamison shook his head and dropped his gaze momentarily toward the deck.

"I'll take the Eagles out, Kyle."

"Jake, that's crazy…you're…you need a few minutes. You've got to calm down." Stara Sinclair's usual controlled tone was a bit shaky.

"Calm down? Calm down? Do you think that's what we need here, Stara? Calm?" Stockton was agitated, and Jamison knew his words were coming out harsher than he'd intended. Especially toward Sinclair. There weren't many officers or spacers on *Dauntless* who didn't know that Sinclair and Stockton were lovers.

"She's right, Jake. The Blues are coming up right behind the Eagles…and they'll need their leader. *I'll* take out the Eagles. You stay here and bring the Blues after."

"But you've got the whole strike force to worry about."

"There's not much I can do sitting around here waiting for

Stara and her people to get these birds refit. You bring the Blues up, and when you get there, I'll leave you both squadrons, and I'll head back to meet up with the rest of the strike force." Jamison had been thinking about taking the Eagles out himself anyway, and he had no intention of letting his friend go back into the fight in his current state.

"Kyle…"

"It's done." He paused. "And, Jake…you had nothing to do with what happened to Warrior. We all know the risks, every time we climb into the cockpit. He wouldn't have made it back without you."

Stockton nodded, not looking entirely convinced.

Jamison turned back toward Sinclair. "Power up all launch tubes, Stara. We're going in three minutes." He reached to the side, where a spacer was handing him a helmet. He nodded toward Sinclair and again to Stockton. "I'll see you out there, buddy." Then he turned and jogged across the deck, toward the single empty fighter at the end of a row of manned and ready craft.

Chapter Nineteen

"All right, we've got Confed fighters coming in. Let's get ready..." Grachus almost said "Dragons," but she held her words. She wasn't leading the Dragons now. She was at the head of thirty-odd fighters drawn from a dozen squadrons, including by her count, exactly two of her Red Dragons. But they were all Alliance warriors, and they were all her responsibility, as were the forty more strung out through the space between the battle zone and the refueling area and the sixty plus still jockeying for position around the tankers. Those ships would come up in small clumps, joining the fight a dozen or half-dozen at a time. She just hoped it would be soon enough.

There were eleven Confed fighters on her screen, coming right from *Dauntless*. Another half dozen or so had launched from the other Confederation battleship, but those were still milling around, clumsily working themselves into a formation. The ships from *Dauntless* were in perfect order, and they were heading right toward her people. *That's a crack squadron.*

She checked her tracer. Nothing. That didn't mean her mysterious adversary—*Stockton*, she reminded herself—wasn't out there. Refitting and refueling a ship could easily shake the trace, not to mention the possibility that he'd switched to another ship, one undamaged or ready to go. But her gut told her he hadn't remerged yet.

That was no cause to relax. *Dauntless*'s fighter wing was full of veteran pilots, men and women who could take on her people on even terms, or worse. But if she had time without Stockton out hunting her people, she intended to use it.

She outnumbered the approaching fighters, almost three to one. But that was misleading. None of her birds had missiles… and the ships launching from the battleship almost certainly did. Five of her ships were bombers, all her makeshift logistics operation had managed to rearm. They were useless in a dog-fight—worse than useless, since they needed to be protected. They were a threat to the enemy battleships, but she knew five wouldn't be enough, certainly not to penetrate *Dauntless*'s vet-eran-manned defenses.

Maybe the other one…

Grachus was obsessed with destroying *Dauntless*, with claim-ing vengeance for Kat. But her duty was clear. If she could take down either of the Confed battleships, she knew she had to do it…even if it meant directing her attack at *Dauntless*'s companion vessel instead of her primary target.

Her eyes shifted back to the cluster of dots moving toward her formation. "Ships 307, 405, 771…" She rattled off a list of a dozen fighters, pulling the IDs from her display. She listed the ships closest to her own, without regard for rank or experience. "You're Force A. On me. All bombers…and all other intercep-tors, you're Force B. You are to attack the Confederation battle-ship at 092.322.205 immediately." The target ship's squadrons were green, she'd realized that in the previous fight. And they were launching slowly, clearly dealing with significant damage in the bays. Her five bombers weren't much of an assault force, but if they could plant one or two of their torpedoes in that ves-sel, it just might be enough.

She more or less ignored the wave of acknowledgements. She knew her people would do what she'd ordered. They were Alliance warriors, after all.

"Force A with me, full thrusters…now." She led her makeshift squadron forward, directly toward the ships launched from *Dauntless*. She wanted to engage them as far from the bomber attack as possible. The quicker she tied up these veteran pilots, the better chance her strike had of reaching the other ship.

She watched the small group of fighters ahead. There was one ship out in front. *The leader?*

Her eyes zeroed in on him. She didn't know if it was Stockton, but whoever it was, she was sure he was dangerous. She angled the thruster, adjusting her vector, heading right for that ship.

Right for the leader…

*   *   *

"I don't have to tell you why we're out here, Eagles. You all know. You know your duty to the Confederation, to *Dauntless*, your comrades…" Jamison paused before he finished his sentence, feeling a twinge of guilt that the sincerity he truly felt was also tinged with a bit of opportunism. "…and you know your duty to *Warrior*." He told himself Timmons would have been the first to use something like that to drive his people. It was true, he knew that, but it only partially salved his guilt.

He watched the Alliance fighters coming right at his tiny formation. He'd expected to be outnumbered badly, at least until Stockton got the Blues launched, but the Alliance force had split. He'd felt relief when he saw the maneuver, followed by a tightness inside when he thought about *Illustrious*. It wasn't his job to keep track of the fleet's capital ships, but it was no secret that *Dauntless's* companion vessel was in bad shape, barely limping along. And its fighters, including the scant half-dozen that had managed to launch, *were* his problem. Commodore Barron had put him in command of every fighter in the expeditionary force, and that meant he was responsible for those six…well, they weren't quite rookies anymore, perhaps, but they weren't a match for the Alliance pilots either.

He'd ordered them to stay in tight, to wait for more ships to launch, and to sit and defend against any approaching bombers until then. But with no interceptors deployed forward to strip the incoming assault ships of their escorts, the enemy bombers would be protected all the way in. He'd only counted five bombers, but against a shattered battleship shielded by inexperienced and outnumbered fighters, five just might be enough.

There's nothing you can do, not now.

He thought about sending half his ships toward Illustrious, but that would leave him outnumbered again, with no reserves to defend *Dauntless* against any waves of Alliance fighters lined up behind the vanguard. No, *Illustrious* and her scant combat space patrol were on their own, at least for now.

"Arm missiles…let's not take these fighters coming in for granted." Timmons's Eagles were no less confident—cocky, some would say—than Stockton's Blues. But Jamison had seen these Alliance squadrons in action too many times.

"Missiles armed."

"We're ready, Thunder."

The acknowledgements were quick and sharp. The Eagles were ready…and the enemy ships were just about to enter range.

*   *   *

"Watch your evasive maneuvers. These Confed missiles are good for four and a half minutes, even five. You've got to keep your distance as long as possible." Grachus was mad. She could feel the heat around her collar, the flush in her cheeks. Two of her people were dead already, victims of the Confederation missile barrage. She'd figured her people were well prepped to evade missile attacks…she'd spent what little time they'd had to train for the mission going over evasive maneuvers. But the Confed missiles were far nastier than the Alliance's, and this squadron was clearly a crack formation. The combination of the two was costing her pilots dearly, and she didn't like it.

She swung hard on her throttle, trying to shake the warhead on her own tail. She wasn't panicking, but she *was* a little nervous. She'd evaded two of the weapons already, but this one had been fired by her chosen target, the pilot she was now sure was in command of the enemy force, if he was not Stockton himself. Her adversary knew his stuff, and he'd closed to much shorter range before loosing the missile on her tail.

She pulled the throttle hard to the starboard, and then down, directing her thrust vector deep into the Z plane. There was science to evading missiles, but to an ace pilot like herself—*and whoever launched this missile*—there was art to it as well. The AI directing the missile's guidance system was hampered by the miniscule delays in transmission of scanner data. When her ship, ten thousand kilometers ahead of the missile, changed its thrust vector, it took a fifteenth of a second for that data to be scanned and returned to the AI. That didn't sound like much, but it *was* something for a pilot to work with. Combined with the fact that the AI, any AI, would ultimately make logical choices in pursuing its target, it made a form of controlled chaos the best way to stay alive in the cockpit. At least when running from a missile.

She glanced down at the small timer on her screen, counting down the seconds of fuel remaining in the missile on her tail. It was an estimate at best, highly dependent on her AI's guesses at the thrust levels and fuel consumption of the weapon. But at least it gave her an idea…thirty-four seconds when her eyes focused on the display.

She could survive that long, she was pretty sure. She could probably make it another fifty seconds, perhaps even a minute total. But that was about the outer limit. The missile had vastly higher acceleration than her fighter, and it would stay on her until it ran out of fuel, or destroyed her.

There was another problem, one potentially as dangerous. A Confed fighter, the one she'd targeted as the leader…was heading right toward her. Normally, in an even exchange, both sides would be equally distracted evading missiles, but her makeshift refueling and rearming setup in the dust cloud did not include heavy weapon resupply. She had one freighter, and a partial round of reloads for her bombers, but her fighters had only been refueled, their laser batteries quickly recharged.

She'd brought the problem down on herself, she knew. Concern that the fighter was Stockton's had sent her heading right for it, signaling a challenge she should have held until the enemy had expended its missiles. Now, she had to stay out of range of the fighter and the missile it had launched, an extra degree of difficulty she didn't need right now.

She pushed the throttle hard forward, decelerating at full thrust. The missile went zipping by, its AI reacting slowly to the sudden and unpredictable move. Now, she hit her positioning jets, spinning the ship around and blasting her engines hard on a vector almost perpendicular to her current course.

The timer had hit zero, but her scanners were still picking up output from the missiles engines. Damn. She'd gained a jump on the enemy fighter, at least, her sudden deceleration increasing the estimated time until firing range by a few seconds…possibly very precious seconds. But the missile was still trying to kill her.

She changed her course again, but even as she did, her AI gave her the report she'd been waiting for. The missile's engines had shut down. It was still moving, very quickly indeed, but it couldn't change course anymore. Unless she crossed its path, at exactly the right time—something shockingly unlikely, even by accident—the weapon was no longer a threat.

The missiles had hurt her people though, badly. Four of her ships were down, and only one of those showed any signs of a successful ditch. That left eight ships besides her own, at least for a while. Her second wave was ten minutes behind the first, give or take, and unless *Dauntless* managed to launch more fighters in that time, its arrival would give her forces an overwhelming advantage.

Her eyes narrowed on the small blip, the fighter that was coming toward her. Her people knew what to do, and they could handle being outnumbered for a while, even against one of *Dauntless*'s crack squadrons. She had her own job to do. She flipped up the small cover on the throttle, exposing the firing stud. She reached down, hitting the row of switches that opened the power conduits and armed her heavy laser cannon.

She watched the enemy ship approaching, her stare cold, focused.

She had a job to do.

*   *   *

"Launch a spread of scanner buoys toward *Illustrious*. I want to see close up what's going on there." Barron sat motionless in his chair, fighting off the growing tension he felt. The Alliance fighters heading toward the immense battleship had just cut through the tiny space patrol Hachet had managed to launch, and the small group of bombers they were escorting was now heading into launch range.

"Launching, sir. Tying in data readout to main display."

Illustrious's defensive batteries were firing, but between damage to the weapons themselves and to the reactors and power lines feeding them energy, only a few guns were active. With some luck, the inexperienced gunners firing them *might* score a hit, but they were never going to take down all five ships, since the attackers were covered by unopposed interceptors.

Barron didn't expect much from *Illustrious*'s evasive maneuvers either. With Captain Reardon wounded and the inexperienced Hachet in command, the situation would have been dire enough with fully-operational engines, but the ship was lucky to have twenty percent output, and even that could fail at any time.

Shit. Barron didn't know what to do. He'd been trying to come up with a plan, and he'd hounded Stara Sinclair three or four times, demanding updates and urging her to find ways to cut time from the refit schedule. She'd humored him, but Barron knew full well, in spite of his pointless inquiries, that his launch operations, run as they were by the brilliant Sinclair and the force of nature known as Chief Nick Evans, *Dauntless*'s legendary flight deck chief, would move at the maximum possible speed whether he spoke a word or not.

It didn't matter anymore, at least not for *Illustrious*. Even if Sinclair and Evans got every ship launched in the next ten seconds, an impossibility of course, it was too late to get to the other battleship, at least before the torpedo attack was long over.

He had to do the one thing he always found hardest. Sit and watch...and hope for the best. And try to ignore the feeling growing colder inside him.

He turned away, focused on the dogfight in front of *Dauntless*. The Eagles were putting up a ferocious fight against what was clearly a force of veteran enemy fighters. They'd scored with their missiles, and they'd held the upper hand since…but the enemy had another group of ships closing fast.

He looked at the chronometer, remembering the last update Sinclair had given him. The enemy fighters would get there before Blue squadron. The tide would turn again, to the enemy this time, and those fresh Alliance fighters would have perhaps six minutes, maybe eight, to wipe out the rest of the Eagles before Blue squadron got to the party.

Barron felt sick—about his fighters suffering so badly, about the danger *Illustrious* was in—but he also knew he *was* getting his job done. The fleet units fleeing across the system were safe, for the moment at least. All but one wounded ship, one of Commander Mellus's, which had fallen behind. Barron's gut told him *that* ship was finished, that there wasn't a chance it would stay ahead of its pursuers. But the rest of the fleet was getting through, and for all the losses and the destruction, *Dauntless* and *Illustrious* were holding back the enemy's encircling force, keeping the trap from slamming shut. The rendezvous with Mellus had proven to be a disaster, and almost certainly the result another information leak. But if Tulus's ships could escape, with even a portion of Mellus's fleet, total catastrophe could still be averted.

Barron watched as the transmissions from the scanner buoys updated the scene around *Illustrious*, sharpening the focus and increasing the detail on the display. The bombers were piloted by crack veterans, he could see that immediately. Their formation was tight, their maneuvers perfectly synchronized. Without interceptors to worry about, or even much in the way of defensive laser turrets, they could focus on their approach vector, lining up for a perfect launch.

And that was just what they did. They came in on a final zigzag approach, taking no chances with *Illustrious*'s few remaining guns, and then they adjusted their vectors, blasting on hard, straight for the stricken ship.

Their launches were synchronized almost as one, and the five torpedoes came in on perfect lines, a web of mutually-supporting courses. A fully-operational vessel might have evaded most of them, perhaps even all. But *Illustrious*'s shattered engines could never get the job done. Hachet might evade two of the plasmas, maybe even three, if he over-performed. But whatever happened, Barron knew in his gut *Illustrious* was in trouble.

"Commodore…"

Barron turned his head, glancing back at the long-range display. He knew before looking. It was Mellus's injured vessel. It had fallen back farther, and the pursuing battleships were opening fire. They were still at long range, and they hadn't scored a hit yet, but any hope Barron had nursed for a miracle was gone. That ship was doomed.

He looked back at the main display, wincing as the five weapons approaching *Illustrious* activated their reactors and converted themselves to plasma. The balls of pure energy were approaching the undefended ship at close to 0.1c. That gave Hachet and his people less than thirty seconds to evade.

The engines fired up, the scans reporting the increased energy level, but the instant Barron saw it, his heart sank. *Illustrious*'s engines weren't at twenty percent, they were at less than ten percent power. The ship was moving, its angles of thrust carefully chosen, but there just wasn't enough thrust to get it done.

The first plasma hit, less than one hundred meters from the ship's aft, tearing into the port engine and knocking out what little maneuvering capability the ship still had.

Then two more slammed, one right behind the other, into the mid-section. One of the landing bays was nearly torn clean off the ship, and a gaping hole opened in the outer hull, exposing a dozen internal compartments to the ravages of space.

Barron let out a short breath as one of the plasmas sailed by, missing the target by a few hundred meters. But the last one hit hard. It slammed into the top of the ship, tearing away a large portion of the superstructure, along with huge sections of the ship itself.

Dauntless's bridge was silent, its crew mesmerized by the nightmare engulfing their companion vessel. Data was coming in from the scanner buoys, but the feeds from *Illustrious* herself were dead. Barron knew immediately, more from instinct and feel than analysis. *Illustrious* was mortally wounded.

"Commander, fleet order to *Illustrious*. Abandon ship." Years at war had taught Barron a valuable lesson. In battle, there was no time for indecision, for wishful thinking. *Illustrious* was done. There was no way she was going to survive what had just happened to her. But her people could still be saved.

Some of them, at least.

Barron had no idea how many were dead already. Hundreds, certainly. But the dead were dead, and Barron's concern now was for the living.

"No response, sir. All comm channels are dead."

Barron shook his head in frustration. He wasn't surprised… actually, he suspected very little was functioning on *Illustrious* right now. But Hachet had almost no combat command experience, and he'd never faced a situation like this. Would he take it on himself to order an evacuation or would he command his people to stay at their doomed stations?

"Keep trying, Commander. Maybe they'll get an emergency channel back online." "Maybe" wasn't a word Barron liked to consider part of his command vocabulary. But it was all he had right now.

"Contact flight control. See if we can launch rescue boats to…" Barron's words stopped abruptly, his eyes fixed on the image of Illustrious on the display. The first explosion was large, from deep within the vessel, a billowing blast that tore a massive hole right through the center. The second and third followed almost immediately just forward and rear of the initial explosion.

The ship was torn open, a cross-section of a dozen decks exposed, shattered bits of equipment pouring out into the vacuum, along with, Barron knew, bodies of her crew. Another series of explosions erupted, and the great ship began to split fully into two pieces, the force from the blast pushing them apart, tearing at the few structural components that still held them together.

Barron's eyes were locked, immovable as he watched the tortured death struggle of the great battleship. Then the spine snapped, and two halves of what had once been the greatest war machine ever produced in the Confederation, drifted apart from each other. *Dauntless*'s scanners reported the rapidly dwindling—and then exhausted—energy of the ship, and within a few seconds there was nothing left. Nothing but two chunks of dead metal, plastic, debris, a grim, frozen tomb for the men and women who had fought inside her.

"Scan for lifeboats or escape pods."

Barron sat motionless as Travis responded, "Yes, sir," and turned to her board to follow the order. He let her do it, but even though he'd given the command, he knew it was a waste of time. He already knew the answer.

Chapter Twenty

Interplanetary Space
Tarantum System
Year 311 AC

"Keep working, all of you. *Illustrious* will still be gone after we get these squadrons launched. Plenty of time to pay your respects an' cry in your beer then." Chief Evans's voice was raw, demanding...and yet somehow compassionate as well. His snarling tones had been reverberating off the walls and rafters of the great launch bay as he drove *Dauntless*'s exhausted flight teams, trying to keep their thoughts off the demise of their companion ship.

Stockton had watched with a certain interest he tried his best to hide, but he'd barely heard the last bit at all. He had been walking across the flight deck when his eyes caught the small scanner screen on the wall, and he stopped dead. He saw two ships fighting, a Confederation Lightning and an Alliance Palatine. The small label next to the Confed ship identified it as "Thunder." *Kyle.*

The enemy ship had no designation beyond RA1—Red Alliance 1—but Stockton felt his stomach go cold as he watched the fighter's wild maneuvers. Jamison was a great pilot, the master in almost any combat he entered. But Stockton could see his friend was in trouble now, the enemy fixed on his tail, chasing him down despite his repeated attempts to break free.

179

Stockton turned and started to run toward his fighter, images of Timmons's brush with death thick in his eyes. "I'm launching, Briggs," he shouted to his flight tech, as he leapt from the deck, reaching out and grabbing hold of the small ladder that led to the cockpit. His grip slipped and he swung around, almost falling back down, but then he climbed up, whipping his legs into the opening.

"Commander, we still have to do your preflight checks. And your missiles haven't been loaded. We need another fifteen minutes, sir." Briggs stood below the fighter, looking up with his hands in the air.

"No time, Briggs. Just get the hell out of the way, and make sure no one is behind me...'cause I'm going now no matter what."

Even as he finished what he was saying, Stara Sinclair's voice same through his comm. "Blue Leader...you're not cleared to launch yet."

Stockton ignored the words, though they came from both his flight control officer and his lover. His hands moved over his fighter's controls, activating the systems and, with a last look to make sure Briggs had sought shelter, he fired up the engines.

"Jake, what's wrong? What is it?" Sinclair's usual professional tone had failed, replaced by undisguised concern.

"I've got to go now, Stara." Then: "I'm sorry."

He flipped the row of activator switches on the dashboard, and he gripped the throttle tightly.

Stara was still talking, her urgency increasing with each word. But he wasn't listening.

I'm coming, Kyle...

He closed his eyes for an instant...and then he stared straight ahead and hit the launch control.

*   *   *

"Shit." Jamison cursed under his breath, bringing his throttle around, increasing the thrust he demanded from his straining engines. Kyle Jamison was one of *Dauntless*'s best, if not quite the natural pilot his friend Jake Stockton was. He was an ace half a dozen times over, and one of the coolest customers every to fly the Lightning fighter. But now he was in trouble.

He'd targeted the Alliance pilot—seemingly the leader of the small group engaging the Eagles—with his missiles the instant his scanners had determined his adversary had no such weapons. And now that pilot was coming for blood.

He angled the controls again, taking a deep breath as he saw how quickly his foe had responded to his last move. *Responded... or read my mind?*

He pulled back on the throttle, maxing out his thrust, and he swung the control to the port, changing his vector yet again. Laser blasts started to go by...right through the space he'd occupied a second or two before. *All right*, he thought grimly. *You're good. Let's see how good.*

He hit his positioning jets, swinging his fighter around, even as he hit his turbos and decelerated at full. His fingers closed around the firing stud, his lasers blasting out...into the open space alongside his target. The enemy fighter had pulled its own maneuver, a rapid response to his. He shook his head, amazed at the sharpness of his enemy's action. Then, he felt something, a coldness running through him, and he jerked his hand to the side...just in time. A pair of laser blasts tore by, no more than a hundred meters from his ship.

His hands were clammy, his normal calm failing him for once. Jamison had commanded *Dauntless*'s entire strike force for more than five years, and that of the entire expeditionary force for six months. He was coldly rational in the cockpit, a man who addressed every aspect of flying, of fighter combat, with the same dispassionate excellence. Until now.

Stockton's pilot...

Jake Stockton had been telling everyone who would listen about an Alliance ace, a pilot he'd fought to a draw during the convoy raid a month before. Jamison had discussed it with his friend, but he also knew Stockton liked a good story. A few embellishments never hurt a tale worth telling.

But now he began to realize Stockton had been deadly serious. Jamison came about abruptly, again just a second or two ahead of the volley his enemy directed his way. He was staring hard at the screen, wracking his mind for the right moves.

His eyes flashed to the side, checking on the rest of the squadron. The battle was a sharp one, brutal, with losses on both sides. His people had the upper hand, courtesy of the missile attack, if nothing else. But the enemy reinforcements were coming into range, and he knew the Eagles would be in trouble.

I'm in trouble.

He tried to let his instincts take over. This pilot was too good to evade with logical tactics. He needed randomness, surprise. He had to break away from this pursuer, turn the tables. This pilot would finish him if he exposed his back, stayed on the defensive. The only way to survive this fight was to take the offensive…destroy his enemy before his enemy destroyed him.

He tried one wild move after another, one crazy, unpredictable change of course. But no matter what he did, his enemy was still there, clinging to him, matching his every maneuver.

He was slick with sweat. It was fear, he knew that well enough. He was losing confidence. The belief that he could win this fight was slipping away. And he knew once he lost that, he'd be dead soon after.

Then his comm crackled. "Thunder?"

Jake…

"Raptor, what the hell? You shouldn't be out here yet." His eyes on the scanner confirmed what he'd guessed. Blue squadron was nowhere to be seen. Only a single Confederation ship, heading toward him at full thrust.

"Yeah, well bust me down to a one stripe spacer if you want, but first I've got something to do."

"I'll have to do that. You've been a discipline problem for a long time now." Then: "Thanks, man. I really need your help."

"Hang in there, Thunder. I'm on my way."

Jamison adjusted his course again, staying just barely ahead of his pursuer. *My hunter…*

Help was on the way. He just had to hold out.

He swerved to the side again, just evading another shot from his enemy.

If I can. Hurry, Raptor…

*   *   *

Grachus gasped for breath as her high g maneuver slammed her hard back into her seat. This Confed pilot was good. No, more than good, he was crack, an ace. But she was almost sure it wasn't Stockton.

There was something missing, a certain innate brilliance… or perhaps it was just semi-controlled craziness. As good as this pilot was, she'd managed to stay on him despite his every attempt to break free. It hadn't been easy, and he'd almost gotten away several times—and once, he'd nearly turned the tables and come a hair's breadth from taking her out. But now, she knew, she had the upper hand. She'd studied his tactics, familiarized herself with his moves. He was cagey, skilled…but he was a touch less unpredictable than Stockton.

She came about again, matching her quarry' every move, slowly—so agonizingly slowly—closing the range between them. She needed to get closer. It would take extraordinary luck to hit a pilot this good at such long range. Grachus didn't depend on luck—she relied on skill, experience…and patience. Which meant she had to get closer.

Time was on her side. Her people had been roughly handled by the single squadron *Dauntless* had launched, but even now, as she chased their obvious commander, her second wave was reaching the battle area. *Dauntless* could launch more ships at any moment—she was far from privy to the happenings on her flight decks—but until she did, the tide would turn in her peoples' favor.

She shifted her controls again, cutting the thrust a bit, giving her target a little room. The closer she got, the tighter her reactions had to be. Rushing things only increased the risk level, and there was no reason she had to…

Her eyes darted to the side and froze. *Another fighter. One. Just launched from* Dauntless.

She looked at her main display and then back to the longer-range scanner. *Still only one.* She waited, checking back again and again, at least five or six times. But there was only one fighter.

Could it be?

She knew she was jumping to conclusions. She checked the tracer, but the result said, "inconclusive." That was to be expected. The ID lock had been unlikely to hold through a landing and refit.

Her mind raced, trying to figure out why a single fighter would launch. *A scout? No, that doesn't make any sense. Perhaps one ship launched and then a malfunction shut down the tubes? That's better, but I still don't buy it.*

She stayed focused on her target, but concerns about that newly launched fighter threatened to break down her single-minded intensity. Whoever it was, the ship was coming right toward her.

She looked back at the target in front of her. She'd had plenty of time...but not anymore. If that was Stockton back there, coming at her, she had to be finished with this fight before he got there. He'd finish her off almost immediately if he caught her tied down in another battle.

She hit the thrust again, trying to ignore the discomfort. There was no time for that. No time for anything except victory.

Her eyes narrowed, and she fired. Then again, angling her shot vector each time. Her blasts went wide, but they were getting closer, bracketing her enemy.

She would finish this now. She had no choice.

*   *   *

Jamison swung his throttle back and forth wildly. He could feel himself slipping, his moves going from controlled chaos to near panic. He knew with each step he took from stone cold control, his chances of victory—of escape—slipped away, but he couldn't stop it. He was tired, his head pounded. His body was drenched, and his legs were shaking. No one would ever call Kyle Jamison a coward, but he had to admit to himself, he'd never been so scared in his life.

He'd been in tough fights before, faced two or three opponents at the same time, but this enemy was something else entirely. If the battle had been more than a duel between a dozen fighters on a side, things might have been different. But he was alone right now. It was a one-on-one struggle here, at least until Stockton arrived.

A one-on-one matchup Jamison realized he couldn't win.

He tried to stay focused, to put his faith in the cool, analytical approach to flying that had made him so deadly. But his resolve was shaken. The fear he kept bottled up deep within had escaped.

He checked the scanner. Stockton was coming on as quickly as he could, but it was still going to be several minutes. He jerked his hand again, moving the throttle to the port, changing his ship's thrust angle yet again. Another evasive maneuver, and another few seconds of survival. But his enemy was still there, relentless, getting closer with each passing second.

"Raptor…" He paused, breathing heavily into the comm unit before he continued. "If this…doesn't…" Another hesitation. "I need you to look after the squadrons. We've got a hell of a fight ahead of us here."

"Cut that shit right now, Thunder. Keep your mind on your ship and the one following you. That's all."

"I mean it, Raptor. If I don't make it, I already told Commodore Barron you're my pick to take my…"

"Stay focused!" Stockton's words were a roar, a command from subordinate to superior, but mostly from friend to friend. "You're going to make it, buddy. Just stay with me…"

But Jamison heard the doubt in his friend's voice. The fear.

*   *   *

You're out of time. You have to finish this…now.

Grachus would have had great respect for her opponent… she did, in fact, save for the hatred she felt for all those who'd played a part in Kat's death. She didn't know this pilot had been at Santis, of course, but he was good. Very good. A veteran for sure, and probably one who'd served aboard *Dauntless* for some time.

She checked the display again, watching the other fighter, the one she was sure was Jake Stockton. He was coming for her, she knew that much. *It will save me the trouble of coming for him.*

She tried to put Stockton out of her mind, let herself slip into the almost trancelike state she adopted in battle. It was intellect and intuition, combining to make her as deadly as she could be.

Her target made a series of wild moves, last-ditch attempts to escape, but she managed to match them all. She was closer now, and her laser blasts were coming within meters of her target. She had worked the fight, pursued relentlessly, anticipated her enemy's moves. It had been a textbook hunt, though the skill of her adversary had made it long, difficult…and in a few instances, very dangerous. But she could feel the victory now.

You have a minute, maybe. By then, if you're still tied up here, Stockton will be on your tail. Then it will be all over.

She altered her thrust, matching her target's move. Then she took a deep breath. Reaction wasn't going to get it done. She had to be more aggressive. She had to guess where her opponent would be.

There were all sorts of standard maneuvers, things the training manuals told you to do in situations like this. But she was facing a crack ace here, and nothing he did would come from the "book."

She pursued for another few seconds, working her way steadily closer. Then, she saw it, an instant before it happened. The move she somehow knew her opponent would make. It was what she would have done.

Her arm moved, almost without conscious thought, angling her engines, nudging forward on the thrust. Her fingers tightened, closing slowly around the firing stud. A shot—close, no more than two meters off. Then another. Just to the other side.

She fired again, her eyes locked with all the intensity she could muster.

It took her scanners a fraction of a second to evaluate the result of her shot and report back, so the AI could update her screen. That instant of time seemed to stretch into a sort of eternity, her eyes moist, her forehead soaked with sweat.

She was still staring at the screen when the blip representing the enemy fighter vanished.

*   *   *

"Noooo!" The scream was raw, primal. Stockton had been looking right at his screen when the final shot hit Jamison's ship. For an instant, Stockton grasped at whatever he could. Perhaps Jamison's ship was just damaged. Maybe his friend had managed to eject. But as he stared at the screen in the seconds after that fateful shot, there was nothing. No ship, no pod, no signals on his comm. Suddenly, coldly, he knew.

Kyle Jamison was dead.

Stockton had always been a man who showed his emotions. Self-assured—many said cocky—he tended to react to things with fiery anger and roaring invective. But after his first stunned outburst, there was nothing but quiet. And the icy cold of a rage deeper and more consuming than any screaming fit.

His hand tightened on the throttle, and his eyes zeroed in on the enemy ship on his scanner. He'd come to save his friend, but he had failed. Now, he had only one purpose, a single thought consuming every corner of his mind and soul.

Vengeance.

He'd already been determined to destroy this enemy, but that had been a rational focus, a goal based on eliminating a danger to his comrades and their cause. Now it was personal, in a way he'd never felt before. Kyle Jamison was the brother he'd never had, his oldest friend. The two had been almost telepathically connected, each seeming to know just what the other needed. They'd faced seemingly endless dangers together, and each had known the day could—likely would—come when one of them lost that last fight. But that knowledge had still not prepared him for what he now felt. Or, perhaps, what he didn't feel. The pain wasn't there yet, not really. Nor the memories of a friend now gone. There was only the need to kill this pilot, a gaping frozen pit inside him, demanding vengeance.

Stockton had always been cold-blooded in combat, able to set aside things like fear and pity in the maelstrom of battle, but what he felt now was new. It would have scared him to death… if he cared enough right now to recognize fear.

He pulled back on the throttle, heading directly toward his enemy. He could see the blip moving, reacting to his approach. For an instant, he thought his deadly adversary was going to run for it…and if that was the case, he was ready to pursue, however far, into whatever dark and danger. But the Alliance fighter was coming about to engage him.

Yes, come to me. You and I have business to finish…

Stockton's fingers were white from the tightness of his fist on the throttle. His eyes were wide, glossy, sparkling like a madman's. Right now, he didn't care about the war, didn't care about *Dauntless* or the other ships of the fleet. Even Stara had been forced from his mind, banished into the recesses along with every vestige of Jake Stockton the man. There was nothing left but a shadow of who he had been, a cold avatar of death with no thought save that of taking its enemy.

"It's time for you to die," he muttered, his tone thick with hatred. *Or for me to die.*

Or both of us…

He knew in that instant, if the price of destroying this enemy and avenging Kyle was his own death, he would pay it in an instant. He could accept his own destruction…in a way, he'd been prepared for it for years. But he could not allow this enemy to live, no matter what. He would destroy this Alliance pilot.

Whatever the cost.

Chapter Twenty-One

Interplanetary Space
Tarantum System
Year 311 AC

Grachus pulled hard on the throttle, a sudden change in thrust angle brought on by intuition, or something else faster than conscious thought. This enemy *was* her old foe, it *was* Stockton. She was sure of it. His moves were similar, yet there was something different now. He was more…reckless? No, that wasn't it, not exactly. He was certainly more driven. He'd come at her three times, blasting away on his turbos, firing relentlessly, like a man possessed. She knew this was a duel between them, that he, as she, saw the other as a threat to comrades and cause. But there was something more there now. Something new.

She watched as a series of laser blasts went by, less than ten meters away. Despite her focus and attention, Stockton had almost taken her down twice. She'd survived this last attack by a second's reaction time. *No*, she thought to herself, *far less than a second*.

She told herself nothing had changed, but she knew something had. Stockton was flying like no pilot she'd ever seen before, almost entirely on intuition, on instinct, it seemed. His maneuvers were wild, unpredictable, even by her standards.

She switched off the safeties on her reactor, firing the power plant to dangerous overload levels. It was something she did once in a while if she had to get somewhere quickly, but she'd never done it in a dogfight. But Stockton had obviously pushed his own reactor into the redline, and that left her no choice.

The pressure slammed into her as she blasted to full thrust, over 12g now, making it a struggle even to breathe. She could pass out at this level, she knew that well enough, but if her enemy was enduring the pain and taking the risk, she was compelled to do the same. This was no opponent she could defeat at a disadvantage. Whatever Stockton had, she had to match.

She spun her fighter around and fired, her shots zipping by her enemy's ship. It had been a sudden maneuver, well-executed. And it had almost succeeded. Her scanner showed the closest shots coming within meters of her target. A good effort…but not quite good enough.

Her stomach clenched, and she swung her arm around hard, a sudden move that almost surprised her as she did it. Then she saw the return shots, burning their way through the space her ship had just occupied. There weren't many pilots who could come back from as close a call as she'd just sent her enemy's way with nearly instant return fire, but clearly Stockton was one of the few who could.

Focus, she thought. *Your instincts saved you there. Don't underestimate this pilot…or whatever is driving him…*

She knew what was driving him. Suddenly, it was obvious. She had killed someone important to him. She knew, because she recognized the symptoms. Her need for vengeance for Kat was no less powerful, but Stockton wasn't the main target of that hatred. Tyler Barron was.

But you are the focus of his rage. He will come at you, with the same single-minded determination that drives you. He will do anything to destroy you…including die himself.

She felt a chill inside. All pilots fought to survive, though they risked their lives on every mission. But this was different. Stockton wasn't just willing to take a risk…he didn't *care* if he survived, not as long as he killed her. She understood, because the same thing consumed her. If she could kill Tyler Barron, avenge her dead friend, her own survival wouldn't even be a consideration. She would die, gratefully, to destroy that most hated of enemies.

And Stockton will die to kill me...

Her enemy had grown far more dangerous. She'd known he could defeat her before, but now she began to truly fear him, what he'd become. What she'd made him. She wasn't scared of death, not for its own sake, at least. But if Stockton defeated her, Kat would go unavenged.

She stared hard at her display, reaching down and turning the small dial farther, driving her reactor and engines beyond the highest overloads she'd ever risked. She couldn't hold back. Not now.

This was a fight for her life, and it would take everything she had. She pulled back on the throttle, trying to ignore the ear-splitting whine from the power plant...and the ribs she could feel cracking in her chest as the g forces climbed...13...14...

*   *   *

"Commodore Barron...get that ship out of there now. You've done your part, held the line. I've got ten fresh squadrons heading your way to take over the holding action." Tulus's voice was loud over the comm, firm. But there was something there Barron hadn't heard before. Was it respect?

"Commander, we can hold while you get your ships out of range." Barron wasn't entirely sure that was true, but he was neck deep in the battle and reluctant to pull back.

"Commodore..." Tulus paused. Barron suspected the Alliance officer had been about to say something along the lines of, "it's an order," but he stopped himself. "...be reasonable. *Illustrious* is already gone...and I can only imagine your fighter groups have suffered brutal losses. Pull them back and get out of there. You've done more than your share. And remember, you've got two more ships back at Sentinel-2. You're Imperator Vennius's conduit to the Confederation. We can't lose you here."

Barron was shocked at Tulus's words. The Alliance officer

had made little effort in the past to hide his disdain for either Barron or the Confederation's aid. But Barron's people had taken terrible losses and stayed in the fight, and from what he'd gathered of the Alliance mindset, there was little they respected more.

Barron glanced at the display, trying to keep track of the losses his squadrons had suffered. He'd already sent out his rescue boats...a dangerous thing to do in the middle of a battle. But he had nearly a dozen pilots who'd ditched, and he wasn't about to leave them behind. His flight crews had finally gotten the last of the fighters launched...and that had equalized things in the dogfight. For a while. There were fresh waves of Red fighters coming on, at least a hundred, blasting at full, from wherever they were refueling. *Dauntless* had thirty-one ships still operational and in the fight, and that included the refugees from *Illustrious* that had found their way into her bays.

The approaching Reds were too far for detailed scans, but if there were bombers there, and they arrived just as *Dauntless's* fighters were exhausting their fuel...

It had only taken five bombers to finish off *Illustrious*. *Dauntless* wasn't as badly damaged as the larger vessel had been, and its squadrons, even depleted and exhausted, were far superior. But if forty or fifty bombers came its way...

"Very well, Commander. It will take me some time to recover my squadrons, but then we will pull back." He didn't like it, but he couldn't argue that it made more tactical sense to match the enemy fighters *with* fighters.

"Hurry, Commodore. We don't want those incoming waves to get there before you withdraw."

"Understood, Commander. Barron out." He still didn't like it, but he knew Tulus was right...and also that the Alliance commander was in charge of the expedition, if not the allied Confederation forces directly.

"Commander Travis...issue recall orders. I want the recovery boats to pick up every pilot confirmed still alive, and then—and only then—the fighters are to break off."

"Yes, sir."

"Let's get *Dauntless* underway. The squadrons can catch us easily enough." *And if we don't put some distance behind us, those incoming waves are going to hit us no matter what we do.*

"Yes, Commodore. Plotting optimal withdrawal course now."

"Proceed as soon as you are ready, Commander." Barron turned and looked over at the main display. His eye caught one tiny speck of blue light, a single ship, far on the fringe of the overall formation, and heading deeper into the heart of the approaching mass of enemy fighters. He punched at the small keyboard on his workstation, pulling up the fighter's ID. But he knew even before the screen displayed a small, "Blue Leader."

Stockton...of course. Barron had watched in horror as Kyle Jamison's ship had been destroyed. He was still hoping—against hope, perhaps—that his strike force commander had managed to eject, that he was floating around out there with a damaged transponder. He knew that was mostly a way to get through the fight without confronting the realization he dreaded. But now, he cursed himself for not immediately realizing that Jake Stockton would go after the enemy that had—likely—killed his friend.

"Atara, get me Commander Stockton. Now."

He couldn't afford to lose Jamison and Stockton, not in the same battle.

*   *   *

"That's an order, Commander. Break off and return to *Dauntless* now."

Stockton listened to Barron on the comm, gritting his teeth against the relentless g forces slamming into him as he continued the duel with his enemy.

"I can't, sir," he said, his voice low, raspy as he forced the words from his tortured lungs. "Have to take down this pilot..."

"Commander...there will be another place, another time. Break off now."

Stockton shook his head, a pointless gesture on audio-only

comm, and one he barely managed with the intense force shoving him down into his seat. He respected Commodore Barron, perhaps more than anyone he had ever known. He didn't take disregarding orders from Barron lightly, but he had to avenge Jamison. He *had* to.

"Commander Stockton," Barron roared on the comm, "listen to me. If you want to avenge Kyle Jamison, you will return to *Dauntless* now. Look at your screen. You've got dozens of enemy fighters approaching, and they'll be on you before the Gray squadrons get there. Stay, and you'll just end up dead… and the pilot who killed Kyle will be laughing as fifty enemy ships swarm all over you."

Stockton could hear Barron's words, and he understood the wisdom behind them…but the rage that had taken him gripped hard. He knew he would likely die if he stayed where he was, but that wasn't reason enough to leave. Not if he could take the pilot who'd killed his friend with him. He craved revenge with an intensity he couldn't resist, and he was ready to die to get it. But Barron's words were haunting, and the reality in front of him was stark. If he didn't win the duel in the next few minutes, he wouldn't win at all. He would be surrounded and hunted down, and his enemy would escape.

Kyle Jamison would go unavenged.

No, I can win this now…

The thought was desperate, a way to justify staying, dying a noble death here and now. But that was the easy way out. He owed Kyle more than to throw his life away. He owed his friend the life of the Alliance flyer who'd killed him.

Even if that meant vengeance had to wait…

He fired a series of shots at his adversary, again coming close, but failing to hit. Even as he took the shots, he knew they were his last chance at immediate satisfaction. The waves of incoming fighters were on his short-range display now, over sixty heading directly toward his location.

His ship and the Alliance fighter were moving at sharp angles to each other now. It was a chance to break free of the combat, to head back to *Dauntless*.

To run…

He gripped the throttle, hesitating, but knowing what he had to do…and hating himself for it. His hand moved slowly, and then, with a last struggled gasp for breath, he slammed the controls to the side, blasting at full thrust and altering his vector away from his enemy.

Away from vengeance…

He fought back against the pain from the bruises, the agony of his dislocated shoulder—another effect of the massive g forces he had endured in the fight. He held his face stony, impassive, even as tears struggled to escape…tears for his lost friend, for his failure, for the coward he labeled himself.

I will avenge you, my friend…whatever it takes, however long…I swear it. I will destroy your killer.

Chapter Twenty-Two

Sector Nine Headquarters
Liberte City
Planet Montmirail, Ghassara IV
Year 62 (311 AC)

"Minister Lille, thank you for coming on such short notice."

Lille looked up at Calavius. The Imperator he'd created sat at a relaxed angle, almost reclining in the throne he'd ordered built for himself.

At least he handled the furniture himself. Lille knew his own machinations had done more to put Calavius into the seat than anything the Palatian had managed to do on his own.

Still, I couldn't have done it without him, without his connections.

"Of course. I am here to assist you any way possible."

He's being too polite. He must need something from me again.

Though, perhaps when you want something, there is a more politic way of sending for me than sending twenty warriors with orders to "fetch me."

"What can I do to aid your great enterprise?" He avoided using a title again. He'd referred to his co-conspirator as "Calavius" when they'd first begun plotting, but that was a bit informal for a head of state, so Lille simply avoided calling the Imperator anything.

"I am concerned, Minister Ricard." A pause. "No, that is

196

not quite correct. I wish to take every precaution. Though victory seems within reach, it is often at such a stage that fatal errors occur."

Lille was surprised. Calavius seemed like just the type to fall victim to hubris, and he'd been watching carefully, ready to intervene to prevent any self-inflicted disasters at this stage. Had the Imperator gained wisdom? Had he had some carefully hidden?

No, more likely he's just scared of Vennius. The Gray Imperator was a vastly better soldier than his former friend and current rival. Tarkus Vennius would have been Ricard's first choice without question, if there had been any way at all to control him. But Vennius was that rare creature, a true man of honor, and Lille's plans had required a degree of moral flexibility.

"Caution is always advisable. There is cause for optimism, but always best to keep it guarded. How can I be of assistance?"

"I would like you to aid my people in something." A pause. "Your Union…your Sector Nine. You have great experience in matters of surveillance…in policing loyalty."

Ah…Mellus's defection has you unnerved, even though her fleet was nearly destroyed and she was killed. You fear more such turncoats…

"Yes, Sector Nine is highly accomplished at ensuring the…" He almost said "obedience," but decided to soften it a bit. "…support of the people. Any great nation must have the backing of its citizens. To allow the few, the disaffected, to jeopardize the interests of the state, is to invite disaster." He felt almost as though his words were coming from some old memories of a Sector Nine training vid. *Perhaps they are.* Maintaining loyalty had never been his specialty in his years of service. He usually got involved after the fact, when such efforts had failed and removal had become necessary. But he figured he could help Calavius. *These Alliance warriors are almost childlike in some ways. In matters of state, at least.*

Lille looked around. He and Calavius were almost alone, save for a dozen guards posted around the room. It was the first time in a long time Lille had seen the Imperator without his officers and advisors gathered around, chattering at him. *And feeding his visions of great personal importance.*

Of course. Those officers and advisors are the ones he wants to watch. That's why they're not here.

"I would like you to work with Gennatus here. He is an admirable warrior, and beyond suspicion, but I'm afraid such matters exceed his expertise. He will supply reliable people, but I am counting on you to develop a prototype organization along the lines of your Sector Nine."

Lille was amazed at how completely power corrupted people. He, himself, had always felt different than those around him. He was driven by success, and by a genuine love for killing, but not at all for the pure accumulation of power, certainly not in excess of what he needed to assure his own position and comfort. He had all he needed now in terms of position and wealth, and he was continually amazed at the risks people took seeking ever more political power, regardless of the risks involved. Calavius already sounded like a Union minister, shedding his Alliance honor and warrior ethics like a serpent's skin.

It will make him far easier to control…

Calavius gestured toward one of the guards, a man in the livery of a high-ranking officer. "Gennatus, you are to fully cooperate with Minister Lille, and provide him any resources he requires."

"Yes, Your Supremacy." The officer turned and nodded deeply toward Lille. "Minister, I look forward to working with you." Gennatus was trying to sound respectful, but Lille didn't buy it. He didn't care, either. He'd be glad to get out of the Alliance once and for all, when his work was done.

"Commander Gennatus," he said, making about as much effort to sound excited about the impending collaboration as the Alliance officer had.

Lille managed not to shake his head as he looked at Gennatus's absurd uniform. It was very un-Alliance-like, even foppish. But one of an Imperator's prerogatives was designing uniforms for his own guard. *All of whom he drew from his estates, from his pool of longtime family retainers. That's smart, but it may be a mistake to rely on them too much.* Old, trusted friends and subordinates were the first ones Lille would seek to suborn if he was making a move against someone, and he had no doubt any other competent enemy would do the same. *People would be surprised how often they can be bought. Often quite cheaply.*

He was amused that lesson was lost on Calavius, the old friend of Vennius that Lille had selected to overthrow the Alliance government.

Lille paused, then he looked back at Calavius. "You must understand, an organization like Sector Nine cannot be built overnight. Sector Nine has millions of operatives, and hundreds of millions of paid informants...not to mention a history of effectiveness that accomplishes much of its work without any direct action. It will take...time...for Alliance culture to adapt."

"I realize nothing worthwhile is built in a day, Minister. However, I would like to see progress as quickly as possible. I feel it is essential to state security, to ensuring we have no... unfortunate...situations that are disruptive to the successful conclusion of this war and the establishment of a strong and lasting government."

"I will see to it at once." Lille nodded, almost a slight bow, holding back the smile struggling to escape his lips. He'd been worried about how he would maintain control over Calavius, ensure that the Imperator honored his commitments after the civil war was won. But the fool had just invited Lille to plant the seeds of his own control in the heart of the Alliance government.

He would do as Calavius asked, and more. Much more. When he was done, he would truly be the power behind the scenes. And when the Grays were defeated, he would see to it himself that every Alliance ship capable of flight joined the invasion, the great offensive that would blast through the Confederation...and ensure Union dominance for generations.

*   *   *

"Commander Grachus, thank you for coming." Lille

watched as the Alliance officer stood in the doorway, hesitating for a moment before she walked fully into the room.

"I was ordered here, Minister." Her tone was curt, professional. Lille didn't suspect she liked him any more than any of the other Alliance officers milling about headquarters, though she seemed smart and capable enough to hide her contempt with some degree of success.

If you only knew the role I played in your promotion...

"Yes, Commander. I believe you can help me...and I can perhaps assist you in attaining one of your own goals."

"How so, Minister? My only desires are to serve, and to see this costly rebellion ended as quickly as possible."

"That's not entirely true now, is it?" He looked up at her, standing next to the table at rigid attention. He reached over and pushed out a chair. "Please, sit. It's making me uncomfortable watching you stand like that."

She hesitated again, but then she put her hand on the back of the chair and slid around, dropping gracefully into place.

"Thank you, Commander. That is so much better, isn't it?" He paused, but she didn't respond, so he continued, "Commander, I have been trying to kill a man, to no avail." His work often involved finesse and deceit, but when he got the chance to be blunt, he rather enjoyed it.

"I am not an assassin, Minister. I doubt I can help you with such a goal." He could hear a hardness in her tone that hadn't been there before.

"Please, Commander, do not misunderstand me. I know you are an Alliance warrior. I would never ask you to skulk in the shadows." *Besides, I've been trying that for close to a year, without success. It's time for something different.*

"Then what is it we are discussing, if you don't mind me asking, Minster?"

"We are discussing *Dauntless*, Commander. We are discussing Tyler Barron."

"He's the man you want killed?" He could hear the attentiveness in her voice now.

"Yes. I want Barron dead. I want his whole damned ship

and everyone on it obliterated." Lille paused for just a second. "I believe we share that desire, Commander. Or am I mistaken?"

Grachus didn't move. "You are not mistaken, Minister." A long silence. "How is such a thing possible?"

"Since Commander Mellus's attempt at defection, the Imperator has become impatient to finish this war, whatever the cost. He doesn't want to risk other officer being led astray by the pretender's propaganda." Lille was astonished occasionally at just how artfully he could lie. Whatever he said, he knew Vennius had the rightful claim, and he was just as aware that the Gray Alliance commander's many talents did not extend into the intricacies of propaganda.

"We will be attacking Sentinel-2?" He could hear the eagerness in her words.

"Yes, soon. And when we do, you will lead the fleet's fighter squadrons." He hesitated, trying to gauge what she was thinking. He was an expert at such things, but he had to admit, Grachus had a good poker face. Her hatred for Barron was clear, but he'd known about that already. Her thoughts on the actual attack were rather more circumspect.

"That is true, I expect. As far as I know, the Imperator was pleased with the performance of my wings at Tarantum."

"He was indeed, Commander. Very pleased." Calavius had been downright giddy over the victory, and of the example made of Mellus, not to mention the destruction of one of the Confederation's newest and most powerful ships. Lille was rather less pleased that *Dauntless* and so much of the Gray fleet had managed to escape, but he held back from blaming Grachus. He knew full well what Barron and his people could do, and by all accounts, their escape had been a near-run thing.

"I believe I can convince the Imperator to authorize you to personally lead a large force of fighters with a single assignment. Destroy *Dauntless*."

"We tried that at Tarantum, Minister."

"With unsupported ships and exhausted pilots, Commander." He could see the defensiveness grow in her expression. "I mean no criticism. Your plan was brilliant, and your people performed magnificently. But your lack of heavy ship support and proper refueling and rearmament facilities was a burden. By the time the main fleet finally pushed the enemy back into Tarantum, it was too late to close the trap. You came close, Commander. Very close." He paused. "I am talking about the same thing this time, but with even more fighters committed, and battleships backing your people." He paused. "Another chance, Commander. That is what I'm offering. You almost succeeded. You almost avenged your mentor." He looked right into her eyes, his stare intense, unyielding. "Do you want to try again?"

Chapter Twenty-Three

AS Ferox
Helios System
En Route Back to Sentinel-2
Year 62 (311 AC)

"I want to thank you for joining me here, Commodore Barron." Tulus was sitting at one end of the table, opposite Barron. They were far enough apart to make conversation difficult, but Barron understood Alliance culture well enough to know Tulus was paying respect to him, the private meeting a way of acknowledging an honored guest.

"It is an honor, Commander. And my great pleasure." He'd always considered his immense experience in acting gracious during uncomfortable social situations one of the more dubious benefits of membership in the celebrated Barron clan, but he couldn't argue it had come in handy many times.

Barron had been surprised at the commander's request. No, more than surprised. Outright shocked was closer to the mark. Tulus hadn't made much effort to hide his contempt for Barron and his Confederation spacers. But there was something different now in the Palatian's demeanor, his tone. Not friendly, exactly, but something quite different than Barron had seen before.

"Commodore, I am not a man given to long drawn out non-

203

sense, so I will simply speak my mind if that is acceptable."

"Of course, Commander. Always."

"I did you a great wrong, Commodore, you and all of your people." The words hit Barron like a hammer. He'd expected Tulus to propose some crazy plan, to complain about the near-disaster they had just suffered...anything but what he'd just said.

"Commander..." Barron didn't often find himself at a loss for words, but he was struggling for them now. "...you did nothing of the sort."

"I appreciate your effort to spare me shame, Commodore, but I am an Alliance officer, and I have lived my entire life by a code of conduct, one which compels me to acknowledge my errors freely and openly. You are a warrior, Commodore, as am I, as are my most trusted officers, and as are your crews. I did you a wrong in treating you otherwise, and I offer my profound apology. I cannot undo what has been done, but I can assure you with utter sincerity that no one under my command shall ever wrong your people so again."

"What has passed between us is as nothing to warriors, Commander. We are bonded, as fighters who have shared the sting and heat of battle." Barron managed to find the appropriate response, the words an Alliance officer would have used to respond.

"I thank you, Commodore. Still, there is an honor debt between us. You have but to call on me, and I shall be there."

Barron was thankful he'd spent as much time as he had studying Alliance customs and ritual. "There can be no debt between brothers who have bled together. You have only to call on *me* in need, and I too shall be at your side." Barron found the Alliance's oaths and customs a bit overwrought, but he felt something as he said the words. Tulus was a man of honor, if one who had been difficult to handle, and Barron knew he said what he did with complete sincerity. That was an assurance he wouldn't feel with many others, even those in his own service.

Tulus looked back at Barron, clearly unable to fully hide his surprise in his guest's reaction and words. "I have done myself a disservice as well, I fear, in denying myself so worthy a comrade for so long. Let us put an end to such foolishness now. Stay. Let us eat, drink, and tell each other tales of our battles…and if we embellish our stories a bit, the gods of war may forgive us."

Barron nodded. "It would be an honor, Commander."

Tulus smiled, and he pressed a small button on the table. The door slid open, and a steward stepped in.

"Yes, sir?"

"Dinner, Volpus. The Commodore and I will be dining together. But first, to my quarters. Bring us two bottles of the '39 Coastal Red." Tulus turned toward Barron. "It is my estate's label, Commodore, from the last case laid down by my father more than twenty years ago. You would honor me by sharing it with me."

"The honor is mine, Commander." Barron held back the sigh. Left to his own, he barely drank…yet he suspected tonight would be an epic bender. It wouldn't be the first time he'd gotten drunk in the line of duty.

*　　　　　*　　　　　*

Barron stood in front of the mirror, fussing with his collar. The dress uniform was uncomfortable—no, worse than that, he was sure it had been designed as an interrogation device—but it was appropriate, and since he'd been forced to don multiple hats—ship captain, fleet commander, ambassador to the Alliance—he'd spent more time considering the various protocols that were appropriate. And his full-dress best was called for in any meeting with a foreign head of state.

He'd met Vennius many times before, wearing only his regular duty uniform, but the long trip back from the disastrous mission to meet Commander Mellus had given him time to think of how to make the alliance work.

He'd not only mended his relationship with Tulus, the two had become something rapidly approaching fast friends. The grizzled Alliance commander had bristled with pride before, but now that Barron knew the man better, he saw other facets. Honesty, faithfulness, courage. He saw much of himself in the

Alliance officer and, truth be told, Tulus reminded him of his grandfather. At least, his childhood recollections of the man he'd loved so dearly…and lost far too soon.

Barron had spent a lot of time with Tulus, discussing battle plans, strategizing on what they intended to propose to Vennius when they got back. He'd also run wild on *Dauntless*, which was his only responsibility at the moment, with *Illustrious* gone and his other two ships still at Sentinel-2 in Captain Eaton's capable hands. He'd haunted the damage control parties, driven Fritzie to the brink, he suspected, and generally involved himself in all manner of ship's affairs, many of them below the rightful focus of a captain, much less a commodore.

He told himself he was just being meticulous, that the military situation was verging on desperate, that there was no room for mistakes. That was all true, no doubt. But in his moments of introspection, of honesty with himself, he knew he was also trying to keep *her* from his mind.

Tyler Barron had quite a reputation in the ports and spacers' retreats that served the Confederation's fleets, but he'd met his match in Andi Lafarge. Unlike all the others, he'd been unable to push her from his mind, at least not for long. She was infuriating in ways…no other woman had ever driven him quite as crazy as she did. But she was extraordinary too, far more interesting than the most beautiful women he'd romanced, hard and strong, but feminine too…and as seductive and enticing as hell when she chose to be.

He'd let her stay at Sentinel-2 far longer than he should have, feeling guilty about it every day that passed. Finally, he'd sent her away. It was too dangerous, he'd told her, and that was certainly true. He wanted to protect her, to keep her from the climactic battle he knew would come to Sentinel-2 as soon as Calavius could mass sufficient forces. But it was more than that. He didn't admit it to her, nor perhaps, except in scattered moments, to himself, but she was a distraction, one he couldn't afford right now. He needed all he had, all he was, to command his forces, to stand with Vennius and somehow defeat the vastly stronger Red Alliance. And Andromeda Lafarge would always consume a massive amount of his attention.

He was right to send her back to Confederation space, but it still gnawed at him. She hadn't given him a hint of disappointment or pain when he'd told her, rather too bluntly, he recalled, she had to leave at once. He wished he'd been gentler, but then his thoughts of the time resurfaced, the realization that she wouldn't have left if he'd tread more softly. Andi was nothing if not stubborn, but she was proud too, and Barron had used that facet of her personality to manipulate her, to give her no choice but to leave. To go where she'd be safe. He hoped he hadn't hurt her too deeply, that eventually she'd see through his tactics well enough to understand.

Of course...she'd never let you know, even if she was hurt. She would hide her pain, showing only that granite-like strength that makes her who she is...

He tried to push the thoughts away yet again, knowing he didn't have time for them now, and yet realizing success at that would be short-lived. They would come back again, as they had for all the months she'd been gone.

But that was tomorrow's problem. Today's was meeting with Imperator Vennius, standing alongside Tulus and explaining why they were returning with seven battleships instead of twelve. Telling the beleaguered leader of the Gray faction, and the Confederation's only hope of preventing an Alliance invasion of the Confederation, that his newest ally was dead. That leaks still plagued his cause...and one of his most trusted subordinates was almost certainly the source of that treason.

Barron smoothed out a stubborn wrinkle in his jacket and did one more pass in the mirror. He'd never had time for such nonsense, but now he represented the Confederation. All of the Confederation, as its highest-ranking officer present. He detested diplomacy and diplomats, and he had great difficultly remembering any successful diplomatic efforts as far as his knowledge of history extended, but he understood treating allies with respect. That wasn't hard with Vennius. Despite their difficult start, the two had become close, and Barron had come to admire the Palatian greatly. He'd felt a kinship with Katrine

Rigellus, though their personal contact had been limited to a single brief exchange. That same feeling extended to Vennius, and now to Tulus as well.

He didn't approve of all aspects of Alliance culture, certainly not the near-worship of war and conquest, but he found he appreciated much of their ethos. He suspected the current split, the war ravaging through their once tightly knit ranks, was especially difficult to endure. The Palatians considered themselves above the corruption and self-dealing so prevalent in the other governments, and their culture was heavily based on an "us vs. everyone else" mentality. They were getting a hard lesson that they weren't as different as they thought they were.

He paused for a moment, then he scooped up the hat that went with his dress grays—*an absurd-looking thing*, he thought, almost tossing it aside. But if he was going to do this, he would do it. He placed the hat on his head, turning it back and forth, trying to get the least ridiculous look from it before giving up with a deep sigh.

He turned and walked toward the door, and out into the corridor toward the launch bay. He was shuttling over to *Ferox*, and he and Tulus planned to go to Sentinel-2 together.

That alone was something he couldn't have imagined a few weeks before.

*   *   *

"That was a close fight, I'll tell you that. The histories have been massaged a bit, but we came close to ..." Tulus had told the story at least two or three times before, but Barron knew enough about comradeship with old warriors to listen as intently as he had the first time. Then Tulus stopped abruptly as the doors at the end of the bay opened, and armed troopers poured into the landing area.

Barron's instincts tightened his hand and arm...and he felt an impulse to reach for his sidearm. But sense prevailed, and he stood stone still, watching.

"Commodore Barron, please step to the side. We do not

wish to risk harming you in any way." The voice came from
an officer who seemed to be in command of the troopers. His
tone was authoritative, but it was clear he was trying to show
respect for the Confederation officer.

Barron glanced at Tulus, and one look told him his Alliance
comrade was as confused as he was. He stood firm, next to
Tulus, silent.

"Please, Commodore Barron. For your own safety, I must
insist that you step away from the traitor."

Barron could see Tulus's body tense, and he knew the rage
his new friend was trying to suppress. Vian Tulus was a lot
of things, arrogant, hard, callous at times…but Barron couldn't
imagine his comrade was capable of betrayal, of treason.

Tulus exchanged glances with Barron and nodded. "Do as
he says, Tyler. I don't know what this is about…" Barron knew
Tulus was trying to protect him, to keep him clear of whatever
was happening. He also received the unspoken message from
the Palatian…an oath that someone would pay for the outrage.
"…but I would not have you risk yourself or the Confederation's alliance with the Gray cause." When Barron didn't move
immediately, Tulus added, "Please, my friend."

Barron returned the nod and stepped slowly to the side. As
he did, a dozen rifle-armed troopers moved toward Tulus, grabbing him by the arms, pulling his sidearm from its holster. They
pushed him down to his knees, something that took four of
them to accomplish, and they pulled his arms behind him, bind-
ing them with a pair of shackles.

Barron wanted to intervene. It took all he had to remain still,
silent, watching as this man, so recently his tormentor, but now
his friend, was thrown to the ground. The bay doors opened
again, and another column of troopers entered, this time escorting several senior officers, and the Imperator himself.

Vennius stood back, not saying a word, looking somber, even
sad. But Hirtius Longinus was in the forefront, animated, a sick
smile on his face. "You tasked me with uncovering the treason
in our midst, Your Supremacy, and so I give you the traitor."

"That is nonsense," Tulus roared. "I will see you on the field of honor for such…" One of the soldiers kneed Tulus in the back at Longinus's signal, sending the officer down to the floor.

"You will do no such thing. Traitors have no honor, nor any recourse to the ways of honorable warriors." Longinus turned toward Vennius, holding up a small datachip in his hand. "Here I have the evidence, Your Supremacy. Incontestable proof that Vian Tulus accessed our primary communications grid and sent a message…just before his fleet departed to meet Commander Mellus. It took some effort to track the endpoint of that transmission, but I can now say without doubt that it was Palatia itself."

Longinus turned and glared at Tulus, who had risen again to one knee. "Do you deny it, traitor? Or will you admit your guilt?"

Tulus was silent. Barron waited for the officer to respond, but there was nothing. Only an angry glare toward Longinus, one that promised retribution but offered no defense.

"You see, Your Supremacy? The traitor does not even try to lie his way out. He is guilty, and the blood of all the warriors we have lost through his treachery cries out for justice."

"I am no traitor." Tulus's tone was defiant, but there was something else there. Barron wondered, for an instant if it could be true, it the man he'd just fought alongside had been working against the cause the whole time. *No*, he decided. It wasn't possible. Whatever evidence Longinus had, it was wrong. Barron could not believe Tulus was a traitor.

"Commander Tulus, this entire episode grieves me." Vennius finally spoke, and Barron could hear the emotion in his voice. "We have served many years together, and we have trusted each other with our lives. Explain this to me, Vian. Tell me whom you sent a message to, whom you contacted in the middle of enemy-held territory. I give you this chance now, as a friend and a comrade of more years than I can easily recount. Speak, clear yourself. I beg you."

But Tulus just stared back at Vennius, silent.

Barron wanted to intervene, but he held himself. This was not his place, not even to be here, and much less to become involved. He just stood and watched as Vennius finally uttered a soft, somber command. "Take him away."

Chapter Twenty-Four

**Command Center
Fleet Base Grimaldi
Orbiting Krakus II
Year 311**

Admiral Van Striker sat at his desk, flipping through the morning comm traffic. It was mostly routine, until he saw the heading on one of the transmissions.

He punched at his keyboard, pulling up the document. It wasn't designated as a formal report, just as a personal message, which was why no one had pointed it out to him right away. But it was encrypted, with the specific code he'd given Tyler Barron when he'd sent him to the Alliance.

There was a buzz at the door. He almost ignored it, he was so interested in the latest from Barron, but finally he looked up and asked his AI, "Who is it?"

"Gary Holsten is at the door, Admiral. Shall I admit him?"

"Yes…of course." He shook his head, wondering if anyone would ever develop an AI that could really think worth a damn. *Yes, probably the old empire. But we'd be wise not to emulate them, at least not in everything.*

The door slid open, and the head of Confederation intelligence stepped into the room. "Van, it's good to see you. It's been, what, four months?" Striker had known the intelligence director was planning to pay a visit, but he'd expected at least some warning.

Though perhaps I shouldn't have…

He knew Holsten often liked to avoid the limelight and travel inconspicuously, not an easy goal for a man who was both the senior intelligence commander for the Confederation and the head of one of its most massive family fortunes.

"Nearer five," the Admiral said, without a doubt in his mind Holsten remembered their last encounter to the minute. Striker was out of his chair, slipping around the desk and extending his hand. "It's good to see you…" He paused. "At least on a personal level. But, I have to tell you, my friend, you travel with a black cloud following you. I'd be thrilled if you walked in here one day and told me you'd just come to see if we could close down all the bars and officers' clubs on Grimaldi, or because you wanted to discuss the navy's excessive use of cleaning products, but I'm not going to hold my breath. Am I right that this is not a social call?"

Holsten walked across the room, gesturing to one of the guest chairs in front of the desk. "Do you mind, Van? I'm afraid it was a rough trip out here—lots of extra acceleration. I just arrived, and I came here directly from the spaceport. My legs are killing me." He sat down without waiting for an answer.

"Of course," Striker replied, now superfluously. "Sore legs? That sounds like g forces to me, all right. I could say you get used to it after a while, but that's only half a truth…and one that requires you to spend a *lot* of time in combat conditions to test out…But you say you were rushing to get here? Which means that cloud behind you is probably a nasty one."

"No, not really. At least, not the worst one we've dealt with. But I wanted to give you as much time and warning as I could."

"Time and warning. That doesn't sound good." Striker turned and moved back to his desk, sitting down himself. His eyes caught the partially decoded communique on his screen. "If it can wait a moment, Van, I was about to read the latest message from Tyler Barron. You might be interested yourself."

"I am indeed. Commodore Barron has done an extraordinary job out there, but we both know we sent him to do an impossible task."

"It is impossible, at least with the resources we gave him." Striker typed in the rest of the encryption code, and watched the jumble of letters move around, gradually forming a readable message.

"What more could we have sent him? Could you really have spared anything from here?"

Striker was reading the message as Holsten talked, and he got about three-fourths of what his friend said. "What? No, of course not. You know what shape we're in here. We'd be in deep trouble without those last three new ships…and the fact that the Union is just as badly battered is our only saving grace." He glanced back at the screen and then to Holsten. "Tyler says he needs reinforcements."

"I didn't need him to tell me that."

"No, but it sounds urgent now. He says the Grays have been limited to hit and run operations against Red supply convoys and the like. They don't have the strength to defend Sentinel-2 properly and mount any more significant operations." Striker looked up from the screen, over toward Holsten. "Gary, Tyler hasn't asked for anything since he's been out there. Reinforcements, extra supplies…nothing. And now he's saying if we don't send more ships, Vennius is going to lose. Soon."

Holsten shook his head. "It's a bad time for that news, Van."

"We've got some new ships coming out of the yards shortly, both new construction and repaired ships. Things have been quiet here. My scouts tell me the Union's gotten some of their new ships up on the line, but no more than six. And we've already put that many new battleships into service. I think we could spare a few in the short term."

"That's because you haven't heard what I came to tell you."

Striker felt his stomach tighten.

"It's the Senate, Van," Holsten continued. "Not just the Senate, but a lot of others too. Anybody remotely connected with military production is getting filthy, stinking rich…and everyone else is bleeding money and paying the taxes to support the war.

Outside the Iron Belt shipyards and mines, people want this war to be over."

"I'd like that too, Gary. So would the men and women fighting it. Dying." Striker had a sour look on his face. He wasn't a big fan of politicians, and he suspected his opinion of them was about to get worse.

"Of course, Van. Your people have done well, worked wonders even, to blunt the initial Union assault, and the price they paid was…" He paused. "I know that, and you know it too. But the civilians are tired of war, that's all they know. They're sick of casualty lists and rationing, and crushing taxes. And the politicians tell them what they want to hear."

"So, where is this going, Gary? I can't exactly will the Union forces to stand down and agree to a peace. I don't suppose any of those brilliant Senators who consider themselves such gifted diplomats have come up with a solution."

"In a manner of speaking, yes. There's a motion pending in the Senate. I've done everything I could to thwart it, including a few things that could get me prosecuted if I'm not damned careful. If I hadn't, you'd have the orders already. But I wanted to come here myself and tell you personally that they're coming. It could be a month, maybe even six, but the Senate is going to order you to go on the offensive, at the latest after you get the next big wave of reinforcements. They're convinced we haven't pressured the Union enough. They think one strong assault will be enough to bring the enemy to the bargaining table to make a peace."

"That's insane, Gary. We're no better off than they are. Maybe in eighteen months, when our higher production levels have really had an effect—and hopefully after the Grays win the Alliance Civil War and come in on our side. But now…it will be a bloodbath, and when it's over, we'll be sitting right back here where we started, with half the strength we have now."

"That may be, my friend, but you don't need to convince me. I've said everything you've just said, to anyone who would listen…and a few who wouldn't. I'm telling you, they're going to pass the resolution sooner or later, if only to look like they're doing something."

"They'll send thousands of spacers to their deaths so they can look like they're *doing something?*" The anger was keen in Striker's voice.

"You know politicians, Van."

"Yes, I know them. Sometimes I wonder if we wouldn't be best served by turning the fleet around and heading straight to Megara. Let them explain themselves to the men and women they're so ready to order to their deaths."

Holsten shook his head. "C'mon, Van. You need to be careful what you say. I understand you're angry, and I agree with you. You can say anything to me, and it won't go farther than these walls. But if the wrong person heard that kind of thing…" He took a breath. "With what's happening in the Alliance, no one in the Senate is likely to look kindly on a senior commander who sounds *too* independent."

"They can eat shit, Gary. A big steaming pile. If they want this job, they can take it and shove it so far…"

"I'm sure it felt good to say that, Van, but think it through. The Senate will order your fleet to attack, and if you bring undue suspicion on yourself, or if you argue too aggressively with their orders, they will replace you with someone more pliable." He stared right at Striker. "And there won't be a thing I can do about it. So, your fleet, your spacers, will still go into the inferno, but they'll do it under some political appointee instead of you." He paused. "Unless you're serious about starting a civil war right now."

Striker looked like he was going to argue, but he just leaned back and nodded, a sour expression on his face. Finally, he said. "I know you're right, Gary, but this is damned hard to take. You know many people we'll lose if we're forced to attack."

"Yes, Van. I know." Holsten's words were somber, almost a whisper. "And this is what puts us in a spot now. We could spare reinforcements for Barron…but not when you could be ordered to take the offensive at any time. We will need every ship we can get into space here when that happens."

Striker shook his head. "No." He paused. "Well, yes, conventional wisdom dictates we get everything we can into the line. But I don't think that's the right move."

"You want to move forward with fewer ships, less strength?"

"I don't want to move forward at all. But if I have to, what do we do? Pour everything we've got, every new ship and patched-together old wreck and push them into the furnace? It's still not going to be enough. We'll take a system, two, maybe even half a dozen. But we won't have enough strength yet to reach anything vital enough to force a peace, not before the whole thing slows down to a bloody crawl. Then we'll just be farther from Grimaldi, at the end of a long supply line through devastated systems. Even if we hold what we take, we'll be a year moving our supply bases forward."

Striker stared hard at Holsten and continued, "Meanwhile, what do we do if the Reds win in the Alliance? Tyler Barron isn't an officer who's bashful about taking on rough odds. If he says they're going to lose, they're going to lose. If the whole fleet is forward, invading the Union, what are we going to use to counter an Alliance attack? We'll be fighting for bullshit frontier planets, and Calavius and his fleet will be in Megara almost unopposed, roasting those timid politicians over a spit."

"So, what do you propose?"

"Well, the weaker we are here, at Grimaldi, perhaps the less likely the Senate will be to order an offensive."

Holsten snorted. "I hope there's more to your plan than that, because I'd hate to bank on that sort of sense prevailing. Know this, whatever you suggest…they're *going to order the assault*, whether you move a single new ship up here or not. And, if they get wind that you're not massing for an invasion, they're just going to order the new construction up here themselves."

"Not if we send the ships to Barron first. Not all the new construction, of course, but enough to make a difference…or at least give Vennius a chance. That will leave some reinforcements for us here, and the temporary diversion of significant forces to the Alliance front at least makes an argument to delay a major offensive. They wouldn't dare order Barron's ships to return. Tyler's become too much of a hero, his grandfather reborn. If the people get the impression the politicians have abandoned him…"

"That may actually work, at least for a little while, but remember, we're talking about Senators here, not sane, rational people. All they know is votes and holding on to power. But if I make sure any hint of ordering forces from the Alliance front sounds like a betrayal of Barron…"

"I'm not saying we can convince them to give up on an attack, but maybe we can gain *some* time that way. A month. Two. Anything is worthwhile."

"You may have something there." Holsten sat quietly for a few seconds. "But once they get word that we sent more battleships to the Alliance front, there will be hell to pay, at least privately."

"If anybody gives you too much trouble, you can let the word out the Senate is waffling on supporting Barron. That should scare the shit out of them, at least temporarily. Let those ships get out there, give Tyler a chance to use them. We'll warn him he's only got them for a short while. Maybe even a few months with extra force can make the difference."

"You're talking about playing rough with the Senate, my friend." Holsten had a troubled look on his face. "You know I almost took the big fall for the shit I pulled to get you named supreme commander. I slipped out of that one by a hair, Van, but you and I are in different positions. Even Senators are afraid to cross me too aggressively, for fear I've got some nasty dirt on them. The combo of Confederation Intelligence's resources and my family's money is enough to shake up even a veteran power broker. But they won't think twice about cashiering a military officer who misleads them or tries to thwart what they want. You could lose your career, Van. You could go to prison."

"You think that scares me? You think I'd miss this job? I've lost count of how many condolence letters I've written, how many funerals I've attended. I've seen almost five years of brutal warfare. I'm supposed to quake in fear because a bunch of fat, corrupt Senators might lock me away? They should live so long."

"I admire your attitude, Van. And, I agree with you…you have to know that. But don't forget, if you go down, your men and women will still have to fight this war, and if the Senate replaces you, they'll put a puppet political commander in your place. How many more of your people will die if a fool like that is in command?"

Striker could feel Holsten's comment hit home. The idea of his fleet going into a desperate fight without him, under the control of some crony admiral, sickened him. "You're right, of course. But we have no choice. We must send at least another task force to Barron. We have to do everything possible to help the Grays survive, even win. If the Reds consolidate control over an even partially intact Alliance fleet, the Confederation could be finished."

Holsten sat for a moment, clearly thinking. Finally, he said, "You're right, Van. There's no choice. But let's be smart about this. I will provide misleading information to the Senate, not you. I want you to send me reports, asking for the new ships to be sent to the front. That way, you've got cover. They can accuse you of improper use of the chain of command, or other nonsense, but you're too famous now for them to sack you over bullshit like that."

"No, Gary. Not a chance. If we do this together, we do it *together*. I'll take the same risks as you."

Holsten shook his head. "You're a good man, Van, and loyal. But you have to let me take point on buying time. First, and let's be brutally honest with each other, you're more important right now to the war effort than I am. If our people have to invade the Union, I damned sure want you leading them…and so does every officer and spacer out there. On the other hand, I've done most of what I can by now…including getting you in that admiral's uniform."

"Gary…"

"No. If you won't listen to me, think of your duty. Not to the Senate or to the chain of command, but to your fleet, to the Confederation as a whole. If we invade, even if it's doomed, we need someone in command who can make good decisions, who won't mindlessly throw our forces away on hopeless attacks."

"I understand what you're saying, but I can't let you take all the…"

"Risk? I'm not taking the risk you'll be taking. My work is less pure than yours, Van. I do many things I'm not proud of. Do you know how many files I have on key Senators? How many dirty deals I've got documents on, how many illicit lovers and illegitimate children I know about? Not to mention how many of those reprobates are in debt to one of the Holsten companies…whether they know it or not. I've bought up every note owed by any Senator, and half the cabinet ministers too. Let's see how pliable they are when loans get called and law-suits are filed to collect." He stared at Striker, a cold look in his eyes. "In battle, you are the warrior. You are ready to fight. In this type of combat, you're naked and unarmed, a sheep led to slaughter. This is my battlefield, Van. You are going to be sent into the Union, no matter what we do, and probably before any ships sent to Barron return. You will face danger, you will have to use your wits to avoid disaster. *That* is your fight. *This* is my battle. Let me fight it."

Striker sat quietly, wrestling with his thoughts. Everything Holsten had said made perfect sense. He knew it was all true. But it still felt too much like abandoning an ally. A friend. Finally, he just nodded and rasped out a soft, "Okay."

"Good." Holsten sighed. "I'd love to give enough to Bar-ron to ensure a Gray victory, but we just don't have the strength for that. If we don't send any of the new construction at all up here, and you're ordered to attack anyway, your people won't stand a chance."

"We'll send him a strong task force. There are two more of the new *Repulse*-class battleships launching at Vandellar, along with two older ships, just fully repaired and out of spacedock. I can spare those, and still assemble enough here at least to avoid disaster if we're ordered to launch an offensive." A pause. "And let's hope Tyler Barron pulls another victory from the jaws of defeat. An invasion would have a lot better chance of suc-cess with his ships, and an expeditionary force from Vennius, attached to it."

"Very well. It is decided. We will send four more battleships to the Rim, and I will do everything possible to delay the orders for you to attack. And when those orders come—and they *will* come—you will move as slowly as you can, do everything possible to reduce losses."

Striker nodded, and then he said what he knew they were both thinking. "And we will pray that Tyler Barron manages to succeed out there. Somehow."

Chapter Twenty-Five

"I have summoned you all here for one reason: to make history. Today, we begin the final offensive. Today, we lay the cornerstone of a new Alliance, rededicated to the ideals of our founders, to the spirit that led the descendants of slaves to strike out and destroy their former oppressors. Too much has been lost over the decades, and now we shall reclaim it all in one glorious battle. At long last, we will launch another assault against the traitors' stronghold at Sentinel-2."

Lille sat and listened to Calavius speak. He hadn't considered the Imperator to be a gifted orator, but he had to admit, the fool had done a credible job. He wondered if Calavius spoke his own words or if he'd had someone write them for him.

The assault Calavius was about to order was the end result of all Lille's planning, the fruition of his plan to bring the Alliance into the war against the Confederation. Gaston Villieneuve, Lille's superior and the closest thing he had to a friend, had approved the operation, though Lille knew the head of Sector Nine had harbored serious doubts. No doubt, Villieneuve had other stratagems in the works, ways to stave off inevitable defeat at the hands of the Confederation's greater production. But success here, a new enemy slicing through the enemy's weakest frontier, would almost ensure victory.

"You are Palatian warriors, and I know that you will fight at Sentinel-2 with your customary zeal...no, with more, with unmatched ferocity. For this final battle shall win us the war. The future."

He definitely had someone write this for him...

No mention of the two battles he lost at Sentinel-2. Or that the enemy in this case are also Palatian warriors, likely to fight like cornered animals.

Lille was optimistic, at least as much as he ever allowed himself to be. But he was still cautious. Calavius had many advantages; numerical superiority, certainly, and the ability to choose the time and method of the attack. But Vennius would be defending, and his men and women would know they were fighting for their lives. They would resist to the death.

Lille had cautiously suggested that Calavius offer an amnesty to the crews of any of Vennius's ships that stood down in the battle. He knew it was wishful thinking, that few Palatians would choose a path they viewed as so dishonorable, but every ship he could save was that much more strength to attack the Confeds. A bloodbath in Sentinel-2, a Pyrrhic victory that destroyed the new Imperator's fleet, would cut the legs out from Lille's plan.

"Step forward, Commander-Altum Battarus." Calavius had been droning on the entire time Lille had drifted off into his own thoughts. But the mention of Battarus jerked the Union operative back to focus. The officer was difficult to handle, easily provoked, and a man he knew Calavius disliked. But Battarus was also powerful and influential. *If Calavius picks a fight here...*

"I hereby relieve you of your rank of commander-altum." Calavius's words echoed slightly in the large, and now silent, chamber.

Lille tensed up. *If Battarus rebels, declares for Vennius...*

"This battle will set the course of history for centuries to come, and the tactical command of our forces cannot be trusted to simply a fleet commander, one among equals. Though I shall accompany the grand fleet as Imperator, you, Kellus Battarus, shall exercise the tactical command. The rank of Commander-Magnus has been stained by treason, and has remained vacant until this moment. I trust you will wash it clean with your own honor and the victory I have no doubt awaits us. Rise Commander-Magnus Battarus. Come forward now, swear your allegiance once again, and accept this rank as the highest of our commanders, and the leader of our military."

Lille watched, surprised again at Calavius's ability to occasionally pull tactical brilliance out of his bag that seemed mostly filled with foolishness and egotism. Calavius didn't like Battarus, that Lille knew for sure, nor did he really trust the man. For that matter, Lille didn't either. But there was more at stake here, and the new Commander Magnus brought many advantages with him. He was a capable commander, one with a strong history of victory, and he was universally respected in the military, something Calavius couldn't claim for himself. Lille had even considered Battarus as the prime mover in his plan, but he'd been uncertain the officer would prove to be corrupt enough to go for it.

"I thank you, Your Supremacy. I am honored…and somewhat stunned." He stepped forward, toward Calavius's massive chair. "I accept, with all my heart, and I swear to uphold the principles of the Alliance, and to defend it with the last of my strength." He knelt down in the proper form, holding still as Calavius reached out and put his hand on the officer's head.

Lille watched, suspecting Battarus hadn't given Calavius exactly what he'd wanted. The officer's words were correct, the proper form for an Alliance warrior accepting a promotion to the highest levels, but Lille was pretty sure Calavius had been hoping for a more personal oath of loyalty.

He's boxed himself in now. He can't come out and demand it, nor can he go back on his decision.

"Rise, Commander-Magnus." Calavius stood himself, and he extended his arms out toward the gathered warriors. "I give you all Commander-Magnus Battarus."

The assembled warriors cheered—a bit too loudly, Lille

suspected. His eyes were on Calavius, on the subtleties in the Imperator's expression. They were details most warriors would miss, but a trained Sector Nine operative did not. Calavius resented every cheer. He had done what he felt he had to do... but Lille could see he didn't like it.

He didn't like it one bit.

*   *   *

Jovi Grachus sat on her cot, looking through a small box. It contained trinkets from her youth, mostly. There was a small tablet, full of photos taken on the Rigellus estate, dozens of images of her with Kat Rigellus, from the time they were babies to the day Grachus had left for flight school.

It was odd, looking at her life that way, remembrances of so much that was gone. Old staff members from the estate. Scallus, the cook, who'd seemed ancient to her then but had lasted another twenty years, even outliving Kat. Wargus, the gamekeeper, who'd taken a liking to her, and showed her remote sections of the estate few had seen. Even Kat had never known about those trips.

By any reasonable measurement, her life was better now. She had achieved rank beyond the loftiest she'd ever dreamed, her family's sins washed away by the stroke of the Imperator's pen. She even had her own estate now, granted by imperial decree. It was small, nothing like the staggering vastness of the Rigellus lands, but it was hers, and that was something she'd never thought possible. She hadn't seen it, and in her gut, she knew there was a good chance she never would, but it was something, at least, to leave to her child. *Assuming he isn't destroyed along with his father's family...*

Still, she found herself longing for much that was gone. Her friend, of course, but also those long past days, the cool lakes and streams of the inland sections of the estate, and the rocky coastline farther east. Nights when she and Kat snuck out and went exploring, finding their way in the dark, guided only by moonlight. Her life then had been troubled, at least on paper, but in reality, there had been happiness, simple joy.

Grachus had always been fearless. Now, she wondered if that courage came as much from having so little to lose, even to live for. It was a feeling that had only increased with Kat's death. Now, she found she wanted to live, to see the lands she'd been granted, to stand before the Imperator and petition for her son to become hers again, removed legally from the disgrace of his father's family and their support of the pretender.

Part of her wanted to give up the obsessive hunt. After all, no vengeance would return her friend to her. But that wasn't possible. She was who she was, and she owed her lost companion something greater than returning to her newly-gained estate. She *had* to have her vengeance, still the restless demon inside, before she could go on. Before she could live a real life.

She flipped through the small pile of old items, each with its own memories attached, but even as she drifted back, the present called to her. She was determined to finish things… but she was scared too. This Confederation pilot, Stockton… he was her equal, a match for her in battle. She knew the next time they met—at Sentinel-2, no doubt—they would finish their business. Either she would defeat him, and lead her squadrons against *Dauntless* to complete her vengeance, or she would lose. She would die.

Either way, it will soon be over.

She found that thought a relief, despite the uncertainty at its core. She had been hunting for so long, and now she was exhausted. She wanted victory, revenge. But mostly, she needed the whole thing to end. She needed rest, quiet…even if that quiet was the icy silence of death.

*   *   *

"I am displeased, Minister Lille."

"Displeased? I do not understand. Things appear to be moving well to fruition. Preparations for the final offensive continue on schedule. Soon, you will be the uncontested leader of the Alliance." Lille was rarely caught by surprise, but Calavius's words were unexpected.

"It is not the military preparations that concern me, nor the expected results of the campaign—though I would caution you, Minister, about your choice of words. I am *already* the uncontested ruler of the Alliance. You will exercise care before you accord legitimacy to a traitor and a rebel."

"I will do so in the future. I meant no disrespect." Lille didn't like the resentment in Calavius's tone. And he noticed the use of the word "ruler," a designation no Alliance Imperator had ever claimed. "If I may ask, then, with what are you displeased?"

"I am displeased with you, Minister." Calavius glared at him.

"May I ask why?" Lille suppressed his anger. *You'd still be following Vennius around, groping in the darkness of his shadow but for me.*

"I asked you to complete a task for me, and to my knowledge it has not been done. I trusted you to create an internal security agency for me, one patterned after your own Sector Nine. Yet, here we are, and nothing has been done."

"That is not true. Much has been done." Lille paused, amazed for about the thousandth time how naïve the Alliance warriors could be about espionage and statecraft. "Sector Nine itself arose over a period of years, decades even, from the partisan groups that founded the Union. And it took even longer for it to develop into its current form. Such things require care, the creation of training and monitoring programs, the imposition of systems for surveillance and counter-surveillance." He paused, unsure how much he wanted to say. "You would not want me to rush such things. The last thing you want is an organization like Sector Nine that you do not completely control." *Or that I do not control…*

"I understand your caution, Minister, but surely you are aware that time is quite sensitive. The prospect of imminent battle holds my officers together, but once the pretender is destroyed…" Calavius paused. "I seek to create a better Alliance, one with stronger leadership. There will no doubt be… resistance. We must be ready to deal with it."

Lille's anger subsided, and now he found himself fighting to hold back a smile. *What an eager totalitarian you've created…*

"I understand your concerns, and I agree with them. But if you rush this project, you will create a danger greater than that posed by any of your commanders. I will expedite things, but I strongly urge caution. We will get there, and when we do you will have a highly efficient organization answerable only to you." *And me.*

"What you say makes sense, but I am still concerned about rooting out any resistance after Vennius is destroyed."

Lille nodded. "Here is my suggestion. I will expedite things as much as I can and still provide reasonable assurances that the agency remains controllable. For your part, make a list, perhaps of the four or five highest ranking officers about whom you are concerned. Any serious trouble is likely to come from them, and a small group will be easier to keep under surveillance. Then, as we further develop the agency, we can add more names, expand the range of operations."

Calavius's face had lost its angry expression. He looked down at Lille and said, "Yes, Minister. Let us proceed as you suggest." He paused, and Lille could see there was something else. "However, I must insist that you have at least some of the agency in operation before the fleet departs." Another pause. "There is one job that cannot wait."

Lille suddenly understood, and the source of Calavius's earlier tension became clear.

"I would like a team to keep Commander Battarus under constant surveillance, Minister." There was another pause, an ominous one this time. "And I would like to ensure that he does not return from the glorious victory." He stared right at Lille. "Do you think you can arrange that for me, Minister?"

Chapter Twenty-Six

Fortress Sentinel-2
Orbiting Planet Varena, Cilian System
Year 62 (311 AC)

"You didn't have to come, you know. The orders were addressed to me, not you." Stockton sat in the shuttle, waiting for the doors to open. "And since you're here, you should put on your launch control hat right now…it's taking these fools far too long to get this shuttle secured. I know they're not combat pilots, but do you enforce any standards at all in the shuttle corps?" His words were coarse, not at all the way he liked to speak to Stara Sinclair. He knew that as they left his mouth. He was angry with himself for treating her badly, for making her suffer for things that had nothing to do with her. But that self-hatred would have to wait, to take its place behind the rage and anger and loathing he felt for himself. For failing to get there in time, failing to save Kyle Jamison.

He knew part of his acting out was an attempt to drive Stara away, at least a subconscious one. He loved her, he was certain about that, but neither did he doubt that all he would bring her in the end was sorrow and pain. He'd lost pilots before, friends. But Kyle Jamison's death had him focused on the true nature of what he did. Pilots died, and the grim career survival statistics in wartime highlighted just how dark a picture it was. They *existed* to die, to sacrifice themselves to save the massive battleships and their crews.

His ego had always resisted the notion that he would be killed in combat one day, despite the odds, despite the fact that *Dauntless* had been in some of the toughest spots again and again. He'd recognized the possibility of course, but now he realized he'd never truly believed it. Jamison's death had changed all that. This enemy pilot, the one who had taken his friend, had stolen his casual confidence. He might very well lose the matchup he knew was coming, but that wasn't going to stop him from hunting down Jamison's killer…no matter what anyone did or said to stop him. He would avenge his friend, or he would die in the attempt. There was no other option, none he could accept.

"We lost our best shuttle pilots to combat training. The fleet is trying to replace losses anyway they can, so all we've got now are rookies." Sinclair's voice was tight, controlled. She was clearly suppressing her own fiery temper, holding back the anger she would normally have thrown at Stockton for speaking to her as he had.

Stockton was almost disappointed she hadn't taken the bait. He didn't want any relationships. No anchors. He would avenge his friend, or he would die in the attempt. Jake Stockton no longer existed, save as the memory of a fool who thought he could be both a man and the angel of death.

"Stara…" He turned and looked at her. "The Commodore wants to see me…I'm perfectly capable of attending that meeting without a minder." He wanted her to go away, to leave him to his misery. She was trying to help, he understood that, but her kindness mocked him, and her soft, caring words clawed at his ears. He wasn't fit to deal with others, and certainly not her.

He could see in her expression that he'd hurt her, but he also knew she'd never admit it, nor even give him the satisfaction of angrily lashing out. "Fine," she said simply, clearly making a herculean effort to keep the emotion from her voice. "I'll see to prepping the shuttle for the return trip. Unless you plan to float back."

"Thank you," he said, trying to soften his tone, with somewhat mixed success.

He turned away and walked across the bay, toward the lift doors, stepping inside as they opened. He made his way as he'd been directed, to the office Barron had been using when aboard the massive station. A pair of Marines stood outside the door, at rigid attention. Probably posing for the Alliance officers. Any Palatian commander worth his salt had guards posted at his door, as much a sign of rank and status as a true security measure. *Though with all the talk of traitors on Sentinel-2…*

"Commander Stockton," he said to the Marine with sergeant's stripes. "Commodore Barron sent for me."

"Yes, Commander. We have orders to admit you at once." The bulky Marine moved to the side as the door opened.

Stockton stepped inside. The room was large, with a high ceiling, certainly a bit of plush luxury in the usually cramped confines of a spaceship or space station. *No doubt the Alliance is trying to impress the cap…commodore.* Barron was seated at a desk on the far side, his face focused on one of the three screens.

Barron remained where he was for perhaps fifteen seconds more. Then he looked up and saw Stockton.

"Oh, Jake…please, come in." He stood up, moving around the table and interrupting Stockton's clumsy attempt at a salute with an outstretched hand. "No salutes, not now. Let's just talk, two old comrades. Friends." He gestured toward one of the guest chairs as he returned to his own seat.

Stockton hesitated for a few seconds. Then he replied, "Thank you, sir." He sat down, looking rather uncomfortable, he suspected.

"Jake, there are no words. I grieve with you. Kyle Jamison was an extraordinary man, and no one will ever replace him."

"No, sir. No one could *ever* take his place."

Barron let out a breath, suddenly looking uncomfortable himself. "Nevertheless, I *do* have to replace him." He paused. "It's perhaps the hardest part of command, but mourning friends is a luxury…and keeping *Dauntless* at full combat readiness is a necessity."

"Yes, sir…I understand." He did, too, at least intellectually.

But he was glad he didn't have to worry about picking someone to fill Jamison's shoes so soon.

"I'm glad to hear you say that, Commander. Because there is only one choice for the job in my mind—and Commander Travis agrees."

Stockton hadn't been entirely focused on the subject, but suddenly his stomach tightened. He'd had no idea what Barron was suggesting...until suddenly it hit him. "Sir, I..."

"I need you to take over the strike force command, Jake. *Dauntless* needs you."

"Commodore, I'm honored, I really am, but I can't. I just can't."

Barron took a deep breath and exhaled. "You have to, Jake. You know it."

"I can't, Commodore. I just can't watch more of them die, not while executing my commands. Ice, Typhoon, Thunder... and dozens of others. All gone."

"And how many more will die if I have to appoint someone less qualified, less capable? Yes, pilots will die under you if you're strike force commander...but how many might live, who would otherwise have died? You know it in your heart, Jake. And you know this is how Kyle would have wanted it."

The last sentence hit Stockton like a sledgehammer. How could he refuse now? He couldn't even lie to himself. Kyle *would have* wanted him to have the job. He'd said as much.

"Sir, I'm not command material. A squadron, yes, but the whole strike force?" But even as he still argued, he knew it was over. Barron had cornered him, the instant he'd brought Jamison into it.

"I have known few men who are more fit for command than you, Commander. You may be a bit unorthodox, but you have what it takes." He paused. "Consider yourself strike force commander, effective immediately. I will let you announce it to the pilots, but if you want me to say something to them, you only have to ask."

"Yes, sir," Stockton said, trying to hide the despair he felt. With little success, he knew.

He took a deep, ragged breath. He would do what Barron had commanded. He would lead the squadrons the best he could. But he would still hunt down that pilot. He would still blast Jamison's killer into dust.

Or end up dust himself.

*   *   *

"Thank you for seeing me on such short notice. I wanted to discuss…"

"You wanted to discuss Commander Tulus. I could see you were distressed from the start of this whole sorry affair, Commodore Barron, though I must confess to some surprise. Tulus gave you nothing but grief. I would have thought you'd find his treason easy to believe." Vennius's tone was somber. It was clear he was still upset by the whole business.

"That is true. Vian Tulus did not easily accept me, but we came together in battle. Tulus came to me, sought my forgiveness, confessed his error. It takes a man of strength and honor to behave that way. We came to know each other rather well on the journey back. Though I do not use this term lightly, and almost never on those of such short acquaintance, I came to call him my friend."

"You're a good man, Commodore. You and I made our way through our differences as well, to something I daresay is also friendship. Vian Tulus was my comrade through many battles. I do not easily accept his treason…but I do accept it. The evidence is damning, and Tulus has offered no defense. There were only six of you in that room, assuming we can all agree that I, myself, am not sabotaging my own cause. The Union is your enemy, and they back Calavius, which places you beyond suspicion… So, who then? Longinus turned up no evidence pointing to anyone else. And Tulus contacted Palatia just before he departed." Vennius looked down, a sad look coming over his face. "I executed the death warrant this morning. We must make an example of him, and there can be no other punishment for betrayal, no thought of mercy."

Barron shifted back and forth on his feet. He couldn't challenge Vennius's decision, and he had no argument to make, save he simply didn't believe Tulus was guilty. *But a death sentence, so quickly?* "Sir…"

"Not now, Commodore. I know you find it difficult to accept this sorry incident. But there is no arguing with the facts." A short pause. "And we have no time to discuss this further now. I have more important matters to speak of to you."

Barron's head snapped up, his eyes finding Vennius's. He had no idea what the Imperator was talking about.

"You know, Commodore, that I also have my sources in the enemy camp. Though they are sadly less well-placed than Calavius's was, they are still useful. I have received intelligence reports. Calavius's forces are on the move, massing for a major attack."

"Sentinel-2?"

"Yes." Barron suddenly fully heard the fatigue in the Imperator's voice. "He is planning to end the war in a single massive battle…and he will succeed. I am too old a soldier to lie to myself. My people will fight with great courage, I have no doubt of that. But the mathematics of war will assert themselves." He looked up. "Even the new Confederation ships you haven't told me about yet will be insufficient to alter that reality."

Barron shook his head slowly. Vennius never ceased to surprise him. He'd only gotten the communique from Striker hours before, and he'd planned to tell the Imperator as soon as he'd made his plea for Tulus. *But clearly there is no need…*

"Yes, sir…four more battleships, two of the new ones, and two older ones, of similar specifications to *Dauntless*."

"Very few ships are similar to that battleship of yours, Commodore."

Barron had to hold back a smile. He didn't particularly care for personal praise, but kudos directed to his crew and his ship—and though he would soon command a fleet of seven battleships, *Dauntless* would always be *his*—were a weakness.

"Thank you, sir. But if Calavius has managed to consolidate control over the rest of the Alliance fleet, you are right. Even my reinforcements will be inadequate."

"You strike at the heart of it, Commodore. I have considered every tactic I know. Unless Calavius's forces fight very poorly—and they are Alliance warriors all, so that is a very unlikely scenario—we are doomed." He paused. "I do not say what I am about to say to impugn your honor in any way, my friend, nor to suggest that the desperation of our plight is too much for you. But, perhaps you should lead your ships back to Confederation space, Tyler. The help is welcome, and greatly appreciated, but if they cannot make the difference, keeping them in the line is little better than throwing them away. You may find them better utilized to begin building a defense against Calavius's ultimate invasion of the Confederation."

Barron bristled at the idea of running off and leaving his ally. If anyone else had said the words, he'd have been offended. But he knew Vennius was only speaking the truth. Tactically, strategically...it made no sense to throw his ships away, and especially not when their loss would leave the Rim frontier naked to invasion.

"I will not leave you, Tarkus. Not while you draw breath or a single ship remains under your flag."

"I have begun to suspect your parentage, my friend. You grandfather's renown of course preceded you here, but I have become convinced there is Palatian blood in you somehow. You have the true spirit of a warrior, my friend, but I must repeat—there is nothing to be gained by the loss of your fleet. And if you remain here, alongside my ships, you will only succeed in being overwhelmed."

Barron opened his mouth, but then he closed it. There was an idea, a wild, crazy gambit, one he'd tried to discount. But it grew despite his efforts, and as it did, in those few seconds of silence, he became convinced. It was the way out, the desperate gamble that offered at least some scant hope of success. Of victory.

"Calavius achieved his dominant position because he has Palatia, because he dominates all the communications lines emanating from there, correct? That is how he was able to discredit you, to spread propaganda and rally the other commanders to his cause."

"Yes. He knew that, of course, which was why his resources were all deployed in the capital. That's why it's taken him so long to consolidate. He was able to use his control of communications to discredit me, to rally fleet units to his side, but it took much longer for him to get truly loyal followers in position from Palatia."

"So, if you'd been able to hold Palatia, you would likely have the upper hand now?"

"If I had been able to hold Palatia, this entire sorry affair would have been over before it began, and Calavius would be a dead traitor instead of a victorious usurper." Vennius looked confused. "But what does that have to do with our current situation? I was barely able to *escape* from Palatia. Holding the planet would have been impossible."

"I wasn't talking about what has already passed."

Vennius stared back. "So, what are you proposing?"

"That we take it back."

Vennius's gazed was fixed on Barron for a few seconds. Then he leaned back and let out a deep laugh. "This is no time for humor, my friend, but it has been long since I've laughed."

"I intended no humor." Barron's stare was cold, his voice firm. "I am deadly serious. I propose that I lead my fleet there, that I take control of the planet, and we retask the communications networks to get your message out. No doubt it is too late to persuade everyone, but I have no doubt there are officers out there prepared to believe what you say...if only they can hear it. They are operating on one side's story only. Perhaps we can change that."

"Tyler, that's impossible. First, an attack force would have to consist of Alliance forces. If a foreign fleet attacked the capital, everyone there would fight to the death...children, the old and infirm. Even the dying in the hospitals would rise from their beds to fight a foreign invader. But all of that is moot, because we don't have the capacity to launch such a strike. Calavius has taken the better part of a year to mass his superior forces against

Sentinel-2. You would have us attack an even stronger target with less than one third the ships he will hurl at us here?" Vennius paused, looking as though in spite of all he'd said, he was considering what Barron had proposed. "No, it's just not possible. Even apart from the massive fleet units stationed there, Palatia's orbital defenses are massive. Attacking battleships would be destroyed before they could close to attack range."

"Alliance battleships would be destroyed." Barron waited, watching as the dawn of understanding appeared in Vennius's gaze. "Palatia's defenses outrange your battleships' guns, not mine. I'd wager my primaries can hit those orbital platforms before they can fire. If I'm right, we can chop them all to scrap before they even get a shot at us." He stared right at Vennius. "And with your Alliance ships massed here, giving all signs to any remaining spies that you are preparing a last-ditch defense, Calavius will come here with all he has to finish this thing between you. He will leave Palatia lightly defended. In his arrogance, he will never imagine that we would make such a bold strike. We can surprise him, and take Palatia by a coup de main."

Vennius didn't say anything for a long while. He just looked back at Barron, as if he was struggling to wrap his head around all he had heard. Finally, he nodded. "I considered every plan I could conceive, my friend, even ordering battleships to make suicide runs. But your bit of pure audacity never occurred to me. It's insanity, a wild gamble...but it offers us something no other strategy can. A chance."

"Then, you will give the authorization?"

"Yes." Vennius paused. "Though never in my life did I imagine I would ever allow, even aid, a foreign force to take the capital." Another hesitation. "I will have to keep most of my ships here to maintain the deception, and to lure Calavius in... but you will have to have an Alliance contingent with you. If you send Confederation Marines down alone to seize key objectives, they will face fanatical resistance at every turn. This must be a joint operation. You must have Alliance troopers with you. It is the only way."

Barron nodded. "I agree."

Vennius looked down, frowning suddenly. "But how will we explain the disappearance of your ships? Calavius's spies will surely be watching them. As arrogant a fool as he is, he surely knows by now how capable your vessels are in a fight."

"That is the simplest part of the plan, my friend." Barron smiled. "We will use Calavius's arrogance against him. We will employ the stratagem you, yourself, suggested."

Vennius look at Barron, confused.

"My ships will leave. Defeat here is assured, and we have a border to protect. My forces will withdraw through the transit point leading toward home, then we will double back and set a course for Palatia. Calavius will assume we have abandoned you, and he will be even more eager to finish things…and more assured of success."

Vennius nodded, a big smile on his face. "Brilliant, my friend. Just brilliant." He took a breath. "I never expected to be at such long odds that so desperate a plan would seem like salvation. But we are where we are." Another pause. "By all means, Commodore. Put your preparations in motion."

Barron nodded. "Yes, sir…" He hesitated. "I have one request…"

"Anything, Tyler. What do you want?"

"I want to see Vian Tulus. I want to see if I can convince him to explain his communication."

Vennius frowned. "Your faith in a comrade does you proud, my friend. But…"

Barron waited, but Vennius's words died out, and none followed. "Sir, just allow me to see him one time. There is little to lose, and it is all I ask from you."

"Very well," Vennius said, still not sounding happy about it. "I will make the arrangements for you to speak privately with the trai…with Tulus." A few seconds later: "I hope you understand how this will look, Tyler, how much blowback I will get from my officers."

Barron smiled. "It's a good thing you're the Imperator then, isn't it?"

Chapter Twenty-Seven

Captain's Log, Andromeda Lafarge, Free Trader Pegasus

We are approaching our destination, I am sure of it. I have reviewed the data and plotted the system three times. I cannot say if we will find the treasure that we seek, for I have seen too many journeys end in frustration.

I have tried to remain focused on our expedition, but my thoughts continue to drift to the devastated site we found. Though I still have no convincing evidence to support my conclusions, I am more certain than ever that what we saw were the remains of a Union operation.

I know their efforts might have been as fruitless as mine may yet prove to be, but my gut tells me otherwise. The scope of the operation, the vastness of the resources deployed—at a time when they have little, if any, to spare—speak of a well-founded lead. I have become convinced they have found something significant, something dangerous.

A weapon. One that can be used against the Confederation fleet. Against *Dauntless*.

Against Tyler.

Unknown World
Uncharted System
Deep in the Badlands
Year 311 AC

"Right here. The readings center on this spot here." Andi Lafarge was standing in the stark, harsh sun of the small planet that lay at the end of her quest. She'd ID'd the system correctly, she was sure enough about that. She was where she was supposed to be, so now the only question was if her intel was worth the coin she'd paid for it. And the scanner readings suggested a big "yes" as the answer to that question.

"You're right...my scanner says the same thing. There is something." Merrick was about ten feet away, squinting in the brightness as he looked back at her. "We should dig here."

"Ross," Andi shouted, looking in the direction where the rest of her crew was gathered. Ross Tarren was closest, and since she'd rushed out of *Pegasus* without any comm gear, he was her default contact. "Start unloading the excavation gear, and get it over here."

"Will do, Andi." Tarren waved an acknowledgement to accompany his shouted reply, and then he turned and jogged back toward *Pegasus*, waving and yelling to the other crew members as he did.

Lafarge didn't like landing her ship, not on barely-explored planets where her data on such things like gravitation, weather, and atmospheric consistency was all rough and hastily-assembled. Bringing a ship down was always a rugged ride, one where many problems that never showed up in spaceflight tended to appear. Nevertheless, it was an occupational hazard. *Pegasus* had a lifeboat of sorts, a small gig that was capable of planetary landings, but it was far from large enough to carry any meaningful amount of equipment, and the items Andi and her crew sought tended to be buried under tons of dirt and rocks.

"I'm getting more than the materials readings, Vig. Some kind of background energy or something too."

"We did a very quick planetary scan, Andi. Our information is spotty at best. This could be anything, radioactives in the crust, the effect of the primary in this atmosphere…"

"True enough, except it's localized. Right where we're about to dig."

Merrick adjusted his scanner, directing it to the spot Andi mentioned. Then he looked up at her. "You don't think this thing could be *operational*, do you? Is that even possible?"

She shook her head. "I seriously doubt that." She paused, staring at the ground. "But you know what it could be? Antimatter decay. Maybe this thing's got one of those canisters to power it."

"If there was an antimatter leak, this entire valley would be a crater."

"Not a leak. But even those storage containers on the planet killer lost a tiny amount of antimatter each year. Not enough to cause a rupture or other damage, but something detectable, a few atoms here and there."

"If you're right, we'd better…"

"Be damned careful where we dig. If we rupture an antimatter storage unit, we'll be blasted to subatomic particles before we realize we've done anything." She looked at Vig, and then behind her, where the others were approaching with a fully loaded grav sled.

"Damned careful is right, Andi."

*   *   *

"We're clear, Andi."

Lafarge let out a deep breath. She felt like she'd been sweating bullets for the last two days, going through each moment as if cataclysm might accompany the next.

"Let's establish orbit, Vig." She wanted nothing more than to blast away at full for home, but she felt she had to wait…and make sure her charges went off.

The readings she'd detected had been a canister of antimatter, the primary fuel for old tech devices. She'd been wildly excited when she first saw it...until she realized it was damaged. The leakage had been minimal so far, but she realized that could change at any moment. She'd asked Lex Righter to take a look, and his ashen face gave her the answer before he spoke a word.

She'd considered taking a chance, loading the canister aboard *Pegasus* and blasting for the Confederation. This find she would keep, parceling off the precious antimatter on the black market, a source of massive wealth for her and her people. She would be as rich as Hephaeseus's most powerful magnates, richer even. But then reality hit her.

"I wouldn't move it," Righter had said. "In fact—and this is assuming we don't just turn and get the hell out of here right now—I would dig around the other side of the device and pull it out that way. I would give the canister as much room as possible. I can only guess, but if we move this thing, put it in the hold, I doubt we've got one chance in four of making it home."

She'd heeded his advice—what she also knew to be the right choice—but it had taken her a while. Finding one cache of antimatter was extraordinary enough, and losing it had been painful. But a second time? She'd tried to convince herself they could do it. They could extract it slowly, pack it carefully, but in the end, she realized that would be a wild gamble with her crew's lives, and worst of all, a bad bet. She was no coward, but the chances she took were measured, calculated.

"How long, Vig?"

"About half a minute, Andi."

She just nodded. The charges had been her idea. If she couldn't take the antimatter, she couldn't leave it behind either, not with Union ships prowling around. No, if she couldn't bring it back—and she couldn't even disturb it or bury it again—there was only one choice. She had to destroy it.

That was easy enough. All she had to do was rupture a container that was barely still holding together. The first significant quantity of antimatter that escaped would vaporize the canister, and in microseconds, the entire thing would go. The explosion would be titanic, though she knew for all her ability to calculate the gigatons of energy released, she couldn't really imagine what something like that would look like…or what it would do to the planet.

The world was uninhabited, though. People had lived there once, but they'd failed to survive the strife known now as the Cataclysm. Whether they'd been blasted from space or wiped out by chemical weapons, they were long gone. Still, it felt strange to unleash such hell on a habitable planet.

"Three, two, one…" Vig's tone suggested he felt similarly. Not regretful, exactly, but there was something eerie about it. Haunted.

She watched as the scanners went wild, the energy readings soaring, the gauges all maxing out. It was done. The peaceful valley where she and her people had landed, where they had dug up their cargo…it was gone now, turned into a radioactive nightmare.

All so there's no chance the Union ends up with that antimatter…

Lafarge felt a pang of regret that she hadn't decided to risk the transport. But it only lasted a moment. She knew she'd made the right decision. Besides, she wasn't going home empty handed, not even close. She'd found what she'd originally come for, and to her cursory inspection, while not operable, it didn't seem to be in bad shape. It was a massive find, a discovery of immense importance and value.

She felt another impulse, a shadowy one from deep inside, an urge to hide it, to keep it until she could find the highest bidder. But she knew she couldn't do that, not with the Confederation at war, and worse, in serious danger of defeat. Not with the Union out there, possibly with a find of their own, one that, from the looks of their expedition, was vastly larger than what her people had found.

No, there was no choice. She would demand a much higher price than her people had gotten last time, but she would bring the thing to Admiral Striker.

"All right, Vig, we did what we had to do here. Take us to Grimaldi, and I do mean with every bit of speed you can coax from the old girl. I have a feeling this thing is important, and we could still very well run into Union ships out here."

Chapter Twenty-Eight

"I consider myself a good judge of character, and in your case, I am not blinded by long friendship and shared memories. You detested me until a few weeks ago, and you took every chance to let me know that. Before we found our common ground, I considered you a pompous ass." Barron sat on a small metal chair in the cell, looking across the meter and a half to where Tulus was perched on his spare-looking bed.

"That may be the worst job of cheering up a prisoner I've ever heard."

"I'm not trying to cheer you up. I'm trying to find out why you won't save yourself. Because, I'd bet my left arm you're not the traitor."

"I am not," Tulus said, matter-of-factly.

"So, why won't you explain what you were doing with the transmission? You have to understand how damning that looks."

Tulus didn't answer. He just sat and looked back at Barron.

"Vian, this is insane. If there is an explanation, you have to give it to Vennius."

"I cannot."

Barron was frustrated. "For God's sake, why not?"

No response.

"Vian, I swear I am not leaving this cell until you tell me what you're hiding." That was a bluff. Vennius had agreed to let him see Tulus, but only for thirty minutes. And he was running out of time.

"Just go, Tyler. You have much to do to prepare for what is to come. Your people need you. Forget about me."

"You dishonor me, Vian." Barron countered with an Alliance-type attack.

"No, my friend. I respect you and all your people. I was wrong before, and I wish you only the best."

"Words are easy. But you do not trust me with your secret. You will not tell me who you were contacting or why."

"It is a personal matter…" Tulus paused. "I cannot elaborate. It is…it would bring shame on my family."

"More shame than you being wrongfully branded a traitor and executed?"

Tulus shifted uncomfortably. "It is difficult to speak of…"

"There is no one else here but us, Vian. The Imperator swore to me that nothing we discussed would be recorded."

"I was sending a message to…a woman."

"A lover? Trapped on Palatia?" Barron hadn't known what to expect, but this definitely wasn't it.

Tulus was silent for a moment. "A lover yes, but more." He hesitated again. "She is the mother of my children."

"You have children? I was told…"

"As far as anyone knows, I do not. Many years ago, my father bade me to engage in matches he arranged, noble mates worthy of the Tullii. But I was in love with a woman…" He paused again. "A Pleb woman." He said the words as if admitting a mortal sin. "I refused other matches and saw her in secret. In time, she became pregnant. Then, several years later, we had a second child. I have a secret family, one no one can know of. My father demanded I have children, a new generation to carry on the traditions of the Tullii…and I could never tell him he already had grandchildren." He paused. "I know it was foolish to contact Palatia, but I was fearful. I had not heard any news of them since the civil war began. I just…had to know that they were alive, that no one had discovered who they were."

"So, you had children with a woman of lower rank. It's not the worst thing anyone has ever done." Barron still had trouble getting used to Alliance courtship rituals. He wasn't aware of another human society that had done away with concepts like marriage entirely, replacing them with a slavish devotion to matching bloodlines and genetic profiles.

"You know many of our ways, Tyler, but not all. You cannot grasp what it is to be a Palatian Patrician of the highest rank. The obligation, the demands. What I did shamed my family. If I had been discovered, my career would have been destroyed. While my father still lived, he would have disowned me, cast me from the Tullii."

"So, you kept it a secret. All these years."

"Yes. She understands. She has understood all along… and I have been able to filter sufficient assets to ensure her and the children—and the rest of her family—a good life." Tulus looked down at the floor, taking a deep breath. "You must understand, Tyler. If this became public, there would be repercussions beyond my shame. It is illegal for a Pleb to bear the children of a Patrician. Plebs can be mistresses, of course, but nothing more. She would be arrested, my children taken by the state, sent to a work facility."

Barron shook his head. He'd come to admire much about Alliance culture, but this was a reminder of the cost his warrior comrades paid to be what they were. It was terrible, and it repelled his Confederation sensibilities.

"You will be condemned for treason to avoid exposing them? You will die at the executioner's hand?"

"I am a Palatian warrior, Tyler, or at least I was. I do not fear death."

"To die in the line of duty, in battle fighting for your people, this I understand. But this way?"

"There is no choice, my friend."

"This is bullshit." Barron shook his head. "Let me tell Vennius."

"No. I forbid it. You would be without honor to betray my confidence."

"You Alliance warriors are pigheaded. You cry on and on about the way, yet you never realize that ways change. Always. They must."

"No…"

"Yes," Barron snapped, cutting his friend off before he'd gotten out more than a word. "What in your 'way' explains what is happening now? Was it written in the sacred book of Alliance warriors that you'd fight each other, that thousands of you would believe false propaganda and swear faith to a usurper? That the Alliance you built over sixty years of struggle would face its destruction?"

Tulus just stared back.

"You owe me an honor debt…you have said so yourself. Very well, I now claim payment. I would have your permission to tell Vennius. He will pardon you, I am sure of this. I will tell no one else, but you must allow me to explain to the Imperator."

"Tyler…" Tulus's voice drifted into silence.

"You are at a crossroads, my friend. I ask for your trust with this secret of yours."

The two men sat silently for a while, several minutes at least. Finally, Tulus looked up, met Barron's eyes. "I will trust you, Tyler. I will show you that my words and oaths on the trip back to Sentinel-2 were not empty."

Barron was about to respond, but Tulus continued, "But I would ask a promise of you."

"What would you have me do?"

"You must promise that you will do everything in your power…everything…to ensure that Attia and my children are not harmed. That you will even take them to the Confederation if you must, if that is what is needed."

Barron looked at the Palatian and nodded, slowly, somberly. "You have my word, Vian, sworn with all of my heart. I am certain Vennius will pardon Attia and your children…but even if he does not, on my honor as a Barron, I will see them taken to my family's estates and cared for as long as they live."

"Thank you, my friend." Then, a few seconds later: "The fates are indeed fickle, that at this stage of life I should meet a foreigner, a man from beyond my culture who has more honor than any Palatian I have stood beside in battle. You are a good man, Tyler Barron, and whatever happens, it has been my privilege to know you."

*   *   *

"Come in, Tyler."

Barron walked into the room, noting immediately that there were no guards, only a pair of children and an old man sitting on a padded bench. "I want to thank you for seeing me."

"None of that. All that is ever required for you to gain admittance is to say you need to see me."

Barron had been struck from the beginning by Vennius's lack of pretension. He'd avoided politics and statesmanship as much as possible, but when he'd had to interact with heads of state, or Senators back home, he'd always found them to be power mad, ego-driven…in essence, the very last people he would have chosen to wield political power. But Vennius was different, and in time, Barron had come to realize the Gray Alliance Imperator had accepted the exalted post over his own deep and profound objections. Vennius was as unlike a typical politician or government administrator as he'd ever seen, and Barron now understood just what it had cost the man to accept the position.

Though he'd done what he had to do, Vennius had not adopted the pomp and other nonsense so many others in his situation would have embraced. He was constantly banishing his guards from his chambers, and whenever possible, he conducted business in the most informal manner possible. Barron found it refreshing, but he was still getting used to it. Alliance culture was so dominated by ritual and custom, it was strange to see their Imperator so unassuming.

"Sir, if I may…"

"There are no other officers present, Tyler. Let us spare the pretense and foolishness. I am Tarkus when it is just the two of us."

Barron turned his head, glanced at the children and man sitting on the large sofa.

"You may speak freely in front of them, Tyler. These are Commander Mellus's children, Ila and Tia." He looked over toward them. "Greet Commodore Barron, children. He is a friend and an ally."

"Hello, Commodore," the two girls said, almost in unison. They were young, but they sat rigid and upright, their posture and behavior both beyond reproach, despite the fact that Barron suspected they had just learned of their mother's death.

"It is a pleasure," he replied, not having any idea of the correct form of response to civilians, and children at that.

"I have just made them my wards. They shall be raised on my estates, as members of the Vennii, and I shall see to their educations and their placements into suitable careers...assuming, that is, that we retake Palatia." A pause. "It is the least I can do after getting their mother killed, wouldn't you say?"

Barron knew the question was not seeking an answer, but he almost gave one. Then he realized nothing he could say would ease Vennius's guilt over Mellus's death in trying to reach him. Not to mention the thousands of her crews who died with her.

"And this is Torba," Vennius continued, gesturing toward the man, "one of Commander Mellus's longest-serving retainers. Torba was the one who secured the children, and got them off Palatia before Calavius could get to them and punish them for their mother's actions."

"Torba." Barron nodded a greeting. The Pleb bowed respectfully in response, a somber look on his face.

"Sir," Barron said, after Vennius had sat silently for a moment.

"Ah, yes, Tyler. You wanted to see me about something. You will have to excuse an old man's wandering thoughts...and indulge his efforts to make right, in some small way, all the pain he has caused."

Barron had never seen Vennius like this. The Imperator was usually totally in control, barely giving a hint as to what he thought about any subject. But he was sad now, almost mournful.

"Sir, I'm sorry, but I must talk to you about Commander Tulus."

"Tulus has been stripped of his rank. He is no longer a commander, nor a warrior."

"Sir, Com...Vian Tulus is innocent. I am sure of it, more now than ever."

"You wish to believe the best in those you like, Tyler. We all do. But that does not change the evidence."

"I know why Tulus would not explain his communications. I know who he was contacting and why."

Vennius was silent for a few seconds. "Tyler, Tulus is facing execution. He might say anything to escape from the scaffold. Once, I would have said a Palatian Patrician would not lie, even to save his life. Now I see the naivety in that thought."

"Is that what you really think? That he would lie to save his life? You've known him longer than I have. And, if that's the case, why didn't he lie right away, when you were demanding an explanation? Do you really think a man of Tulus's experience and intelligence wouldn't have been ready to deal with accusations if he was truly guilty?"

Vennius didn't look convinced, but he didn't argue further. Finally, he nodded. "What did he tell you?"

Barron explained all Tulus had said.

Vennius sighed softly. "That has the ring of truth to it. And I seem to remember rumors of some sort that Tulus had fathered a child with a Pleb woman. I always assumed they were rumors spread by his rivals to discredit him. If it were true, he would be spared the scaffold, but his career would be over."

"Sir..." Barron had settled on "sir" as a sufficiently respectful form of address for his interactions with Vennius. "...I mean no disrespect to your laws and customs, and as a foreigner, I am unfamiliar with your social structures..." He paused, thinking for a moment exactly how he wanted to phrase what he wanted to say, but Vennius interrupted.

"Our customs are rigid...and sometimes foolish. We speak

of the way, and yet often we fail to understand its true meaning, focusing instead on superficialities of no real importance." He looked up at Barron. "We are a proud people, Tyler, but we are as capable as any of being fools, resisting change out of reflex instead of judgment."

Barron wasn't sure exactly where Vennius was going, but he had a good feeling. "Things have changed, sir. This war is proof of that. Can you really spare a man of Tulus's capabilities?"

Vennius didn't reply at first. He just sat, staring straight ahead, but obviously deep in thought. "No," he finally said, "I cannot." Another pause. "I will speak with him myself. If he can convince me that this story you have told me is true, I will drop all charges of treason, and I will pardon him for his… crime." His face darkened. "But I fear I may lose his services anyway, Tyler. I cannot openly state my reasons for clearing Tulus. Our ways may be rigid, sometimes foolish, but our warriors are raised to follow them. Were it known that Tulus had fathered children with one so beneath his class, he would be ridiculed. The officers and spacers would not follow him. And if I do not give reason for his exoneration, doubts will persist, whispers of treason. It will undermine his ability to command."

Barron was silent now. He hadn't fully considered the complexities of what he had proposed. Then he said, "Perhaps there is a solution. Exonerate Tulus without explanation. You are the Imperator, after all. Assign Tulus's old ships, the ones he commanded before the war, as the Alliance contingent for the Palatia operation. I will publicly show confidence in him, and the crews of those ships are the ones least likely to believe the accusations of treason. If we are successful at Palatia, the glory of victory and Tulus's role in it will extinguish suspicions." Barron paused, looking down at the floor, a sudden grim look on his face. "And if we are not successful…will it even matter?"

Vennius nodded. "You are an Alliance warrior my friend, deep in that raging heart of yours, that much is clear. I don't know how you ended up misplaced in the Confederation, but as long as I am Imperator, you will always have a place with us, Tyler Barron. I name you now and always, a Palatian warrior."

"Thank you, sir. That is…extremely gratifying." Barron had grown to like and respect Vennius more each time they'd met. Then: "So, you agree?"

"Yes, absolutely. If Tulus can convince me this whole story is the truth."

Barron smiled. He had no doubt Vennius would believe what Tulus told him. *As long as I can get Tulus to come clean. It was hard enough pulling it out of him the first time…*

"My thanks, sir."

"Tulus owes you his thanks." Vennius paused, then he looked right back at Barron. "I have one request of my own, Tyler. Something I can ask of you but not command."

"Sir?"

Vennius looked across the room at the two children, still sitting quietly along the far wall. "When you land your forces on Palatia…" There was pain in his voice now, and he paused, gathering himself. "When I was forced to flee, I was able to rescue the Imperatrix, but there was no time to…" His words failed again.

Barron opened his mouth, but he closed it again, holding his tongue, waiting on Vennius.

"Kat's children, Tyler. They are on Palatia. There were on the Rigellus estate, not in Victorum. There was no way for me to get to them…" His words were heavy with self-condemnation.

Barron's impulse was to try and comfort his friend, but again, he decided silence was the right choice. He had to let Vennius get it all out.

"I left them, Tyler, protected only by house guards." Another pause. "They are as my own grandchildren…and they are on Palatia, at the mercy of Calavius and his pack of traitors."

"Katrine Rigellus is a hero of the Alliance, sir. Calavius wouldn't dare harm them."

"No, perhaps not. But he would use them, lie to them, poison their minds. And if he is pushed to the last extent, if defeat is imminent…I am sure he would kill them, if only because he knows how dear they are to me." Vennius took a deep breath. "When your forces land, Tyler, find them for me. Please. Secure their safety. I know your resources are too small for even what you must already do, but I cannot fail Kat again."

Barron stepped forward, reaching out and putting his hand on Vennius's shoulders. It was a breach of protocol for sure, and if there'd been any guards present, they'd no doubt be on him already. But, for a moment, there were just two men, friends, one comforting the other during a moment when the facades dropped and an Imperator and warrior became just a man, burdened by a lifetime of pain.

"Of course, Tarkus…I will do everything possible to rescue the Rigellus children."

Vennius looked up, and forced a small smile. "Thank you, my friend. My gratitude to you is eternal. If you need anything of me, ever, all you need do is ask."

Barron nodded and returned the smile. "I'd best be going now. There is much to prepare."

"Fortune go with you, Commodore Barron."

Barron turned and walked toward the door, and as he faced away from Vennius, the smile slipped from his face.

How am I supposed to find two children on an entire planet plunged into war?

Chapter Twenty-Nine

"I want six squadrons on scouting duty, deployed five hundred thousand kilometers in front of the fleet. Just because the enemy is pinned down at Sentinel-2, it doesn't mean they don't have scoutships out. I have no doubt they know we're coming, but I do not intend to make a gift to them of our exact position and timing." Kellus Battarus sat on *Gladius*'s bridge, snapping out orders. He treated most of his officers with the respect that was their due, but his voice was harsher, edgier when speaking to Jovi Grachus. The Imperator's decree absolved her of her family's prior shame, but it was still hard for Battarus to forget she was the grandchild of a traitor.

"Yes, Commander-Magnus." Grachus's voice was crisp, proper. She even used his full rank designation, though "commander" would have sufficed. "I have implemented regular rotation, two replacement squadrons launching every hour, and two returning for refit."

"Very well, Commander. That is all for now." He closed the line abruptly, though he had to admit, his dislike for Grachus was fading, washed partly away by the unmistakable competence she displayed.

He looked out across the bridge. He was still shocked to be where he was, at the helm of the grand fleet's flagship, commanding more than fifty battleships and a massive swarm of escorts. He'd rallied to Calavius reluctantly, mostly because of what he'd heard about Vennius's attempted coup, of his abduction of the Imperatrix. Battarus had always respected the former Commander-Magnus, but attempting to seize power, moving against the Imperatrix...these were things he could never condone.

"Fleet status, Commander?"

"All ships report fully operational. All formations intact. Scouting forces and scanners report clear, sir. No contacts."

"Very well." Battarus's first action as Commander-Magnus had been to transfer Commander Perticas to act as his aide. Marcus Perticas was one of the top ship commanders in the fleet, and he'd hated to pull him from his crew, but there was no one more qualified...and no one he trusted more. The Red forces might very well be on the verge of victory, but even if that transpired, Battarus was uneasy. He was an Alliance warrior, and he would follow Calavius's orders, but something about the Imperator troubled him. And instead of alleviating his concern, the unexpected elevation to Commander-Magnus only increased his worries. He couldn't explain why, but he was on edge, and for reasons beyond the impending battle.

"Time to Caprius transit point?"

"Projected arrival in four hours, sixteen minutes."

"Very well...proceed on current course." Battarus pushed aside the concerns. There was a battle to win before he could start worrying about Calavius and the new regime. And whatever Tarkus Vennius had become, he had no doubts—none at all—about his former friend's tactical skill. Even with vast numerical superiority, he was sure he faced an epic struggle before the victory could be won.

*   *   *

"Is everything in motion?" Calavius sat on a large chair—more of a couch, really—leaning on one elbow as he looked out across the room. As always, he was flanked by his guards, four on each side.

Lille stood facing the Imperator he'd created with the same confused sense of satisfaction and concern he always had about Calavius. The pompous fool had done well in many ways, exceeding expectations on a number of fronts. *But he looks more ridiculous here, on this couch, than he did on that ludicrous throne he had built.*

His ego and hunger for power could still come back to bite us…

"Yes. I drafted the plan myself, and reviewed it thoroughly. However, I must state that, despite our preparation, this is a difficult mission. Assassinating Battarus outright would be relatively simple. But you need it to appear he was killed in battle." Lille looked to the side, at the row of absurdly uniformed warriors. He knew they were all lifetime retainers of Calavius—whose families would suffer horrors unimaginable if they ever betrayed their master—but he disliked speaking of such matters in front of anyone not vital to the operation. Leaks were poison to espionage and assassination. Secrecy wasn't everything, but it was close.

"Please continue, Minister." Calavius flashed a glance toward the troops. "You may speak freely in front of these men. They are utterly trustworthy."

No one is utterly trustworthy, you damned fool…

"It is simply that the Agency is in its infancy. We only have a very few operatives ready for action, and only one I felt capable of executing this mission." Lille paused. "I do not like proceeding without a backup plan."

"Since we do not appear to have a backup plan, there is little choice but to move forward without one. I was compelled to appoint Battarus to quell the unrest among my officers…but I do not trust his allegiance. He is a troublemaker, and if we do not rid ourselves of him in the final stages of the battle, it will be extremely difficult afterward."

Lille was surprised again at the clarity of Calavius's logic. Battarus *would* be a problem, Lille agreed completely. And his appointment *had* silenced the grumbling that had grown louder among the Red officers.

"I will supervise the operation personally, every step of the way. When you give the word, I will see it done." It was better to give Calavius unconditional assurances, but Lille knew better than to take anything as a certainty. Failure to kill Battarus would be bad enough, but what concerned him most was his operative getting caught. If the other officers found out Calavius was trying to kill his Commander-Magnus…

"Very well, Minister. See it done."

Lille hesitated. "There is something else."

"Yes?"

"The assassination will simulate battle damage. There are two potential problems with that. First, the order must be given while fighting is still in progress—and *Gladius* is still in the combat zone."

"That should not be too great of an issue. For all his faults, Vennius had many loyal followers. No doubt a large number of them will choose to fight to the death. That should allow us a time when the battle has been decided, but combat continues."

Lille nodded. "Yes, that is true." A pause, then: "The other issue may pose more of a problem to you. To simulate damage in combat, we must detonate sizable charges, not only on the bridge, but in other compartments that would be damaged by incoming enemy fire. Many of your officers and crew will be killed, hundreds, perhaps. And *Gladius* will be very seriously damaged."

"Will the ship be salvageable?"

"Yes. We were very careful in locating the charges. The ship will retain maneuvering capability and at least minimal power generation."

Calavius looked over at Lille, his face devoid of emotion. "Then I see no problem, Minister. None at all."

*   *   *

"Get back on that comm and tell *Teratus*'s flight control that schedule is unacceptable. They will have two squadrons launched in thirty minutes or less, or I'll be over there to find out why." Grachus stood in the middle of *Gladius*'s flight control center, shouting out commands to the makeshift crew she'd managed to put together. She hadn't had the time to build any kind of real staff, and that meant most of the work landed on her shoulders, even the routine items.

She loathed this part of her new job; the administrative duties, the supervision of an entire fleet's fighter squadrons. It was a position that hadn't even existed before. Alliance squadrons had always been directed by the commanders of their mother ships, and in gross, by the fleet commander. A chaotic command structure, perhaps poorly thought out to begin with, had become downright insane with a fleet this large. Grachus had only led a large fighter force once before, and that had been two hundred forty ships. Grand fleet had one hundred twenty squadrons.

Eighteen hundred fighters...every one of them my responsibility...

She looked up at the large display, recently installed so she could keep track of her far flung fighter wings. She'd been tense, waiting for someone to suggest that she remain aboard *Gladius*, direct her squadrons from there. That would probably make sense...how much could one pilot do in a battle this size? But her cockpit was the place she felt most at home, and she dreaded the thought of being barred from it. She would lead from her fighter, unless the Imperator himself forbade her.

She *had* to be out there with the attack. She had business to conclude. With *Dauntless*, and Tyler Barron, the man who killed Kat Rigellus.

And with Jake Stockton. She knew the next time the two of them met, only one would leave the fight. It would be the most desperate battle she'd ever experienced, and one that chilled her to the bones. She almost felt as though she were matched against herself, facing another pilot born to the cockpit. She would bring all she had to that fight, every trick, every bit of strength she possessed.

Hopefully that will be enough…

Chapter Thirty

Captain's Log, Andromeda Lafarge, Free Trader Pegasus

The device we found is largely intact, though it is now without a power source. I am hopeful Admiral Striker and his team can adapt something quickly and see if it is operational. It is worth a king's ransom, of that I have no doubt. The trinkets and bits and pieces of ancient junk my people and I have traded on for so many years do not even compare. I fully intended to demand my price in advance, hiding the device and not agreeing to turn it over until we were paid. But how can I do that? How can I delay needlessly, knowing the contents of *Pegasus*'s cargo hold could be vital to the war effort?

I don't know what it is, at least not with any degree of certainty. It appears to be a generator of some kind, and Lex Righter has suggested it may produce an energy field that blocks scanners. If it is a stealth device of some kind, the tactical implications are extraordinary.

I must rely on my negotiating ability to ensure my people are compensated for the risks and efforts they have endured. I find myself more drawn to patriotic endeavors than I would ever have imagined possible, but this small band of men and women, who have followed me through danger and hardship and strife...I owe them my first loyalty. Bringing the device with me to Grimaldi is poor bargaining, but Striker is an honorable man...and no doubt, I can use that against him in some way that puts well-earned coin in my crew's pockets.

Free Trader Pegasus
Docked at Fleet Base Grimaldi
Orbiting Krakus II
Year 311 AC

"Stay with the ship, Vig. All of you stay. If anyone tries to come aboard…do what you can." She was about to say "stop them," but she caught herself before such an absurdity came out of her mouth. She'd willingly docked at the largest naval base in the Confederation, one with thousands of Marines on it, not to mention ship crews, security personnel, and just about every type of weapon imaginable. What did she think her crew could do if anyone really wanted to board *Pegasus*?

"Good luck, Andi." She wasn't sure if she caught a tone of discontent in her friend's voice or if it was just her own doubt manifesting itself. She was pretty sure Merrick had expected to stash the device they'd recovered, keeping it safe from confiscation, at least until they'd been paid their price, but he hadn't argued with her when she stated her intention to go directly to Grimaldi without any stops. That was Vig's way, but she was far from sure he didn't resent her subordinating the interests of the crew yet again.

"I'll be back as soon as I can." She turned and saw a small group of Marines moving forward. "Captain Lafarge?" one of them asked as he walked toward her.

"Yes, Lieutenant. I am Andi Lafarge."

"Admiral Striker sent me to bring you to him."

"Lead the way, Lieutenant." She glanced back toward Merrick, still unsure of the emotions behind the look on his face. She didn't doubt her people's loyalty, and certainly never Vig's, but she didn't like the idea of them feeling unappreciated or ill-treated by her. She had to admit to herself, the closeness she'd once enjoyed with them all wasn't as easy anymore. She'd been distracted for the last two years—by the war, of course, and most of all, by Tyler Barron. Her affections for her people hadn't changed, but now she asked herself, how would she react if she was one of them, watching their comrade suddenly so friendly with naval types and more interested in the war effort than in profits?

She followed the Marine through the hatch and into the hall, tracing the familiar route toward Striker's office. But then the lieutenant turned off from the course she remembered and down a hall to a large set of double doors. "I am here with Captain Lafarge, sir," he said into the comm unit alongside the door.

The hatch opened, revealing a large conference room. "Come in, Andi." It was Striker's voice, but there was something there, tension? Distraction? Then: "That will be all, Lieutenant."

Lafarge stepped inside, the doors closing behind her. "Admiral it's…" She froze, staring down to the end of the conference table. It was a man, but not Striker. She recognized him, at least she thought she did.

"Gary Holsten, Captain. We've never been formally introduced, though we have run into each other before." He stood up and walked toward Lafarge.

"I am sorry, Andi." She turned as Holsten approached. The last words had come from the side, and Striker was standing there, in front of a massive screen. "I didn't mean to blindside you. Mr. Holsten and I are dealing with something…important. But when they told me you said you had to see me, I ordered them to bring you here at once."

Andi turned back toward Holsten, who was next to her now, holding his hand out. "Van has told me all about what you did out in the Badlands, Captain." He forced a smile over his otherwise deadly serious expression. "Please, call me Gary."

"Yes, Mr…Gary." She reached out and took his hand. Then she turned back toward Striker. "Thank you for seeing me, Admiral. I can see that you're…occupied." Her eyes darted around by instinct, normal curiosity. But then she realized everything in the room was probably highly classified, and she looked back toward the door.

"Don't worry, Andi," Striker said softly. "Yes, everything in here is top secret, but if I didn't trust you, you wouldn't be here. And besides, it won't be secret much longer." He sighed softly.

"Ah…yes, Admiral…well, I have something I needed to discuss with you."

Striker gestured toward one of the chairs around the table. "As you have said. Please, sit." Striker did the same, followed by Holsten, who took one of the closer chairs instead of going back to his old spot. "You can say anything in front of Gary," he said, noting Lafarge's hesitancy and repeated glances toward the other man.

"Well, Admiral…Gary…you are aware of what my crew and I do for a living."

"Indeed, Captain…or may I call you Andi? You have had a very interesting career."

Striker shook his head. "You have to understand Gary here. He is the head of Confederation Intelligence. Chances are, if hamburgers give you a stomachache, he knows about it."

The whole thought gave Lafarge a shiver. She'd never really thought about what kind of files the intelligence services might have on her and her people. Now, she wondered what Sector Nine had…

"Well," she continued tentatively, "we found something… something I think may have military potential. And I wanted to give you first crack at it before I sell it." She looked over at Holsten. "And yes, please call me Andi."

"Sell it on the black market, no doubt," Holsten said, more amusement than accusation in his voice.

"To the highest bidder," Lafarge replied, mustering her defiance, "wherever that may be."

"I trust that would not include the Sector Nine agents infesting the border ports now, would it?"

"No! I would never…" She was upset at the suggestion that she would sell her cargo to the enemy.

"Yet you have in the past, have you not?"

Lafarge suddenly felt strange, a combination of unease and anger. "If I did, it was long before the war, and nothing of any real importance. Your operatives may not approve of what my people do, Mr. Holsten, but we are no traitors."

"Gary didn't mean anything by that, Andi. He just has a hard time dropping the grim intelligence chief bit."

"I apologize...Andi. I did not mean to impugn your patriotism. Indeed, your efforts involving the planet killer may very well have saved the Confederation from destruction. We all owe you our heartfelt thanks."

"So, what did you find now, Andi?" Striker looked right at her, an anxious expression on his face.

"I am not sure, but I think it is some kind of interference generator, something that blocks scanners. It seems to be intact, or at least relatively so."

"Functional?" Striker sounds surprised.

"No, but it had an antimatter power source with it when we found it. The canister was damaged, and we couldn't risk taking it with us."

"There's a canister of antimatter out where you found this?" Holsten's voice this time, concerned.

"No, not anymore. We destroyed it."

Striker shook his head. "All that antimatter...I'm surprised you didn't leave it so you could come back." He paused. "Or did you?"

"No, Admiral...I might have done that, but I didn't think we could leave it there for just anyone to find."

"You must have been way out there...why were you so concerned?"

She sighed. "Because I think there was a Union expedition two systems away."

"You ran into Union ships?" Striker and Holsten both sat bolt upright.

"No...not exactly. On the way there, we found a system. There were residual fuel traces everywhere, and the surface of one of the planets was massively scarred. Someone had excavated there—a massive project—and they covered their tracks with a nuclear bombardment."

"Are you sure? Could it have been an asteroid collision or something natural?"

"I'm sure." She reached into her pocket and pulled out a data chip. "Here are the scanner readings. *Someone* was definitely there, and they didn't want anyone to find out why." She slid the chip across the table toward Striker.

He reached out and scooped it up, looking down at it in his hand.

"Who else knows about this, Andi?" Holsten's voice had some edge to it now, a sense of urgency.

"No one but my crew."

"Where are they now?"

She tensed up. "Why?"

"I mean them no harm, Andi…but can you order them to stay on your ship, what is it, *Pegasus*?" He paused. "Just until we can check this out. If the Union has made a major find in the Badlands…"

"I told them all to stay put until I came back. And though I suspect it was the Union, I have no real evidence."

"The fact that you found what you did is pretty strong evidence. Who else would be out there in flagrant violation of international law?" Holsten looked across the table at Striker. "I'll have that analyzed immediately, Van." He reached out across the table, and Striker dropped the chip into his hand.

"I'd have brought a copy if I knew there'd be two of you here." It had been an attempt at levity, but it came out dark and deadpan instead. "That chip has a complete scan of the blast site, as well as the fuel trails and other remnants of the expedition. You can study what someone else did or did not find there, but I have a real piece of old tech, and I'm looking to sell it. You were fair to my people last time, Admiral, and I want to help the war effort. That is why I am here. But I cannot just give away what I found."

"I will do what I can, Andi," Striker said, cautiously. "Unfortunately, I am limited in my ability to requisition funds."

"I'm not," Holsten interrupted. "I give you my word, Andi. Whatever you have, whatever condition it is in, Holsten Interests will purchase it for its full black market value. Just give it to Van and his people so they can begin researching it. If it is of military value, it might make a difference in the war…and if not, my people will repurpose it for civilian use, and I'll get that much richer. And you and your people will wealthier than you've ever imagined."

Andi was silent. She didn't know Holsten, at least not well. She looked over at Striker.

"I trust Gary with my life, Andi. If you would rely on me, you can rely on him."

She turned back and forth, looking at each of them in turn. Finally, she said, "All right. I will trust both of you." *Since you could just take it away from me, and neither of you have threatened to do that. Yet.*

But watch your words, friend…you have no idea how much wealth I've imagined…

"I will send a team to offload the device. We'll do it late, when the night duty shift is on. We want to keep this quiet, of course."

Andi nodded.

"I will leave authorization for you to stay for as long as you wish, and you can refuel and refit if you want."

"Leave authorization?"

A shadow passed over Striker's face. "Yes, I'm afraid Gary is going back to Megara on government business…and I will be leaving with the fleet."

"The fleet?"

"Yes…I'm afraid the Senate has ordered an immediate offensive to break through the Union defenses and end the war."

Striker's tone told her all she needed to know about his hopes for success.

God help us all…

Chapter Thirty-One

From the Journal of Commodore Tyler Barron

We are on the way to Palatia. The desperate, crazy gamble has begun. I have seven battleships, a dozen escorts, and just over four hundred fighters. Commander Tulus commands another three capital ships, and eight frigates. It is an impressive fleet by any standard...any standard save the invasion and conquest of the capital of a race that worships strength and victory in combat. A race that is driven by an obsession to ensure their homeworld in never again subject to any enemy. I am haunted not only by what lies ahead, but also by the knowledge that this whole insane effort was my idea.

Though my thoughts lie forward, on the battle before us, and on the men and women who will fight it with me, they are also behind, at Sentinel-2, where Vennius and his forces will stand and face the furious onslaught of Calavius and his Red fleet.

Vennius would have been outnumbered even with every ship under my command arrayed alongside his forces. Now, without my ships and Tulus's, his position is utterly hopeless. But he is not there to win, nor to save Sentinel-2. He is the bait, drawing in Calavius and as much of his fleet as possible. Every ship that attacks Vennius is one less defending Palatia. One less standing in the way of our desperate assault.

We discussed the plan, a hundred times, it seems. I urged the Imperator to withdraw almost as soon as the Reds appeared, to flee and follow after my ships, having done their job of diverting the enemy's strength. But I fear he will fight far too long, that he will do all he can to keep the enemy tied down in Palatia, to buy more time for our desperate bid to end the war.

I only hope he breaks off soon enough, that he does not allow himself to be trapped. For he is not expendable, and no matter what success my arms achieve, I cannot long control Palatia without him. He must divert the enemy...and then he must get here, before his pursuers. Before my meager ground forces are defeated.

Vennius is a good man, brave and trustworthy. I have seen too many like him lost, dead in battle. I pray he does not join that list.

Bridge
CFS Dauntless
Sistari System, En Route to Palatia
Year 311 AC

"Bryan, come in." Barron looked up from where he sat at the small desk in the corner of his quarters. His office off the bridge was a roomier workspace, but his quarters were quieter, farther from the nexus of activities on the ship. He'd suggested the attack on Palatia on an impulse, the only thing he could think of to ward off imminent defeat. But the reality of what he was attempting had since sunken in, and he realized what a desperate gamble the whole thing was. If Calavius didn't commit most of his forces to the attack on Sentinel-2, all was lost. If he was wrong about the range of the Palatian orbital defenses, all was lost. If his small force of Marines and troopers couldn't secure and hold the most vital installations on the ground, all was lost.

"Commodore." Bryan Rogan had been the commander of *Dauntless*'s Marine contingent since Barron had taken command. Despite years of service together, Rogan was still stiff around Barron, formal. He stood at attention for a few seconds, hesitating to sit in his commander's presence. But then he obeyed, and he dropped into the chair, managing to look as tense and rigid sitting as he had standing.

"Bryan, I want you to command the landing forces on this operation. You've got *Dauntless*'s Marines as well as the contingents from the other ships…and the Alliance troopers as well." Rogan's Marines had fought a harrowing battle against Alliance soldiers at Santis, and Barron knew asking the officer to fight alongside, to *command*, the troopers, was a heavy lift. But the ground action was vital to success, and there was no one in the fleet Barron considered a replacement for the Marine captain sitting across the desk from him.

"Yes, sir." The response was crisp, proper, but even the dour Marine was unable to completely hide the emotions Barron's words had stirred.

"I know this will be difficult for you, Bryan. I'm also confident you can do the job." Barron reached out and grabbed a small box. "But it is not a posting for a captain. This has been long overdue, Bryan. I'm only sorry I allowed it to take so long." He pushed the box across the desk. "I'm afraid I had to have these made in *Dauntless*'s metal shop…apologies if they're not quite up to normal standards.

Rogan picked up the small box and opened it, staring down in dumbstruck shock. Finally, he stammered, "Sir…I don't know what to say." He pulled out a shiny platinum eagle, the insignia of a Marine colonel.

"It's well deserved, Bryan." A pause. "I'm afraid it's just a brevet bump for now, at least officially. But the high command will make it permanent as soon as we get back, I have no doubt of that."

"Thank you, Commodore."

"Now that we got that out of the way, let's talk shop. You won't have any problems with the other Marine contingents. You'll have just under sixteen hundred, and eleven vital objectives. You'll have to take control of them…and hold them for an indeterminate period." That was the part of the plan that most worried Barron. A surprise attack *could* be successful, even against overwhelming odds, but unless Vennius managed to break off in Sentinel-2 as planned and get back to Palatia before Calavius—or, for that matter, just get back before the troops on the planet managed to reorganize and counterattack—it was all academic. A force as small as the one Barron was landing could only hold out so long.

"Understood, sir. Resources will be thin, but we'll make it work."

"You have my every confidence, Bryan." Barron paused. "You will have about eight hundred troopers as well. They will also be under your command. You, better than anyone, know how well they can fight."

"Yes, sir." There was a vast pool of emotion behind the Marine's clipped reply.

"Well, this time they're on your side. And, Bryan…you've got to use them effectively. All your strike teams need to be integrated. We don't want the entire planet rising up against us, and I think you have some idea how the Palatians would respond to a foreign invader. With their history, they would lose their minds. You'd have young kids strapping bombs to themselves. Your troopers are your cover against that. Deploy them in the most visible spots, use their officers to interact with the locals. They've gotten a lot of propaganda against the Grays, but that will be nothing compared to how they would react to foreign officers and troops. If any of your Marines sneaks out to take a leak, he's got to have a trooper with him. Understood?"

Rogan paused briefly. Then he nodded. "Yes, sir. I understand."

Barron hesitated now, an uneasy look coming over his face. "Bryan, there is one more thing."

"Sir?"

"I know your people will be spread thin as it is, but I need you to handle one more mission for me."

"Of course, Commodore."

"I don't know where, not yet, but as soon as we secure control of the data storage systems, we should be able to find a location."

"A location, sir?"

"Yes. As soon as our data people can identify the spot…I need you to send a team to rescue two Palatians. Your people are to find and safeguard Katrine Rigellus's children. Imperator Vennius is concerned the Reds will kill them if it looks like they're about to lose. And I...I promised him we would try to save them."

"Of course, Commodore."

"Thank you, Bryan. And be sure you include some Alliance troopers in that operation too. Otherwise your people might find themselves fighting Rigellus family retainers."

"Understood, sir."

Barron looked across the table at Rogan. He knew how difficult the Palatia assault would be for the Marine and his people, and the losses they were likely to take. The challenges they would face fighting alongside the Alliance stormtroopers. *And those stormtroopers won't have the easiest time of it either...they'll be fighting their former comrades as well as standing alongside old enemies...*

Barron took a deep breath. Then he tapped the controls on the edge of his desk, bringing up a series of maps on the built-in display. "Okay, let's go over each of these objectives..."

*   *   *

"Jake..." Stara Sinclair stuck her head through the door.

Stockton was sitting on his bunk, staring at the wall on the other side of the small cabin. He'd almost told the AI to send Stara away, but when it came to it, he just said, "Open."

The bunk was on the opposite wall from the door, but still no more than two meters away. Squadron leaders had private cabins, which was a luxury on any spaceship, but they were small, cramped. The strike force commander's quarters were substantially plusher, but he wasn't even close to ready to take Kyle Jamison's cabin.

"What?" He answered, his tone far harsher than he'd intended. He knew his grief, and his fatalism, were trying to force him to drive Stara away. He was angry with himself for the callousness, but despite his best efforts, he hadn't been able to stop. He was trying to spare her, to protect her from the toxic creature he'd become. To save her from the grief at his all too likely death in the fight that lay ahead. But he knew it just came out as cruelty, and it added to his already-considerable self-loathing.

"I know how much you're hurting, Jake." Stara Sinclair had a temper of her own, one Stockton had seen up close many times. She'd turned down his advances for more than a year, and during that time—and even after they'd gotten together—she let him have it whenever he gave her a hard time. But not now. Since Jamison's death, she'd taken all he could dish out, and given him nothing but patience and affection in return. All he wanted was for her to leave him alone, to his misery and the dark thoughts that had taken control of him...and that was the one thing she wouldn't give him. He knew he should be grateful, but the shadow inside him took control when he spoke, hurling hurtful remarks.

"Stara, I'm just fine. Okay?" He spun around, sitting on the edge of the bed and banging his fist on the wall. "I know you mean well, but I just want to be alone. Please...just leave me be." He felt the rage taking control again, and he tried to bite down, to leave it at what he'd said already, but to no avail. "Is that so much to ask, that you leave me the hell alone? I don't need your concern, and I damned well don't need your pity. Don't you have enough to keep you busy? We're going to lose at least half our fighters in the battles ahead of us. Maybe you could go get started on the, 'I regret to inform you' letters? I figure now that Barron's a commodore, he might delegate that to the one who sends us all out there, who's got all the screens to watch the pilots die."

Sinclair stared back at him, clearly struggling with her own emotions. He could see the anger, her impulsive response, and one he knew was well-deserved. But she held that back, and for a few seconds, all he could see was the pain in her face, the hurt he'd so skillfully inflicted. She pushed that aside too, and she stood there defiantly, the slight smile returning. "You're not going to drive me away, Jake Stockton. I know you want to, and maybe I understand, at least a little, but I'm in this to stay. I'll leave you alone now, but I'll be here. When you're ready to find your way back, my hand will be there to lead you."

She stood where she was for another few seconds, almost daring him to hurl another wave of invective at her. Then she turned around and walked back out into the corridor, the door closing behind her.

Stockton leaned back, cursing himself for yet another round of self-indulgent and hurtful behavior. He was in a bad place, his rage at Jamison's death and his burning need for revenge consuming him whole. But there was more, something else he struggled to admit, even to himself. He was scared.

He'd never met an enemy as good as he was...perhaps even better. He knew he would go after his adversary, pursue the revenge for his oldest friend. But he didn't know he'd get that vengeance, that he would win the battle. He was as likely to die as to succeed. Part of him was ready for that, but inside, where the Stockton who would never hurt Stara or shirk his command duties for a vendetta still lurked, he was terrified.

It will be over soon...one way or another...

Chapter Thirty-Two

AFS Bellator
Orbiting Planet Varena, Cilian System
Year 62 (311 AC)

"Welcome aboard, your Supremacy…" Brutus Egilius leapt out of his chair, gesturing for Vennius to take the command station. "I am honored that you have chosen to transfer your flag to *Bellator*."

"Where else would I go, Brutus? Your ship was the first to come to my aid, the first to rally to my cause. A man who forgets such things is not worthy of loyalty…and certainly has no right to expect warriors to die for him." Vennius waved his arm. "Back to your station, Brutus. You have not only *Bellator*, but an entire wing to command. I am but an observer, who can sit as well at any station."

Vennius gestured again when his subordinate just stood where he was, and he watched as Egilius reluctantly returned to his seat. "I can have something brought to the bridge, something more…"

"This seat here will be fine," Vennius said, turning toward one of the spare stations. He walked over and sat down. "You have far more important things to worry about than my comfort. No doubt you've been monitoring the activity at the transit point. The battle we've been waiting for is almost upon us."

"Yes, sir. I have ordered all ships to hold their positions as directed."

Vennius nodded. He knew his people would want to rush forward to meet the enemy as they came through, taking advantage of the short time before transiting ships regained control of their systems. That would be the correct strategy—if he planned to fight to the finish. But he didn't want to meet the enemy at the transit point. He wanted them deep in-system, their courses right for Sentinel-2, their velocities as high as possible. Once the enemy was committed, he could execute his escape...and get the head start he needed before the enemy figured out what he was doing.

He turned and looked at the display, at the large blue oval representing Sentinel-2. The battle station had served him well, its massive defenses crucial to the survival of his cause in the early months of the war. But now he was abandoning it. He'd hesitated before boarding the shuttle, and he'd looked back over the bay, at the skeleton crew he was leaving behind. They were volunteers, every one of them, but that didn't make it easier to leave them. He told himself many of them would escape— the flight crews, for example, would board shuttles and escape pods as soon as they launched Sentinel's contingent of fighters. His commands had been clear...everyone whose presence was not absolutely vital to the battle underway was to evacuate. But climbing into a shuttle and making it across a war zone to one of the retreating battleships were two entirely different things. And he knew Calavius well enough to realize there would be no prisoners in this fight. His crews caught in unarmed shuttles and pods would be blasted out of existence.

He looked around the bridge, watching the cool efficiency of *Bellator*'s crew. Egilius had created one of the most efficient and capable teams in the fleet, and they'd proven that again and again.

The lift doors opened, and a tall man walked in, wearing the uniform of a Commander-Princeps. "Your Supremacy," he said, snapping to attention as he did.

"Ah, Jarus, thank you for coming." Vennius turned and

looked over at Egilius. "I am going to use your office, Brutus."

"Certainly, Your Supremacy. I will see you are not disturbed."

Vennius stood up and gestured toward the back of the bridge. "Let us speak privately, Jarus."

"Of course, Your Supremacy. Your word is my command."

The two men walked to the end of the bridge, a single hatch sliding to the side as they approached. When they had both entered the room and the door had closed, Vennius gestured toward a chair and said, "I appreciate your loyalty, Jarus, and I do not doubt your obedience, but this is not something I can order you to do. At least it is not something I *will* order. I only ask for your help."

"How can I serve you, Your Supremacy?"

"There is a pilot on the Red side, apparently now in some position of considerable command authority. The descriptions, of her tactics, her flying style—many things—that have reached my ears remind me of someone important to me, someone who blames me for the death of her closest friend. A warrior who should, by all rights, be serving alongside us, but who, it appears, has instead declared for the Reds. I suspected she held me responsible for Kat's death, but I had not realized the depth of her anger…her hatred."

Jarus nodded slowly. "Jovi." His voice was mostly devoid of emotion, but Vennius caught a hint of concern, perhaps even affection.

"Yes."

"We do not have…or I should say, we did not have much contact, Your Supremacy. Only when she came to visit our son, Jarus, and I'm afraid certain members of my family made it difficult for her to visit frequently."

"Yes, I know the match was not a favorable one for you. I believe Kat Rigellus exerted considerable pressure to arrange it."

"Yes, she did." He paused for a few seconds, and when he continued, his voice was softer. "My coupling with Jovi canceled a longstanding honor debt between our families." Another pause. "My father and brother were horrified, though they had little choice but to agree. It never bothered me, though, certainly not like it did them. Jovi and I…enjoyed each other's company. Despite her grandfather's disgrace, her DNA profile was highly favorable, and our son…he is a good boy, Your Supremacy, smart and strong. One day he will be a fine warrior."

"Of that I have no doubt, Jarus." Vennius hesitated now, struggling with old pain. "You know Kat Rigellus was like a daughter to me. I curse myself for not doing more to save her, but I did not see her defeat as likely when I executed the orders for her to probe the Confederation's border. I didn't relish the thought of war with the Confeds, but I never imagined whatever force they could quickly deploy to the frontier could destroy *Invictus*. The orders didn't come from me…they came from the Council, and from the Imperatrix herself. It was ill-conceived, certainly, but no one betrayed Kat, nor sent her knowingly to her death. Yet, I fear that is precisely what Jovi believes."

"She was devoted to Katrine, Your Supremacy, as I'm sure you know. Everything she attained in life, she owed to opportunities Katrine provided her."

"Yes, I know. I understand her need for vengeance, but while I will never forgive myself for Kat's death, her rage is ill-directed. She has sworn herself to a traitor, one we must destroy." Another pause. "I fear that she will die in the fighting before this war ends. And I would save her if I could."

"I would save her also, Your Supremacy. What can I do to help?"

"When the fighting starts in earnest, our scanner teams will try to identify her fighter. From the previous reports, it is clear she will be leading some or all of the Red squadrons. If… when…we find her, we will establish a direct comm line, using the full power of the Sentinel-2 nexus. I would speak to her, but she is so enraged at me, I fear she would not listen. But perhaps if it is you…" He paused, looking for a moment, very much like a lost old man. "Try to explain to her, tell her no one is as distraught as I at Kat's death. It may be a hopeless effort, but do all you can to convince her she has made the wrong choice."

"I will try, Your Supremacy. I will do it for you, of course, but I would also save Jovi if I can. She is my son's mother…and

I retain some affection for her. My family has treated her badly, and I would make that right if I can." He paused, a troubled look on his face. "But, she is infuriatingly stubborn. If she has sworn to the Red cause, it will be very difficult to get her to switch sides."

"I am well aware, Jarus. She is more like Kat in that way than she probably imagines. But if we cannot persuade her, we will likely have to kill her." Vennius was silent for a moment. "I failed Kat, five years ago…I do not wish to fail her again. I want to save Jovi Grachus if there is any way to do so, because she is a worthy officer and an honorable Palatian. But more than that…I would save her for Kat. Just perhaps, I can avoid letting her down again."

Jarus stood silently for a moment, looking back at Vennius. Then he said, "I will do my best, Your Supremacy…for you, of course, and also for Jovi. I, too, would see her saved."

"Thank you, Jarus. I would spare myself yet another ghost haunting my sleep."

*   *   *

"Let the attack begin." Calavius was well into his address to the fleet. He spoke loudly, his voice echoing off the walls of the chamber he'd turned into a makeshift throne room. "And let it not stop until the traitors are vanquished, until every man or woman who has risen in arms against the legitimate government of the Alliance is dead. We shall take no prisoners, accept no surrenders, show no quarter. Go now, my warriors, and see it done. And from the broken wreckage of Sentinel-2 we shall build the future."

Calavius nodded to the communications officer, a signal to cut the line. He'd spoken for just over three minutes, his words broadcast to every ship in the fleet. He hadn't written the speech, but he knew he'd delivered it well, an Imperator's charge to his warriors, the men and women who would now secure his rule. Many would die, he knew—such was the cost of war—but as he looked at the display, at the ragged line of ships in front of Sentinel-2, outnumbered more than three to one by his own vessels, he almost felt sorry for his old friend.

I have you now, Vennius. You placed your trust in the Confeds, and they abandoned you when things became difficult...

He hadn't been surprised when he'd been advised that the Confederation forces had departed. The Confeds had a massive economy, and that gave them strength. But they were shopkeepers, builders, and traders...not warriors.

He had been cautious, his earlier defeats still fresh in his mind. He'd pulled together every ship he could, stripping even Palatia's defenses to build an invincible fleet, one that could overcome even Vennius's skill in battle. He could take no chances now. He *would* take none. He was committing all, and on the massive screen he'd had installed on the wall, he saw the overwhelming numbers he had led to this place...to win an empire.

Goodbye, Vennius. I am sorry you could not just swear faith to me. We could have done great things together...but instead, you will die as a traitor...

*   *   *

"Your Supremacy...I'm getting a report of unauthorized comm usage. Somewhere on deck twenty-three."

Vennius had been sitting in Egilius's office since his meeting with Jarus. He didn't know if the officer's efforts would work... in fact, he thought it more likely they wouldn't. But he had to try. The thought of watching his people gun down Kat's closest friend was difficult to endure, even for a warrior who had seen so much death and suffering.

"Shut down all external comm at once! Do you have the source localized?" He leapt up from his chair, moving toward the door.

"Not yet, Your Supremacy. We're working on it now."

Vennius slipped through the door and out onto *Bellator*'s bridge. "Have you confirmed it is not normal housekeeping traffic?" He raised his voice so it would carry across the bridge as he walked toward Egilius's chair.

"Yes, sir. It is nothing I have authorized, nor anyone in the command structure. All non-essential comm is restricted now, per your order."

Vennius had done all he could to tighten control over communications since he'd released Tulus. The officer had told him the same story he'd told Barron. He'd even had pictures, of the children and their mother. Vennius suspected he would have been appalled at the breach of the vaunted "way" when he was younger, but all he felt now was empathy for his longtime friend, and the family he had struggled to protect. Most importantly, he believed Tulus. Completely. There was no conclusive evidence to prove what the officer claimed, but Vennius had always been a man who trusted his judgment. Still, his release created a dangerous problem. If Tulus was innocent, that meant the traitor was still out there. Every earlier attempt to tighten security had failed to stop the devastating leaks, without a trace of the treacherous party. Perhaps until now.

"Get security down there, now. Close off deck twenty-three. Seal all compartments." If it *was* the traitor, if he had finally caught whoever was responsible in the act, Vennius had no intention of allowing his enemy to escape.

"Yes, sir."

"Captain, we've got enemy fighters inbound." Vennius had never heard Egilius sound scared…until this moment. "Dozens of squadrons, sir. Heading toward Sentinel-2 and toward us. Shall I order all ships to launch?"

Vennius stood stone still, his eyes focused on the display. "No, Commander. If we launch, our ships will just be outnumbered and overwhelmed…and they'll have trouble breaking off. We'll end up having to abandon half of the survivors. Order the fleet to pull back. Edge us closer to our exit transit point… but not directly. We don't want to tip our hand…not yet."

"Yes, Your Supremacy."

Vennius jumped up.

"You see to the fleet, Brutus. Send the order to the other wing commanders."

"Yes, sir…where are you going? Your Supremacy?" Egilius

jumped out of his seat as Vennius moved toward the lift.

"I'm going to deck twenty-three, Commander."

"No...it's too dangerous. Please...let security handle it. Or let me go. You can't risk yourself."

"Brutus, my friend...you have duties here. You cannot leave the bridge. I have already set our strategy. My only role now is sitting in the background, watching."

"You're the Imperator. We cannot risk you!"

"The way is the way, Brutus. Palatian warriors do not allow fear to rule their actions, even Imperators." He paused, and when he continued, his voice was distant, somber. "Besides, if there is a traitor down there, it is someone close to me, someone I trusted. As I once did Calavius. I must see this through." Vennius turned and walked toward the lift.

"Go with the Imperator." Egilius was shouting to the two guards posted on the bridge. "I charge you with his safety."

Vennius ignored Egilius's command, and the two storm-troopers falling in behind him as he stepped into the lift. Egilius's concern was gratifying, in its way. But Vennius's thoughts were elsewhere...and save for the traitor he was sure he'd find down on deck twenty-three, he doubted anyone on *Bellator* cared less for his own safety than he did.

His life was over, at least all that retained any satisfaction, any joy. Everything that was important to Tarkus Vennius, the man, was gone. He had lived, loved, fought...once he'd tasted a sweetness in life. But now there was only bitterness and obligation. And the disillusionment of treachery from those he'd called friends.

He existed now only for duty, a revenant condemned to do a job he despised until he died. He couldn't run, couldn't stop. He owed it to the Imperatrix, to his warriors...to all Palatians.

And now it is time to deal once again with treachery, with the black sickness our arrogance made us believe could never plague us.

Chapter Thirty-Three

"We're through, Commodore. Systems rebooting now."

Barron listened to Travis's report. It was the same one he'd heard countless times. Just as in every battle they'd fought together, the initial transit was potentially one of the most dangerous moments in a fight. Normally, Barron would have sent scoutships, or even drones, through, but that wasn't an option here. Surprise was a crucial element of his plan. He was counting on the arrogance of the Alliance forces, on their inability to quickly believe that anyone would dare assault their homeworld. Sending drones through would be giving up precious time, warning the enemy something was coming.

"Very well. As soon as intraship comm is reestablished, issue launch orders to flight control." *Dauntless* had every fighter that could fly ready to go. Battleships often transited with their squadrons on alert, their flight teams ready to scramble at a moment's notice, but Barron had ordered every pilot in the fleet to his or her fighter *before* he'd ordered the final approach to the transit point. Each captain had the same order...launch fighters the instant sufficient systems control returned to permit it.

"Yes, sir. Launch support systems are still down."

The bridge was silent, Travis hunched over her station, monitoring the gradual return of *Dauntless* to operational status. Most of the other bridge officers were sitting, trying to look occupied, though they had little to do before their workstations restarted. Barron knew his people understood what lay ahead, the desperate, daring assault they were attempting. Whatever chance they had of success, he knew it was better than the almost certain defeat that had awaited them at Sentinel-2. But he couldn't shake the same tension he knew was preying on his crew, the cold feeling of they'd forced a decision, that victory or defeat was coming right now.

"The central AI is back online, sir. Branch systems booting now." Travis's words didn't call for a response. They were directed at Barron, in the remote case that his own eyes weren't glued to the screens, watching for himself.

Barron was focused as the main display lit up, the massive hologram in the center of *Dauntless's* bridge, streaked with ribbons of light as the AI recalibrated the projection. Barron watched, trying to take his mind off the fear that enemy ships would be posted near enough to the transit point to engage while his ships were still helpless. That was rarely the case, at least when an assault wasn't well expected, but he'd learned not to assume anything with Alliance warriors as the enemy. The Palatians were masters at war, and if they'd had the Confederation's size, tech, and economy, he shuddered to think of the wave of conquest they could have unleashed.

"Commodore, intraship and fleet communications active. Flight control advises launch systems will be operational imminently. Captain Eaton reports *Repulse* has commenced launch operations."

Barron allowed himself a little smile. Eaton had gotten there first, launching before *Dauntless*. He knew it had less to do with skill and effort, and more with the vagaries of the sub-atomic charges the ships had picked up in the transit between systems, but he was glad to cede the honor to his comrade. He had nothing but respect for his Eaton, and he still admitted openly, commodore's stars or not, that she and *Intrepid* had saved everyone on *Dauntless* back in Arcturon years before.

"Flight control reports launch operations underway."

The report was superfluous. Barron knew his ship like the back of his hand. He'd felt the distant vibrations, the feeling of fighters rocketing down the launch catapults.

His battle plan was aggressive, almost reckless, but he knew there was no choice. There wasn't a fighter in the fleet held back in reserve or committed to space patrol duties. Every squadron, every ship, had an offensive mission. The entire operation was based on speed and surprise. Each hour that passed lessened the chance of success, gave the stunned enemy more time to react, to call for reserves. Barron had ten battleships, a powerful force by any measure, but his target was nothing less than the capital planet of the most militarized nation in known space. If he gave them time to organize, every Palatian over the age of five would be formed up, waiting to fight his people.

Bryan Rogan and sixteen hundred Marines, backed up by fewer than one thousand allied Alliance stormtroopers. That was the army that would invade Palatia. In space, Barron could hope, at least, that most of the Red Alliance ships had been committed to the attack on Sentinel-2. But whatever had happened, there would still be tens of thousands of soldiers down on the surface of Palatia. Hundreds of thousands. With luck, they would be spread out, unprepared—perhaps even mixed in their commitments to the Red cause. Rogan and his people would have to move fast, strike directly against vital targets, but still, even if they were successful, how long could they hold on?

"All squadrons launched, sir. Scanner reports coming in. Enemy dispositions on the display." Barron could hear the tone in Travis's voice, and it gripped him, shook him from his gloomy ramblings. He'd expected a grim tone, word of vast enemy forces lined up between the transit point and the planet, but her words had been light, excited.

He turned quickly, looking at the display. He could hardly believe what he was seeing. There were only six battleships, and they were scattered all over the system. Three of them were close enough to respond, and one had started launching fighters, but in general Barron realized his attack had caught the Alliance forces flatfooted. It appeared Calavius had indeed deployed almost all of his strength to the final assault on Sentinel-2, a battle that would be little more than a diversion if Vennius was able to successfully extricate his fleet and make a run back to Palatia. Barron had a lot of faith in the Gray Imperator, but he also knew just how difficult a maneuver a fighting withdrawal could be.

"It appears that Imperator Vennius's diversion has done its job," he said. "Now, let's do ours. All squadrons, deploy and attack, tactical plan Beta-2. All battleships, full thrust as soon as system restarts permit. There are three battleships close enough to interfere with our move against the planet…"

Barron stared ahead, feeling the excitement inside, the controlled rage that took him in battle.

"Let's go get them."

*   *   *

Stockton stared out his screen, watching the hopelessly disorganized Alliance squadrons trying to form up into something resembling a battle line. The three ships closest to the invading fleet had all launched, but their strike teams were strung out, their fighters racing to link up, to put up at least some kind of credible defense amid the total surprise of the Gray invasion.

Stockton led *Dauntless*'s fighters in, pushing them to the max, directing each squadron with meticulous accuracy. He'd felt uneasy at first when he sat down, ready to launch at the head of the ship's entire strike force, but then it occurred to him he was sitting in Jamison's seat, figuratively at least, and a sense of pride came over him. He wouldn't allow himself to let his friend down. Jamison would have picked him to take over, just as Barron did, there wasn't a doubt in his mind, and that realization laid a heavy burden on him.

You can live up to what Kyle thought of you…or you can fail. Those are your choices.

Stockton shook his head. He would not fail. Whatever it took.

I'll do this, Kyle, for you...

He angled his controls, bringing his ship around onto a vector toward the closest enemy fighter. A quick glance at the screen confirmed Blue and Scarlet Eagle squadrons were right behind him, the two elite formations escorting the Greens, who were outfitted for bombing strikes. Torpedo attacks were cantankerous beasts, sometimes hitting with deadly effect, and others foundering on a well-conceived defense. But with the disorder in the enemy ranks, and the two best squadrons in the Confed fleet leading them in, he had no doubt the Greens would hit hard.

His eyes shot over to the side. Olya "Lynx" Federov was leading her own Red squadron, along with *Dauntless*'s Yellows. Stockton had faith in his new number two, an officer who had long fought beside him. But he couldn't help but think of how many comrades were gone. "Ice" Krill, Corinne "Talon" Steele, Kyle...all dead. And Dirk Timmons, the feared and admired "Warrior," his greatest rival for the position of top ace in the fleet. Timmons was lying in sickbay, nearly half his body gone, just barely alive. Federov was a good pilot—more than good, she was a decorated ace...but her road to number two on *Dauntless* had been paved with the loss of far too many friends.

"You know what to do, Lynx. What you've always done. What we've been doing for five years now." He held his voice firm, like a rock. *Like Kyle always did.* Federov could handle her assignment, there was no question in his mind. But she was his responsibility now, not just his comrade, and he was determined to send her into the fight the best way he could.

"Roger than." A short pause. "And thanks, Raptor."

Stockton turned back toward the screen, watching as the line of enemy fighters firmed up...slightly. His people would be in range in just over a minute. Then the fight for Palatia would really begin.

"Blues, Eagles...arm missiles now. You all know what to do, so let's get it done!"

*   *   *

"All ships, continue deceleration. Dead stop at sixty thousand kilometers from geosynchronous orbit. Prepare to fire on my command." Barron leaned forward in his chair, staring ahead, watching as the range to Palatia counted down slowly. His fighter wings had obliterated the three enemy battleships that had attempted to delay his forces, and his entire line had raced across the system, heading right for the Alliance capital.

"All ships decelerating, sir. All batteries armed and ready to fire on your command."

Barron sat quietly, watching, waiting. The range countdown display slowed as his ships' velocities reduced, the time to range dropping ever more agonizingly slowly. He wished there was a way to move faster. The sooner he could get to Palatia, the better chance Rogan and his people had of taking and holding the crucial installations. The ground forces had time now to fortify, but he was betting again that Alliance pride would intervene. The troops on the planet, already disorganized by the civil war, might count on the forts to defeat the invaders. He didn't like all the assumptions and hopes…they were the kind of things he tried to keep out of battle plans. But they were all he had now.

The three remaining enemy capital ships, plus a dozen or so escort vessels, were on the defensive. They had pulled back, forming a last-ditch defense just inside the range of the planetary defenses. Those powerful guns, mounted on eighteen massive orbital fortresses, were the lynchpin of the Red defenses. They could outrange anything in the Alliance fleet, and their massive, six-barreled turrets could blast an approaching fleet into slag.

But they didn't outrange *Dauntless* and the other Confederation battleships…at least Barron was gambling they didn't. He'd reviewed the schematics with Vennius before he'd left Sentinel-2, and he was convinced his primaries could blast the fortresses to atoms before he exposed his fleet to their deadly return fire.

He was still a little concerned, despite all his preparations. The range of the enemy guns was about only five to ten thousand kilometers below that of his big batteries…and one look told him that was because their power transmission systems were a generation behind the Confederation's. He'd had Fritzie take a look just to confirm his suspicions, and she agreed. With a bit of rerouting of the conduits and a few upgrades, those forts could tear his fleet apart. Not for the first time, he gave thanks for the Confederation's status as the most technologically advanced power in space.

He'd had a fleeting thought, an image of the weapons upgraded by his engineer, a way to hold Palatia even if Calavius's forces returned ahead of Vennius's. But there was no way to get close enough to capture the platforms, not without having his ships blasted to slag. No, as much as he wished he could seize the forts, he knew he had to destroy them utterly…and he had to do it as quickly as possible.

He could feel *Dauntless*'s thrust lessening…and then stopping entirely, the bridge filled with the weightlessness of freefall. Zero grav was far from an ideal working environment, but Barron needed to keep his ships in a narrow strip of space, a few thousand kilometers wide at best, which meant he had to fight this round at a dead stop.

"All vessels in position, sir." Travis turned and looked across the few meters from her station to Barron's.

He sat still for a few seconds, his eyes on the display, the tense feeling in his gut fading as the enemy guns remained silent. He'd checked and rechecked, but the margin was so small, he'd been nervous anyway, concerned the great batteries would open up, that their range would be greater than he'd expected. His eyes caught Tulus's three ships and their escorts, positioned just behind his line, ready to move up and engage any of the Red ships that advanced.

The seven Confederation battleships stood where they were, engines off, waiting for his word. He turned toward Travis and the two shared a fragile smile. Then he said simply, "Fire."

He heard Travis repeat the one-word order into her comm unit. Within a few seconds, *Dauntless*'s bridge lights dimmed, and her deadly primaries lashed out toward the hulking fortresses. One glance at the display told him the other ships had fired as well, the quad mounts of the four new *Repulse*-class monsters making *Dauntless*'s dual turrets seem almost puny by comparison.

He watched as the scanning data came in, updating the display. The ships were firing at extreme range, but the fortresses weren't ships. They had only minimal repositioning thrusters to avoid incoming shots…and it was clear from the start that none of them had expected to be under fire before they could respond with their own guns.

Close to half of the blasts from Barron's ships hit, slamming into the great stations, melting armor and ripping deep through the structures. But each platform was double the size of even Barron's giant new ships, and the heavy particle accelerator batteries were at the very edge of their effective range. The beams would have hit with more than double the impact just another twenty thousand kilometers closer, but then the hundreds of guns on the stations would be returning their fire, blasting Barron's ships to slag.

"All ships report batteries rearming."

Barron glanced over toward his exec and nodded. The recharge time was the greatest weakness of the Confederation's primaries, and it meant it would take some time for his fleet to reduce the forts. The firepower of the Palatian defense grid was too great to risk moving forward, not before every fort was gone.

The enemy emplacements opened up now, trying without success to return the fire. But the beams didn't reach the Confederation line, or they missed. The few that actually hit were too weak to cause damage. At worst, they could scramble an antenna or a scanner dish, and that only with a perfect shot. They needed the invasion force to close, to come within their own effective range…and that was the one thing Barron wasn't going to do, not until every one of those gun emplacements was blasted to bits or melted into useless junk.

"*Repulse* is firing again, sir. And *Majestic*." The new battleships had upgraded reactors and transmission systems, and their recharge time was better than half a minute faster than *Dauntless*'s.

Barron watched as another barrage of beams slammed into the fortresses. Even more of them hit this time, and he could see the damage building. The enemy platforms were still firing ineffectually, but Barron could see the intensity dropping as more and more guns were destroyed. He was still staring right at the display when *Dauntless*'s bridge lights flickered again, its own primaries lashing out a second time, tearing into one of the great platforms.

Barron was excited to see his plan working—so far, at least— but he couldn't help but think of the suffering on those stations, the thousands being killed and maimed. How many had chosen to follow Calavius, and how many were just acting on the orders of their superiors? And even among the Red Imperator's directly-declared adherents, how many had made their decisions under the influence of carefully-directed propaganda? Commander Mellus was a prime example. She'd rallied to the Reds, fought alongside them…and after she'd realized she'd been lied to, she'd tried to switch sides.

The closer Barron saw the Red Alliance leadership, the more convinced he became that the Union was involved. The slick propaganda machine, the polished efforts to suborn the military, to discredit Vennius, the rightful successor…it reeked of the Union. And they had every reason to intervene. A Red victory meant an Alliance invasion of the Confederation, and that meant disaster, an almost open route, directly into the Iron Belt and the Core.

But there was no escape for the men and women on those platforms. Diehard Red or trapped spacer, it didn't matter… they would all die. Barron had considered trying to spare the platforms themselves, just silencing the guns and then capturing the actual structures, but he'd quickly given up on that idea. Any attack sure to destroy the guns would already leave the fortresses wrecked, and besides, he didn't have close to enough Marines for his ground assault. He had none at all to spare for taking shattered orbital stations.

"Commodore…"

Travis's voice pulled Barron from his thoughts. He looked over toward her, but as he did he saw it himself, on the display. The remaining Alliance ships were advancing, moving against his line. It was suicide, a battle the Red forces couldn't win. But he knew they had no alternative. If they stayed where they were they would see their forts all destroyed, and then they would have two options…fighting to the death or running…and for Alliance warriors, he knew that was no choice.

He was about to issue orders, to command his ships to cease fire against the forts, to redirect their guns at the incoming battleships. But then Travis turned toward him again. "I have Commander Tulus on the line, sir."

Barron waved his arm, a signal his exec knew very well meant "put it through." "Vian, we've got battleships moving up," he said into the headset.

"Yes, Commodore." A short pause. "Let me take them. It'll be an even match…and your people can keep pounding the stations. We've got to get to Palatia and commence landing operations as soon as we can. Every hour they delay us lowers our chances of taking the objectives."

"Are you sure?" Barron had doubts. For once his fleet had numerical superiority, but Tulus's force alone would be an almost dead even match for the approaching ships. The Gray Alliance vessels would take serious losses…but if they could hold up the Red fleet units, Barron's ships could finish off the forts that much sooner.

"My people can do it, Tyler. Just give us the go ahead."

Barron could hear the anxious tone in his friend's voice, and he wondered how many spacers would die so Tulus could heal his shame and bruised ego in the inferno of combat. Amid all he admired about his new allies, there were some things he didn't like. Still, there were tactical reasons for the strategy as well…and Tulus was right, every moment sooner he could land his Marines increased the chances of success.

"Go, Vian. May the fortunes of war be with you, and all those who serve you."

"Thank you, sir." There was gratitude in Tulus's voice.

Barron was amazed at how well the proud Alliance officer had fallen into accepting him as the mission commander. No matter how well he thought he understood Palatian warriors, they continually surprised him. He'd never seen people who could so instantly transition from contempt to warm admiration the instant you won their respect.

"Maintain fire on orbital platforms," he said needlessly, more of a reaction to his own abortive intent to cease fire than anything else.

"All ships maintaining maximum fire, sir."

Barron watched on the display as Tulus's ships moved forward to meet the approaching Red vessels. He thought about launching fighters to support—about half his squadrons were already refit and ready to go—but he couldn't spare them. He needed his full wings to launch as soon as the platforms were down, to blast any remaining defenses and clear the way for the troop landings.

Tulus was on his own.

Barron's eyes caught a bright flash on the screen, then another one. Two platforms destroyed outright.

Sixteen to go…

Chapter Thirty-Four

Near Planet Varena
Cilian System
Year 62 (311 AC)

Grachus could feel the tension, the acid feeling burning into her stomach lining as her eyes darted all around her screens. Vennius's fleet was lined up, ready for battle. But the Confed ships weren't there.

They must be hiding somewhere...

"Slashers, Condors, Warhammers, break off and explore the asteroid belt. Black Tigers, Stormbringers, Blasters...check the far side of planet two."

She turned back to her screens, looking for any other places ships could be hiding. But there was nothing. It didn't make any sense. Where were they?

She'd heard rumors there was trouble between Vennius and his Confed allies, but Grachus hadn't believed them. Nonsense, she'd said. Wishful thinking. But now she began to wonder.

If the Confeds were really gone, the Red victory was even more certain. That was good news, for Calavius, at least. For her, it meant the duel she'd expected to fight would not happen, at least not here and now. She would not face Stockton. But her chance to avenge Kat would be gone as well. If *Dauntless* had fled home, if the Confeds had shown their true, cowardly colors, Kat's soul would still cry out for vengeance.

Her mind was in disarray, distracted by the worries that her primary target had eluded her. But she still had her duty, and she forced herself to set aside thoughts of retribution, at least against the Confeds. Her eyes locked on the large icon representing the Sentinel-2 station. She could still destroy the man who'd sent Kat to her death. It was far from enough, but it *was* something.

"Main strike force, on me. We're going directly for the station. Flanking force A, engage enemy ships out-system from Sentinel-2. Force B, engage all forces in-system."

Acknowledgements streamed in, dozens of them. As far as she knew, no Alliance officer had ever commanded so many fighters in battle. She'd organized her 120 squadrons into wings, each under the command of the senior squadron commander present. But she hadn't had time for more reorganization, and she knew she'd only be able to exercise superficial control over the unwieldy formation.

They're Alliance warriors. They know what to do…

Her eyes looked straight forward, locked on the display, on the small oval labeled, 'Sentinel-2.' It was time for Vennius to pay for Kat's death.

Suddenly, her readings went wild. Something had hit her ship. Not a piece of debris, nor a shot from a weapon, but something that almost overloaded her receptors.

A comm beam?

She flipped a row of switches, recalibrating her scanners. But they were blank, almost burnt out.

"Jovi?" The voice on the comm unit was familiar. She shook her head, ignoring what she heard. Thought she heard. But then it came again. "Jovi, is that you?"

Am I losing my mind…it can't be. Not him.

"Jovi, it's me. Jarus. If you hear me, please respond."

She reached out, her hands working her controls, reorienting her scanners to get a read on the communications beam. It came from one of the enemy vessels, a battleship positioned near the flank of the Gray line.

Perhaps it truly *was* Jarus. He and his entire family had rallied to Vennius's flag. *Traitor…*

She felt a rush of emotion, confusion trying to divert her from her purpose, but she resisted it, ignoring Jarus's words. She almost turned off her comm, but she couldn't do it without cutting contact with her strike formations. The beam was too strong, and it was coming in on all channels.

"Jovi, listen to me. I know you're angry. I understand what Kat's death did to you. But you're wrong about Imp…about Tarkus Vennius. He loved Kat as much as you did. She was like a daughter to him. He would never have betrayed her."

Grachus felt the anger growing inside her. She relived the moment she got the news about Kat, the fury that grew as she tried to determine what happened, how the Confeds had destroyed her. *Dauntless* couldn't possibly have defeated Kat in a fair fight. It *had* to be rigged. Vennius had set her up…there was no other explanation.

She poked at the buttons on her console, angling her antennae, trying to break off the incoming signal. But whatever she did, it adjusted almost immediately. *Whoever's controlling that thing must have an entire ship's comm staff working on it…*

"Main force, fire up turbos. We're going in now, and we're going in hot. Target…Sentinel-2." Her voice was coarse, raw.

She felt thoughts in her mind turning to doubt. She still had feelings for Jarus, affection she'd never lost, even when his family had treated her like dirt, keeping her from her son. Memories surfaced, the two of them alone, dining together…intertwined in the quiet darkness, the only light the flicker from the fireplace. Jarus had been compelled to couple with her, she knew that. But she was also sure he had felt something, even as she had. *Would he lie to me? To set me up? To distract me?*

She wanted to say no, to believe the father of her child would not engage in such deceit. They were on opposite sides in this conflict, but Jarus was still an honorable warrior.

No, it's a trick. The other side of her mind, the dark cloud formed from her rage and her lust for revenge, argued back. *Will you betray Kat now, so close to avenging her? Will you turn your back on the only person who ever truly cared about you? Abandon her when she can no longer stand for herself?*

"No!" she shouted, the word echoing in the cockpit. She felt a rush of determination. She would ignore Jarus. She would lead the attack in…and her squadrons would destroy Sentinel-2. Tarkus Vennius would pay for what he did.

"Main force…turbos on full. Missiles armed and ready."

"Jovi…I am telling you the truth. On my honor." A pause. "I swear it, on our son's life, my mate. Our son is safe, Jovi. He's hidden away, far from the fighting. I beg you…join us. Let go of this misguided quest for revenge. Deep in your heart, you know Vennius is the rightful Imperator. Push aside your rage, and listen to your honor. Please…"

Grachus's mind exploded again, voices inside, all her, arguing with themselves. The dark side was still in control, but its grip had weakened. Jarus's mention of her son had hit her like a punch to the gut, and she ached to see young Varus. For an instant, a passing moment, she considered breaking off from the formation, flying toward the ship Jarus was on. If she yielded to his words, she would see her son again! But then the cold determination slammed back into place. It was too late. She had chosen her path, and her course was set.

She looked at the cluster of dots on her scanner, the station's hopelessly outnumbered fighters. It looked like the squadrons from the battleships hadn't launched yet. It didn't make sense to her…by rights they should mass and try to gain local superiority at some location on the battlefield. But it wasn't her place to correct the enemy's mistakes.

Or to listen to their propaganda, to the treachery of those who would do anything to mislead…even dig up old lovers to try to confuse an adversary. *You have no honor, Tarkus Vennius.*

"Main force, prepare to engage enemy fighters…now!"

*   *   *

Vennius had been somber as he rode the lift down to deck twenty-three. He couldn't be sure the unexplained comm activity was the traitor, but he didn't have any real doubt either. He'd been waiting, expecting his hidden nemesis to strike again. He'd kept the destination of Barron's and Tulus's forces as secret as possible, but he'd done that before, restricted the most important intel only to his inner circle…and the information leaked anyway. He didn't know who he would find, but he was sure of one thing. There would be more pain, the bitterness of betrayal by one he had trusted.

The doors opened and he stepped out, one of the two guards slipping in front of him, pushing past in as respectful a way as possible. There were half a dozen other troopers waiting outside the door—Egilius's doing, no doubt. Barron appreciated his subordinate's concern, and he understood that as Imperator, he had no place there, exposing himself to a traitor. But he was still a Palatian warrior, and this was personal. He would deal with whoever had betrayed him, cost the lives of so many of his people.

"What is the status?" he asked to the highest ranking of the troopers, an optiomagis.

"We have the renegade penned in, Your Supremacy. We are searching compartment by compartment now. We will have him soon." A pause. "With respect, Your Supremacy, I implore you to remain here until we have apprehended the fugitive. We believe he is armed."

"That is of no consequence." Vennius knew the officer was thinking only of his safety, but the truth was, he didn't give a damn. "I am going forward now, Optiomagis. You and your people can come along if you wish, but do not get in my way."

He turned and reached out his hand. "Your scanner, Optiomagis."

The officer hesitated, but only for a second. It wasn't in him to disobey Vennius, no matter how horrified he was by the Imperator's orders.

Vennius took the small scanner and looked down at it, turning and moving swiftly down the corridor. His other hand dropped to his side, brushing against the sidearm hanging from his belt.

The scanner updated, several compartments becoming shaded, as the hunting troopers worked their way through, gradually shrinking the search area. Vennius headed for the center of the still-unexplored area, but before he got more than a few steps, he heard the distant sounds of gunfire. He increased his pace, no doubt surprising his guards with how quickly an old man could move. But before he'd gotten a dozen steps, the optiomagis's comm unit crackled to life.

"We've apprehended the suspect, sir. He is wounded but alive, and he insists he is innocent."

Vennius almost asked for an ID, but a quick glance at the updated scanner told him the prisoner was only a few compartments away. He hurried forward, turning the corner after about twenty meters, and then slipping through an open hatch. His eyes fixed on the scene: at least a dozen troopers, and one man, roughly his age, his right hand grasping his left arm, and blood dripping through his fingers from a gunshot wound.

Hirtius Longinus.

Vennius had been prepared for betrayal, for treachery at the hands of someone he'd trusted, but Longinus had been the last one he suspected.

"Hirtius," he said, his voice deep with disillusionment.

"This is a mistake, Tarkus." The old officer was trying, at least, that was no surprise. But now that Vennius's blindness had lifted, the trust of old friendship stripped away, he could see the officer's guilt, written plain on his face.

"Would you add to your treachery with lies, Hirtius? You're a traitor. We've been friends since we endured the Ordeal together. We've served for half a century, and I have denied you nothing." Vennius could feel himself hardening inside, the pain turning to a deep coldness.

"You denied me nothing?" Longinus's attempt at denial collapsed, and his voice became angry, accusatory. "You, who took my place, my position?" The guards surrounding Longinus reached out, grabbed his arms at his outburst.

"Release him. Let him speak." Vennius stared at his old friend. "I will hear what he has to say."

"Commander-Magnus," Longinus spat. "You held the rank that should have been mine. You worked your way closer to the Imperatrix, poisoned her mind against me. You stole what should have been mine. Did you steal my rank in her bed, when you were unable to claim it by deeds on the battlefield?"

"You are a fool, Longinus. I never spoke an ill word about you, to anyone, and least of all the Imperatrix. And if you think she would have been moved by a lover's words, you knew her less even that I'd thought. You are so bitter, so envious. You let a lifetime of friendship turn to hate and betrayal, and for what? Lust for an office I took but despised. I never wanted to be Commander-Magnus, Hirtius, as I do not now want to be Imperator. But we must do our duty, without regard to personal desires. I pity you, old friend, for you lost yourself. You traded adherence to the way for petty ambition and jealousy."

Vennius paused, staring at Longinus with anger, but even more, with sadness, with pity. "You could have lived—and died—a hero to your people, respected and admired long after your death. But now you will die as a traitor, your name stricken from every honor you have won, every accomplishment you once called your own…and your family shall carry your shame, as a millstone. How many times have we sat together, drank long into the night, talking of days past…when the entire time, your mind was consumed with envy and hatred? How you must have laughed at me when I entrusted you to seek out the traitor in our midst. What a fool I was."

He reached down and pulled the pistol from his holster. "It is duty now that I answer. You will pay for what you have done, for the treachery against me, but even more for the brave and noble warriors dead in battle because of your treason. I can only be thankful that you were stopped before you could divulge our plan here. That secret will die now, with you."

Longinus looked back, his face defiant. Whatever his former friend had become, Barron knew Hirtius Longinus had never been a coward.

Vennius extended his arm, his hand gripped tightly on the pistol. He knew what he had to do, understood how Longinus had betrayed him...but fifty years of friendship welled up from the recesses of his mind, mixing with images of Calavius. He could handle battle, strife, pain...but not much more treachery from those close to him. Cynicism was his armor, but even that had a limit. He was a man who valued loyalty about all else, and staring into the hate filled eyes of one who had been as a brother to him pushed him near his limit.

His finger tightened, defying every doubt, every pang of rage and sorrow inside. He felt the kick as the gun fired, the spray of blood, spattering over the two closest guards, and on him too... even as Hirtius Longinus fell to the deck with a sickening thud.

Vennius looked down, the pistol dropping to his side, at the motionless form of his officer, his friend, lying on his back, open eyes staring at him in one last accusatory gaze.

He looked for a long while, silent. The troopers standing around him were still, not saying a word. Vennius knew he was a dinosaur, a creature of a past that was gone. *You damned old fool, still living in a world that doesn't exist anymore. That probably never existed...*

He wondered how many old friends had harbored resentments and anger when he recalled only comradeship. He was tired, and he felt cold, alone. But still, duty called.

"Take him away...throw the body out of the airlock." A traitor deserved no ceremony.

"Yes, sir," the captain replied, just as *Bellator*'s klaxon's sounded.

The battle had begun.

Chapter Thirty-Five

"Commodore, perhaps we should conduct a higher-intensity bombardment. Enough to be sure we've taken out any military forces that could respond in the short term to our operations." Captain Eaton's voice was crisp in Barron's ear, firm, but he could also tell she was at least somewhat uncomfortable with what she was suggesting. Barron had created a short list of key ground installations to be targeted, for the most part, the ones that could shoot down the Confed landers. There was no shortage of other potential targets, though each one added to the list also increased the likely numbers of civilian casualties and collateral damage.

"No, Captain, we're not going to do that." He caught himself before the words came out too hard, too accusatory. He suspected Eaton was the most conservative of his captains, that the rest of them wanted to unleash hell so the Marines could land in the middle of flattened target zones, without a live enemy in sight. He like the idea of reducing the losses of his ground troops as much as anyone, but he wasn't about to flatten an ally's capital city to do it.

And, despite the current Red control, that was exactly what Victorum was, the capital of the Alliance, both Red and Gray, the home to millions of Palatian Citizens. He knew the vast majority of people on the ground were there by the vagaries of geography and politics, and not by passionate commitment to Calavius and his Union backers. Killing them, blasting their streets and buildings to rubble, would only increase the animosity. He needed to destroy the Red upper echelons, but he had to turn the rest of the warriors down there into future allies… which would be a lot easier if he didn't blast them to cinders.

"I want all of you to remember, this is not an enemy planet we're attacking. We have to look at it more as we would a hostage situation. We must go down, gain control, and hold for as long as we need to…and we need to do it without blasting the place back to the stone age."

Barron couldn't even imagine the mood on the ground. The Palatians down there, unopposed conquerors for three generations, coming to terms with the fact that their orbital defenses had been destroyed, that an invading fleet was in complete control of the space above the planet. Some cultures would surrender, but he knew the Palatians would never behave that way. They would fight.

"But, sir, we just don't have the forces to land in the teeth of heavy resistance and take and hold even the most vital of our objectives."

It was Captain Fitzsimmons who'd responded first, but Barron knew he spoke for all the others…and he was right, at least to a point.

"I understand the difficulties, Captain, but we're just going to have to do the best we can."

"Your officers are correct, Commodore." It was Tulus. Barron had included the Alliance officer in the comm line for the conference.

"Commander Tulus, those are your people down there. We can't just blast them to bits." Barron paused, not particularly liking the extent to which his empathy was coming from the goal of securing Palatian allies against the Union, and not from basic decency. "They will never be able to be allies with us if we do this."

"*My* ships will attack, Commodore. It will be Alliance forces against Alliance forces."

"I appreciate the distinction, Commander, but you don't have the strength to take on every ground defense installation on Palatia, or even just those around Victorum." Tulus's ships had endured a vicious fight against the Red vessels. All three battleships had survived, mostly because Barron's ships had finished off the orbital stations and intervened toward the end of the fight, but a trio of battered warships was simply not enough to make a difference, at least not without indiscriminate nuclear carpet bombing, which Barron wouldn't allow even if Tulus were willing to do it.

"My ships will target the main anti-assault batteries around the capital. There will be collateral damage, but it will be relatively controlled. Once those defenses are neutralized, we can launch fighter squadrons to attack ground targets with far greater precision that we could achieve with ship-based batteries." Tulus paused. "I believe your Lightnings can be adapted to use in atmosphere, just like our Palatines."

"Yes, they can." *But none of my pilots have likely practiced atmospheric operations since their Academy days…*

"That could work." It was Eaton again, a new enthusiasm in her tone. "Our squadrons took out all the defensive fighter squadrons before we reached orbit. Am I correct, Commander Tulus, that most of the planet's wings were based in orbit?"

"Yes, Captain Eaton, that is correct. There could be isolated ground-based squadrons, but not many. We'd need to keep a few wings on patrol, but most of our forces would be free to focus on vital targets."

Barron could feel the situation slipping out of his grasp. He was hesitant to send his pilots on a mission he knew they were ill-prepared for, but he quickly realized there wasn't a choice. Unless he could soften up the ground forces for Rogan and his people, the ground invasion would be a massacre.

"Very well," he said, trying to sound less edgy than he felt.

"But we've got to do it quickly. We have no idea what is happening at Sentinel-2, or how long it might be before fresh Red fleet units return…and we'll need our squadrons ready and on alert when that happens." A pause. "All captains, prepare your fighters for atmospheric operations. I want two squadrons per ship held back in reserve. You'll have to drive your flight crews hard, because we launch in one hour."

Barron knew the timetable was a tight one, but he was pretty sure all of his ships could hit it with enough effort. And he wasn't about to bet against Vian Tulus driving his own people to match that performance.

"Commander Travis, I want attack plans ready with squadrons assigned to specific target lists. And I want mixed formations on this, with both Confederation and Alliance fighters assigned to each operational area. Wherever a Palatian is getting shot, I want there to be Alliance warriors there alongside our people."

"Understood, sir." An instant later. "All captains will have operational plans within thirty minutes."

"All squadrons will be ready to launch in sixty minutes. And no screw-ups. Your flight crews are going to be rusty with atmospheric mods…I know they'll be rushing, but they have to get it right too. I'll skin anybody who messes up and gets a pilot killed through carelessness. Is that clear?"

Barron didn't wait for responses. He didn't need any. He'd made his point.

*   *   *

"All right, I want everybody to be careful. It's been a long time since most of you flew in an atmosphere, and you can get yourselves killed half a dozen ways if you're not focused. You've got gravity to worry about, and when we get a little lower into the atmosphere, you're going to be dealing with a lot of air drag. If you blast your turbos too hard, you can incinerate yourself damned fast, so forget all that hotshot stuff you pull in space." *Take your own counsel on that one, Raptor.* "Oh yeah, and three dimensions only go so far…there's solid ground down there too, and you're not going to like it much if you slam into it."

"Roger that, Raptor."

"We're good to go, sir."

Stockton listened to the wave of acknowledgements. His people were veterans—mostly, at least. Casualties like those *Dauntless* had taken over the last few years meant there were always a few replacements floating around. He just didn't want them to get cocky, to let their confidence morph from strength into something harmful. He knew all about that, better perhaps than anyone. But his own belief in his invincibility, battered when he'd almost died crashing into *Dauntless*'s landing bay, was gone. He'd always known he could be overwhelmed by numbers, killed by mechanical failure or damage to his ship. But he'd never really believed his match was out there, a pilot who could take him one on one. Not until now.

"Let's go…and keep those insertion angles in line with mission parameters. No pushing it like in space, because here you'll just burn yourself to slag."

Stockton eased his throttle down, watching as the glowing blue of Palatia grew in front of his eyes. He'd had the standard Academy training in atmospheric flying, but since then he'd only flown a few atmospheric missions, and none of them that promised to be as vital and difficult as this one. He didn't expect much in the way of ground-based air defenses. According to Commander Tulus, almost all the Alliance squadrons had been based on the orbital forts. Most of the dedicated atmospheric craft were transport planes and the like. Since the Palatians had expelled their oppressors sixty years before, the thought of fighting again on their home world had become anathema to them, and their productive resources had been directed into their massive fleet and space-based squadrons.

That didn't mean there were *no* defenses. Tulus had laid out a detailed list, along with maps and notes. Stockton had reviewed it as much as he could in the twenty minutes or so he'd had, but the bottom line was, his people would be dodging missile launchers and rocket batteries all around the capital.

His fighter shook hard, skipping on the upper atmosphere. It was a rough ride, the feeling completely different from that in space. He cut his thrusters, dropping back to one-tenth power, as he angled around into a bank of high-altitude clouds. He had to keep reminding himself he was in atmosphere, that his velocity would decline rapidly when he eased off the thrust. A quick glance at the ragged formation, a wild cluster of dots where his ordered and crisp squadrons should be, told him all his pilots were struggling with the change.

His eyes flashed to the screen, where an altimeter readout had appeared next to his coordinates. He was coming down quickly. He checked the temperature readings. The skin of his ship was hot, over eight hundred degrees, but nowhere near critical yet. He took a deep breath and fired his thrusters again, and a few seconds later he popped out of the cloud cover, looking down over a wide valley, and behind the far range of hills, a coastline, with a mass of distant lights. Victorum.

"We're beginning final approach. All squadrons…you know your targets. We shouldn't hit much in the way of resistance until we're about ten kilometers out, but I want all of you keeping your eyes open. You're going to have a harder time dodging incoming missiles in atmosphere, so you've got to pick them off right away."

He angled his controls again, changing his course to a direct approach. Blue squadron had the most important target, the fortifications right around the military HQ, and he was with them. "Optio Tillus, would you care to lead us in?" Tillus was a wing leader, and the commander of the three Alliance fighters attached to Blue squadron. Stockton wasn't sure how much good it would do in the end. People getting blasted on the ground were unlikely to notice whose ships were firing. Still, Barron's orders were clear. Alliance personnel were to take the lead in all attacks.

"Yes, Commander. Commencing final run…now."

The three Palatine craft blasted their thrusters hard— at least, hard by atmospheric standards—and they shot to the head of the formation. "Let's go Blues, follow them in." Stockton fired his own engines, his fighter lurching forward after the three Alliance craft.

The lights of Victorum grew closer, rapidly approaching as the fighters streaked in low, barely clearing the last range of hills before the coast. Tulus had recommended the tactic as the best way to undermine the defensive tracking systems, but in spite of the ground-hugging flight in, Stockton could hear his alarm systems going off. Missiles were coming in from the outskirts of the city. Only a few at first, but then dozens moved up, perhaps a hundred or more in total.

"Incoming," Stockton snapped as he angled his throttle, bringing in his ship into a sharp dive to the right. He only held it for a few seconds, the ground racing up at him, as he pulled back and reversed into a sharp climb. He looked across the display, at the fighters from *Dauntless* and the other ships. He was going to lose people here. His fighters were crammed together, mere dozens of meters apart, as opposed to the great distances common in space combat. The clustering of the approaching fighters made the missiles' work easier, and Stockton was watching as his first ship went down. It was Righetti, a replacement in Yellow squadron, and he was followed quickly by another. Then two more. All across the line, the attacking fighters were slicing right across the frontage of the missile attack…and paying the price.

Stockton hated the losses, whether they were his own, or more distant comrades from the other Confederation ships. Or even the Alliance pilots. He watched as one of his three attached Palatines was blown into two sections by a missile, each of them crashing in its own fireball a few seconds later.

The cost was high, but perhaps not as bad as he'd feared. The defensive fire was heavy, but it was confused, disordered. Stockton knew those ground installations had sat idle for more than half a century, and he suspected the third line troops deployed to man them had never expected to see action.

"All right, we should be through the frontline missiles, but watch out. Commander Tulus says there are short-ranged rockets deployed around the key installations. Stay sharp, let's take out the targets we're here for, and then let's get the hell out in one piece."

Stockton flipped on the targeting computer, bringing up the designated ground installations. The city was just ahead now, but the vast sea of lights was gone, blacked out against the coming attack. There was a faint glow of moon and star light, but Stockton and his people would rely on their scanners, as they did in space. That was just as well. Half his targets were weapons systems, scanning towers, depots, communication nexuses…but the others were barracks and fortified infantry positions. Stockton knew he had to clear those away, slice through the fixed defenses if Rogan's Marines were going to have any chance at all, but he'd just as soon be covered by darkness as he blasted hundreds of soldiers to charred crisps.

"Arm missiles…prepare to engage against primary targets." Stockton flipped the series of switches on his panel, arming the weapons. The missiles were primarily designed for ship to ship action, so he'd had his people hold them to the last moment. The closer in the launch, the likelier the birds would all hit home.

His eyes were fixed on the targets he'd chosen for himself, a cluster of scanning dishes tied right into the high command's headquarters. If Tulus was correct, the destruction of those dishes would go a long way toward crippling planet-wide command and control. And since the rest of his fighters were slamming all the backup systems, with any luck, any defending officers who survived would have immense difficulty in calling in reinforcements…or directing whatever remained of their deployed formations.

He squeezed his finger, firing the first missile, and a few seconds later, he sent the second one on his way. The weapons streaked across the sky, burning fuel at three or four times the rate they did in space. But it didn't matter. They'd either hit or miss in the next fifteen seconds.

Even as he watched the scanner, tracking his shots as they went in, he banked around, lining his ship up for its second attack run. The missiles had been locked on fixed facilities, but the rest of the raid would be a series of strafing runs, using his quad lasers to blast every defensive position, every bunker, every place Red troops could be hunkered down waiting for Rogan and his people.

The thought of smoking corpses, lying in great heaps, roasted at knife range by lasers powerful enough to send great beams thousands of kilometers in space, sickened him. But he'd been sent there to do a job, and he was damned sure going to do it. He owed that to Commodore Barron, if not to the Marines who would be coming down any moment.

And he owed it to Kyle Jamison, who would have been in his place if…

Stockton struggled to hold his focus, to push aside the thoughts of his friend…and of the match up that still awaited him. He had no doubt the Red fleet would be back, that they would return to retake Palatia. And when they did, Stockton knew what he had to do.

Chapter Thirty-Six

CFS Renown
Comara System
311 AC

"The enemy is pulling back, Admiral Striker. All ships appear to be withdrawing toward the Formara transit point."

"Very well, Commander. All squadrons with sufficient fuel reserves are to maintain contact and pursue until target ships have transited. The battle line will cut thrust until enemy ships are out of their fire range. Then set a course to remain in primary battery range." Striker wasn't at all surprised that the Union fleet was retreating. They'd fallen back out of three systems already...and the next was Formara, known colloquially as "The Bottleneck."

"Yes, sir. Relaying orders now." Commander Hogan had proven to be a tremendous aide, and the two had worked seamlessly together.

Striker stared at the display, at the star map of nearby systems. The border here condensed from an average of three systems in width to just single one. It was a natural spot to mount an aggressive defense, and Striker had no doubt the Union would have everything they could muster there waiting for him. He had tried to come up with a tactical plan, anything but a headlong charge forward into the enemy's toughest defense, but he'd come up blank. The real choice was not to attack at all, not until he had a hell of a lot more strength ready. But that was the one option the Senate had expressly denied him.

The entire offensive had gone better than he'd expected, far better. He'd pushed forward, fighting sharp, pitched battles in each system along the way. But the fights had been lopsided, odd, and each time he'd been matched against outnumbered Union fleets that seemed to be playing cat and mouse with him. He'd done damage, inflicted losses…but not all that many in the end calculation. The whole thing was starting to feel orchestrated. *They're enticing us forward, pulling us to somewhere. The Bottleneck, it has to be. They want us to dash our fleet against their defenses, to throw away our new construction and cripple our growing offensive capability.*

And courtesy of the Confederation Senate, we're going to do just that.

The success of the assault had only worsened his situation, not with the enemy, but with the politicians back on Megara. He'd sent two requests, the last one entrusted to no less capable hands than Gary Holsten's, entreaties to pause, to allow him time to regroup, to consolidate the captured systems. Both had been soundly rejected. The rapid advance had only reinforced the Senators' belief that they had been right, that Striker's earlier caution had only prolonged the war.

He'd recovered two worlds lost to the Union over half a century before, planets the Confederation still considered their own, even though they'd been compelled to cede them in the first war between the nations, the conflict Confed history books still called "The War of Shame."

Striker himself wondered how much of the old Confed societies remained after so long under a government expert in breaking down individuality and peoples' will to resist, but he knew enough about politics to understand what great headlines the recoveries of such planets made for the populations back home.

Recovery was a strong word. If they'd have let him stop, they might have been actually *been* recovered, or at least have begun the long, painful process. As it was, the fleet just sailed by, doing nothing more than announcing that the populations were liberated, something Striker figured did little more than give ample warning to the Sector Nine sleeper teams no doubt infesting both worlds.

Striker watched as the Union forces continued their withdrawal, with considerable skill, he had to admit. *If that wasn't planned, and I mean well in advance, I'm a damned fool.*

His fighters, faster and more maneuverable, were able to stay close, for a while at least, before they were gradually forced to turn back to refuel. They managed to cripple one more enemy battleship, an old hulk Striker couldn't believe had survived the war this far. But still, any capital ship destroyed was a step toward victory, if a small one. The rest of the enemy fleet made good their escape, with varying degrees of damage, and then, suddenly, he was in uncontested possession of the fourth system since he'd set out from Grimaldi. It was a success, by some measure, he supposed, though he saw only the problems. His supply lines were strung out and tenuous, his main fleet base now five transits back. His own fleet had suffered losses, and though they were far less serious than he'd feared, every crippled ship had to limp all the way back to Grimaldi, or further, and every new fighter or tanker full of fuel had to travel forward on an increasingly longer—and to Striker's way of thinking, vulnerable—logistical tail. He suspected Union treachery of some kind was out there, waiting to ensnare him. In fact, he was sure of it. He just didn't know what.

But I bet I know where...

His eyes focused on the transwarp portal, the one the Union fleet had used to escape. *Escape my ass, they want me to follow.* He suspected the enemy had constructed bases and laid minefields, everything possible to attrite his forces as they attacked. He didn't like paying for victory with blood, at least not more than he had to, especially when brainpower could shift the cost balance. But his hands were tied. Whatever bloodbath awaited his people in Formara, it was a date he couldn't stop. All he could do was be as ready as possible, for whatever lay ahead.

*   *   *

"Now we know why they fell back, don't we?" Striker turned slightly, his eyes moving to Admiral Jaravick. Jaravick was old school Confed navy, a veteran long retired when the disastrous initial months of the war brought him back to the colors to serve any way he could. At first, that had been as Striker's aide, a strange role reversal for two men who'd once served in the same positions switched. Striker had gone along with that for a short while, when survival in the war seemed to hang by a thread. But then he'd seen that Jaravick got his stars back, and an appointment to his staff to go with them. There was no one whose opinion Striker valued more highly, save perhaps Holsten's and Tyler Barron's, and he'd asked Jaravick to sit with him on the bridge to consult.

"That's a strong force out there, Admiral, but take a look at those dispositions. Is that how you would have deployed?"

Striker stared at the display. "No, perhaps not…but maybe they've got some hidden defenses, something we don't know about." He shook his head. "But we've got no choice." *None but mutiny.* He'd come close to that dreaded word a few years back, when Holsten had hatched his plot to retire Admiral Winston and put him in the old fleet commander's place. He'd never grown comfortable with that whole episode, despite the fact that he didn't have a doubt doddering old Winston would have lost the war in those fateful months. But disobeying a direct Senatorial order, there would be no question about that. It would be textbook mutiny, and treason to boot.

"Let's get the fleet formed up for attack, Commander."

"Yes, sir."

Striker had come through in an unorthodox formation, one designed to bring as much fighting strength as possible to bear against any enemies positioned near the transit point. He would have placed a screen of fast escorts there himself if he'd been defending, ships capable of opening up on the invaders as they trickled through with scrambled systems, but also of making a hasty withdrawal when the relative strengths shifted. But the

Union had nothing waiting. Not a line of pickets, not a cluster of laser buoys. Not a thing.

Striker was gratified not to take any losses on the transit, but the whole thing just made him even more uncomfortable. Something was wrong, something beyond the heavy force concentrations waiting deeper in-system. He felt as though he were walking into a trap, but he couldn't see it, no matter how hard he looked.

"All ships are ready, Admiral. Awaiting the orders to advance."

Striker sat for a moment, feeling as though his mouth had gone dry. It was one word, but it stuck there, refusing for a moment to come out. Then, without detectable emotion, "Advance."

"Yes, sir."

Striker had already given the orders, the specifics. His fleet would accelerate full into the system, closing to primary range of the enemy and then decelerating to a stop. His line would stand firm and bombard their targets from outside the enemy's range. If the Union forces wanted to fire back, they could close with his ships. With any luck, the fearsome primaries, especially the gigantic quad mounts on the new ships, would gain an edge before the enemy vessels could bring their own laser cannons into the action.

"All ships, prepare to launch fighters." He wanted his squadrons in space, with plenty of room to push forward and intercept any bombing attacks. He'd outfitted all of his strike teams as interceptors. It cost him the chance to launch bombing runs at the enemy ships, but he just couldn't be sure how many fighters the enemy had stashed in orbit around the system's planets. His wings could handle anything the Union ships themselves launched, he was sure of that. But if hundreds of fighters suddenly emerged from one of the planets…he wanted to be ready.

He felt the pressure from *Renown*'s engines, but the crushing force he'd expected for about the twentieth time still didn't appear. His flagship was one of the newest to roll out of the shipyards, and her dampening systems were leading edge.

Renown's engines were putting out close to 12g of thrust, but on her bridge, it felt like no more than three. That wasn't comfortable, not by any means, but it wasn't the relentless, crushing hell that usually made his bones feel like they were about to poke through his skin either.

He was impressed by his new flagship, as he was by all the recent construction, though he tried not to think any more than he had already about what had happened to the last ship that had been called *Renown*.

"All task forces report ready to launch, sir."

Striker started out at the display. It was a battle he hadn't wanted, and the fact that it was about to take place a few systems farther along from where he'd expected did nothing to change that. He wanted to cancel the launch order, command his ships to reverse course, to fall back to the previous system. To truly liberate those reclaimed worlds while he built supply bases and forts, and waited for more of the new construction. Anything but what he knew he had to do. Here. Now.

"Launch all squadrons," he said, trying not to sound as grim as he felt. Something was wrong. He didn't know what, but he was sure of it.

"Launch all squadrons." Commander Hogan repeated the order as he passed it on to the task force and ship commanders. Seconds later, *Renown*'s main display began to show clouds of tiny dots, hundreds of fighters blasting out from the main battle line, heading toward the enemy positions.

"The fleet will advance. Attack plan Alpha."

"Attack plan Alpha...executing."

Striker could hear *Renown*'s engines, feel the giant ship moving forward. If he'd had his way, his vessel would have been in the front of the line, but the Senate's instructions were clear. He was to maintain a position behind the main force, where he could direct the entire operation. It made sense, of course, but it stuck in his craw. Van Striker wasn't the kind of admiral who led from behind. He understood how that kind of thing came naturally to the political hacks and careerists back on Megara, but he liked to stand alongside the officers and spacers he ordered into hell. But this entire operation was a concession to obeying commands, and he'd glumly placed *Renown* ten thousand kilometers behind his main force. That was a lot closer than the intent of the Senate's instructions, but taking advantage of vagueness was not a court martial offense.

He sat quietly, watching, waiting as the fleet neared combat range. The odd positioning of the enemy formation was still gnawing at him, Jaravick's words playing again in his head. His eyes panned across the display over and over. *Those ships don't look like they're ready to defend. They look like...*

He shook his head. *They look like they're ready to counterattack... or retreat.*

But why would they retreat? They've got as much strength as they're going to muster anywhere...and we'd have to backtrack a dozen systems to get around the Bottleneck if we can't take it.

A counter attack? Beyond thwarting his own ships' effort to benefit from their longer range, there was no tactical reason for the Union forces to attack. They were positioned deep in the system they held, in range of whatever planet-based assets they had.

So, what then?

"Admiral..."

Hogan's voice cut through Striker's thoughts, almost like an answer to his question.

"...we're picking something up on the scanners. It's big... and the energy readings. I've checked three times, sir, but it still has to be a mistake..."

Before Hogan could finish, the display flashed, and every eye on the bridge darted toward the image. It was *Majestic*, an old battleship just returned from complete rehab. She'd been along the edge of the fleet's left flank...but now she was gone, nothing left but energy and a cloud of hard radiation.

Striker felt like he was going to vomit. He didn't understand what was happening, but he knew it was bad.

Damned bad.

"I want full scanner readings from..."

Another flash.

"*Resounding* was hit by something, sir." Hogan turned toward the command station, his face white as a sheet. "She's gone, sir. She was completely destroyed…"

Chapter Thirty-Seven

AFS Bellator
Near Planet Varena
Cilian System
Year 62 (311 AC)

"Your Supremacy...shall I order the withdrawal?"

Vennius sat at the workstation. It was an odd place, perhaps, for an Imperator to be during a battle that would determine if his cause would endure, or if he and his followers would all die. He was silent, lost in thought, Egilius's words floating at the edges of his gloom. Vennius was a warrior, and he'd been prepared to face death for more years that he could remember. But he'd never understood what a dangerous enemy fatigue could be, or the relentless disillusionment of too much betrayal and deceit.

He had believed in the way, body and soul, and even as age brought some doubts and questions, he'd never questioned the essential rightness of what he had done during his long career. The Alliance was aggressive, and it could be merciless as well. But the Palatians were honorable, a people who had come together from unimaginable suffering to rise up, stand together. He'd always known one day his people might meet an enemy they couldn't defeat, that they could fall in battle. But he'd never had the slightest question they would stand or fall together.

Now, that belief was shattered. The civil war was bad enough, but the seemingly endless sequence of treachery and dishonor had almost broken him. *Was I really so naïve all my life? Was I a fool to believe all I did, only to see it crumble before my eyes?*

He knew he had to press on, that he owed it, if not to Palatia and the future, to those warriors who had rallied to him, fought, bled, and died in his name. But he wasn't sure he knew how anymore.

Bellator shook hard, the second time in the last few moments. And again, the familiar voice, at the periphery of his thoughts, but louder, more urgent, sinking through this time.

"Your Supremacy…the enemy line is closing. If we don't begin our withdrawal soon…" Egilius let his words trail off, but his meaning was clear.

"Yes," Vennius said, his voice hoarse. "Initiate withdrawal phase one."

"Yes, sir."

Phase one…we're not just running, we have a complex and well-conceived plan on how to run. Vennius knew his assessment was unfair. He wasn't fleeing from the fight with Calavius. His retreat here would draw his enemy after him…to the final showdown at the capital itself, the heart of the Alliance. If the two Imperators were to fight for the future, that battle should be at Palatia, not some remote base. *Assuming Commodore Barron has somehow managed to succeed, to take control of Palatia.*

Vennius sat and watched Egilius, his admiration for the young officer growing by the minute. Egilius had not only been the first ship commander to swear to his cause, he had proven himself to be a master tactician and strategist as well. Vennius had pushed Egilius as fast as he dared, into the command of one of his wings. He'd have given the officer operational command of the entire fleet if he'd thought he could pull it off. But that would leapfrog over too many senior commanders, all men and women who had also sworn to him…and Vennius had learned one lesson very well over the past months. Never to take loyalty for granted.

He watched as the entire fleet began falling back, a move that looked, at first at least, like a direct withdrawal. But in a few minutes, he would order phase two...and Calavius and his people would know his ships were not heading for the outer transit portals, the routes they would take if they were fleeing. No, Vennius's fleet would make a run for the link deep insystem... and it wouldn't take long for the Red Imperator and his people to figure out where they were heading.

The Red fleet's approach vectors were far from ideal for pursuit, especially if they didn't anticipate his intentions before his ships changed course. With any luck, Vennius and his people would get a head start. But Calavius and his people would figure out what was happening, and they would pursue, hot on Vennius's heels. He was sure of it.

In fact, he was counting on it.

*   *   *

Something is wrong. Why aren't they launching their fighters?

Jovi Grachus sat in her cockpit, her eyes darting back and forth, directing the massive force under her command. It was almost impossible to fully track so many fighters. She'd divided them up into strike wings of four or five squadrons each, but it was still taking all she had to stay on top of the attack. She knew it was sapping her efficiency, that as prepared as she was, the assault was sluggish and slow...but she struggled to push things forward.

It's a good thing Dauntless isn't here. There's no way I could have focused on an attack against only one ship. Another day...

Her anger was still there, but Jarus's words echoed in her mind too, driving against the resolve that had hardened in her over the past five years. Was it possible she *had* been wrong about Vennius? She'd known the old officer since childhood, and while he'd mostly come to the estate to see Kat, he'd always been kind to her.

He came to see Kat so many times, and he always seemed so fond of her. And when Lucius Rigellus was killed...he stayed for weeks. He must have dropped every duty he had to come to the estate. How could he have betrayed her? Conspired to sacrifice her to his machinations with the Confeds?

She exhaled hard, pushing the distracting thoughts away yet again. She couldn't accept the possibility of being wrong. Her eyes went back to her scanner, watching as her wings pushed forward, absolutely shattering the Gray fighter forces…what there were of them, at least.

She'd expected hundreds more fighters to oppose her attack. She'd pushed her bombers to the back of her formation, intending to allow time to crush the defending interceptors before going against the battle line for the kill. But there were no interceptors, not from the battleships, at least. Just a thin line of fighters, perhaps three hundred in all.

All from the station, and none from the battleships…

It had taken her some time to realize that all the squadrons her people faced had indeed launched from Sentinel-2. Her mind raced, trying to divine what Vennius was up to. Was he trying to pull her forces in before he launched? Divert her attack toward the base, and then send his fighters out behind them? A desperate attempt to sneak an attack in against the Red battleships? It didn't seem likely. In fact, none of it made much sense. But as each minute passed, and no fighters launched, she became more and more worried.

She almost wanted to call off her attack, to pull her ships back until she knew what was happening. But that wasn't an option…and if Vennius wanted to leave his ships undefended, so be it.

"All bomber squadrons, accelerate at full. Prepare to commence attack runs." She wasn't going to let any doubts interfere with her duty. Not vestigial emotions for Jarus. Not uncertainty he seeded in her head. *And not endless worries about what Vennius might be up to.*

"Wings three and four, isolate and pursue remaining enemy squadrons." Whatever thoughts raced through her mind, she had nothing but respect and admiration for the pilots of Sentinel-2's squadrons. They had thrown themselves into a hopeless attack, and they'd battled to the bitter end, losing more than half their strength so far and still fighting. But she wasn't going to play their game anymore. She wasn't going to let them tie up her whole attack. *As they did so well already…*

She looked up at her screen, at the Gray battleline. Her face was hard, her stare fixed. She was ready.

But something was wrong.

The Gray battleships were blasting their thrusters suddenly, accelerating at full thrust. Away from the attack.

Were they retreating? *That makes no sense. Where can they go that they will be stronger than here? If they abandon the base, we'll destroy it, and then they'll be fighting us someplace else without it.*

But there was no question. The entire Gray battle line was on the move, directly away from the Red fleet. Directly away from her fighters.

*   *   *

"We seem to have gotten the jump on them, Your Supremacy."

Vennius nodded. "Yes, Brutus, at least to some extent." He was watching as Egilius and his staff directed not only *Bellator*, but an entire wing of the fleet. The Gray Imperator wasn't surprised at the enemy's apparent confusion. It made no tactical sense for his forces to withdraw from Sentinel-2. Their position was hopeless even with the base, but without it the Red fleet would crush them even more certainly. His only concern had been the fighters. His decision to hold them back had been a difficult one, and certainly a choice a lot of his people disagreed with…but there had really been no option in his analysis. His fleet would fight again, the final battle, and that combat would take place in a location Calavius would never suspect.

Assuming Commodore Barron and his people succeed. Somehow.

Vennius knew Barron's mission was difficult, a longshot by any system of measurement. But he also found himself believing in the Confed officer…and he decided there was a chance after all. A good one.

He looked back at the display, at the large orb representing

Sentinel-2. The great base had become his home, and the rallying point of his cause. It felt wrong to abandon the facility, to leave it to be destroyed by the enemy…along with the skeleton crew of volunteers he'd left behind.

And the fighters…

Vennius closed his eyes as he looked at the ragged, sparse clusters of small dots. One-third or less of Sentinel-2's fighter complement remained. Holding back his ships' squadrons, allowing those pilots to go into battle alone, unsupported, it had been one of the hardest things he'd ever had to do. But he knew he would need his battleships' fighters at Palatia.

When we settle this, once and for all…

He looked back at the Red ships on the display. They hadn't yet responded to his fleet's abrupt run for the transwarp point. They were still pounding Sentinel-2 and chasing down the last survivors of the station's fighter wings. Vennius had ordered his own ships to pause briefly and land as many of the scattered ships as they could. In the end, they'd recovered forty-one; not a lot, at least not by the standards of the casualties this civil war had already caused. But there was a point, in Vennius's view, where rationality and expediency had to be abandoned, at least momentarily. Those men and women had fought for him, and he'd felt he had no choice but to save them if he could. He was leaving hundreds of other behind, the volunteers manning Sentinel-2, firing the last of its guns as the Red fleet blew it to bits, the pilots who'd already been lost, and the seventy or so that remained but were too far away to retrieve. They were all going to die in the next twenty minutes or so, Vennius knew, even as he watched them continue their desperate and hopeless battle.

He saw the large white dot on the screen, the transwarp point, growing closer with each passing moment. *Bellator* would transit in less than ten minutes, and within an hour, every one of his ships would have left the system…or they would be drifting fields of rapidly-cooling wreckage.

One more battle, my old comrade, Calavius. One more, at a place of my choosing. I will see you to hell, if I must take you there myself.

Chapter Thirty-Eight

Above Planet Palatia
Astara System
311 AC

"All right Marines, we've got sixteen minutes 'til we land. Let's not waste it. Check your weapons, your ammo…and say whatever the hell you want to whatever god you think gives a shit, because when we hit ground, it's on." Bryan Rogan's voice was coarse, his words harder than his usual.

A chorus of half-gripes came back over his comm—pretty standard from Marines who'd just been told to check their kits for third time—but Rogan wasn't in the mood for it, and he shut them down with a savage, "That's enough…you've got your orders."

Rogan was usually in far tighter control of himself, but right now he felt out of his depth. He was a Marine, through and through, and he'd see any mission to the end. But this time he was invading a planet—not just any planet, but one renowned for its warrior culture. And he was doing it with less than three thousand combat personnel. If he hadn't gotten the orders directly from Commodore Barron, he'd have been sure some-one was pulling some kind of prank on him.

You're not invading a whole planet, just grabbing a few key installations, mostly in the capital. Which the fighter wings were

325

kind enough to soften up for you. And you've got surprise on your side, and the fact that these Alliance troopers have to be on edge, split in their loyalties…

Rogan had already been deployed with his people in the landers when the fighters broke off and returned to their ships, but he'd heard enough back and forth chatter on the comm to be pretty sure they'd taken some nasty casualties from the ground defenses. *Defenses that won't get a shot at us, thanks to the fighter jocks, and the risks they took flying in so close.* Rogan generally subscribed to the notion common in the Corps that there were Marines and then there was everybody else, but he was about ready to relax that a bit, and make some of those pilots honorary leathernecks.

It was still night over the main target area, though Rogan knew it would be less than an hour before predawn light began to cut through the darkness. The city was completely blacked out—Rogan wasn't sure how much of that was a defensive measure and how much was the result of the fighter wings pounding the hell out of the power grid. But there *was* light, coming from what looked like thirty or forty different fires still burning. None of them were massive conflagrations, and that, he suspected, was a testament to the accuracy and restraint of the attacking squadrons. If the pilots had been as precise as it appeared to Rogan, maybe his people had a chance after all.

The assault shuttle shook hard as it entered the thicker atmosphere. Rogan was with the central force, tasked with securing the main military command structures—and if they were lucky, capturing some of the high-level Red officers. His orders on that account were clear. He was to take them alive. The attack on Palatia was about military success, but it was about diplomacy too, at least of a sort. There were Red officers who had chosen their allegiance based on lies and propaganda…and the idea was to undo some of that, to win back adherents to the Gray cause.

Rogan didn't know much about that kind of thing, but Barron had explained it carefully, mostly in the context of trying not to blast officers that could be turned. It seemed like a reach to him, and his recollections of fighting Alliance troops didn't especially bode well for taking prisoners. But he realized that the overall purpose of the entire operation was to get Imperator Vennius's word out to the Red fighters, to try to shift their allegiance. He didn't much like the sound of it, but that wasn't his call, and he had enough to worry about already.

He glanced to the side, to a small group of three landers on the flank of the main formation. Clete Hargraves was over there, in command of a reinforced platoon, sixty of the hardest veterans Rogan had. The grizzled old sergeant wasn't leading an assault on enemy military headquarters or a crucial transport junction. No, he was on a mission to find and rescue two children. Rogan had been stunned when Barron had given him the orders. The whole attack was desperate enough, but five dozen Marines, going off alone, hundreds of kilometers from support—to find two kids? It was insane. But Rogan respected Commodore Barron more than any man he'd ever met, and he would carry out any order he was given, however hopeless, however insane.

And this one was both.

I'm sorry, Clete...you're the toughest Marine I've ever known. And I had to send my best on this, whatever the risk.

*   *   *

"First squad, up on point. These kids are probably under guard, and even if the Reds don't have any troops there, the family retainers will likely put up a fight." The Marines were there to safeguard the children, to rescue them, but Hargraves knew that in actual practice, what they were doing would be very like kidnapping them.

He moved forward a few meters, to the edge of the woods. The manor house was off in the distance, on a large hill about two kilometers south. Part of the approach was covered by tall grasses and a stretch of something that looked like vineyards, at least from his position. But the last thousand meters stretched over open, manicured hillsides. If anyone was watching—and with the planet under attack, he had to assume *everything* was being watched—his people would get pegged before they were close to the house.

He watched as the ten Marines of his first squad moved past him, slipping out beyond the tree line, crouched down below the shoulder-high grass. He waited a few seconds, letting his scouts get about a hundred meters up, and then he turned and gestured to the clump of Marines behind him. "Let's go," he said, speaking loudly enough for them to hear, but not yelling. He had everybody on communications silence. The invasion and the fight for control of vital targets was hundreds of meters away, mostly in and around Victorum. But it wouldn't take more than an intercepted comm transmission to truly raise the alert here.

Hargraves slipped around the tree he'd been behind and moved ahead. He had a pair of pistols at his side, but right now he held a heavy assault rifle in his hands. He wore a shoulder strap holding a dozen reloads, and three grenades. He had a protective vest and some other light body armor, but he and his people had sacrificed a level of protective gear for speed. They had to get in, grab the kids, and get out. Fast. The shuttles would be there in an hour, and if he and his Marines weren't there waiting…well, it was a long walk back to the capital, through hostile country.

Hargraves was a sergeant, low in the overall hierarchy of the invasion of Palatia. But that didn't tell the whole story. He was a hardcore veteran of thirty years, respected by privates and generals alike. It felt strange to be relegated to some fringe theater, away from the fighting that would decide if the invasion succeeded. He might have been offended, annoyed to be so misutilized, but he was too accustomed to following orders to allow himself such thoughts. Besides, these orders came directly from Commodore Barron, and in the years since he'd been plucked from his posting at Santis and made part of *Dauntless*'s complement, he'd fallen under the same spell as the rest of the crew and Marine contingent. Tyler Barron was a natural leader, and in all his decades of service, Hargraves had never admired an officer more. He would do anything Barron commanded, even lead a crack team away from the main fight to rescue two kids.

He moved steadily forward, eyes darting back and forth,

making sure the Marines on both sides of him were staying down, using the cover as long as they had it. He could see his squad up on point stopping, hesitating at the edge of the high grass, waiting for his orders to rush the house.

"Your Marines maintain their order very well, Sergeant." Optio Hursus and ten of his stormtroopers had been attached to Hargraves's command. He understood the logic of including Palatian troops with each ground force, but he still didn't like it. Truth be told, he found Hursus to be quite likable, and clearly a good soldier, not terribly unlike Marine sergeants he'd known, or even himself. But he'd seen almost his entire command destroyed fighting the troopers on Santis, and despite the Palatian's clear efforts and his willingness to submit to Hargraves's orders, the old Marine still couldn't see anything but an enemy standing there.

"They're well trained." His tone was curt, and it didn't invite further discussion. He didn't have time to deal with Hursus now. He'd kept the Palatians at the rear of the formation, something he suspected they might take as an insult, but he didn't want to deal with them, not now. And he didn't give a shit if they were offended.

He pulled out his comm unit. Everything was ready. With any luck, the radio silence had kept their presence and approach a secret. But now they were going to be spotted no matter what. He knew enough about the Alliance to be sure if there were troops here watching the children, they'd have sentries posted… especially after the invasion commenced.

"All squads, here's the deal. We're going to rush the house. First and fourth squads, cover the flanks and look out for enemy snipers and fire positions in and around the house. Second and third squads, with me. We go right in, no stopping. Any Red troopers are to be shot on sight…" *Like there's any way to know if someone we run into is a Red.* "Any retainers…try to spare them if you can, but if they're armed and they come at you, you're authorized to shoot to kill. But make sure you know what you're shooting at before you fire. The Marine who hits one of the kids we're here for is in a world of shit." Hargraves had gone over all this before, but in his thirty years, he'd never seen an instance where a reminder wasn't worthwhile. "We're here for the two kids, period. Once we grab them, we get out and head to the extraction point."

He paused, but just for a couple seconds. His transmission would most likely be detected, and he had no intention of standing around until the enemy reacted.

"Let's go…forward!"

*   *   *

"They're both still asleep. I just checked." Vilia Drovus walked out of the hallway into the Blue Room. At least, that was what the household staff had told her the sitting room was called, named, she guessed, for the blue wall coverings. The manor house of the Rigellus estate was vast, enormous. She'd known the family was rich, but now she saw up close what that truly meant. *And all just for those two kids…*

It occurred to her that there were only two Rigellus heirs because every other member of the family, three generations at least, had been killed fighting the Alliance's wars. But still.

"That's good." Firtus Mascius was her partner, assigned to Rigellus Manor the same day she had been. They hadn't met before, but she'd found him easy enough to work with, if a little hard-edged. "With everything going on tonight, I'd just as soon not have to deal with them. Unless…"

"Yes." Drovus had thought this assignment—her first as a member of the new Alliance First Bureau—would be easy, almost effortless. Keeping the kids in line had been somewhat annoying, but there were more than enough family retainers to see to the brats' everyday needs. She and Mascius were there for one reason, and one reason only. If the Red Alliance fell, they were to see that the Rigellus kid were taken care of…and that *did not* mean clothed and fed. They were to kill both of them and dump their bodies in the sea.

That had seemed a remote prospect, with the relative fleet sizes and strengths…at least until a couple hours before when, from what they'd been able to gather, enemy fighter squadrons laid waste to Victorum's defenses, followed by what was starting to look very much like a ground invasion.

Now, suddenly, the destruction of the Red cause seemed at least possible, and Drovus knew Calavius's defeat would mean the end of the fledgling agency, and very likely severe punishment for all who had been involved in it. She'd signed up mostly because of the promise of rapid advancement, but now she wasn't so sure. If they didn't follow their orders, if they spared the children, would the invading Grays show mercy?

It was doubtful. And letting the kids go would backfire horribly if the Reds, as was likely, repelled the invasion.

Drovus had signed on with the Reds because they were on Palatia and in control. They appeared to be the clear favorite, and if Drovus knew one thing, it was that it was better to be on the winning side. It wasn't a very Palatian attitude, but she had always been more focused on her own needs than some overarching sense of duty. She'd often wondered how many of her comrades spent their lives playacting adherence to the way while nursing their own self-centered thoughts.

"Vilia…I'm getting something on the outside scanners. I think it's…"

The sound of automatic weapons fire from the guard post outside cut him off.

*   *   *

"Keep moving…we've got to take that position now." Bryan Rogan was near the front of his line—something he knew would have earned him a severe *talking to* from Commodore Barron. He stood firm, firing his rifle toward the half-shattered wall of the strongpoint. The intel Tulus and his people had provided had proven to be completely accurate, but unfortunately, it also appeared that Calavius's people had added some fortifications not on the maps Rogan's people had been given.

It was about standard for any mission, Rogan figured, foul ups and information shortfalls being endemic in operations like this. But he hadn't led many assaults so absurdly weak relative to the strength of the target, and he simply had neither time nor personnel to waste dealing with the unexpected. His people not only had to take the target positions, they had to hold them for an indeterminate amount of time. He simply couldn't afford losses like this, not so early.

The fortifications weren't elaborate, but they were directly in the path of his attack. He doubted they had been built to ward off an invasion of the sort his people had launched. The Palatians could never have brought themselves to believe any enemy would actually dare to attack their capital. *They were probably worried about Vennius loyalists onplanet when they built those...but the damned things are coming in pretty damned handy against us.*

He had almost a hundred casualties already, just around the main military headquarters, and if he let his Marines stop advancing and get caught out in the open, it would make that toll look like a walk on the beach. He thought about falling back, grabbing some cover and fighting it out, but there just wasn't time. He had all the forces he was going to get, at least until Vennius's fleet arrived, and his enemies had a whole planet to draw on. He had to take those objectives, and he had to do it now.

There was wreckage all around from the strafing runs, and Rogan knew his forces would have been crushed already save for the massive damage inflicted by the fighter squadrons. But he'd never seen an air attack, short of a thermonuclear strike, that eliminated all ground resistance, and that was again proving to be the case. So, unexpected fortifications or not, his people were just going to have to go in there and take these objectives the hard way. One at a time.

"Forward, all of you. Over the wall...now!"

Chapter Thirty-Nine

UWS Banniere
Formara System
Year 62 (311 AC)

"Another hit, Minister. Heavy damage to the target, readings of internal explosions, leakage of atmosphere and fluids."

Villieneuve stood quietly on *Banniere*'s bridge, watching his plan unfold on the display. It had been a long effort, one that had entailed great expense, and not a little personal risk. The last thing Villieneuve had wanted to do after returning from the grueling trip to the Badlands was get back onboard a ship, but he wasn't about to miss his great victory.

He smiled as he watched the Confederation fleet, and he tried to imagine Admiral Striker's frantic efforts to determine what was happening...and how to deal with it. Should he advance, seek to get his own ships into range of the Union fleet? *Yes, please...do that.* The weapon wreaking havoc on the Confed ranks was twenty thousand kilometers behind the Union battle line. If Striker took the bait, if he pushed forward, his fleet would be trapped in range of the great weapon that much longer. The entire Confed battle line could be destroyed.

Villieneuve had gambled and lost with the planet-killer. He'd committed irreplaceable reserves and almost incalculable resources, only to have the great artifact destroyed by Tyler Barron. But like any skilled gambler, he recognized bad beats, and he knew, save for fortune's intervention, his plan could have worked. Would have worked.

He knew the Confederation would respond as they always did, to relax their guard after the immediate threat was gone. He had done the opposite. He'd sent his operatives into every port on the edge of the Badlands, throwing whatever it took to gather all the rumors, tall tales, and whatever else a border rogue might reveal under the heavy persuasion of drink, bribery, or the opposite sex.

He hadn't found another planet-killer. That would have been too much to hope for. But in the two years following the destruction of his previous find, his people discovered something else. There had been rumor combined with fact, guesswork mixed with real exploration. His people had analyzed it all…and when he'd finally launched the expedition, luck had shone on his efforts. They'd found what they were looking for.

It was an energy weapon, akin to a laser, but far more complex…and powerful. It had needed repairs, but fortunately, the central core was completely intact. The tech in there would take years to decipher, and perhaps decades to effectively replicate. His scientists had told him it used some of the same systems as the transwarp links that connected solar systems, and that the core laser blast was enhanced by some form of energy drawn from the alternate universe that made faster than light travel possible. It was all beyond him—beyond his scientists too, he suspected—but they'd managed to get the thing functioning—another bit of luck. Whether by skill, luck, or some combination, the thing worked, and that was all that mattered.

Villieneuve knew he'd been fortunate that the most complicated parts of the system had remained fully operational. The biggest problem had been replacing the antimatter power source. The weapon required astonishing amounts of energy to function. Villieneuve had solved that problem in a straightforward manner. He'd directed his engineers to rig up a cluster of fusion power plants, as many as it took. And when it appeared the construction of enough facilities would take two years or more, he'd confiscated a hundred reactors from Union planets, an action that inflicted severe power rationing on the inhabitants. If reducing a few billion citizens to four or six hours a day of electricity was what it took to win the war, so be it. The resulting string of fusion plants was unwieldy, exposed, but it was enough to get the weapon working.

He still didn't understand the weapon, but he'd grown tired of his scientists trying to come up with a label that described its functionality. Finally, he'd simply give it a name himself. The Pulsar.

He watched as another Confed ship was almost torn in two by a single hit. He'd chafed for years at the power of the Confederation's primaries, outranging and outpowering his ships' guns. But his new weapon was exponentially more powerful than his enemy's particle accelerators. The first two shots had taken the Confeds by surprise, and with no evasive maneuvers to deal with, both had been direct hits, nearly vaporizing their massive targets. Villieneuve had never seen anything as large as a battleship destroyed with one shot, and even his own iron control failed him for a moment as he watched, and almost giddy smile slipping onto his lips.

The Confeds were in disarray now, trying to decide how to react. *Wait until they pull back and see that we held our fire for thirty thousand kilometers to draw them in…*

Villieneuve was extremely satisfied. He'd suckered Striker in, and now he would make the Confeds pay for that mistake. He suspected he owed political pressure for his adversary's unusual lack of caution, but that too had been part of his plan. There were operatives on Megara, and a sizable amount of Union funding had found its way into the hands of numerous special interest groups, feeding their demands for an offensive to end the war. He'd fenced a match with Gary Holsten on that one, and he had to admit, his opponent had played a skilled hand. But in the end, the Confederation's republican government, and its spoiled, unappreciative masses had been too large a burden, even for the gifted head of Confederation Intelligence. The Senate had at last cast the die…and Van Striker and his spacers had set forth into enemy space.

And now they will pay the price…

Unless the Confeds withdrew. The Pulsar itself could likely destroy any attacking ship before it could get into firing range, but lack of mobility made his superweapon useful purely on the defensive. He'd suckered the Confeds in now, but he knew he'd never fool Striker again. The Bottleneck was the sole route between the powers on this section of border, but there were other points of contact, farther Rimward. If enough of the Confederation fleet escaped, it could pose an invasion threat elsewhere. He had to take down as many ships now as he could.

He closed his eyes and took a deep breath. What he really needed was a system that could move the pulsar and its vast train of reactors. If he could make his ancient tech into an offensive weapon, he could invade the Confederation and drive straight to Megara. His fleet would be invincible with the great ancient gun before it.

He had his people working on it, thousands of engineers and technicians, hundreds of designs and proposals. He'd offered a vast reward to the team that gave him what he needed…and he'd threatened to unleash the full wrath of Sector Nine on those who failed.

But that was tomorrow's problem. Today, he would enjoy all he had worked for, all he'd pursued for so long. He would watch the Confederation fleet shattered.

*   *   *

"We have to do something, Admiral…and now." Jaravick was standing next to Striker in the middle of *Renown*'s bridge. "We either commit one hundred percent, and accelerate forward full…or we turn and run at full thrust. If we stay here, we're finished."

The old admiral was remarkably calm. Striker was a man who rarely lost his focus, but the instant one of his immense battleships was blasted out of space, he'd come close. He'd pulled himself together quickly enough to order a random pattern of evasive maneuvers, but not before a second vessel had been blasted to atoms.

He looked back at Jaravick. For an instant, his impulse was to order the fleet forward at full thrust. Then he shook his head. He had no idea what that was out there, but one thing was certain. It could destroy every ship he had.

He turned toward Hogan. "Fleet order retreat. All ships are to set a course directly for the transit point. Full thrust." Even as he spoke, he could see the Union fleet, every ship, blasting their engines and advancing toward his ships.

It was a trap. The whole thing was a setup, a plan to lure him to the Bottleneck. He'd known…deep down he'd known the whole time something was wrong. Now the quick retreats from system to system, the lack of resistance…it made perfect sense.

"All ships acknowledge, sir." Just as Hogan snapped out his report, Striker saw yet another of his ships vanish from the display. *Indomitable.* One of the newest ships.

Whatever that thing is out there, not even our biggest ships can withstand a hit.

He looked at the screen, at the two damaged ships. They'd taken less than direct hits, but now Striker could see that while the vessels hadn't been destroyed, the damage they had suffered was catastrophic. He knew immediately both ships were total losses. Worse, he realized almost at once that there was no time to send rescue ships or to pick up lifeboats. He would have to leave any survivors behind.

He wrestled with that knowledge, trying to think of some desperate measure to save his spacers. But there was none. His only concern now, the only thing that mattered, that *could* matter, was making sure there still *was* a Confederation fleet when this engagement was over.

"I want maximum evasive maneuvers during withdrawal. We have no idea of the range of that…whatever is firing at us." He turned and looked at the display, running calculations in his mind. The Union ships were accelerating from a dead stop, while his were still trying to overcome their inbound velocity. He knew the answer in his gut before his head confirmed it.

Those Union ships were going to get into firing range before his fleet got away.

Damn.

He turned and glanced at Jaravick. One look into the older man's eyes confirmed he had reached the same conclusion.

"Admiral, the Union ships are launching fighters."

Striker could almost feel the weight pushing down on him. He was caught well and truly in a trap. All he could hope for was to avoid total destruction. If he couldn't pull out some reasonable portion of the fleet, the entire border would lie open to the Union. The war would be as good as lost.

"Center task force, cut thrust to one-quarter. Increase spacing between ships five hundred percent." The words had just blurted out, and they were met with only silence, for a few seconds at least before Hogan managed a fragile, "Yes, sir."

Striker knew what he was doing, and so did his crew. He'd turned the center third of his fleet into a rearguard, a desperate line to hold back the enemy while the others escaped. His ships would be exposed to the deadly new enemy weapon, but their primaries would be in firing range long before the approaching Union ships could respond.

"Center force, all ships arm primaries." His fleeing ships couldn't fire their main guns, not while blasting their engines at full thrust. Not even his newest ships produced enough energy for that.

"Yes, Admiral. All battleships, arm primary batteries." Hogan had gotten more of a grip on himself, and his words were steady. A few seconds later. "All ships confirm, sir."

Striker stared straight ahead, his eyes fixed on the display. "All other vessels are to go to overloads on reactors and engines. I want the fleet out of here."

"Yes, sir."

Out of here…while we stand in the breach and hold off hell…

Chapter Forty

"First squad, keep up that covering fire. Fifth squad, move up to support first. We need to hold that line until we get the objectives." Objectives. It sounded ridiculous to Hargraves to speak in such cryptic terms, even as he said it. Anybody inside that building knew why his people were there.

He was crouched out in the field, far too in the open for his tastes, but first squad's heavy fire had pinned down the enemy troops on the left. There were four or five, Hargraves had figured, up on the roof of an outbuilding. *It was less resistance than he'd feared, but still dangerous, and it was astride his exit route. And you've still got no idea what's inside.*

He watched as his Marines pushed forward, moving through the shattered remnants of the main door. He ran up, pressing himself against the front of the building as he waved the rest of his people in. He could hear their boots inside, on some kind of hard floor, but there hadn't been any shooting. Yet.

He swung around as the last of Hursus's people slipped through. The entry was massive, the ceiling three stories above the great marble floor, with balconies overlooking from the second and third levels. *This would have been a great spot to mount a*

339

defense. He was glad, at least, that there were no enemy troopers lined up on those upper floors, hosing down the main entry.

"You know what to do," he said, realizing it was unnecessary. He'd reviewed the plan with his people three times. They all knew why they were there. Hargraves didn't like splitting his people up in small groups of three or four, but there wasn't any other option. He had no idea where the kids might be, or what other personnel might be in the house somewhere. And it was a big house to search.

Hursus was standing next to him. All the Gray Alliance troopers had dispersed, sometimes only a single one accompanying a group of his Marines. *I guess Hursus is my minder…*

Hargraves knew it made sense to keep the Alliance troopers dispersed throughout his formation. If anyone had a chance of convincing the Regullii retainers not to resist, it was them.

"Let's go," Hargraves said sharply. The three Marines clustered around him, and the Palatian non-com snapped into place alongside. The group moved up the main stairs, rifles out, alert for any enemy troopers that might turn up. Hargraves didn't have any solid intel on where the two children might be, but the second level seemed like a fair bet.

He came up to the top of the stairs, and spun around, his combat instincts reacting to the threat before his mind even processed it. He fired half a dozen shots, and the Marines with him did as well. The trooper coming down the hall had started to bring his rifle around, but the blast of fire threw his bloodied and clearly dead body back against the wall before he got off a shot.

"Stay sharp…and watch the fire. We get those two kids out of here alive, whatever the cost. Don't forget that."

The group moved down the wide corridor, stopping again after twenty meters or so, as more enemy troops poured into the hall. There were half a dozen, at least, but the Marines, and Hursus, opened fire immediately, taking half their attackers down in the first second or two. Then the enemy survivors dove to the side, one ducking in an open doorway, and the other two dropping behind heavy pieces of furniture.

"Grab some cover," Hargraves shouted, as he pressed himself against the wall, maintaining his fire. *Shit. We don't have time to get bogged down.*

His comm crackled to life. "Sarge...it's Cooper here. We're just down the hall from you, bracketing the enemy troops. I think we found the kids, but there's somebody else in there too. I hear scuffling around."

"Stay where you are, Coop. Don't even think about going in there until we get through to you. If you get a shot at these guys in the hall, take it."

"Got it, Sarge."

Hargraves fired another burst and then ducked back into his makeshift cover. He'd been in fights like this before, and he knew a standoff like this could last for hours...or at least until somebody ran out of ammo. His people didn't have that kind of time, and the longer they were bogged down the more chance the enemy would get reinforcements. He knew he had to do something, now."

He held the comm to his mouth, speaking softly. "All right, listen up. On three, we're all rushing that position. Just push forward full speed, firing every step."

He popped the clip in his rifle, replacing it with a fresh one. "One."

He took a deep breath and exhaled. "Two." Rushing an enemy in cover was his last choice of tactics...but it was also his only one right now.

His rifle was tight in his hands, and he lunged forward, just an instant before he said, "Three."

He stumbled down the hall, his momentum taking him forward and to the left. He fired, and then again as he caught a glimpse of one of the enemy troopers. He saw a spray of blood, and then the shadow of his enemy's body falling. He heard a sickening thud as it hit the ground.

Fire tore down the hallway, and he saw as one of his Marines fell forward, his left leg giving out as a pair of shots came close to tearing it off.

Hargraves was still moving, though he could feel himself

stumbling forward, his momentum pushing through his balance. His rifle continued spitting out rounds on full auto, ripping into the fine paneling of the walls, sending shards of wood flying everywhere. Another enemy trooper fell victim to his assault, dropping hard into the center of the hall.

He tried to right himself, to keep up on his feet, but the strength in his legs failed him. He fell to the ground, landing on a long, ornate carpet, and gasped for breath, feeling a sharp pain in his side as he did. He reached down and then pulled up his hand. It was covered with a sheen of bright red blood.

He'd been wounded before, almost more times than he could recount, and he knew almost immediately this was serious. But he didn't have time to be out of action. Not now. He tried to get up, but he couldn't, not until he felt a hand on his shoulder, helping him to his feet.

He wobbled as he stood, gritting his teeth against the pain. He glanced to the side to see Hursus standing next to him, the Alliance soldier's hand still on his shoulder. He nodded his acknowledgement, and then he moved slowly forward, limping.

The Alliance troopers were all down, and a small group of his and Cooper's Marines were clustered outside the doorway. He made his way forward and looked inside.

There were two children, a boy, perhaps twelve, and a girl two or three years younger. They were sitting on the edge of a bed, the boy leaning forward in front of the girl, holding a knife. Two adults, a man and a woman, were standing on the opposite side of the room, both holding guns pointed at the children. There was an old man in between, clearly trying to shield the kids with his own body.

"This is your last warning, old man. Get out of the way, or you die too." It was the man speaking. He turned to his companion. "Vilia, cover the door." Then, turning slightly toward where Hargraves and his people stood, "Stay back, all of you. One move, and we open up."

"You're trapped in here," Hargraves said, struggling more to get the words out than he'd expected. "Drop the guns, and we won't harm you. We're just here for the children."

"I said stay where you are. And who's trapped? How long do you think it will be before this house is surrounded?"

Hargraves could see the old man, his eyes darting back and forth.

"Imperator Vennius sent us for the children. We have no quarrel with you," Hargraves's voice was strained, but still threatening, "but we will kill you if you force us to."

Hargraves caught an odd look in the old man's face, as if he'd been trying to come to a decision and finally had. Barely a second or two later, he turned directly toward the man who had spoken. He pulled a small pistol out from under his shirt, and brought it to bear. Even as he did, the man and woman opened fire. Hargraves could see the impacts, four shots taking him in the chest, throwing his frail body backward toward the bed. But not before his pistol fired. A single shot.

Hargraves snapped his head around, watching as a large red circle appeared in the man's head. The old man had sacrificed himself to save the children, his shot perfect, dead on. Hargraves reacted immediately, instinctively. He would see the man's sacrifice was not in vain.

His hand snapped up, bringing one of his pistols to bear, even as two of the other marines opened fire. The woman had started to speak, and Hargraves thought she might have been trying to surrender...but it was too late. Her body was riddled with bullets, and she crashed into the far wall, falling dead to the ground.

The two children leapt off the bed, rushing to the crumpled body of the old man. The boy kept his knife pointed toward Hargraves and the Marines, looking as though he intended to defend the man against them. Hargraves opened his mouth, but before he got anything out, the old man muttered, "Go with them, Lucius, Ariane. Your Uncle Tarkus sent them to save you." The voice was weak, frail, and Hargraves could hear the gurgling sound of blood in the man's lungs.

"We can't leave without you, Yuricus. We won't." The boy reached down, put his hand behind the man's neck, pulling his head up. But there was no response. The old man was dead.

"You two have to come now. We've got transport coming, but if we don't get out of here now, we never will." Hargraves looked up at Hursus. "Take them," he said, wincing again in pain. He watched to see if the children resisted as the trooper put his hand gently on their shoulders, guiding them toward the door. They didn't.

Hargraves turned to the entire group, wobbling on his feet and catching himself on the edge of the bed. "Let's get the hell out of here."

*   *   *

"I want those positions manned right now." Bryan Rogan was yelling into his comm, the urgency of the situation clear with every word he spoke. His people had taken the primary targets, somehow. He'd almost given up for a few minutes, but his people had pushed forward, beyond endurance, beyond reasonable expectation, and once they'd taken the main line of defenses it had become a turkey shoot, his enraged Marines chasing down every now-exposed enemy survivor they could find.

Rogan didn't approve of casual brutality, and he'd ordered his Marines to take prisoners of any enemy troops who surrendered, but he wasn't surprised when no live Reds were rounded up. He couldn't fault his people, not knowing the ethos of the Alliance. You couldn't mandate taking prisoners from an enemy who rarely surrendered.

"Yes, sir. We've got all approaches covered…but, sir, we've got multiple sightings of enemy troops inbound. I'd say we've got a massive counterattack forming."

Rogan cursed under his breath. He'd had similar reports coming in from all across the line. He knew his people would have to defend the ground they'd taken, but he'd hoped to have longer to prepare. His forces had blasted the makeshift defenses relentlessly when they took them, and he needed a day, twelve hours, at least, to get them back into some semblance of shape.

But it didn't look like he was going to get it. He stared at the portable scanner his aide had just set up. Things were worse than he'd thought. There were thousands of Red troopers, approaching from all around his perimeter.

"What's the status of that comm link?" He turned toward the engineers working on the electronics panel behind him. The main Alliance communications nexus had been his number one objective, the sole point Barron had labeled as essential. The Marines had taken it, along with all the others, but the equipment had been pretty badly shot up in the fighting.

"We're working on it, Colonel. The Alliance systems don't work the way ours do." A pause. "We'll get it back online, sir."

"As soon as possible," Rogan said. Then he looked at the screen again. *There's no way we're going to hold back that attack, not without more time to dig in.* He pulled the comm unit from his belt and stared at it for a few seconds. Commodore Barron had sent him down here to do a job...and now he had to tell his commander that he was going to fail.

"*Dauntless*, this is Colonel Rogan. I need to speak to the commodore."

"Hold, Colonel." Rogan recognized Commander Travis's voice.

"Colonel, report." Barron came on the line within a second or two.

"We've taken all major objectives, sir, but..." Rogan was as no nonsense a Marine as the Corps made, but he was having trouble telling Barron his people weren't going to hold what they'd taken, at least not for more than an hour.

"Speak, Colonel. Give it to me straight."

"We've got a major counterattack forming, sir. Thousands of troopers, and I'm betting they're first line types. We're digging in, but we haven't had enough time. I don't think we can..." Rogan's eyes caught the scanner again, the huge groups of enemy troops gathering together. They were formidable for sure...but they were also forming up out in the open. "Sir, if you can launch another fighter strike...they're all out in the clear. If we can hit them quickly enough..."

"On the way, Colonel. You and your people just do what you can. Help is coming."

Chapter Forty-One

UWS Banniere
Formara System
Year 62 (311 AC)

"All ships are to continue to advance at full thrust!" Villeneuve had his hands on the back of Mies's chair, hovering over *Banniere*'s captain. His elation at the trap he'd sprung had given way momentarily to anger. "I want those ships destroyed!" His superweapon had earned its keep, justified every resource he'd poured into acquiring it. The makeshift power facility his technicians had put together was another matter entirely. The weapon had taken down seven enemy ships, four destroyed outright and three crippled, gutted. But the power feeds kept giving out, shutting down the superweapon's fire while emergency repairs were made. His engineers had warned him they needed more time to complete their work, and he had to admit they *were* repairing things in almost astonishing time, but still, he was furious. Seven destroyed Confed ships should have been twelve, and now he'd lost two of his own vessels as they moved toward the enemy, running the gauntlet though the Confed's deadly primary battery range.

"Yes, Minister." Mies was just *Banniere*'s captain, but Villeneuve's presence made her a sort of staff officer to the entire fleet. The head of Sector Nine didn't hold a position in the

346

naval hierarchy, of course, but no one would refuse his command. He'd learned his lesson earlier in the war about trusting too much power into any single officer's hands, and the combined fleet was commanded by three different admirals, each in their own ships. Militarily, he knew it was a cumbersome structure, and tactically inefficient, but the last thing he needed now was a naval hero with visions of political power. It was another reason he was there, at the front in *Banniere*. If someone was going to be revered as the hero of the Union, it was going to be him. He didn't crave the adoration, but he couldn't dispute the political utility of it all.

He had every reason to be pleased, to rejoice in the great victory his arms had won…but now his eyes caught the enemy rearguard, and the columns of ships behind them, moving steadily through the transit point. Every Confed ship that escaped was one he'd have to fight another day. He'd never expected to bag the whole enemy fleet—Striker was too smart for that. But the initial phase of the battle had gone so well, he'd gotten greedy. He'd had images of pursuing a crushed and broken force, his own fleet winning the war, in the next system…or the one after that. But that wasn't going to happen. The Confederation fleet would be battered here, hurt badly. But it would not be destroyed. And his deadly weapon, the tool that taunted him with the promise of total victory, was stuck, unable to pursue its prey and complete its work of destruction.

At least until his engineers managed to do as he'd charged them to do. His face tightened. They *would* build some kind of structure to move the Pulsar, no matter how much pressure he had to put on them, how many dire threats he need to hurl their way. And they would do it quickly. There was no more time. The Union was on the verge of collapse, its economy utterly devastated, unrest building on dozens of its worlds. It was time to win the war…or lose it. And which it would be hinged on whether he could turn his superweapon into something mobile…and bring the war to the enemy.

*   *   *

"The left flank has begun transiting, Admiral."

Hogan's words were a fleeting solace to Striker in his misery. At least some of his ships would escape this deathtrap...*the one I led them to.*

He knew he'd had no choice, that he'd been expressly ordered to do as he'd done. In a Senatorial chamber, testifying before the miserable band of politicians who'd sent his people into this nightmare, he'd have proclaimed it loud and clear, laid the blame at the feet of the pompous fools. But sitting on *Renown*'s bridge, watching his people die, it sounded like an excuse. Those men and women being burned and crushed and blasted to bits had followed *him* here...and they would blame him for what had happened. But none of them would blame him with more bitterness than he did himself.

"Admiral, we're getting requests from fighter squadrons all over the task force. They are requesting permission to launch."

Striker stared at the display, at the waves of Union strike craft approaching his wavering line. There were hundreds of fighters, and a second line that looked very much like bomber squadrons. He could only imagine what they would do to his ships unopposed. But he'd held back from launching his own fighters. He knew full well, sending a pilot out there was a death sentence. As soon as the other ships had transited, his rearguard would make a run for it...and there would be no time to retrieve fighters.

We just might make it out ahead of those bomber squadrons...

He'd sent his people into deadly situations before, and, he had to admit, more than one nearly suicidal mission. But ordering his fighters out when he knew without doubt that he was sending them to their deaths...could he even make himself do that?

"Volunteers only, Commander. Each ship may launch volunteers, but only up to one-fourth of their complements." He hated himself as the words came out of his mouth. He knew the roster would be full on every ship, even oversubscribed.

And he also knew those doomed pilots might hold back in the incoming assault wave...maybe even just long enough.

He turned toward the far end of the display. His battleships were moving through the transwarp point. They were almost on top of each other, far closer than safety regs required. But regulations weren't important now. Whatever escaped from this trap would be the Confederation's sole defense, and Striker would do anything that got more of his people out.

He saw the escort ships clustered around the portal. Not one of them would transit before the battleships had all gone through. The big motherships were the heart of the fleet. They *had* to survive. If that meant a few dozen escort vessels and their crews had to be sacrificed then so be it.

His eye caught the clouds of tiny dots, his doomed squadrons launching. The math was simple—if the fighters could hold back the enemy attack long enough to save even one more battleship, it was worth it. But there was more to this equation than simply numbers. These were loyal officers, pilots who had served faithfully, and who now were giving all they had left.

There was another flash on the display. The enemy's big gun was firing again. This time it was *Monarch*. The old ship took a hit amidships. She hung in space for a few seconds, and then she disappeared in a massive explosion.

Striker almost looked away. *No*, he said, holding his head firm. *You owe it to them to watch, to see.*

Renown's bridge lights blinked again as her quad primaries fired. Striker turned his head to the targeting screen just as the heavy particle beams slammed into a Union battleship. The vessel was badly damaged already, and the direct hit proved to be too much. It didn't explode...the reactors scragged instead of losing containment, but the scanning reports quickly confirmed Striker's guess. It was dead.

That's three...and we've lost nine, counting the cripples that will never leave this system. And we're still in the fight.

He felt anger building toward the politicians who'd ordered him into this disastrous invasion. How many men and women would die here because of their ill-conceived action? *Will it be enough to cost us even our defense? Will the Confederation fall because of their foolishness?*

He saw another bright light on the display, the enemy weapon firing again. A clean miss this time. He let out a deep breath, thankful for the salvation of another thousand of his people. At least for a few moments.

"Admiral, the right wing is going through, and the escorts are lined up behind."

Striker turned and looked, confirming what his aide told him.

"Very well, the rearguard will pull back. All ships without primaries are to move at flank speed to the transit point. The rest of the formation will conduct a fighting withdrawal."

"Yes, sir." Hogan turned back to his station and passed on Striker's orders.

Striker watched as his volunteers flew their fighters forward into the approaching Union strike force. They were vastly outnumbered, but as he sat there and stared at the screen, they sliced into the masses of enemy ships, cutting through like a bloody scythe. They ignored their own losses, and they plunged straight through the Union interceptors to the bombers behind.

It was a sight to see, but all Striker could think of was so many of his best people sacrificing themselves, buying time for the fleet to escape. Even as his eyes were fixed on the fighter battle, he knew battleships were pouring out of the system. He didn't know if the enemy would pursue, or what was involved with moving their new gun, but he understood one thing. The war had just changed, dramatically. The enemy had a weapon his forces couldn't face, and he had no idea how to deal with that.

"The rest of the rearguard will fall back now, Commander." Striker pushed aside worries about tomorrow. All that mattered right now was getting his people out of there.

He felt the pressure as *Renown* accelerated at full speed, its course a zigzag pattern toward the transit point. He had the urge to order the engines to halt, to stay back and try to pick up some of the fighters closest to the flagship. But all that would do was doom *Renown* and its twelve hundred crew members. If it had just been him, he would have stayed. But battleships came first...and every pilot in the fleet knew that.

He watched the remnants of his fighter force, now surrounded, the enemy's numbers finally coming into play. Then *Renown* shook hard, a massive cracking sound reverberating throughout her hull. He knew immediately his flagship had been hit by the new weapon, that she had suffered damage all down her spine.

And then he was lying on the ground, looking up at Hogan. His aide was leaning over him, saying something, but he couldn't hear. There was nothing but the cold metal of the deck below him...and the massive structural support that had crushed his chair.

Was there pain? He wasn't sure. All he knew for certain was despair, for his spacers, his ships...the Confederation. And then there was only blackness.

Chapter Forty-Two

"Let's go. You've all got your coverage areas. Let's get in and do this, and take some of the pressure off those Marines on the ground." Stockton nudged his throttle to the side gently, lining his ship up parallel with a long line of enemy troops. At least he hoped they were enemies. Colonel Rogan had been advised to keep his people in a tight perimeter, but if any of them slipped out of that, they could end up getting wasted by their own air support.

Stockton hadn't been surprised when the call came to lead another strike. His people had obliterated the ground defenses, but those were Alliance troops down there, not Union conscripts, or even FRs. He suspected those formations had forced marched from every surviving barracks within fifty kilometers, and they'd done so in an almost impossible amount of time. Stockton had known Rogan's people would be up against it, and soon. But not *this* soon.

He'd hoped to avoid the necessity of running close support missions. For one thing, they were hard on the city, and Commodore Barron had been clear about avoiding unnecessary collateral damage. But now there was no choice. Either he and his

352

pilots could break up those advancing formations…or Rogan's entire ground force would be overwhelmed and destroyed before they even had a chance to fortify.

He adjusted his angle again. The previous mission had refreshed his memories of flying in atmosphere, but it was still difficult, very different from handling a fighter in space. He knew at least some of the casualties on the last sortie had resulted from pilot errors. The attack had been made from low altitude, and it didn't take much for a fighter jock used to open 3D surroundings to slam into the ground.

This attack should be easier, and a lot less costly. Last time, his people had flown straight into the ground defenses, but now those missile launchers and rocket batteries were nothing but piles of rehardened slag. The troops on the ground might have some portable rockets, but that was nothing compared to the firestorm his pilots had faced last time.

"Remember, the atmosphere's bleeding off your laser power fast, so get in close and make those shots count." Stockton could see the dense groupings of troops up ahead. It looked like Rogan's forces were already under heavy attack. He was tempted to fly in close to Rogan's line, to try to relieve the immediate pressure. But there was too big a risk of hitting friendlies. No, he had to take out the advancing units behind, cut off the flow of fresh forces and leave it to the Marines to take care of the enemies already in their faces.

"Let's do this!" He angled his fighter down, cutting through the air at as sharp an angle as he dared. He saw the troops down below, watched as they stopped and looked up…and then began to run in different directions, seeking cover.

"There's nowhere to run, you bastards," he said as he tightened his finger around the firing stud. His laser cannons fired, again and again as he swooped down less than half a kilometer over the enemy formations. He could see the bursts slamming into the ground, wiping away enemy troopers in clumps. Then he pulled back on his throttle, angling his ship up sharply into the sky.

He looked down at the scanner, watching as his squadrons

followed behind, a line of fighters, as close to wing to wing, he suspected, as any fighter force had ever come. And on the ground, chaos, death and destruction almost unimaginable.

But the units didn't break. They didn't run. Even where there were the greatest gaps, where as much as half a formation's strength had been lost, the survivors regrouped and continued to advance. Stockton shook his head. No matter how much he hated his enemies, it was hard not to admire these Alliance warriors.

"Let's come around and make another run here. I want those units running for the hills…or I want them wiped out. Follow me."

He angled his controls again and brought his fighter into position. He was going to see this done, here and now. He was going to do it for Bryan Rogan and the Marines. And he was going to do it so he didn't have to come back a third time. He was getting used to flying in atmosphere, but he had his own business, elsewhere. One day, probably soon, the Red fleet was going to transit into the system, and he had to be ready. Then the final battle would begin.

His battle would begin.

        *   *   *

"No, Lieutenant. You can send out a harassing force for a few hundred meters, but I want no general pursuit. Position your company along the main line of fortifications. I want one-third on watch, one-third repairing the line, and one-third resting."

"Yes, sir." He could hear the disappointment in the young officer's voice, and he understood it. His Marines had gone from staring certain defeat in the face to pursuing a broken enemy. It was only natural to want to exploit such a change in fortune, but he knew full well his people didn't have the strength for moves like that. He needed every Marine he had, and then some, if he was going to hold back everything the Reds were likely to throw at him.

He switched his comm unit to ground to orbit and called up *Dauntless*. A few seconds later, Commander Travis was on the line. "Looks like you've got things under control down there, Bryan. Well done. Hold for the commodore."

Rogan was going to thank Travis for her words, and admit that the fighter attack had at least as much to do with the result of the battle as anything his people had done, but she was gone before he could get it out.

"Nice job, Bryan." It was Barron's voice.

"Thank you, sir. We couldn't have done it without the fighter strike. Those birds tore apart the entire attack."

"And they'll do it again if they have to, Colonel. I've got six squadrons on alert at all times, ready to launch when you give the word. You've got air support whenever you need it." Barron's tone grew more serious. "What shape are you in down there, Bryan?"

Rogan sighed softly. "It's not good, sir. We took heavy losses taking the objectives, and more fighting off the counterattack. I've got maybe fifty percent of my strength still in the line, maybe another hundred fifty walking wounded who can fight in a pinch." He paused. "Sir, if you can get some shuttles down here, I'd love to evac some wounded. It would free up the Marines I've got guarding the aid stations, and if we could get some of our most shot up cases to sickbay, we might save a few."

"Consider it done, Bryan. I'll send down two squadrons to escort the shuttles, just in case."

"Thank you, sir."

"What's the status on that comm setup? We're going to need that when Imperator Vennius gets here."

Barron didn't even hint at a doubt about Vennius arriving, but Rogan knew better, and he heard the unspoken "if" in the statement. "The engineers are working on it, sir. I'm afraid it got pretty badly shot up."

"Stay on the engineering team, Colonel. Get them anything they need. We *have* to have that comm up and running. Our side's been getting smeared so far, and this is our chance to even the score on that, maybe persuade a few Reds to switch to our side."

"Yes, sir. I'll do all I can."

"And, Bryan…"

"Sir?"

"That's your last stand. We need everything you've taken down there, but if it comes down to the and the shit hits it, you hold that comm center and the emergency power source. It's the only absolutely vital position. You understand?"

"Yes, sir. I understand."

He did understand. Completely. And he would do everything in his power to hold it for Barron. Those Red bastards would have to kill the last Marine on Palatia before they took the comm center back.

Which they just might do…

*   *   *

"We're taking you out of here, Lucius, Ariane. We'll get you off-planet, where it's safe." Hursus was sitting in the front of the shuttle with the two children. Hargraves had expected them to fall to pieces, crying for the loss of the man he'd been told had been their caretaker since they'd been born. The old man had died well, Hargraves had to admit that. He'd given his life to save his charges, and there was something to admire in that.

"Leave Palatia? Never! We are the Rigellii, Optio. No usurper will drive us from our home like defeated cowards. We would die before we would suffer such dishonor."

"Lucius, your Uncle Vennius was forced to leave Palatia. Do you consider him a coward? There is no dishonor in following the orders of your Imperator, is there?"

The boy leaned back, relaxing the tension he'd worked himself into, but still with a sullen expression.

Hargraves shook his head. As long as the little shit shut the hell up, he was satisfied. He knew the child was just a product of his culture, that his outburst had shown considerable courage for someone his age…but he was sick of Alliance attitudes despite the fact that, on a level he couldn't quite wrap his head around, he knew they were not that different than those that drove his own beloved Marine Corps.

He was lying in the back of the shuttle, and the medic was working on him. He knew his wound was bad, but he could tell from the med tech's silence, and the tension in his hands, his body language, it was even worse than he thought.

He was weak, lightheaded, and he found it increasingly difficult to breath. The medic leaned over and pulled an oxygen mask over his face.

I'm in trouble, he thought, suddenly finding it much more difficult to stay conscious. He knew the shuttle only had rudimentary medical facilities, but he'd figured he'd be okay until they got into orbit and docked with *Dauntless*. Now, he wasn't so sure.

He'd stared death in the face more than once in his career, lying in the mud and filth of one battlefield or another. He'd been sure he was dying on his third assignment, his small force completely surrounded by FRs. That had been the war before the current one, and he'd survived that day, and many more since then. He almost laughed at the thought of dying on some mission to retrieve two spoiled kids. For a few seconds...then the whole thing stopped seeming funny.

He felt farther from the shuttle, and a strange floating feeling took him. He couldn't hear the kids anymore, just strange, distant sounds. The medic? Was he yelling, waving his arms?

His thoughts drifted back to Santis. Bryan Rogan had gotten them all through it, somehow. *Not all...we left more than half our number there, dead on the frozen ground. Considerably more than half...*

He realized somehow, in a way that only seemed partly real...he was dying. A lifetime at war, a history of brutality and battles, and he was going to die here, escorting two Alliance kids to safety, fifteen minutes from a sickbay that could save his life.

War, he thought. *We can fight it, endure it, master it...but in the end, do any of us really survive it?*

He was mostly satisfied with his life, his service. He had given all he had, done all he could. He thought back decades, to the half-frozen mud of his first training camp, the grizzled old non-coms who had trained him, told him what a disappointment he was bound to be. He'd been so scared of those Marines. They seemed so hard, so strong. Yet, he'd become one of them, and he'd gone on to terrify legions of young Marines himself. He dared to think those who had trained him would have been pleased at how he'd turned out, that they would have welcomed him to their Corps.

As they will welcome me again...

He'd fought for an entire lifetime, never yielding, never giving up. But he was tired, his strength gone. For the first time since he'd donned the uniform, Clete Hargraves stopped fighting and just slipped away.

Chapter Forty-Three

"We have a new report from Colonel Rogan, Commodore. He advises his people are holding, though they're sorely pressed at several points. He's requesting another airstrike." Atara Travis sat on the opposite side of Barron's desk, one hand pressed against her portable headset, looking across at him.

"I've told him three times, he doesn't have to ask. All he has to do is advise flight control to launch whatever he needs." Barron shook his head. Rogan had always been enormously deferential to him, flawlessly respectful. He'd written it off to Marine discipline, but over time he'd come to realize that Rogan truly admired him. As an officer who'd grown up amid the often insincere praise hurled at the descendant of the Confederation's greatest hero, he'd developed a habit of insinuating a certain amount of cynicism in his view of such behavior. But not in Rogan's case.

"You know Bryan." Travis leaned back in the chair, trying to get comfortable. She tended to be a little less formal when it was just the two of them, something Barron always encouraged. His promotion to commodore had cost him some portion of the easy relationship he'd had with Travis, and, in truth, he missed it.

She looked tired. She'd been going through the motions, taking regular off-duty periods to "rest," but Barron doubted she'd actually managed to sleep any more than he had. The mission had gone well so far, vastly better than they'd had any right to expect. They'd taken Palatia totally by surprise and found that Calavius had indeed stripped the defenses to bolster his attack fleet. The wild gamble had paid off, and they'd swept away the enemy flotilla and obliterated the vaunted Palatian orbital defenses without losing so much as a single ship. Then they'd taken control of every vital ground installation, and they still held them all nearly a week later, despite half a dozen counter attacks. It had taken countless sorties by the fighter squadrons to prop up the Marines, but the fleet's strike teams had proven up to the task, even if the first run had been costly. Since that initial attack had obliterated the ground-based missile and rocket batteries, however, the enemy defenses had been minimal. The subsequent waves had faced little danger from the enemy, even if unfamiliarity with atmospheric operations had killed nearly a dozen and a half pilots.

But none of that mattered, not if the rest of the operation didn't go according to plan. If Vennius and his ships didn't manage to escape from Sentinel-2, it was over. If they didn't get ahead of Calavius's Red fleet, it was over. If the engineers on the surface didn't have the Alliance's comm nexus functioning in time, it was over. There were a hundred ways things could go wrong…and only one winding path toward victory. But, against the odds, that path was still open.

"Let's send a double strike force down there," Barron said. "Maybe we can buy some extra time for the Marines before…"

The main klaxon sounded, and Barron's comm crackled to life. "Commodore, we're picking up activity at the transit point. We've got ships inbound."

Barron exchanged glances with his exec, and then almost as one, they snapped up to their feet. "On the way," he said into the comm unit on the desk, and then the two of them walked through the opening hatch and onto the bridge.

"I want IDs as soon as possible." Barron could feel the tension in his gut, the uncertainty. "And bring the fleet to battlestations, Commander." *Just in case.* Either Vennius's fleet was about to emerge, ahead of the Red forces which were no doubt in hot pursuit. *Or the Reds got here first.*

Or they already destroyed Vennius...

"Yes, Commodore," Travis said crisply, sliding into her seat as she did. About half a minute later: "Sir, we've got ships coming through. We're picking up ID beacons now. I think it's..."

*   *   *

"We're through, Your Supremacy. The rest of the fleet is right behind us." Brutus Egilius was staring at the display as he made his report. Vennius knew his new fleet commander—he'd issued Egilius's promotion to Commander-Altum during the trip from Sentinel-2 to Palatia—was concerned about *Bellator* being the first ship to transit. Egilius seemed to have taken on the responsibility for keeping the Imperator safe, which suggested a position farther back in the line. But Vennius would have no part of it. He knew very well *Bellator* might emerge into the teeth of Red ships, fresh from the defeat of Barron's force, but that was of no consequence. If the Confederation ships hadn't managed to seize Palatia, defeat was a virtual certainty anyway. Vennius had no wish to outlive his cause...or to see what a victorious Calavius would make of his beloved Alliance.

"I want a full report as soon as possible." Vennius knew his words were needless. There wasn't a set of eyes on *Bellator*'s bridge not trained on the still-dark main display. Vennius knew his warriors were courageous, that they would never let fear overcome them, or, for that matter, admit to feeling any. But he was also well aware that staring into the unknown was often worse than the face of any enemy.

"Of course, Your Supremacy," Egilius replied.

Vennius watched as the screens illuminated, a black and white static pattern appearing at first, and then a slow creep of color, in vibrating patterns. But first, the comm came to life, recovering from the disorientation of translight travel before the display showed clear readings.

"*Bellator*, this is *Dauntless*. Welcome to Palatia."

Vennius closed his eyes, exhaling the breath he hadn't even realized he was holding. The flight from Sentinel-2 had been a tense one, his forces barely ahead of the pursuing Reds. Reaching Palatia first, sticking to the desperate plan he and Barron had conceived, had forced him to make some painful choices. Leaving Sentinel-2 and its volunteer crew behind, almost certainly to their deaths. Abandoning three of his battleships during the chase, vessels with damage that made it impossible for them to stay ahead of the enemy. Each of those three ships had fought to the finish, hopeless battles against the entire Red fleet...and all three had done so still within scanner range of *Bellator*. Vennius had watched his people die, fighting for his cause to the last. He'd almost failed in his resolve, the order to turn about and fight it out with Calavius hanging in his throat for a moment. But he knew his duty. Thousands of his people had already died. The Imperatrix had died. If he failed, all that would have been for nothing. He drew strength from that realization, and he watched wordlessly, almost soundlessly, as those three ships died.

They'd served a last purpose, holding back portions of the enemy fleet, buying time for Vennius's forces to escape. He wasn't sure if that had been the difference, if those ships' deaths had saved the rest of the fleet, but he chose to believe it. He had never been prone to such self-indulgent thoughts before, but right now he needed something.

"*Dauntless*, this is..." Egilius began to respond. It was a breach of protocol for an Imperator to answer an initial contact, but Vennius didn't care. More than pointless etiquette and formality would be cast aside before this fight was done.

"This is Imperator Vennius. I must speak with Commodore Barron."

"Barron here." The response was almost immediate, at least after calculating for the distance involved.

"Commodore, we don't have the time we'd hoped for. The

Red fleet is as little as one hour behind my force."

Vennius could hear Barron's voice in the background, shouting out orders to bring the fleet to battlestations. "We'll be ready, sir."

"Tyler…was your mission a success?"

"Yes." A short pause. "The enemy left only a token fleet behind, and we were able to destroy it, along with the orbital defenses." Another hesitation, and then Barron continued, his voice more subdued. "We were also able to take all primary ground targets and hold them. But the cost…" His voice tailed off. The casualties didn't matter, not now. Vennius knew it pained Barron to lose people, but he also knew, if the Confed leader been certain only one Marine would have survived to hold the vital installations, he'd have sent his people in anyway. As Vennius himself would have done.

"We've got to be ready. I'll bring my ships in closer to the planet. There's no way we're going to set up a transit point defense. Not in the time we've got. Better to let them through… and then hope our plan succeeds."

"I agree completely." Barron's voice was tentative. *He's not telling me something…*

"I think the transmission will be best done closer to Palatia. If Calavius's people try to block the signals, the closer we are, the better chance we have of powering through their jamming."

Silence. Vennius felt a tightness growing in his gut. *Something is wrong.* He was just about to ask Barron when the commodore finally responded.

"We have a potential problem. The communication nexus was badly damaged during the initial attack. I've had my best engineers working on it for the last week, but I'm afraid it's still non-functional."

Vennius felt like the air had been sucked from his lungs. Barron had somehow managed to get past the system's considerable defenses and utilize that surprise to seize control of Palatia's core installations…only to have the one facility vital to the plan damaged in the battle. There was going to be a fight, here, a bloody one hard fought. But Vennius knew, unless he could communicate with the ships in the system, his forces would lose. They were simply too outnumbered.

He had a speech prepared. He had video of the Imperatrix and him together before she died, evidencing that she hadn't been killed on Palatia, that the two had been friendly to the end. He had all the evidence he'd been able to put together to refute Calavius's lies and propaganda…but the main comm nexus was the only broadcast facility powerful enough to burn through jamming efforts and reach every ship. The only one with over-rides on all encryption programs and security measures.

*   *   *

"Fritzie, we need that communications facility back online… and I mean now." Barron was talking into the small microphone on his headset. He'd only sent Fritz down the day before, and now he was cursing himself for not doing it sooner. She was his most gifted engineer, the most capable he'd ever known. But he hated the idea of her leaving *Dauntless* on the eve of a potential battle, so much so that it had prevented him from even thinking about sending her…until Atara Travis suggested it.

"Sir, this thing is infernally complicated. It's a bunch of sto-len high tech mixed with complicated lower tech workarounds. I'd wager the Palatians took what they could from conquered planets and made up the rest as they went along. It's powerful, there's no doubt about that, but I've never seen a more mixed up circuit architecture in my life."

"Fritzie, I've seen you pull *Dauntless* back from the brink of total destruction. I know you can do this." He knew that wasn't a fair comparison. Fritz knew *Dauntless* like she knew her own body. Every crevice, every crawlspace, every ornery circuit or conduit. But now she was trying to decipher foreign tech and fix it in short order. He knew it was a *lot* to ask, but he'd asked much of her in the past, and she'd always delivered.

"I'm trying, sir."

Barron paused a few seconds. "Fritzie…we've got the whole Red fleet inbound. We'll be in battle in ninety minutes, maybe less. We're outnumbered up here…badly. And I don't know how much longer Bryan Rogan and his people can hold out down there, especially now that I need to pull their air support and redeploy it against the enemy fleet." He hesitated again. "You've got two hours, Fritzie…*maybe*. After that it's going to be too late. So, take whatever chances you need to…but give it your best shot."

"Yes, Commodore."

"Get it done, Fritzie. Barron out."

Barron knew he was asking for something close to impossible…but somehow in his gut, he believed she would pull it off. He wasn't sure if it was memories of so many times she and her band of engineers had pulled his butt out of the fire before… or just his decision that, with nothing else to do, he would just believe in his people.

C'mon, Fritzie…you can do this.

*   *   *

Dauntless's Alpha bay was a madhouse, technicians running around, small utility vehicles carrying away the atmospheric flight attachments as quickly as the flight crews could pull them off. The fleet's squadrons had been running ground assaults around the clock for a week, holding back the steady but disorganized wave of assaults at the planetary beachheads. But now, the final battle had come, and every fighter was needed to meet the enemy fleet. Back in space, where *Dauntless*'s pilots were at home.

Jake Stockton sat in his fighter, focusing thoughtfully on each breath he inhaled and exhaled. He was as nervous as he'd ever been—scared shitless, actually—but something stronger was in control of him now, and it would not be deterred, would not be denied.

He'd been a key part of managing the ground attack missions, and he'd been grateful for the distraction, the scant few minutes when his mind had been pulled from the obsession that had ruled him since he'd seen his best friend killed before his eyes. But now it was time. He had his duty to *Dauntless*'s strike force, and he would see to their dispositions, their move forward into battle. When they got there, though, he had one purpose and one alone. He had a date with a single enemy, and he had no doubt that Red pilot would be as focused on him. They had fought multiple times, pushed each other to the limit. But this battle would be different, Stockton swore to himself. Only one of them would leave the battlefield this time.

"Scarlet Eagle squadron, you are cleared to launch from Beta bay. Blue squadron, you are clear to launch from Alpha bay."

Stockton listened to Stara Sinclair's voice on the comm, the strength in it, but also the slight crack when she mentioned Blue squadron. It wasn't much, and he doubted anyone else had picked up on it. But he knew her better than anyone.

He took a deep breath. He'd left her a letter, on the computer, one that would be delivered if he didn't return. He was ready to face his greatest test, to die if need be…but he still held on to enough of himself to leave her kind words, and a confirmation that he loved her, that he had always loved her. He wasn't sure if that would help her or hurt her, and he'd thought for a moment it would be more merciful to leave things as they were, to help her get over him. But in the end, he knew what he had to do.

He waited for the indicator light on his board to turn green. Then he said, "All right, Blues. Just one more battle…like a hundred others." He was in command of *Dauntless*'s entire strike force now, but he hadn't given up Blue squadron yet. He knew he'd have to…if he returned. If any of them survived. But that had been too much to contemplate in the days leading up to this final showdown. The Blues were his family, and leaving them, even just to move up a rung in the command ranks, was going to rip his guts out.

"Blue squadron…launch."

He hit the launch controls, and his body slammed back as the magnetic catapult blasted his ship down the tube at almost 14g. An instant later, the gray metal of the landing bay was replaced by the cold black of space.

He looked down at the scanner, watching as the Blues, followed quickly by the rest of *Dauntless*'s wings, shook down into formation. There were holes in the OB, gaps in the formation where comrades had once been. Friends. But he knew those who remained would fight, to the death if necessary. The Grays were hopelessly outnumbered—the fight would be a desperate one, and very possibly it would end in defeat. But part of him almost pitied the Alliance pilots who came up against his Blues…and the rest of *Dauntless*'s strike force. The Reds would pay for any victory today, they would pay dearly.

He looked down at the long-range screen. The Red fleet was launching too, hundreds of fighters forming up, moving forward. He watched the clouds of tiny dots on the scanner, looking, waiting.

He had a date with one of those fighters.

Chapter Forty-Four

Victorum, Alliance Capital
Palatia, Astara II
Year 311 AC

"Get out there, Tommy. You too, Cass. We need every Marine we've got left." Bryan Rogan looked over toward his two aides. They had served him well for the past week, running orders to his various commanders when enemy jamming interfered with the comm, helping him keep the whole, teetering position together for just a little longer. But that was almost over now. The arrival of the Red fleet had energized the forces surrounding his strongholds, and they were throwing themselves against the remains of his defenses with renewed energy, almost with abandon. *No doubt some of the fence sitters committing themselves, now that they see Calavius about to return and retake the planet.* His two assistants could serve him better now on the line with rifles in their hands than running messages to the few survivors of his force.

"Yes, Colonel," the two responded almost as one. They snapped to attention and gave him a crisp salute. That wasn't normal procedure for the battlefield, but he knew it for what it was. A goodbye. They would all be dead by nightfall…or if not, by dawn. His aides knew that as well as he did.

And it's better for them to die like Marines, fighting…

He clutched his own rifle, fully committed that, when the moment came, he too would go down in combat. He looked over the makeshift barricade, the last defense of the command post, thinking it wouldn't be long.

He turned toward the small group of engineers on the far side of the room. "Commander Fritz...my perimeter is being overwhelmed at multiple points. I cannot guarantee the safety of your people any longer. Perhaps you should pack up and get back to *Dauntless* while we can still get your shuttle launched." Rogan was commanding a full-scale ground operation, but protecting *Dauntless*'s crew members still struck close to his heart. Fritz and her people were revered by the rest of the battleship's complement, Marines included. They all knew just how many times her wizardry had saved their lives.

"No, Colonel. We're here to the end." Fritz didn't look up from her work as she spoke. "This is where Commodore Barron needs us the most...where we might be able to make a difference." A short pause. "If you have any spare side arms, perhaps you can issue them to my people. That way if the enemy gets in here..." She didn't finish. She didn't have to.

"Of course, Commander." Rogan almost argued with her, tried to convince her to go. He'd been watching engineers work on the shattered comm system for a week, though Fritz's people had only been there since the day before. He'd given up hope that they could repair it, and without it, the battle in the system was just about hopeless.

Rogan actually considered it *completely* hopeless, as he did his own fight on the ground, which was why he didn't argue with Fritz. Her people could die here carrying out Barron's last orders to them, or they could go back and die on the ship. It wasn't his call to try to influence her decision on that.

Dauntless was a home to Rogan, as he knew it was to Fritz... to virtually every member of her crew. He had only intended to do a two-year rotation as a shipboard Marine, but then Captain Barron took command...and Rogan had been mesmerized, his dedication to his new commander growing almost instantly. He'd stayed on through five years of war, turning down every opportunity for a transfer, despite the fact that he'd almost certainly cost himself at least one step up in rank. Of course, Barron had made up for that too, moving him up to full bird colonel in one fell swoop. Even if he'd only carry the rank for a week.

He found himself wondering if Barron had sent a communique back to the Confederation with a report of the promotion…whether he would be noted on the Corps roles as a dead colonel or captain. He scolded himself for such pointless thoughts, but still, it was there. In the end, he liked to think of himself as someone who wouldn't care about such things, certainly not here in the middle of the fight of his life…but he was human too…no matter how much a few of his drill instructors had tried to beat it out of him.

He could hear the fighting outside, explosions and gunfire from down the hallway. The enemy was inside the building.

I'm sorry, Commodore…I'm sorry I couldn't hold things here for you. At least for a while longer…

*   *   *

"We've matched velocity and acceleration with Imperator Vennius's forces, sir. Project movement into primary battery range in twenty-seven minutes."

"Very well, Commander." Barron glanced over at Travis. His steadfast second was at her post, stone-faced as always in battle. Whatever fears, whatever realizations that this was likely their last battle, she kept them well hidden.

He looked at the display, watching as the cluster of transports approached Palatia. Those ships contained every trooper on Vennius's ships, bound to reinforce Bryan Rogan's shattered Marines. But they were still at least an hour from the planet, and from the reports he'd been getting, Barron was far from sure his people could hold out that long.

"Fighter squadrons about to engage, sir." Travis's report pulled his thoughts from his almost-doomed ground force. The battle in space didn't look much better, and his fighters were facing a hard battle.

Barron looked at the display. The array of tiny dots was sparser than usual. His wings had suffered badly in the recent campaigns, and he had squadrons at sixty percent strength, seventy. Even a few below fifty. The approaching mass of Red fighters outnumbered the combined Gray force by more than two to one. His people had faced odds like that more than once, but these weren't Union conscripts this time. They were Alliance warriors, and most of them were veterans.

His eyes were fixed on the five small formations *Dauntless* had launched. He knew his people would perform well, that they would face whatever came at them and give better than they got. *You fool…they're all your people now, not just Dauntless's pilots.* He knew the mostly green pilots on the other ships would have a hard time standing against their Alliance opponents. Sara Eaton had some of her people from *Intrepid* with her on Repulse, but the rest of his ships were loaded up with pilots fresh from flight school. They'd been blooded in the battles of the past six months, but they were far from ready to face the best of the Alliance.

"Put me on the main squadron channel, Atara." His voice was grim. The thought that he'd led his people here, defeated the enemy forces present, gotten past the vaunted Palatian defense grid, and seized every important objective on the ground—only to fall short because the comm nexus they needed so desperately was damaged—it was almost too much to bear. He had no idea if Vennius's appeal to the Red forces would have worked. Even if they'd succeeded in capturing the nexus intact, there was no assurance the Gray Imperator would have managed to sway enough of his countrymen. But Barron believed he would have, he believed the plan would have worked. Vennius was a hero of his people, a name every warrior knew. He'd been toppled by lies and propaganda, an assault that, for the most part, he'd been unable to counter.

"On your headset, Commodore."

"All squadrons, this is Commodore Barron." He still wasn't used to that, or to commanding more than one ship and strike force of fighters. "We all know the odds we face, the desperation of the situation. For those of you from *Dauntless*, you know we have never let the odds concern us. For the rest of you, I will not try to sugarcoat things. We have a difficult fight before us, so all I ask of each of you is to give your absolute best, to fight with all the strength you can muster…and to think only from moment to moment, combat to combat. The road is traversed one step at a time. My heart is with you all."

He turned toward Travis and made a cutting motion under his chin. He knew his pilots would fight hard, even the rookies. They would give the Alliance wings one hell of a scrap.

But in the end, he also knew they would lose.

*   *   *

"All squadrons, break!" Stockton angled his throttle, bringing his fighter around, toward the edge of the approaching Alliance formation. There was a gap in the line coming toward his people. Not a large one, but enough to turn to his advantage.

His people had managed to get the best of the missile exchange, despite the enemy numbers, a tiny victory he owed half to his people and half the Confederation's superior ordnance. He'd lost four ships—none of his Blues—though only two had been destroyed. *Not that the ones who ditched have a chance of pickup.* He knew the fleet was in dire trouble, and he wasn't in the mood to fool himself with uplifting nonsense. His pilots floating in their survival gear would sit there helplessly, watching the destruction of their allies as their life support slowly waned.

He fired his lasers, taking out an enemy fighter almost immediately. He was flying better than he ever had in his life. There was almost no conscious thought, just pure instinct, fueled by his rage. He didn't have a doubt he was going to die today, but he had something he had to do first, and by God, he was going to see it done.

He fell in behind a second enemy ship, firing again. A near miss, followed a few seconds later by another hit. That was three, counting the one he'd taken down with one of his missiles. But the usual elation wasn't there. He wasn't out here to rack up pointless kills. Only one victory mattered. He had an engagement, one that had been long in coming.

His eyes moved over his scanners, searching the massive enemy formation, looking for his target. He was determined, his focus unshakeable. In the bay, his mind had wandered, to Stara, to the battle, to *Dauntless* and her crew. After launch, he'd seen to the dispositions of his squadrons, done the job Commodore Barron had entrusted to him…Kyle's job. But now his fighters were engaged, and each pilot was more or less on his own. This was a fight to the finish, one where there could be no thought of retreat. So, his obligations were finished, and that left one thing on his mind.

Vengeance.

He scoured the scanner, looking for his enemy. His eyes locked on an Alliance ship that had just destroyed one of *Repulse*'s fighters. The pilot was highly skilled, clearly an ace, and for a moment he thought he'd found his opponent. But something wasn't right. A capable pilot, yes, but not the one he was looking for.

Not the one who killed Kyle. Who crippled Dirk.

His hands gripped tightly on the controls, his finger closing on the firing stud, blasting another ship out of existence.

Maybe if I kill enough of your pilots, you'll find me…

* * *

"Commodore, I've got Commander Fritz on the comm."

Barron's head snapped around. There was anticipation on his face, but he didn't dare to allow it to blossom into hope. "On my line."

Travis turned and nodded. "On your line."

"Fritzie, tell me you've got some good news." Barron could hear noise in the background, fighting. Explosions, shouts. Too close to Fritz. Far too close.

"I think we've got it working, sir." Her voice was tentative, and she was almost shouting, trying to be heard over the chaos in the background. "I mean I'm sure we've got it working, but I don't know how long we can keep it up."

"I have every confidence in your engineers, Fritzie."

"It's not my engineers, sir. It's the Marines. They're holding on, but I don't know how much longer they can keep the enemy back. If we lose the building, there's no comm. If we lose the power plant, there's no comm. If we lose the uplink antenna, there's no comm."

"We've got Alliance troopers inbound, Fritzie. Tell Bryan his people they just have to hold out another hour."

"He's not here, sir. He's up fighting with his people. The enemy's in the building, Commodore. My people are all armed, but I doubt we'll be able to hold out an hour. So, if you're going to use this thing, I suggest you do it now."

"Roger that, Fritzie." He felt the pain cut at him, the thought of Rogan and his Marines being wiped out, of falling just before help arrived. "You'd better get your people on the shuttle now, Fritzie. You've done your work." A few armed engineers weren't going to make the difference for the Marines…and Barron wanted his ace engineer back onboard.

"Not so fast, sir. I said we've got it working, and we do. But it's in shit shape. If you want to transmit anything at full power, my team and I will have to be right here. If we leave this thing unattended, it will melt down the instant a full charge goes through it."

Barron felt a pain inside at the sudden realization that he faced a stark choice. If he wanted to use the comm nexus, it meant leaving Fritz and her people on Palatia. Likely leaving them to their deaths.

He paused, wasting seconds he knew he didn't have. He understood almost immediately what he had to do…but he couldn't accept it. Couldn't say the words.

Finally, he took a deep breath. "Fritzie, keep that thing working. Whatever it takes."

He turned toward Travis, about to signal her to cut the line. Before he changed his mind and ordered Fritz back to *Dauntless*. But he paused, the sudden fear taking him that this was the last time he'd talk to his engineer. His friend. "Well done, Fritzie, as always. Give your people my respect…and my thanks. For everything."

"Yes, sir." He could hear the emotion in her normally cool voice. They both knew the situation.

He almost said something else, but then he turned and gestured to Travis, and he listened as the soft click signaled that the line was closed.

If he was going to sacrifice Fritzie and her people, it could *not* be in vain.

Barron looked over at his second in command. "Get me Imperator Vennius, Atara. Immediately."

Chapter Forty-Five

"It is time, Ricard. Vennius and his allies have proven themselves to be more deceitful than we'd anticipated, but now they're trapped. There will be no escape. Here I shall vanquish my old friend, now my enemy. Here I will secure my dynasty for a thousand years."

Lille took a deep breath, cringing inside at the carelessness of Calavius's words. His Palatian followers, many of whom served him only because of Lille's superbly crafted lies, would not react well to talk of "dynasties." The Palatian Patricians had a virtual monopoly on the highest offices, but within that select group, the leaders were chosen on merit. Or at least that was what was widely believed.

Lille struggled to understand Calavius. He usually figured people out in an instant, but the Alliance Imperator was almost schizophrenic. One moment he was an arrogant fool, spouting off without discipline…and the next he was shrewd, calculating. Worst of all, it seemed impossible to tell which version would surface at any given time.

He's mad now. Lille knew Calavius was upset that Vennius

fooled him, lured him to Sentinel-2 and then slipped away to join his Confederation allies…forces that had not withdrawn and gone home, but had instead executed a daring and brilliant strike to seize Palatia. Whatever happened, however the battle ended, Lille knew that would be a particularly cutting shame for Calavius. The Palatians' history of enslavement and oppression made the idea of losing control of the homeworld, even for a brief time, a particularly touchy subject.

"Yes, it is time. We have done much work to come to this pass…and soon you will be the uncontested Imperator of the Alliance." Lille knew that Calavius's forces greatly outnumbered their opponents, that even with the Confederation ships and their superior tech—and Tyler Barron—the battle would almost certainly be won. But he was worried about what Vennius and Barron had planned. They *had* to know they could never hold Palatia…so, for all they had managed to pull their plan off almost flawlessly, one question remained. Why?

They almost certainly would have been better off fighting it out at Sentinel-2, with the fortress and all its resources backing them up. Taking Palatia humiliated Calavius, but Lille couldn't believe that was the sole purpose.

Calavius sat with his eyes glued to the massive screen he'd had installed. *Princeps* was his newest ship, one he'd taken over almost-finished in the shipyard. It was the biggest vessel in the Alliance navy, the sister ship of Katrine Rigellus's ill-fated Invictus. Lille thought the name was a bit foolish. *Though better than* Princeps Calavius, *at least.*

He was tense, waiting to see what he hadn't been able to anticipate. Lille was accustomed to being smarter than his opponents, but he had to admit that Tyler Barron had proven to be quite the match for him. And Vennius was no slouch either. Whatever they had planned, he knew he had to be ready… because Calavius wouldn't be.

He was still thinking that when the speakers in the room crackled loudly…and a few seconds later a voice came blasting through at full volume.

*   *   *

"Epsilon Wing, tighten up those formations. You need to cut a hole through those fighters so the bombers can get through." Jovi Grachus was staring at her dashboard, at the extra screens her flight crew had installed. The very idea of commanding almost two thousand fighters in battle was something that had never occurred to her. Less than a year ago, she had been a squadron commander with little hope of rising any higher.

Imperator Calavius made all this happen…

She was trying to reassure herself, to banish the doubts Jarus had instilled in her. *He's a fool*, she told herself. *He allowed himself to be seduced by Vennius's lies.* But she knew Jarus was no fool. He was one of the smartest men she'd ever met, and the most honorable, aspects that had been central to her consideration of him as a mate…beyond of course, the—far less important—facts that he was good-looking and charming.

"Sigma Wing, you've got the flank. Watch those Confed squadrons slipping around your coverage area. We've got numbers, so there's no excuse for slipups…none of them get by. Do you understand?"

"Yes, Commander."

Even as the acknowledgement came through, her thoughts had returned to the confused morass that had taken control of her mind. She'd been devastated by Kat's death, and she'd sworn revenge against the Confeds the moment she'd gotten the news. But her rage toward Vennius had grown more slowly… and now she began to realize how much she'd listened to Calavius's announcements, his proclamations. He had declared the Commander-Maximus guilty of a litany of crimes…treason, connivance with the Confederation, the murder of the Imperatrix. It all came together when she'd heard that. Kat couldn't have lost a straight up battle. She'd been lured in by the Confeds, and set up by her oldest family friend, who had sold out his people for Confed support. It had all seemed so clear.

But is any of it true?

Her speakers suddenly blasted out a loud wave of feedback, hurting her ears, shaking her from her thoughts. She reached out, tried to adjust her comm unit, but then, a voice blared out, the signal strong, so powerful it overwhelmed every other incoming feed.

"Alliance warriors, this is Tarkus Vennius. To some of you Imperator, to others the enemy…and no doubt to your view, a traitor."

She stared at the display in shock. How was this possible? She tried to ignore his words, tried to cultivate the rage that had sustained her, but doubt had blunted her anger.

"I know many of you have been told that I sought to gain control of the government, that I conspired with foreign powers…" There was a brief hesitation, a bit of pain slipping into the otherwise firm voice. "…that I killed the Imperatrix." Another pause. "I am here to tell you all that you have been listening to lies…lies told by my old friend, and now my blackest enemy, the man you call Imperator. Calavius. And lies told by his allies from the Union."

Grachus sat listening in stunned silence. Her eyes moved to the display, but even the battle raging all around her had slowed almost to a stop. Whatever Vennius had to say, whatever the thousands of warriors now engaged in a struggle to the death thought of it…they were all listening.

Grachus felt herself plunged into confusion. She didn't know what to think. She mistrusted Vennius's words, but now they piled on those of Jarus. She shook her head, and sucked in a deep, ragged breath. She didn't know what to believe.

"Kat," she said softly to herself, feeling a tear slipping from her eye as she did. "What do I do? How can I honor you best, my old friend?"

*　　　　*　　　　*

"I want that signal jammed at once!" Calavius was on his feet, his hands balled into fists, screaming at the cluster of officers, mostly sycophants, gathered around him.

Lille watched the functionaries, those who had fed off Calavius's favor, standing in shock, their attention divided between the screaming of the man they had all sworn to follow, and the calm, authoritative voice coming through every speaker in the ship.

"We're trying, Your Supremacy," an officer yelled from against the wall, where he was crouched over a comm panel. "It's being broadcast from the main nexus on Palatia."

"Shut down the speakers then. Everywhere on the ship. Everywhere on every ship!"

"We can't, Your Supremacy. The nexus AI has systems override authority. I'm afraid we can't disengage…we can't even shut down the comm system."

"I am transmitting evidence, recordings of the Imperatrix, with me after I rescued her from Palatia. As she lay dying from the wounds inflicted by Calavius's soldiers. I am also sending proof that I had no contact with the Confederation until after Calavius assumed control on Palatia…even my certified log entries as testimony that I was against the dispatching of *Invictus* to the Confederation five years ago, that I merely obeyed the orders of the Council and the Imperatrix at the time…a command our ruler came to regret in the months and years following."

"Then burn out every comm circuit on the ship!" Calavius was screaming at the top of his lungs.

Lille stood to the side, silent, watching. He held his poker face firm, but inside he was reeling. He thought he'd been familiar with every crucial aspect of the Alliance's military, but now he suddenly understood the reason for Barron's desperate attack on Palatia.

The Alliance was so dedicated to the defense of its homeworld, so sure no enemy could ever invade it again…they'd developed a communications system like no other. Their comm nexus was powerful enough to broadcast to anything in their system, strong enough to burn through any jamming attempt. And, perhaps worse, the AI that operated it had override codes for all Alliance ships. Even the communications officer of a vessel couldn't stop the receipt of the transmissions…couldn't even turn down the volume.

It was a disaster, and even as he still pondered the implications, he knew it. Everything could fall apart here. He'd done his best to connect as many officers as possible to Calavius, to tie their wealth and influence to the Red Imperator's reign, to implicate them deeply enough that there was no way to go back. But he'd only been able to reach a portion of those adhering to the Red cause. The rest had been influenced by propaganda… a wave of lies that Vennius—curse him—was now countering.

It was impossible to be sure how many would listen to Vennius's words. The Gray Imperator had been a hero to his people for decades. It was one thing to turn people against a figure who wasn't there, one who seemed guilty merely by his absence, and quite another for that brainwashing to hold under the impassioned words of that old hero.

"I know many of you opposed me with honor, believing the lies you were told. I hold no grudges, and I welcome any of you now who wish to switch sides…or even adopt neutrality until you are able to analyze the situation with care. I will pardon any who rally to me now…and I will respect the non-combatant status of any who claim neutrality. I seek no vengeance, save against the traitor, Calavius, and those who still adhere to him, knowing now what he is. His claims are built on lies, and he is but a puppet of the vile Union."

Lille listened to the words, gritting his teeth and shaking his head. Vennius was good, very good. He wished again that he'd been able to corrupt the old Commander-Maximus, that he could have used Vennius instead of Calavius. But there was nothing to be gained by such thoughts. He had to make a decision, and soon. Could he salvage the situation? Or was it time to slip away, to accept defeat and escape back to the Union.

Fleeing now meant near total disaster. His plan to bring the Alliance into the war on the Union side was not only in ruins, it was likely to backfire terribly. The Confederation had come to Vennius's aid with forces they couldn't spare. Lille couldn't see any way they'd have done that without assurances from the

Gray Imperator that the Alliance would reciprocate if he was victorious.

The battle wasn't over. It was still unclear how many would listen to Vennius's plea, and how many would stay in the ranks. Certainly, those deeply involved with Calavius, the ones who had taken bribes, who had been complicit in spreading lies and propaganda…they had no choice but to fight alongside their master. No one who knew anything about Vennius could doubt how such warriors would fare at his hands.

"Your Supremacy," Lille said, the first time he had used the form of address. "With your permission, I would go to the communications center. We must prepare a response to this outrage."

"Yes, yes," Calavius roared. "Go. Do that. At least some-one here is doing something."

Lille nodded his head respectfully…and then he slipped out into the hall and headed toward the lift. He paused a moment, finally saying, "Deck thirty-one." He watched the lights move downward, past deck nine, the comm center…and all the way to thirty-one, where his private shuttle was docked. Lille still held *some* hope that Calavius would prevail, but he had serious doubts now. And if things went badly, if the Union faced war with the Alliance, Villieneuve had to know as soon as possible.

Though Lille dreaded delivering that message…

He moved swiftly toward his ship. There was a guard there—evidently Calavius wanted to ensure his commitment. *One guard? You needed more than that.*

He moved up silently, behind his prey, pulling the carbon fiber blade from his leg-sheath and slicing through the guard's throat in one swift motion.

Then he moved around, hopping over the body.

It was time to hedge his bets. Time to get out of there.

*   *   *

"We're getting communications from multiple Red ships. They're offering their allegiance, Your Supremacy. They're requesting permission to join our formation."

Vennius let out a deep exhale. He'd been waiting to see if his words had exerted their desired effect. He'd been pretty sure he'd get to some of Calavius's people, or at least hopeful he would. After all, he'd been their commander, led them for years. Lies were infectious, and people were too willing to believe things they were told without asking for proof. He had provided proof, or at least something like it. The Imperatrix's final recording was clear and convincing, at least to those who didn't just assume it was a fabrication.

He'd suspected that he could undo *some* of the damage Calavius's lies had done, at least. And it seemed that was happening. But the question remained. Would it be enough?

"Give all ship commanders requesting to join us my compliments." A pause. "And request that they take position off the right flank of the fleet." Vennius didn't like distrusting those who appeared to be rallying to him. He was sincere about his offer of pardon, but he wasn't about to fall for any trickery… not now. Not when the disastrous civil war was about to be decided. One way or another. It was best to keep his new converts segregated, at least until he could be sure of the sincerity of their submission.

"We have other ships moving off to the far flank as well, Your Supremacy. They are broadcasting declarations of neutrality."

"Send all such ships messages that they are safe from us. As long as they do not power up weapons systems, we will not attack them."

"Yes, sir."

Vennius took a deep breath. He was a veteran of many battles, but now his stomach was twisted into knots. He could feel the sweat pouring down his neck, his back. The next moments would determine if he would survive, but it would also decide something far more important than that to him. The confusion in the fleets, the shifting of loyalties…what was happening now would set the destiny for the Alliance's future. Either the nation he'd served his entire life would endure, or Calavius and his Union puppeteers would take control…and all he'd fought a lifetime to preserve would be lost.

"Fleet order, all ships. No one is to fire on any vessel that does not initiate hostilities. These are our comrades out there. They have been lied to, misled...and we now welcome them back, as loyal Palatians. Only those who continue to fight, who stand by the usurper knowing what he is, are our enemies." His voice hardened, and he could feel his fists clenching as he sat there. "For them, there is no mercy. Any ship that fires on us is to be destroyed."

Chapter Forty-Six

"Keep firing, Walt…cover me while I reload."

"I've got it, Corporal."

Bryan Rogan was watching as his Marine—Tompkins—spoke to the man standing next to him, firing an assault rifle while he reloaded his autocannon. The heavy weapon was the lynchpin of the defense right there, the last stand before the mobs of Palatian warriors broke through and stormed the control center of the communications tower.

The man covering the gunner wasn't a Marine, nor was he a Palatian stormtrooper. Anya Fritz had sent her people to back up the Marines while she stayed and singlehandedly kept the communications tower functioning. He'd been skeptical of the real impact thirty or so techs and engineers could have on the fight, but he shook his head as he watched the man in front of him—Billings, he thought his name was—gun down every trooper who tried to advance the instant the autocannon's fire ceased.

He was impressed by Fritz too. He didn't know how she'd managed to keep the communications nexus operating by herself, but somehow she had. Vennius had made his speech, sent his video files and other evidence out to every receiver in the system. Rogan had no idea what effect it would have, if Commodore Barron's plan would work, but that wasn't his concern. Somehow, despite the odds, his people had completed their mission. They'd held, long enough at least, and that filled him with a somber pride.

The realization that they had succeeded was bittersweet, of course. Even if they had won the war by holding, none of them would survive to see the fruits of victory. They were surrounded, outnumbered fifty to one. They were dead, all of them, except for the formalities.

He'd gotten signals from several of the other strongpoints which had fallen, but then the enemy jamming came closer, and once again he was cut off. The main comm tower that broadcasted Vennius's words was impossible to jam, but his Marines' portable units were hopelessly blanketed with static. He didn't know if any of his other units were still fighting, or if the sixty or so Marines and stormtroopers he had left with him were all that remained of the invasion force.

It won't matter in twenty minutes...it will all be over by then...

He heard the autocannon open up again, and his head snapped around, his eyes looking out over the scene. It was only then he noticed the blood red circle on Billings' shirt. The engineer wasn't only fighting alongside his Marines, he was doing it wounded, with so little notice of his injury that Rogan hadn't even realized. He scolded himself for thinking so little of the fighting abilities of Fritz's people. Walt Billings could fight at his side any day.

If there are any more days...

He took a few steps forward. The enemy was about to launch their final push. He could see it in their dispositions, the direction their fire was coming from, but mostly, he could *feel* it.

He pulled his rifle from his shoulder. The barrel was still warm. He'd been in the fight, at half a dozen vulnerable spots on his shrinking line, but this was where the final assault would come. And this is where he would meet it.

"Let's stay focused, Mar...everyone." He was used to leading only Marines, but in addition to his engineers turned make-shift soldiers, he still had perhaps twenty troopers in the line. He'd had trouble accepting the Palatians at first, but they had fought with all the ferocity of his Marines...and *they* faced the burden of killing their own people as they did it. He'd looked at them as enemies when they'd first landed, but now his attitude was a hopeless, contradictory jumble.

He knelt down, behind a chunk of half-shattered concrete, and pushed his rifle out in front of him. But then he heard it. Sounds, voices. Screaming...normal tones at first and then anger. Then the shooting started. Not among his people and their tattered line, but behind the enemy front, and out in the street.

The troopers facing his people were still there, but their fire on his position was diminishing gradually...and then it virtually stopped, replaced by the sounds of intense fighting outside.

Rogan exhaled hard. He couldn't believe it. It took him time to truly understand what was happening. The troopers outside, the warriors who had been about to wipe out the last of his command...they were fighting each other.

My God...it's working. Commodore Barron's plan is actually working...

He couldn't believe it. He'd already respected Barron, but now he was beginning to believe all the legends, the foolish talk that he was the second coming of his grandfather, that he was destined to lead the Confederation to greatness. Rogan had never been one for such nonsense...but he'd never served a leader like Tyler Barron either.

Keep control of yourself...you're not out of this yet. The fighting was taking the pressure off his people, but there was still some sporadic incoming fire. And he had no idea what was going on outside, if the newly pro-Vennius forces, enraged that they had been manipulated and lied to, would sweep away the Red loyal-ists...or if a few converts would be shortly overwhelmed and destroyed.

The battle wasn't over, not by a longshot. But he had some-thing new, something he'd lacked since the moment his force had launched.

Hope.

*   *   *

Grachus sat in her fighter, staring at the screen, at the confused mass of fighters, some continuing on their previous courses, others moving on their preexisting vectors, their thrusters powered down. Confusion was everywhere, and nowhere stronger than in her own cockpit.

Silent tears streamed down her cheeks as she slowly let herself realize the terrible error she had made. Kat's death had crushed her, and in her grief, she'd sought some way to deal with the pain. She'd found that in vengeance, in an obsession to make those who'd killed her friend pay. That need had turned her against Vennius, convinced her that the then-Commander-Maximus had betrayed Kat. She'd found a twisted comfort in that, and her focus on revenge pulled her from the pain that was too hard to bear. But Vennius's words now rang true...and those of the Imperatrix had left little room for doubt. Now, the agony of losing Kat was compounded with the realization of what she'd done.

Jarus had been right, and his family's steadfast allegiance did them proud. But for her there was nothing save grief and shame. *I have been so wrong, my actions so twisted. I allowed myself to become the tool of a traitor, of one who would destroy all we are...*

She didn't know how she could endure. She glanced down at her panels, her mind focused on the reactor controls. One overload, and all her pain would be over. She felt the sensation of movement, her hand drifting a few centimeters toward the board. But she stopped. Foolishness and pain did not justify cowardice. She was responsible for hundreds of pilots, many following her blindly, looking to her for leadership. Her own death would be a mercy, but how many of them, too, would fall if she left them behind, in a disorganized mass?

She had been a fool, and a traitor. She detested herself, but even in her state of mind, abandoning her command was unthinkable. She reached down, flipped on the comm.

"All Red fleet fighters, this is Commander Grachus. You have listened to the broadcast from Imperator Vennius, and the evidence he has supplied. You must all decide for yourselves what to make of it, what to believe. For me, there is naught now but regret, and shame for the choices I have made. Before all of you, I swear my allegiance to Imperator Vennius, and I denounce Calavius, the usurper, the liar. I believed propaganda, deliberate lies...to my everlasting shame. But what remains of the warrior inside me, what I retain of the shreds of my honor, leave me no choice. I urge all of you to follow me, to rally to Imperator Vennius."

She shut down the comm, and she pitched forward, retching, almost vomiting right there in the cockpit. It was stress, tension, shame...the full realization of all that had happened. She didn't know what would come next. Would her people follow her? Would they repudiate her, and remain loyal to the Red cause?

Or worse, will they split, will the next moments see the start of a fight between those I just led, squadron against squadron, pilot against pilot?

She watched, reminding herself to breathe, as she waited to see what her people did. She tapped her own throttle forward, toward Vennius's formation...and as her eyes stayed fixed on the screen, she saw other fighters, hundreds, doing the same.

Some clusters remained, and in a few places combat broke out between scattered groups, but ultimately, it was clear. Better than eighty percent of her people were with her.

She looked at the long-range scanner, her eyes stopping on *Dauntless*. Tyler Barron and his ship had been the target of his revenge. For as long as she could remember, it seemed, she had hated him, ached to avenge her friend. She had refused to believe that Barron and his ship had beaten Kat without treachery of some kind. But now she saw that Barron and his people had accomplished nothing less staggering than the invasion of Palatia. Realization flooded into her mind, of the skill of this officer, of the fighting abilities of his people, and for the first time, she imagined her friend *had* been simply defeated...not betrayed, not deceived. It was painful, but it also stripped away a burden that had weighed on her so long she couldn't remember what it was like to be free of it.

She would spend the rest of her life atoning for what she had done, there was no question in her mind about that. But, at least, she felt relief. She could see past the present strife, past the regret and mistakes…to the future. A future she suddenly realized would have been Kat's fervent hope for her friend.

Goodbye, my sister. You will live in my heart forever.

The tears increased, a torrent washing down her face, the pain pouring out. She felt the burden lifting away, the dark shadow replaced by warm remembrance. The ghost driving her was gone.

*   *   *

Stockton stared at his screen, watching the astonishing spectacle unfolding in the system. His squadrons were decelerating, holding back, by Commodore Barron's fleetwide order. The epic battle was paused. *But not over…*

He saw a group of battleships clustering together, the vessels that remained loyal to Calavius. For all the defectors, and the neutral ships moving to the edges of the battle area, there was still a powerful force. They no longer had numerical superiority, nor any kind of advantage now, save perhaps one. *They* were the desperate ones now, those who faced a stark choice: victory or death.

Stockton reached down and flipped on the comm unit. The enemy fighters were in total disarray, most of them moving off, signaling that they were rallying to Vennius. But Raptor's eyes were on the battleships, now stripped of their fighter cover. Almost two dozen warships were still in the Red battleline.

"All Gray fighters," he said into the comm, his voice cold, hard. "There are still battleships serving our enemy here. Form on me, all of you…it is time to finish this." Stockton had no authority over the Confederation forces beyond *Dauntless*'s squadrons, and certainly not over the Gray Alliance ships…but as he blasted his engines and headed toward the enemy ships, he could see fighters following him all across the line. He was Raptor, the Confederation's greatest ace, and now he was seeing just how far his reputation had spread. In small groups, then whole squadrons, entire wings, the Gray strike forces followed him, all of them.

"Interceptors, take out those remaining enemy fighters. Bomber groups...we'll get you a clear run at the targets. Take them down!"

Stockton felt the fury take him. He wasn't a man now, nor an officer. Not even a pilot. He was an executioner, plain and simple. And it was time to end this.

*   *   *

"The battle line will advance now. Right behind the squadrons." Barron had listened to Stockton's amazing speech. He'd known *Dauntless*'s top ace was a leader, but even he was stunned at the audacity of what Raptor had done...and more so that every squadron in the fleet appeared to be obeying him as though his urgings had been the word of God.

Stockton had violated a whole pile of regulations, of course, vastly exceeding his authority. But Barron sat there with a smile on his face, watching the whole thing unfold. He was proud of his officer, and he knew Kyle Jamison would have been too.

"All battleships advancing, sir."

The situation had changed dramatically. There was still a substantial force loyal to Calavius, but the odds had shifted. Victory was in reach, if it still promised to exact a high cost.

"Commodore, I have Imperator Vennius."

"Sir," Barron said into his headset.

"It appears the situation had improved, Commodore."

"Yes, sir...it has."

"Your pilot is to be commended. The strike force has no significant opposition...the attack against the remains of Calavius's battleline is likely to be devastating."

"If Commander Stockton has his way, you can bet it will be.

I've ordered my ships to move forward. It is time to end this."

"I agree, Commodore. I, too, have ordered all fleet units to advance." His voice became lower, somber. "We may have found an unlikely route to victory, my friend, but hard and costly work remains ahead of us."

"Yes, sir. Victory is rarely cheap."

"It is not, Commodore. I find I crave peace, in a way I have never understood before...but what must be done must be done. Those who remain before us have chosen treason of their own free will. There can be no mercy, no quarter."

Barron could hear the regret in Vennius's voice, but there was hardness there too. He wasn't sure if he would have come to the same conclusion, but he knew in the Alliance, his ally had no choice. If he allowed traitors to live, he would be perceived as weak...and he would lose much of what they had all fought to gain.

"No quarter...yes, sir." Barron paused. "Fortune go with you, Imperator Vennius."

"And with you, Commodore Barron."

Barron turned and looked toward Atara Travis. "We have our orders, Commander. Let's end this nightmare."

Chapter Forty-Seven

CFS Dauntless
Astara System
Year 311 AC

Vennius sat at the spare workstation on *Bellator*, out of the way, like some observer or staff officer there to watch Egilius and his crew in action. He'd stayed out of the routine operation of the ship, and even of the task force his protégé was commanding. He'd known every level of service, and he was well aware how much damage he could do by micromanaging, by interfering in things well handled by his officers. But now, he looked out over the bridge, his eyes locking on the display, on the battle that was still shaping up before him.

The final battle...

"Commander Egilius," he said, his voice loud, firm, "the fleet will advance. It is time to finish this."

"Yes, Your Supremacy."

Vennius could see the situation, so suddenly transformed from virtually hopeless to nearly certain victory. His words, and the evidence he had so diligently prepared, had worked. He'd hoped they would, trying to depend on the honor and pragmatism of the Alliance's warriors, but, truth be told, he'd been far from sure. He'd sat on the bridge, silent, his insides twisted into knots, as he watched those agonizing moments to see the effect his broadcast had on the Red Alliance forces.

Now, he felt the pressure of acceleration as *Bellator* moved toward the remnants of Calavius's force. The advantage had shifted completely, the forces remaining to the usurper hopelessly outnumbered...but they were Alliance warriors, all, and Vennius knew they were well aware this would be a fight to the death. No one would retreat, nor fall back...and those who had been willing to accept amnesty had already done so. The next hours would see hard and bloody work, and it would not come free. He would lose ships and warriors, far too many...and when it was all over and he had the victory, he knew there would be no joy, no sweetness. The whole sorry affair had been a waste, of resources, of warriors' lives. The emergence of greed and lust for power in officers he'd served with was disillusioning. It was a rite of passage perhaps, a reality a maturing Alliance needed to face, but Vennius regretted it nevertheless.

He watched as the remaining Red battleships fired their own engines, accelerating toward his approaching ships. They were traitors, corrupt, at least the officers in command were...but Vennius wondered how many spacers on those ships would have switched sides if they could have, how many were even now preparing to die at the behest of officers unfit for their loyalty.

"Entering primary battery range in twenty seconds, sir."

Vennius nodded at Egilius's report. Barron's ships, their massive particle accelerators vastly outranging anything his Alliance forces possessed, had opened up. One Red battleship was already gone, and two more were holed in half a dozen places each, freezing fluids and atmosphere gushing out into space.

Vennius had lived a warrior's life, and for the past year he'd sent his forces into battle to kill thousands of their former comrades. But he'd seen too much of brother fighting brother, and he'd secretly been glad this would be the last fight...either way. Now, he had one last task to perform, one word that would commence the beginning of the end.

He paused, staring out at the ships moving toward his fleet, his mind placing the images of officers with the ship names.

Commanders who had served under him as Commander-Magnus, men and women he'd known, at whose sides he'd fought.

He took a deep breath, pushing back the pain, the doubts. There was no time for that now. There was only time for duty.

He looked over at Egilius, nodding. "Fire," he said emotionlessly. "All ships, open fire."

*   *   *

"Damage is extensive, Commodore, but there are no fires, and all systems are at least marginally operational."

"Very well, Commander." Barron was exhausted, and relieved. The battle had been ferocious, the Red warriors aware that their choice was stark...victory or death. Barron's forces had ensured it would be the latter, though they had paid their own price. He'd lost another of his new battleships. *Resolution* had been caught between three Red Alliance ships and destroyed before help could reach her. Every one of his remaining six ships was damaged, and all of them had suffered heavy casualties. But there wasn't an enemy ship left in front of his force. Nothing but floating debris, and dead, lifeless hulks.

He had not offered quarter, but neither had the enemy requested any. He considered those fighting his people to be traitors, but they had proven they were still Alliance warriors. They had died for their cause...and they had taken hundreds of his people with them.

"I've got Commander Tulus on the comm, sir."

Barron gestured for Travis to connect the Palatian. "I am glad to see you made it through, Vian."

"And I you, my friend. The battle was hard...yet I feel victory is near."

The battle *was* all but over, only one ship remaining...Calavius's. Vennius himself was in pursuit, in *Bellator*, with half a dozen other ships. Calavius's flagship seemed to be making a run for the transit point, but now her engines had been blasted to scrap. Whatever the Red Imperator, the usurper, had intended, was immaterial. He was trapped, his fate rapidly approaching.

"Yes. Vennius will have much work to do. I fear it will be more difficult to heal the Alliance's wounds than simply declaring amnesty. Mistrust, once deeply embedded, is hard to wash away."

"You speak wisely, my friend. Yet, I believe we can achieve it, and much else…with your help."

"I will provide it…any way I can."

"And we shall prove that honor is not lost to us. You have helped us win our war…now we shall stand at your side, until your own enemy is crushed."

Barron nodded, but he didn't answer right away. It would be Vennius's decision whether to intervene in the war. Barron didn't doubt the Imperator would honor his promises, but the Alliance fleet was badly battered, and the job of meshing its warriors back into one force would be long and hard. Just how much Vennius would be able to send to aid the Confederation remained an open question. But at least there would be no second front, no invasion through the Confederation's soft underbelly.

"We will be fortunate indeed to have such allies, Vian Tulus."

*   *   *

The battle was over. All but over. Only a single Red ship remained, and the space of Palatia's system was littered with debris, with floating clouds of radioactive dust that had once been Alliance warships. Thousands had died, despite the fact that the result of the battle had been all but predetermined. It was waste, pure and simple, and yet it had proved to be unavoidable.

The battle had raged for hours, the doomed Red ships fighting with a ferocity Barron could only respect, despite the terrible toll it extracted from his forces. Even when two-thirds of their ships were gone, the survivors closed their ranks and fought on, moving to point blank range, even as Vennius's units clustered all around, virtually surrounding them.

Laser batteries fired again and again, concentrated pulse of high-energy light slamming into hulls, melting and vaporizing the dense metals. Compartments erupted as they were exposed to the vacuum of space, debris—and men and women—blown out into the frozen void. And still, even as their batteries were slowly silenced, the Red ships battled on, firing what guns remained operational. Near the end, the last few vessels closed to a few thousand kilometers—almost adjacent in space combat—and fired with their small, anti-fighter turrets, the only weapons that remained to them.

Vennius's ships, too, suffered, some destroyed, others blasted into crippled wrecks. In all his storied career, of all the vicious fights he'd seen, none had been this brutal, this painful. And yet, it had continued on, longer than he'd thought he could endure. But finally, the shooting had ceased, the last of the enemy destroyed.

Almost the last…

"I will grant you a concession to long comradeship, my old friend." Vennius stared at the face in the screen, that of his former companion, now turned enemy. Calavius's eyes showed his fear, and his shock at his defeat. Barron had ordered the cessation of fire, the communication with the last ship serving the Red cause. Even through the rage, the fiery need to avenge so much death and pain, he'd wanted to speak one last time to the man who had been the architect of such tragedy, a man he had once called friend.

"You will spare me?" It was an undignified question, one unbefitting to a Palatian.

"Do not bring further shame on yourself, Calavius. Try to reclaim some part of what you once were, here at the end." Vennius's words were hard. He'd ached enough at his old friend's treason, agonized all he was going to over fighting one who'd once been close. Too many had died needlessly. Whatever mercy he might have felt, or pity, was gone.

"What do you intend?" Calavius's voice was shaky. He was clearly trying to remain firm, but it eluded him.

"Fight your ship, Calavius. Finish this like a Palatian. Die on your bridge, with some shred of honor, and not as my prisoner, tried before all of Palatia and executed while throngs scream for your blood. Die as the man I knew so long ago, not the detestable creature you have become."

Vennius turned toward Egilius. "Commander, prepare to fire all batteries. Advise the other ships." He looked back toward the screen, saw the terror in Calavius's face...and then something else. His enemy nodded, and looked back with a calm that had not been there an instant before.

"You have won, Vennius," he said simply. "There was a time I could not have imagined facing you as an enemy. I will not apologize, nor will I ask again pointlessly for mercy. What has passed between us cannot be undone, and I die as your enemy... but even among enemies, there can be respect. I thank you for granting me a warrior's death. Accept now this farewell, from one who fought at your side for far longer than he struggled against you."

"And farewell to you Gratian of the Calavii." Vennius felt anger, rage...a hatred he knew would never leave him for all his old friend had done. But there was remembrance too, of a different time, and for this moment, he focused on that. "May you find in death what eluded you in life."

He turned toward Egilius, his eyes cold, and he said grimly, "Open fire."

*   *   *

Grachus leaned forward in her cockpit, feeling utterly drained. Not so much physically—she'd been rested and ready for a protracted combat that never came. But emotionally, she had come a long way in a short time, through self-doubt and anger, and the realization of the damage she had done.

Most of the squadrons had sided with her, convinced by her words, and those of Vennius, that they had sworn themselves not to the just Imperator, but to a traitor and a liar. She suspected they all felt a dose of the shame that tormented her, and she was proud that they'd risen above it, done the right thing in spite of the fact that it required them to admit their own foolishness.

Let them blame it on me. It is my fault, after all, at least partly. Many of them followed me, trusting in my judgment…my judgment that proved so horribly bad in this case.

She glanced at the screen, her eyes on the splinter of her force, the pilots who remained loyal to the Red cause. They had pulled back from their former comrades…and the new Grays let them go. Grachus had almost ordered her people to stand down—the idea of shooting at those who had launched as comrades was repugnant to her—but before she could issue the command it became clear to her that none of her pilots had the stomach to fire upon their former allies, at least not unless they were fired upon. Which they weren't.

She reached out, extending her hand toward the comm unit's control panel. She had one more duty, one she dreaded. It was one thing to speak to her people, to urge them to stand down. But the situation was still uncertain. Vennius's words had suggested he would welcome any Red warriors who wished to switch sides, but she was responsible for almost two thousand pilots. She needed to make sure. She needed to formalize things…and the closest ship was *Dauntless*.

She hesitated. It was no longer hatred of Barron that ate away at her. It was shame. But there was no choice, and failing to do what duty demanded would only make things worse.

She flipped on the unit switching to the Confederation command channel. "This is Commander-Princeps Jovi Grachus, commanding the former Red Alliance fighter wings. I wish to formally accept Imperator Vennius's offer and confirm that all fighters currently standing down along the line wish to submit." Word like "submit" were never easy for an Alliance warrior, and she felt a twinge as she said it, despite her certainty that it was the right thing to do.

"Commander Grachus, your communication is acknowledged. Advise your forces to remain in place, with weapons systems down until we are able to provide more specific instructions." There was a pause, and then: "Commander, please hold for Commodore Barron."

She was startled by the words. Contacting *Dauntless* had been difficult enough, but facing Barron himself…well, not "facing," exactly, but…

"Commander Grachus, this is Commodore Barron. I just wanted to thank you for ordering your forces to stand down. You saved many lives today, and if I may be so bold as to say, you did the right thing for your people."

She was stunned. This was the man she'd pursued, whose death she had sworn, and imagined too many times to count. Now he was on her comm unit, no animosity in his voice, no recrimination.

"Thank you, Commodore. I was…" She hesitated, not sure what to say. "…wrong in my earlier allegiance and actions. I made a deep error, and I fear it caused much damage before it was rectified."

"We have all made mistakes, Commander. You had the courage to correct yours, and for that, you have my admiration. I welcome you to the Gray Alliance, and I hope we are able to meet in person soon."

Grachus was struck again by Barron's graciousness. She'd built him up in her mind to be a monster, imagined him as some devious Confederation killer, devoid of honor. "I thank you for your wisdom, Commodore Barron. I blamed you for years, held you accountable for Katrine's death, but I was wrong." Grachus had chosen *Dauntless* as her contact to arrange for the transfer of her forces to Vennius's Gray fleet. She preferred not to think of it as a surrender, but whatever it was, she'd compelled herself to go through *Dauntless* to arrange it, a bit of self-flagellation she felt lay on the road to redemption. She hadn't expected to speak with Barron himself, but as soon as she'd given her name, he'd come on the comm line immediately.

"Thank *you*, Commander. I didn't know Commander Rigellus, but even in the brief moments I spoke to her, I could tell she was an extraordinary officer. I regret that we met as enemies, and not as friends." Barron paused for a few seconds. "You showed tremendous leadership today, Commander, in following your conscience, in leading your people to what you knew was right…and the vast numbers in which they followed you speaks volumes about your abilities as a leader. I hope we may serve together in the future…and if it is not too much to ask, perhaps one day we can sit down, and you can tell me about Katrine Rigellus."

"It would be an honor, Commodore. I look…" Her voice trailed off. There was something on the scanner, a tiny blip—a fighter. It was moving toward her, at high speed. The battle was over, the forces had all stood down. Except this…suddenly she understood. It was Stockton.

"Commander?" Barron's voice echoed in her headset, but she ignored him, her eyes fixed on the display, on the grim death that approached her.

Stockton had to know the battle was over, that she and her people had sworn to Vennius's service. *Unless…yes, of course. That other pilot.* She'd fought an epic struggle with another Confederation flyer, and Stockton had been racing to intervene. Suddenly, it was completely clear. Stockton wasn't fighting the Grays' battle, nor the Confederation's. He was fighting his own. He wasn't attacking on Barron's orders. He was coming for *her.* He was avenging his comrade.

Most likely his friend…yes, certainly his friend…

She slammed her hand to the side, hard, pulling back to fire up her engines. The battle *wasn't* over. She hadn't survived, at least not yet.

She threw her ship into a wild evasive maneuver, moving her vector to a nearly perpendicular angle from her attacker. She didn't know what to do. Should she fight, try to destroy Stockton? They were on the same side now…could she begin her service to Vennius by killing one of his pilots?

"Commander Grachus…is something wrong?" She could hear the concern in Barron's voice, but her thoughts were elsewhere, trying to decide how to deal with the deadly threat heading toward her.

Against any other flyer, she might have simply tried to evade. But Stockton was far too good for that. If she didn't fight him with everything she had, struggle with all her skill to destroy him, he would finish her for sure.

Perhaps death is still the price you will have to pay for your foolishness…

*   *   *

Stockton's eyes were fixed on the tiny dot on his scanner. His fighter was ripping through space, his reactor's safeties completely shut down. The g forces pressed into him, going beyond discomfort, to outright pain. He struggled to inhale, forcing his chest to expand, to push against the pressure almost crushing him. But he ignored it all.

The battle was over—most of it, at least. But he still had a score to settle. The dozens of squadrons, the battleships all around the system, the lines of escort ships…had all stood down. But there was one enemy left, a single fight that remained, one that would be finished only when one of the combatants was dead.

Stockton's mind was clear, no thoughts save those relevant to the battle. He'd tracked his enemy down, and now he was heading into the fight. *Soon, Kyle…I will avenge you, my brother.*

He could almost feel the radiation leaking from his tortured reactor, a tingling sensation on his back. But radiation poisoning was of no concern to him, not now. He could get a cleanse if he survived the fight…or perhaps he would take a lethal dose and he would die. No matter. Whatever happened, it would be after the battle, after he had avenged Jamison. Or after he died.

He knew his ship couldn't take much of the punishment he was inflicting, but he'd decided it was worth the risk. His enemy was too good…a normal engagement between the two could go on forever. And if he ran out of fuel before the fight was decided, he wouldn't get another chance. Not with the civil war over and Calavius dead.

It had to be *now*…and that meant pouring everything he had into it. All his skill, and all his ship had to give as well.

He gritted his teeth against the pain, his hand tight around the throttle as he watched the range count down. The Alliance pilot was reacting now, trying to evade his attack.

His lips twisted against the pressure, into a crooked smile. His enemy wasn't coming right at him, trying to take him down immediately. That was a mistake. By evading, his adversary was yielding the initiative. And that was all the edge he needed...

*   *   *

"It's Commander Stockton, sir." Travis's tone told Barron his second in command understood what was happening, just as he did. Jake Stockton was going to attack Jovi Grachus. He was going to avenge Kyle Jamison.

"Get him on my comm now," Barron snapped. He understood Stockton's anger and frustration, but Grachus and her people had yielded...and his people did not kill warriors who had given up the fight, much less those who had joined them as allies.

"On your line, sir."

"Jake, this is Tyler Barron..." There was no room for formality now. He had to reach Stockton, somehow...and his top pilot had never been one who'd shown particular deference to rank or orders.

There was no response.

"Jake, answer me..."

Still nothing.

"Jake, I know what you're doing, but I need you to break off...now. You are not to attack Commander Grachus." A pause. "That's an order." It was worth a try.

The comm was still silent. Barron was about to try again, to repeat himself, when Stockton's voice came through.

"I'm sorry, sir." The pilot's words were soft, forced. One look at the scanner, at the output of Stockton's engines, explained that. "This pilot—Grachus, you say—killed Kyle. I'm going to avenge him."

"No, Jake...you can't. Commander Grachus has yielded. She led almost the entire Red fighter force over to our side. You are *not* to attack her."

Silence again. Then: "I am sorry, sir...but I have to do this.

I have to avenge my friend…my brother. I owe him more than I can ever repay."

"Jake, I am ordering you to stand down."

Nothing.

"Jake, don't do this. Don't throw your career away."

Silence.

Barron turned toward Travis as though he was about to issue some kind of order. But what? Could he command his fighters to intercept Stockton, to shoot him down? He didn't know if he could bring himself to do that…and he was far from sure any of his people would obey if he did.

He felt his hands ball up into fists as his frustration grew. He wracked his brain, trying to come up with some way to reach Stockton, to get the pilot to listen. Then: "Get Stara Sinclair on the line, Atara. Now!"

Chapter Forty-Eight

Interplanetary Space
Astara System
Year 311 AC

Grachus swung her ship hard to the side, evading again as a barrage of laser fire ripped by, no more than a few meters from her starboard side. She'd known Stockton was good, but right now the Confed pilot was downright possessed. He was tight on her now, closing in…and it wouldn't be long before he had her.

Unless you fight back…

She'd held back, unwilling to engage, but now she saw her choice clearly. She'd heard Barron's efforts to call off his ace pilot, and Stockton's refusal to obey. Everything was right there in front of her. She had killed Stockton's best friend, a man he'd considered a brother. Grachus understood her adversary's motivations now, perhaps better than anyone else could. The irony tugged at her, and she knew she had to make a choice. She now faced the same anger and hatred she had felt for so long, the irresistible need for vengeance. All she could do now was turn and fight, and try to destroy this man who should now be her ally…or stay her course, struggle to escape, and almost certainly die in the attempt.

Her impulse was to fight, though she was far from sure even

407

then she could prevail. But the realization of what she had done weighed on her. Had she not been mired in her own misguided pursuit of revenge, she never would have fought the Gray Alliance forces and their allies. She would never have faced Stockton's friend. She would never have killed him.

She angled her ship again, and then back, trying to stay a step ahead of her attacker. *Half a step…*

She wrestled with her thoughts, her motivations. She'd been crushed by Kat's death, and ready to die herself in pursuit of vengeance. But now she'd allowed herself to see a future serving under the man she'd wronged, an Imperator worthy of loyalty. And her son…the future offered to be one where she could be more a part of his life. Jarus had shown he had at least some genuine admiration for her…and with her new rank and status—assuming Vennius allowed her to keep it—he could stand up to his family. She found she wanted to live.

But we can't always have what we want…

The warrior inside her ached to fight back. But her guilt restrained her. Stockton's rage had spawned from her own foolishness, her misguided hatred for Vennius and Barron.

Perhaps this is my destiny…the price I must pay…

She pushed forward hard on the throttle, decelerating rapidly, a wildly unpredictable maneuver, and a chance to buy a little more time.

But only a little…Stockton is too good. I can't elude him, not for long…

The two sides in her head battled mightily…and then the urge to survive, deeply instinctive, won out. She accelerated hard, and then spun her ship around, opening fire with her laser cannons. Her targeting had been dead on for Stockton's location…but her target wasn't there. She'd expected her move to be a surprise, perhaps a chance to catch her opponent unaware and end this deadly struggle. But it was almost as if he'd read her mind. Worse, he'd shifted to the side, and he opened fire himself, his laser blasts ripping right past her ship, a meter to port, a meter to starboard…and then her fighter lurched hard, spinning end over end as one of her engines flamed out.

She had waited too long. Her move to fight back, to kill Stockton if that was the only way to survive, was late…and now she would pay the price.

She frantically pulled at her throttle, ran her hands over the controls on her board. Her ship still responded, but the glancing hit had left her less than half normal power. She'd never evade a pilot of Stockton's skill with half thrust. Worse, her laser batteries were dead. *Probably a power conduit…*

She sighed softly, still gripping the throttle. She would do everything she could, use every trick she knew…but there was one inescapable fact.

It was over. It was just a matter of time. Very little time.

*   *   *

Stockton stared at his screen, his eyes cold, focused. He wasn't a man, at least not now. He was an animal, a predator. He had no pity, no emotion, save the need to destroy his enemy.

His hands gripped tightly on the controls, and he angled his fighter, coming around for another attack. The final attack.

He'd watched silently, emotionlessly, as his last shot had hit his target. For an instant, he'd thought the fight was over, that he'd destroyed his enemy. But the hit had been a partial one, the damage bad but not complete. Jamison's killer was still alive… even if her ship was crippled. This time, he would finish her. He would avenge his friend.

He'd come in fast, and it was taking time to alter his vector to make another run. He stared at the scanners, watching for any of the other fighters, to see if they were coming to stop him. He wasn't sure if Barron would actually send fighters to stop him, or if he did, if the Confed pilots would come at him. He was the pride of the fighter corps, and he knew it. He had nothing but respect for those who wore the same uniform he did…but he was ready to kill any pilot with the audacity to try to stop him. Even a comrade.

He suspected the Gray Alliance pilots would follow any orders to attack, if Vennius gave them, but he didn't see any movement in his direction. Still, he knew it could come, and even blinded as he was by incoherent rage, he knew he could only hold off so many.

It's time to finish this…now…

"Jake…"

The voice cut through his focus, his cold obsession. He'd ignored Commodore Barron's repeated attempts to reach him… but this got his attention.

"Jake, it's me…Stara. Jake, please don't do this. I know you're angry, I know you miss Kyle…but this is wrong."

He didn't respond, trying to ignore all she said. But he couldn't. It was there, pushing its way into his closed mind, trying to reach some deeply buried part of him.

"Jake, I know you don't care about your career, and I'm not enough of a fool to believe fear of court martial would matter to you. But what about the pilots, Jake? What about the squadrons? They lost Kyle too, you know. They followed him for more than five years…and now they have to go into battle without him. Will you make them go without you too? You know we'll be heading back to the Union front soon."

His eyes were still on the screen, on the crippled Alliance fighter, as he came around, his vector changing gradually. In a few seconds, perhaps half a minute, it would be time. He could begin his final run.

But Stara's words were well-chosen, and they sliced deeply into him. He moved his hand, toward the comm unit, intending to turn it off. But he paused. If the civil war in the Alliance was truly over, *Dauntless would* be heading back to the Union front. His pilots would be heading back not to a respite, but to more war. There would be no peace, no break in the fighting. And more of them would die…they would die because he wasn't there.

No, that's not your responsibility…your obligation is to Kyle, to avenge him.

What would Kyle say about abandoning the squadrons?

The voices in his head went back and forth, a bitter argument raging. He felt like he would go mad. And all the while,

Stara was still there. He desperately wanted to shut her out, to stop her words from tormenting him...but he couldn't bring himself to turn off the comm.

He saw his enemy in front of him. She was doing everything possible, her ship altering course wildly. But she didn't have the tools anymore. Her ship was half dead, her quest to escape his wrath hopeless.

Finish this, the voice from within cried out. *Finish this now...*

"Jake, please...you know I love you. I don't know if you care anymore, but if I ever meant anything to you, please listen to me now. Don't do this. Don't leave your pilots." A pause, and then, her voice cracking, "Don't leave me..."

Jake felt the words like a series of punches right to his gut. He hated himself for the pain he had caused her, and the doubt she'd expressed about his current feelings tore at him. But the monster inside was still there. Kyle Jamison's face, from a thousand times they'd been together, staring at him. The thought that he'd never see his friend again filled him with renewed rage. He screamed, slamming his hand against the edge of the cockpit. But his hand was still on the throttle, moving it slightly, lining up right behind his target.

It's time. Do it...

The words were unspoken, but to Stockton, the volume was deafening, drowning out Stara's continued pleas on the comm.

"Do it," he said softly to himself, as his hand tightened on the throttle.

His eyes narrowed, focused on his enemy. She was right ahead...she was in point blank range. There was no escape, not with her damaged engines. His vengeance was at hand.

Do it...

Chapter Forty-Nine

**Fleet Hospital
Grimaldi Base
Orbiting Krakus II
Year 312**

"I brought you just the thing to get those new legs humming…" Stockton stepped through the door, into the small hospital room. Dirk Timmons was not in the bed, as he'd been every time Stockton had visited him before. He was sitting up in a chair next to the window, his biomechanical legs covered with a small blanket. Or at least what passed for a window, five hundred meters deep inside a space station. It was really a screen, but one with the advantage of programmability, meaning Timmons could have any view he wanted, the ocean, the desert, the mountains. At the moment, it was set to display a thick forest, looking very much like autumn in northern Megara. Stockton vaguely recalled that Timmons had been born and raised on the Confederation's capital.

Stockton turned and looked to the side of the room. He stopped dead. There was a woman standing there, clearly in the middle of a visit with Timmons.

"I see you're busy," he said, a cold tone in his voice. "I'll come back later."

"Jake…"

412

"No, please don't go." The woman's voice was soft, sad. She turned toward Timmons. "I will visit you again, Commander Timmons. I'm pleased you're doing so well." She looked in Stockton's direction, but she didn't make eye contact. "Commander," she said, respectfully. Then she slipped out into the hall without another word.

Stockton stood where he was, looking down at the floor. It had been nearly six months since that day around Palatia, the day the civil war ended. The day he'd had revenge in his grasp... and let it go. He still wasn't sure how he felt about it, even now, but in the end, he'd realized he just couldn't leave them, all of them. The pilots, Timmons...and most of all, Stara. His hand had been on the firing stud, a tenth of a second from finishing things. But then his strength left him. He'd flown by, sparing the pilot who'd killed Kyle Jamison.

He'd struggled with his choice ever since, and as fate's cruelty would have it, Jovi Grachus had been assigned to command the fighter squadrons attached to the Alliance Expeditionary Force. She had followed *Dauntless* to Grimaldi, haunting him like some specter. Even his expectation that at least he'd never have to see her again had been dashed, and finding her here, in Timmons's room, the man she'd crippled...

"She's really not so bad, Jake."

"Not so bad? She put you in that bed. You're in here because of her."

"She's a warrior, Jake. Just like us. Do you think you haven't killed peoples important to others? Mothers, father, sisters, brothers? You think none of the pilots you've gunned down had lovers, friends? War is war, Jake. Leave it there." A pause. "Kyle would have."

The last words sliced at him, but he just nodded. "I just wanted to drop this off," he said, setting a small container down on the table next to Timmons's chair and then moving back toward the door. "I've got to go..."

"Jake," Timmons said, "stay...please. I could use some company." He looked over at the small package. "What did you bring me? You can tell me that, at least."

Stockton turned and looked behind him, as if checking for any hospital personnel...or to be sure Grachus was no longer there. "It's a burger, the greasiest one I could find down on the promenade. I remember enough from flight school to know that's how you like them."

"And fries?" Timmons smiled hungrily, leaning forward, opening the small package.

"Of course...what kind of half-assed operation do you think I'm running here?" He looked back behind him again. "But be quiet...and eat it now, before the staff gets here with your normal slop and takes it away."

Timmons smiled and nodded. "You know I'm going to eat it now." He reached in and pulled out an enormous burger, dripping all around, and he took a massive bite.

"My God, that's good," he said, his words barely intelligible with his mouth jammed full. "I can't remember the last time I tasted something that good."

Stockton smiled, the tension he'd felt earlier starting to fade. He sat down on the edge of the bed and nodded. "I knew you'd like it." Then, a few seconds later, "So, I hear you'll be getting out of here soon..."

*   *   *

Tyler Barron stood next to the large medpod. The room was silent, save for the pumping sounds of the machinery that kept the pod working...and the man inside alive.

He reached out, touched the metal of the canister. It was cold, the cryogenic gasses inside refrigerating even the outside of the heavily insulated pod. It was a miracle Van Striker was even alive, Barron had been told. The wounds were massive, his condition beyond critical. He would have been dead, if Admiral Jaravick hadn't acted quickly, taking command and ordering Striker placed in cryostatis. The admiral could still die, indeed, that was the likeliest outcome, but some cutting-edge treatments at least offered some hope. Barron tried to cling to such thoughts, but he found it difficult.

He stared down at the pod. All he could see was Striker's face, beneath the small, clear panel on the top. He looked dead. *Or sleeping?* Barron didn't know what to think. But he knew he had to be there. He had to pay his respects.

"Vennius was true to his word, sir. Commander Tulus is in command of the expeditionary force. We've got six Alliance battleships here already…with more on the way. Your plan worked, Admiral." Of course, even the presence of Alliance allies was overshadowed by the ever-present gloom, the fear of the still barely-understood superweapon the enemy had somehow produced…or, more likely, found.

Still, he'd come to respect the Alliance fighters greatly, and whatever lay ahead, he was glad to have them at his side. He took a deep breath, remembering his last meeting with Vennius. He'd brought Kat Rigellus's children to him, safe and unharmed. The rescue had cost him several good Marines, and one great one. Clete Hargraves had survived decades of service, but duty had finally claimed him. Barron had been glad to see Rigellus's son and daughter safe—he felt as though he had repaid a debt of his own as well as honoring Vennius's request—but it still hurt to lose people.

Vennius had been a committed ally anyway, of course, but the return of the children had seemed to energize him, to hold back the despair and exhaustion that had grown heavy on him. He'd given his word he would send every ship he could spare, and Barron didn't doubt it at all.

"I just wish we could have been with you, Admiral…at the Bottleneck…"

"That would have served nothing, Commodore. The Bottleneck was a trap, one Striker and his people were forced to walk into."

Barron turned abruptly, startled, as Gary Holsten walked into the room.

"He managed to get the fleet out of there, though. His quick action saved thousands of spacers. It saved the Confederation."

"Mr. Holsten, I didn't…"

"Please…I'm Gary. There's no rank insignia on my shoulder, no need for formality between us."

Barron nodded. "Gary…I don't doubt he saved the fleet. Nor am I surprised that he was there in the rearguard, holding the line while everyone else escaped. That was…*is*…him, through and through."

"He's an admirable man…may I call you Tyler?"

Barron nodded.

"Tyler. He's one of the few in my life I have truly called a friend." Holsten paused, and Barron only then realized the pain in the intelligence chief's voice. "I think you might understand that to some extent. You know what it's like."

"What do you mean?"

"Oh, you have friends…certainly Atara Travis. And you are close with your crew. But that's not the same thing, is it? However much affection they have for you, and you for them, you're their leader. They look to you, draw from you. It's not quite the same thing as a true friend, is it?"

Barron didn't answer, but Holsten's words were hitting close to home.

"You're the heir of the greatest hero in the Confederation's history. You've carried that burden your entire life. It insulates you, isolates you. It makes it hard to truly share anything with someone else, doesn't it?"

Barron looked over at Holsten, fishing for something to say. He'd never thought about it in the abrupt terms Holsten was using, but the spymaster was right. However close he was to anyone else, in some ways he always felt alone.

"I understand, Tyler, at least on some level. I'm also the scion of one of the most well-known families in the Confederation, though I'm at least spared the shadow of any ancestors quite as revered as your grandfather. I live a false life, I do a job few know about. It is difficult." He looked back toward the pod. "I was able to talk about things with Van, things I couldn't share with anyone else. I don't want to lose him."

Barron could sense a vulnerability in Holsten he'd never seen before. He wasn't one for false optimism or invented hope, but perhaps there was a time for everything. "He'll make it, Gary. I know he will."

Holsten looked up. Barron could feel that his companion sensed his uncertainty, but he could also see the words had helped. "I hope so," Holsten said softly.

The two men stood, staring at the canister for a moment. "You know, people like us, so singular, so alone…we have to try to recognize those few people who are truly special to us, truly close. The war still rages, and the enemy has gained a massive advantage with their new weapon. We have no idea what to expect…so, we do not have time to waste."

Barron just nodded.

The two stood silent for a few moments. Then, Holsten said, "Did you know that Captain Lafarge is on Grimaldi, Tyler?"

Barron held his head where it was, trying not to react. "Is she?" he asked, as casually as he could manage.

"Yes. She and her people found an artifact of significant value, a stealth generator. While it is not a match for the enemy's new weapon, it has considerable military potential." He paused. "She is quite a woman, Andi Lafarge…" He looked over at Barron.

"Yes, she is," he replied.

"I believe she's staying in Blue section. Room 2707, if I remember correctly." He turned toward Barron. "I think I'll stay with Van for a while. There is no need for both of us to stand here…"

Barron nodded, realizing how utterly useless his nonchalance was around Holsten. "Perhaps I will go and say hello then…"

Holsten nodded and smiled. "Yes, why don't you do that?"

*   *   *

"Tyler Barron is at the door."

Lafarge looked up, startled at the AI's words. She paused, feeling uncharacteristically flustered. She'd faced countless dangers, stared down some of the most notorious scum on the frontier, and yet the mere mention of Barron's name unsettled her.

"Let him in."

The door slid open, and Tyler Barron stepped in. "Hello," he said, clearly trying to appear calm.

"Hello," she replied. "I had heard you'd docked. I hear congratulations are in order. They're calling you the hero of the Rim."

He frowned. "Are they?" He sounded more concerned about it than glad. "You as well. Gary Holsten told me about your discovery…" Barron hesitated, then he stepped toward her. "Andi, I'm sorry about everything. I didn't want you out there. We were so outnumbered, the odds so against us. And *Pegasus* is such a small ship. I couldn't put you in that danger… and I knew there would be no way to keep you out of it if you stayed." A wave of emotion poured out with his words. "I am sorry if I hurt you, if I seemed callous. I wasn't sure you'd listen to me any other way."

She stood, trying to stay firm, cool, even as she realized how much she wanted to hear what he was saying. "You didn't hurt me," she lied. "You had work to do, and so did I." But even as she faced him, trying to maintain her façade, a smile broke through. "It *is* good to see you, Tyler. I was worried about you."

He returned the smile. "And if I'd had any idea what you were up to, I'd have been more than worried. From what Gary tells me, you and your people really made a find…one that may be hugely important."

"It looks like. I figured one day one of these leads would amount to something."

Barron took a step forward. "It's some kind of stealth device?"

She looked at him and smiled. "I'm not sure I can divulge that, Commodore. The entire project is highly classified."

"Oh, is it?" He returned her smile, looking right at her. "Perhaps I should show you my security clearance then?"

She returned his gaze. "Yes…I think you should."

Epilogue

"You've done well, Colonel. I commend you." Gaston Villieneuve looked out over the massive structure, a complex web of metal girders with a series of compartments attached. It had cost a fortune, one Villieneuve had somehow managed to extract from the Union's collapsing finances, and now it was ready.

"Thank you, Minister." The engineer nodded respectfully, clearly nervous to be in the presence of a member of the Presidium...not to mention, the dreaded leader of Sector Nine. "My entire team is grateful for the opportunity, sir."

"You have served the state well, and you will be suitably rewarded." Villieneuve held his gaze. The thing was ugly. It was clumsy in design, and it was pig slow. Worse, it had to be split into ten sections to get it through transwarp points. But it moved, and when it did, it carried the Pulsar with it, along with the almost endless series of fusion plants that powered it.

Villieneuve knew he was looking at victory itself. The lumbering monster would be vulnerable to attack...but the massive gun it carried could destroy anything that came at it, from ranges far beyond that of any other know weapon. It wasn't elegant, nor was it quick...but it could more forward, steadily, unstoppably. It would engage whatever forces the Confederation put in its way, blast their vaunted Grimaldi base to radioactive debris... destroy everything in its path, until it reached Megara itself, and he dictated his peace terms in the rubble of the Confederation

419

Senate House.

The war had been long, hard...a far greater struggle than he'd envisioned at its outset. But now victory was finally his for the taking. The economy was about to fall into the abyss, and Ricard Lille's efforts had not only failed, it had brought the Alliance in the war on the Confederation's side. But none of that mattered, not now. Confederation, Alliance...none of their ships could face the Pulsar. None could stop it

"It is ready then, Colonel? Fully operational?"

"Yes, sir."

Villieneuve smiled. "Then the invasion will begin at once. And it will not stop until the victory is won."

Blood on the Stars Will Continue With

Dauntless

January, 2018

Also By Jay Allan

Marines (Crimson Worlds I)
The Cost of Victory (Crimson Worlds II)
A Little Rebellion (Crimson Worlds III)
The First Imperium (Crimson Worlds IV)
The Line Must Hold (Crimson Worlds V)
To Hell's Heart (Crimson Worlds VI)
The Shadow Legions(Crimson Worlds VII)
Even Legends Die (Crimson Worlds VIII)
The Fall (Crimson Worlds IX)
War Stories (Crimson World Prequels)
MERCS (Successors I)
The Prisoner of Eldaron (Successors II)
Into the Darkness (Refugees I)
Shadows of the Gods (Refugees II)
Revenge of the Ancients (Refugees III)
Winds of Vengeance (Refugees IV)
Shadow of Empire (Far Stars I)
Enemy in the Dark (Far Stars II)
Funeral Games (Far Stars III)
Blackhawk (Far Stars Legends I)
The Dragon's Banner
Gehenna Dawn (Portal Wars I)
The Ten Thousand (Portal Wars II)
Homefront (Portal Wars III)
Red Team Alpha (CW Adventures I)
Duel in the Dark (Blood on the Stars I)
Call to Arms (Blood on the Stars II)
Ruins of Empire (Blood on the Stars III)
Echoes of Glory (Blood on the Stars IV)
Flames of Rebellion (Flames of Rebellion I)

www.jayallanbooks.com

Made in the USA
San Bernardino, CA
07 February 2018